I0760952

PAINFUL DELIVERANCE

Books 1-3

ANN M PRATLEY

ISBN 978-1-99-116468-1

CONTENTS

PAINFUL DELIVERANCE

~~ Book One ~~

CHAPTER 1

~~ The Departure ~~

'He won't find me. He won't find me. He won't find me,' Alexis chanted inside her head. Over and over, she repeated those four words silently as the bus pulled out of the terminal. She looked around her like a small animal who knows there's a predator nearby - a hunter - but doesn't know where it is, or in what form it will take.

As her eyes skimmed over the other passengers on the bus, an elderly woman caught her eye and gave her a sympathetic smile. The movement startled Alexis and made her turn away. It made no logical sense that the woman would be on the bus, planted only as a way to find her, but her paranoia had reached a level that was intensely terrifying to her. She knew she could trust no-one. That meant pulling into herself and making herself invisible.

Alexis looked out the window. She'd purposely decided to travel in daylight. She didn't want to be in a situation where someone could be lurking in the dark and seeing into the light bus without her equally seeing them. Her eyes remained alert to everywhere and every movement. As her paranoia pushed her to sink deeper down into her seat, she pulled her cap lower over her eyes.

That morning she'd gone to a second-hand charity store to buy a man's overnight bag and as many second-hand clothes as she could fit into it. Being so well worn, she knew they wouldn't have any digital way of being tracked. They'd have no digital footprint. She knew such thinking made no logical sense. It was illogical that he could use something like a store item recording system to follow her if she bought new things from a clothing store. Knowing just how rich and powerful he was, she wouldn't put it past him to use technology in whatever way he could to try and locate her. He'd done it before. She had to expect that he would do it again.

After writing down phone numbers of friends and family members on the small piece of paper that she now clutched tightly, she'd discarded her mobile phone and SIM card. She'd changed her voicemail greeting to say that she had the flu and would return calls the next day. That would take care of what he would hear when he dialled her number. It would provide a reason why she wasn't answering.

When she'd reset the phone and ensured everything on it had been deleted, she had snapped it in two and drove a hammer through both halves of it. The SIM card had suffered the same fate before half was tossed into one rubbish bin in the central city and the other half was thrown into another two blocks away. The pieces were spread far away from where she had been living, but equally far away from the bus terminal. It was an extreme move that would make no sense to anyone else, but she had reached a level of paranoia to demand it - just in case.

As she sat back and felt the bus moving forward on its journey, she absorbed the soothing vibration through her body. She fought the urge to sleep. 'Not yet', she continued to say to herself in the darkness of her mind. She hadn't slept for two nights, driven by fear of what would happen if she did. No, she needed to get away first. She just needed to get somewhere new - somewhere safe. Then she would sleep. He was still too close, and he was determined. He had proven the lengths he would go to, to keep her close by his side. Not close enough so that everyone knew she was a part of his life, but close enough so that when he wanted her to be somewhere, he expected her to be so. If she wasn't, he made sure she fully understood and felt the consequence of that decision.

Thinking back over the previous three years, she wondered how she hadn't seen the signs right at the start. It was a mystery to her how she'd come to miss identifying the depths of his nature. He was an expert of disguise, she had come to realise, albeit much too late. He was a chameleon. He could charm and delight in the presence of others, and he could smile and impress to the world at large. But in the dark of night - in privacy away from almost everyone - there was another side to him. That side wasn't charming or delightful, or even impressive. To her, it was just *evil.*

She clutched her hands tighter around her purse. In it was all the money she had been able to save in preceding months as she'd planned her escape. It was all the cash she had saved, siphoning a little here and there as she'd purchased things. Even the day to day things such as food she had mastered into her plan of using a card to pay for the item, then withdraw some cash on the same transaction. That would ensure that if he investigated her bank records, he wouldn't see any excessive cash having been withdrawn from ATMs. It was her money, but he knew people everywhere, and he had access to resources. He'd already proven in the past that he could find ways to see what she was doing financially. He could recite to her all of the shops, cafés, and other locations she'd been to in the past day … the past week … even the past month.

He watched her carefully, even though he had no legal right to. At least he'd been forward about that - not in a friendly, informative way, but rather in a mocking, know-it-all way. In revealing the lengths he went to, to monitor every little thing she did, he had helped her to think about every action she took. Listening to him share that knowledge had helped her to plan different ways to do things. His having money or not, she'd had to find a way to create a digital footprint that wasn't accurate about what she was doing.

She'd had to make him believe that everything was normal … that she was happy … and that she certainly had no desire whatsoever to leave.

~~~~~

Over the previous week, she had put in place ideas for making it seem like she wouldn't have left, for as long as possible. She'd had to design a plan that would enable her to be long gone by the time he even noticed she wasn't around.

He ran his life on a tight schedule. Over the three years that she'd been seeing him, she had come to know how he lived. On Tuesday and Thursday mornings, he met with members of his company's board to discuss ideas for future growth. At 4pm on Wednesday, he hosted a meeting for senior management at company headquarters, here in Melbourne. Afterwards, he extended that to an expensive dinner that took him through till at least 9pm before he would head back to his apartment.

Today, Friday, he flew from Melbourne to Brisbane. It was a two-hour flight each way, and he stayed there for the whole day. For the duration, he'd keep his phone turned off. He would then return on the 7pm flight back to Melbourne. He wouldn't turn his phone back on until at least 9pm.

Alexis looked at the watch on her small wrist. It was now 11am. He would already be in a meeting that would run all day long. He wouldn't check his phone at all. Giving those clients his full attention on this day each week was of utmost importance to him. He wouldn't try and call her. She was a distraction that he wouldn't indulge in when he was so wrapped up in his business. He knew, as well as she did, that even when they only talked now, three years into this 'relationship', it was like lighting a match to a fuse. There was no respite from the friction and the tenseness that came with the two of them being in the same room together. Even speaking on the phone together had started to result in the same. It had never been his preference to call her for long chats. It was his way instead to only give clear, concise and direct instructions to her before abruptly hanging up.

For weeks, Alexis had been analysing possible places to go on this very day. Her research was never done in one place, and never in her home or on her phone. She had taken to using cash to catch various buses to different suburbs around Melbourne. Over time, she had used library computers to do the research she wanted. He might think to delve into library computers to see if she had discretely been looking at anything there. If he did, at least it would take him time to track down *all* the
~~~~~

computers she had used throughout the sprawling city.

She hadn't leaned on any of her friends or family to provide her with assistance. To do so could have put them in danger and she couldn't risk that. Even if they told him they hadn't heard from her, she knew he could check their phone records to see if they were lying. If they were lying, what he would do to them was not something Alexis could even bear to think about. No, this was something she had to do completely alone.

She'd purposely not called anyone over preceding weeks. She knew there was a chance they would be worried - even more so if he contacted any of them to ask where she was. Still she dared not make any kind of contact with them - not even a letter sent via 'snail mail', not even a postcard, and certainly not any message through any kind of technology.

She cursed herself for having indulged him at the start, all that time ago. Thinking back now to when they first saw each other, she could still remember how she'd felt at that moment they'd met in person. It was easy for her to remember the extreme level of nervousness she had experienced. She could almost taste the sense of importance and desperation she'd felt for him to like her. She could still feel the power of her intense need for him to look at her and want her.

Those things she had wanted, desired, and dreamed of. All of them, she had received - in abundance.

In reality, they were completely mismatched, she realised as she sat on the bus and took some time to contemplate how she'd ended up in her current place and time. She had never quite understood how they came to see each other a second time after that initial meet. How was it that he'd happened to be driving near her at the right time, in the right place?

For a moment, she just thought about him as a person. He possessed wealth, and he exuded power. He had a charisma about him that lured people toward him naturally - women and men.

Alexis, in contrast, had always been an introvert. She remained in her own world, afraid of what other people would do to her emotionally if she let them get too close. She came from an area others would call a slum. She was awkward in company. She worked as a checkout operator at a small supermarket in what was known to be a bad part of the city.

She was a good employee. Where she came from had only built in her a resolve that resulted in an impeccable work ethic. She was the one called upon to clean up the spills or do any jobs that other people who worked around her would say no to.

Even though she couldn't easily be among people, she could force herself to smile and greet customers at checkout. It was a different way of interacting with people. The faces that passed by her every day in that job, probably wouldn't see her again, so they were safe. They wouldn't want to know anything about who she was, or where she was from. She could smile quietly at them, and they would often smile back. They might even ask her how her day was going. The comfort came from knowing that as soon as they walked away, they would completely forget about her. That level of interaction, Alexis could handle. That was acceptable, in return for earning money so she could have a roof over her head and food in her stomach.

Walking away from her job was her biggest regret of having to leave. Her job was a good job. It wasn't everyone's dream job, but it was a *good* job. From it, she had gained regular hours of work and regular pay. It suited her to be an anonymous face that no-one would remember by the time each day ended, and the world reset once more.

Breaking her out of her daze and thoughts was the sound of the bus driver. His voice boomed over the loudspeaker, informing passengers that they would be at their destination in twenty minutes. Alexis was startled. It seemed as though she'd only just got on board. When she looked at her watch, she saw that three hours had passed. She sighed to herself. The upcoming stop wouldn't be her destination. It was only the beginning of her journey. She had much more road travel ahead of her yet.

~~~~~

As she felt the bus come to a stop, she immediately noticed her nerves kick in once again. The hairs on her arms stood up in paranoid fear. Before stepping off the bus, she took a few minutes to look through all of the windows. She took her time to look in all directions. It made no sound sense that he could be there. He wouldn't even know she'd left Melbourne yet. Regardless of acknowledging that truth, she was driven to be cautious. It had been part of her nature before she'd even met him. That level of need for caution had intensified since he had entered her world. It had grown further to colossal proportions in the weeks since she'd started to think about getting away.

When she was sure it was safe to leave the confines of the vehicle, Alexis stepped down into the sunlight. In Brisbane, it would be 2pm. He'd have now finished lunch and would be guiding the client back into the conference room he always had set up for that purpose each week. He held control of everything about such days - the location, the time, and even the catering. The client was far too important to him in his work. He wouldn't risk offending them by even pulling his phone out of his pocket to look at it during lunch. It would be turned off, and it would stay turned off - until 9pm. At 9pm he would call her with an instruction. That was his thing, and he reliably did it every single Friday.

Alexis looked around her and took a moment to inhale deeply as she embraced the sunlight hitting her face. She didn't know the name of the town she'd arrived in. She didn't *want* to know. She wanted to pass
~~~~~

through silently and leave no impression on anyone so that if anyone asked, no-one would have noticed her.

She made her way to an information centre and picked up a small map to find out where longer distance buses would leave from. There she assessed timetables to pick the next town she would go to. She had already investigated bus timetables and routes, but she hadn't booked anything. She had avoided choosing any particular town for any particular purpose. It was her belief that if she wanted to leave no trace, it would be best to not make any definite plans. She would deal with every decision as it had to be made, and just keep moving forward as she could.

After viewing the timetable and looking at her watch to see the time, Alexis walked inside. She asked to pay cash for a ticket on the bus that looked most attractive to her. It gave her just under two hours to wait. That was time enough to find a public bathroom. In there she could use a sink to do whatever washing up she could to freshen up and change her appearance slightly. After that, she would venture into the small supermarket she could see, to buy enough food to get her through the next leg of her journey.

In the public bathroom, she looked at her reflection. The mousy brown hair she saw was her natural colour. For the moment, she wouldn't think of colouring or cutting it. That was a step she would only take when she finally reached wherever it was that she would end up.

Out of her bag, she pulled out another cap she had bought. She'd purchased four in total at the used clothing store, all quite different from one another. She didn't know if it would make any difference or not in concealing herself. Having paid only 50c for each one, it was worth a try.

She pulled her hair tight and wove it around her hand, forming it into a tight ball. Slipping the cap over it made it seem like she had short hair. She had already washed away all trace of any makeup that might have been residual. She'd put on a bulky old jersey and jeans that were tidy enough not to be overly noticed for being too shabby. She didn't want to be noticed for good *or* for bad.

Standing back and looking in the mirror, she saw a nobody. She was slender in physique, having lost so much weight over the past year or so. She suspected she could be construed as a woman or a man from a distance - and under the view of a security camera. Taking a deep breath, she stepped out into the sunlight again and walked into the supermarket, eyes straight ahead. She wouldn't face upward, revealing her face, nor downward, like someone purposely trying to avoid security cameras.

In the supermarket, she stocked up on a large bottle of water and a healthy supply of fruit and baked goods to keep her going. It was a nervous hour more before the bus appeared that she would next jump onto. It would take her through the night and deliver her to another town early the following morning.

Once again she settled down into a seat, this time for a much longer period. Now she would let herself sleep. If he found her on the bus, she would be woken anyway. She'd gotten away. There was nothing more she could do. She may as well try and recuperate some of the lost slumber while she had a long journey of many hours ahead of her.

The bus moved forward. Alexis watched out the window, silently saying goodbye and thank you to a town that unknowingly had let a woman on the run slip right through it. Through that town had passed a woman with a determination to get what she wanted - to start a brand new life. A life without pain. A life that would enable her to start rebuilding her soul once again.

In Brisbane, it was now 4pm. He would call her in five hours. In five hours, he would know that she was, at that moment, not accessible to him. In five hours, his questions would begin.

In five hours, Alexis would still be asleep, on a bus, in the middle of nowhere. It was a terrifying thought, but she would sleep, because what else could she do?

~~~~~

"Wake up, little lady," Alexis heard a man's voice saying to her as she felt a gentle prod on her arm.

Immediately she jumped. The driver saw a terrified look cross her face before she seemed to grow alert and realise where she was.

"I'm sorry to have startled you, but it's time for you to get off the bus now," the man continued.

Alexis looked at him. She saw nothing but kindness in his eyes, even though she was wary of him.

"I'm sorry," she mumbled quietly before gathering her things and making her way off the bus.

In her confusion, she forgot her plan to look through the windows first. She'd wanted to make sure no-one was nearby who looked like they might be looking or waiting for her. As her feet touched the ground, she cursed at herself inwardly for overlooking what she considered to be such an important thing. She then forced herself to relax. If he was going to find her, he was going to find her - if he was even likely to come after her. As she travelled further away from Melbourne, she could feel just a sliver of relaxation falling over her. That wasn't what she wanted. She needed to always be alert and never get complacent.

Her mind began to consider other outcomes. What if he *didn't* bother to look for her? What if she wasn't that important to him after all? What if his extreme levels of power and financial status made him not even care if she was gone from his life for good?

She let the questions flow over her. For a few minutes, she felt a sense
~~~~~

of complete freedom at the possibility. After she'd indulged in that fantasy for long enough, she made sure to bring her mind back to the here and now. There was no time for complacency in her thinking. If he never sought her out again, that was fine. She still had to keep moving forward as if he would - as if he most *definitely* would.

~~~~~

Looking around the bus destination, she saw she was in a small town with a long but quiet main street. Dotted around the outside of that were buildings and houses of all shapes and sizes. In the distance, Alexis could see vast land beyond the border of the mismatched structures.

Once again she determined to seek out public toilets and somewhere that sold bus tickets. As she walked around, she realised that despite her predicament, she had enjoyed a good night's sleep. The result was a new sense of energy and empowerment.

She was alone. Some people would hate being in that situation, but she was alone and, at least for the moment, she loved it.

Walking through the main street, she sought out the locations of the supermarket and the public restrooms. There was no bus terminal in sight, nor anything that seemed to be advertising a bus service.

Tentatively she stood still, wondering what to do next. As she considered her options, a man who appeared to be around her age walked up to her.

"You look lost," he said, smiling at her.

Alexis jumped backward in surprise. The voice was remarkably similar to *his*. The man immediately looked apologetic.

"I'm sorry," he continued with a cheerful voice. "I wasn't trying to cause you to have a heart attack". It was a voice that told her he was only trying to be easy going and friendly.

Alexis looked at him carefully, the same paranoia immediately jumping into her mind. Was *he* planted to find her and take her back? If so, he wouldn't know everything about the town already. In desperation, she resolved to test him to see if he would hesitate in answering a question.

"I was hoping to find somewhere to buy a bus ticket. Can you tell me where I can do that?" she asked.

She held her head up while maintaining a strong gaze on his face. She was determined to read anything that might suggest he wasn't the town local he appeared to be. All she saw on his face was immediate confusion.

"You only just set foot off that bus over there, and already you want to go back to where you just came from?" he asked. His facial expression changed from one of confusion to one of amusement. "What have we done in such a short time to make you want to return to wherever you've
~~~~~

just travelled from?"

Alexis couldn't help it. For the first time in a long while, she thought that, for once, she could just enjoy an interaction without worrying if there was a consequence to come from it. She wanted to be carefree, but she still fought the natural desire to laugh along with him. She could not let herself be so easily convinced that everything was normal.

"I ..." she stuttered. "I was hoping to catch a bus somewhere else."

He looked closely at her face. The woman before him had definitely not done her homework. He could see her growing increasingly distraught by the minute. Although it was his nature to tease, her expression indicated that teasing might not be the right thing to do at that moment.

"Lady, this is an end of the line town as far as the bus goes," he said. "It comes here from one town, and then it goes back to the same town shortly afterwards. It does that five days a week. No other buses come here."

Alexis felt a deep feeling of regret in her heart. She had spent money on the bus fare, and now would have to backtrack with another ticket? How had her research not identified that it was a town she should avoid if she wanted to keep moving in one direction?

Suddenly the young man smiled at her, as if he'd told a great joke.

"But there is a train that comes three days a week. Would that suffice?"

He heard her breathe a deep sigh of relief. That relief seemed to be mixed in with what appeared to be an equal measure of anger.

"Three days a week?" Alexis asked timidly. She felt slightly relieved but already knew in her heart what the answer to her next question would be. "Is there one coming today?"

He smiled at her with such an easy-going smile that Alexis realised she'd forgotten what it was like to be so at ease in the world. To not worry so much. To not be afraid. To not feel like every little thing she did was a cause of pain to someone.

"One did pass through this morning, but won't be coming back today," the man continued. "If you want to catch the next one, you'll have to stay here for two nights. Otherwise, you'll have to get right back on that bus over there that you just arrived on, and scadoodle back to where you just came from."

Alexis forgot herself for a moment and laughed at him.

"Scadoodle?" she asked.

Without thinking, she found herself suddenly giggling uncontrollably. She then realised she'd forgotten just how good it *felt* to laugh - to *really* laugh. Why had she let all of her humour be taken from her? How had she let herself become so serious in her life? She was 21 years old. She felt like she was at least 50.

She focused on him once more and saw on his face that same look of amusement. With a slight grin and one eyebrow raised, it was as if he were asking 'what on Earth is this girl about? It wasn't that funny.'

As Alexis felt her laughter subside, she discovered another small amount of her stress had melted away. She resolved to not let that happen too often. For the moment, however, there was someone in front of her who seemed happy to help her. Even more importantly, for the first time in a long while, she felt relaxed around another human being.

"Okay," she said. "Where can I buy a train ticket?"

He looked at her, seeing her face transform from happy to serious.

"At the train station. Would you like me to walk you there?" he asked.

Reading her mood change and not wanting to upset her, he forced himself to move down a gear into polite mode. He saw her nod while maintaining a look of reluctance on her face.

"Only if I'm not holding you up from your work, or whatever you're supposed to be doing," Alexis replied. "If you want, you can just point me in the..."

"It's no bother. At this time of day, I don't have anywhere I need to be. Come this way," he said and began walking away with Alexis following behind him.

Noticing her slowness, he slowed in his walking, expecting they would then be walking side by side. Instead, he saw her walk slower still, so she was still behind him. Out of his natural curiosity, he took his walking to an excessively slow speed. He slowed almost as if he were making fun, or in a slow-motion movie, just to see what she would do. Yet again she slowed right down. There was no doubt - for whatever reason, she seemed determined to stay behind him.

Finally, he stopped and turned to her. Startled, Alexis looked down at her feet, not raising her eyes to him. He found himself perplexed at the situation.

"Are you alright?" he asked her. Straight away, something about the sound of his voice made her still, serene and non-responsive, like she was waiting for something. "Hey, lady!" he said, more aggressively. That seemed to wake her up from whatever trance she had been in.

Alexis looked at him in confusion. For a few moments, she had felt like she was somewhere else, with some*one* else.

"I'm sorry," she muttered. "What did you say?"

He looked at her with an expression of utter amazement.

"Where were you just then?" he asked, dumbfounded. "You seemed to just ... zone out."

He watched her face as she appeared to have difficulty processing what he had said. He resolved to wait patiently and not press her for any information. Finally, he saw her face clear entirely.

"I'm fine," she mumbled. "Thank you."

She moved forward, so she was beside him, and they continued their walk toward the train station. Nothing more was said between them.

As Alexis stood and read through the train timetable, she tried to assess each name on the long list of places the train would stop at. None of them looked familiar, leaving her unsure where she should buy a ticket to. All of a sudden, she felt an overwhelming sense of uselessness flow over her. Her mind started to kick at her through her thoughts. In her head she could hear the cursing, 'you are so stupid', over and over again.

Behind her, she could sense the man who had offered to help her. She didn't even know his name, but she was very aware of him.

"Do you know where you want to go?" he asked gently, speaking in a voice that was too much like…

Alexis jumped and moved away quickly, not letting herself be pulled into her fears at that moment. She wanted to be strong, but his voice being so similar brought out in her too many memories. She stood aside, apart from him. She had to focus her eyes on him to reassure her mind that the man before her was not *him*. After a few minutes of them looking at each other, she found the strength to speak.

"Have you been to any of these places?" she asked as she pointed to the train schedule. She saw him nod in response. "Which do you think will be the most populated?"

He didn't speak but was surprised by her questions. His finger raised and pointed at the name on the list that he felt would most suit her needs.

Alexis nodded and moved indoors to purchase the ticket. When she paid for it, she felt tearful. It would take a fair amount of the cash she had on her, but at least she would be further away. She just had to hold on and move forward. Once she was far enough away, she'd be able to focus on rebuilding a new life.

Ticket in her hand, she felt a brief sense of renewal. It was short-lived.

"What will you do until you can catch the train?" the man before her asked. "Do you have somewhere you can stay?"

The feeling of renewal and hope faded in Alexis as she realised she would have to find accommodation. That would take even more of her limited money. She was angry at herself for not having just withdrawn all of her cash that morning, instead of purposely leaving it in her bank account. It had seemed a good idea at the time. She hadn't wanted to make it so obvious that she'd left Melbourne and didn't intend to go back. Now that she had limited funds to survive on, she questioned whether it had been wise at all.

"I don't. Where do you suggest?" she asked the man in front of her.

Once again, she was greeted with a further look of disbelief.

"There's only a pub to stay in, here in town. It's most likely full, but we can go and check," he said softly.

Alexis nodded and followed him.

Hearing that there were no rooms for rent when they reached the pub, Alexis felt exhaustion set in. She found herself wanting to just sit down, go to sleep, and not bother waking up again. It was a new level of deflation, even for her. What stupid situation had she now gotten herself into? Stuck in a town for two nights without somewhere to stay?

"I have a spare room at my house," the man said. "Come with me, and you can stay there." Once more, the likeness of his voice startled her. "Now, don't look like that. I can see that you're running away from something that might not be pleasant. I'm only offering you a roof over your head for two nights. You can't sleep out here on the streets. It might look like a sleepy town, but it has its bad folk, just as all towns do."

Alexis looked at him, dreading she was about to get herself into the same situation she'd just run from, but what was the alternative? Like he had said, sleeping on the streets wouldn't likely be any safer. Determined to at least be gracious and not let him know her fears inside, she looked directly at him.

"Thank you," she said.

He nodded in response, looked away from her, and began walking. He was glad to see her at ease as she walked beside him. It was a twenty-minute walk to his home. In that time, they said nothing. Questions started to emerge in his head. He determined to keep them quiet, afraid of startling her.

As they began walking up a long path to an old homestead, Alexis felt her breath catch. For several minutes, she was transported outside of her mind and the thoughts that plagued her there. All she could see and be aware of was the beauty around her.

"Oh!" she breathed out, taking in the beauty of the house before her. The verandah seemed to engulf it on all sides that she could see. Various colours of rose bushes were climbing up a long trellis along the front of the verandah.

The man stopped walking and looked at her, thinking for a moment that she was in pain, or had remembered something awful. When he looked closely at her, he was surprised that she seemed to have changed again. Now she looked like she wasn't afraid or downhearted at all. She'd changed into someone who was looking at something she considered amazing.

Alexis turned to him and looked him directly in the eye.

"This is your home?" she asked. She saw him nod, with a confused look on his face. It was clear that he didn't understand why she was being affected so much. "It's so beautiful," she whispered, turning her view back to the homestead in front of her.

Never in her life had she seen anything as beautiful and welcoming. She'd never lived, or even visited, anywhere with the kind of heritage and standing that the house in front of her had.

He laughed softly at her, still with a sense of confusion about who she was and what was intriguing her so much. To him, it was the house he grew up in - nothing more, nothing less.

"Come inside," he said, turning away and beginning to walk again. It was only when he went to put the key in the front door that he realised she wasn't beside him. He turned around and saw her standing exactly where she had been, still seeming to drink in the sight before her.

"Oy!" he yelled out at her in amusement to wake her up out of her daze. Surprisingly it seemed to work. He saw her blink and refocus before beginning to walk up the path toward him.

Despite her previous moment of relaxation and joy, Alexis found herself growing highly agitated and extremely hesitant when she stood at the front entrance to the home. What was she doing? Why was she going into the house of a man she didn't know?

He sensed her fear and spoke to her as he would to a stray kitten.

"I am going to go inside, and I'm going to leave this door open," he said gently. "If you want to come inside, please do. If you don't want to, that's okay too."

Then he was gone, leaving Alexis alone on the verandah.

She took a few minutes to decide what to do. She didn't have any feeling about this man that told her he was like *him*. Then again, she hadn't had any feelings about *him* either before things had changed, and in doing so, had begun to change her. It was only two nights of shelter that she needed. What could happen in two nights?

Feeling a chill move through her, Alexis noticed that the weather was turning. She didn't want to be out in the cold and rain when it did. Indecisive, she moved to an outdoor sofa she saw along the verandah, and sat on it. As she relaxed back into it, she looked out at the rose bushes and breathed in the heavenly scent emanating from them.

Inside, under a blanket of confusion about the strangeness of the woman he had met, the man did as he'd told her he would. Two cups of coffee were made and carried out to the verandah on a tray, along with milk, sugar and cookies. He wasn't sure she would still be there when he got outside. He was relieved to see that she was, given the fear growing in him that she was going to try and sleep rough that night, which could lead to any bad situation.

Alexis heard him come out and watched as he put the tray on the low coffee table in front of the sofa. Seeing the cups of coffee, she felt the hairs on her arms and back of her neck rise instantly. At that moment, she realised the fear she had about drinking anything she hadn't prepared herself.

"How many sugars do you have?" he asked as if nothing were odd about the situation they had both found themselves in.

"I..." she stuttered. "I don't want any coffee," she continued, even though the smell of it was divine.

Alexis saw him shrug it off as if it were no big deal. As she watched, he put sugar and milk into his cup and then sat down beside her. He made sure not to sit too close, but as far along as the arms of the sofa would allow. After he took a long drink, she heard him let out an appreciative sigh.

When he looked at her, he saw her looking at the cup longingly.

"Do you want some?" he asked again. She looked uncertain. The thought popped into his head about why she might not accept it from him. "If you're worried that I put something in your cup, here, take this one. Look," he said, taking another sip so she could see it was alright. "It's fine."

Alexis found the cup handed out to her. Finally, she accepted it. She watched him put sugar and milk into the remaining cup, and take it for himself.

"Now, Missy, I can see that you probably don't want to talk about whatever is going on with you," he said. "I do think, though, that if you do want to stay here, we can at least exchange names. Do you agree?" he asked.

Alexis sat quiet, not wanting to do that at all.

"Well, whether you want to tell me who you are or not, I'm Anthony," he continued as he held out his hand.

Alexis shrunk back from the hand at first. It was an automatic reaction for her. As she realised what he was doing, she took a deep breath and placed her hand in his.

"Anthony," she breathed out. It was a brand new name for her to hear.

She'd never met anyone in person who had that name. It provided a brief moment of excitement before she saw him looking at her expectantly. It panicked her. She didn't want to disclose her name at all. She also didn't want to lie and find herself in a situation where he spoke to her and called her by that name, and she wouldn't remember to respond to it.

He had always insisted on calling her Lexi, rather than her full name of Alexis. Considering her name in her head, she decided she could probably live with using the first half of her name from that moment forward. That wouldn't be too difficult to remember when spoken to. In a vague memory, she could even remember her mother calling her by it.

"I'm Allie," she said quietly, trying the name on for size and finding it was comfortable. Perhaps if anyone should come to the town looking for her, *he* might have forgotten her full name and not make the connection at all.

"Allie," Anthony said quietly, looking at her face. It was easy to read conflict and pain on it. "Well, welcome to my home, Allie," he continued.

For a moment, he continued to hold her hand tightly before she pulled it away.

They sat in silence, drinking their coffee while both deep in thought. He wanted to ask her questions, but didn't want to push her when she already seemed so wound up over whatever had happened to her.

The further away from Melbourne she was getting, the more Alexis felt like some of her humanity was returning. She wanted to show appreciation for the man's kindness if that was what it would turn out to be, but everything seemed difficult since she was afraid to speak and say too much.

"What *can* you talk about, Allie?" he asked so gently that she almost spoke without thinking first. "Or, if you don't want to talk about yourself, what would you like to ask me? What would you want to know, that would help you feel more at ease?"

Alexis took some time to formulate words in her head. She was well used to assembling and assessing her thoughts before she verbalised them. Over time, she had taught herself how to consider how every single word she said could be perceived. It was now a natural thing for her to do.

Although she'd never been a natural conversationalist, she had always believed in good manners. She wouldn't immediately ignore someone being kind to her. Despite her natural apprehension, she had to at least try and trust the person beside her.

"Do you live here alone?" she asked tentatively, finding her way toward conversation.

"Yep," Anthony replied as he nodded. "This was my family home. I grew up here. Since my parents died, I've just kept living here. My brother was living here with me, but moved to Sydney earlier this year. It's a big house for one person, I know, but it's home."

"Do you … work?" she asked, slowly relaxing more and more.

"I do," he replied, smiling at her. "I'm a baker. I work in the bakery section of the town supermarket."

Alexis picked up one of the cookies in front of her. When she looked at him with a question posed on her face, she saw him laugh softly.

"Yeah, I baked those. I like baking. It relaxes me," he said, feeling the armour next to him falling back ever so slightly. "And it tastes so good, too!"

He saw a glimmer of a slight laugh almost escape her. It was immediately suppressed. He sat silent, waiting for her courage to build up again.

"Are you … curious … about me?" she asked quietly. She couldn't help but wonder what he was thinking about her situation and her inability to talk to him confidently.

Anthony studied her face for a few minutes. Her eyes were downcast. He wasn't sure if it indicated she felt she shouldn't look at him, or if she was too afraid to look at him. He perceived that with the woman facing him, formulating the right words might be extremely important. He took his time.

"Of course I am," he said, letting a moment pass before he continued. "You seem so … troubled. But I can see you don't want to talk about it, and I'm fine with that. It's just a part of life that sometimes we have things happen to us, that we just want to keep to ourselves. I don't think there's anything wrong with that."

"Will you … want me to … do things, while I'm here?" she asked as if it were the most natural question in the world.

Anthony only felt confused by her words.

"Do you mean, like, wash your dishes and make your bed?"

He saw her face take on a look of frustration as she continued to keep her eyes down.

"No, I mean, *do* things," she said.

"Allie, you might need to be a bit more straight up with me. What is your real question?"

"Please you," she said.

Anthony gulped heavily in surprise.

"*Please* me?" he asked, trying to ascertain what she meant. He let the words roll around in his mind and could only come up with one thing she could mean, surely. "Do you mean … *sexually?*" he blurted out in horror, sincerely hoping that he must be wrong.

Alexis heard the question and nodded. All the while, she kept her eyes down, just as she'd had drummed into her she must do when talking to a man. She found that the sound of his voice was so like *his* that by listening to it, she'd unknowingly fallen under his spell.

"No!" he said forcefully. Straight away, he saw her wilt and yet also become rigid at the same time. Before his eyes, he could see her completely shut down. "Why would you think that?" he asked, feeling uncertain about how that question had made him feel. He waited for her answer. Receiving none, he studied her for a long while, still waiting. When no response came, he spoke again. "And why won't you look at me now?" he asked further. All he saw on her face was confusion.

"I..." Alexis started to say before giving up.

Before Anthony's eyes she seemed to deflate even further, the life going out of her all of a sudden. He put his cup on the table and reached over. After seeing an initial shock on her part, he took her cup and moved it out of the way.

"Allie, can you look at me?" he asked tentatively. It was an effort to try something to gain a better understanding of who the woman sitting beside him was. When she didn't look up, he purposely changed his tone. "Allie, look at me!"

Instantly he saw her raise her head and look into his eyes. Without her having to say any more, he understood then a great deal about her. He didn't want to force her to do anything. What he could see, however, was that the only way he might be able to keep her safe for the following two nights, might be to speak to her in that way. He stood up and reached out toward her.

"Stand up and take my hand," he said. He watched her obey, as if in a trance. "Walk with me," he continued.

They moved into the house. She didn't even seem to have any awareness of the fact that she'd been afraid to enter the house earlier.

Anthony led her to his lounge area. After instructing her to sit on the sofa, he went outside to bring in her bag and the coffee tray. He closed the front door on the way back in. When he returned, he saw she was down on her knees on the floor with her head hung low.

"Get up," he said.

Anthony watched as she did as commanded. She stood before him, head down and eyes down. It was almost as if she was a robot, void of any humanity.

Stepping up to her, he gently and slowly raised his hand toward her chin. He couldn't miss her flinch as his hand moved closer. Despite her obvious discomfort, he persisted. Softly he touched his hand to her chin and raised her face so that she was looking at him.

"Allie, stop!" he said to her forcefully.

Something about his voice, and seeing his face, startled Alexis. She seemed to break out of whatever trance she'd been in, as if waking from a hazy dream. She had been thinking she was somewhere else - with *someone* else. Thinking about what had just happened scared her.

"Are you back with me now?" Anthony asked and saw her nod in response. "Sit down here and talk to me."

Alexis felt disoriented but did as he suggested.

"What happened to you just then? You seemed to shut down and not hear me asking you anything," he started. He was glad that at least she seemed to be looking directly at him. "You only responded when I commanded you. What's that about?"

Alexis felt deep anguish inside of her. She'd had moments like that at different times over the previous three years. Some of them, she'd lost time in. She hadn't since remembered what she'd done, or what had been done to her. Until now, she hadn't even considered that it might be a part of who she was, and not only directly related to who she'd been with.

Anthony saw her start to look down once more. Fearful that he would lose her again, he instructed her to keep looking right at him.

"Keep your eyes on me, Allie, so you remember who you are talking to," he said.

She looked into his eyes and nodded, still alarmed at what was happening to her.

"Do you even know that you just tuned out for the past few minutes, like you didn't know I was here?" he asked. He saw her head shake, confirming what he had already thought. "You shouldn't be travelling by yourself if you fall into trances like that. If someone else sees as easily as I could that you're willing to do anything that they tell you to - Allie, you won't be safe."

She nodded at him, knowing he was right.

"What has happened to you, to make you act like that?" he asked quietly. With each word he spoke, he purposely held her gaze so she wouldn't slip away from him.

Continuing to look into his eyes, Alexis breathed out heavily. She didn't want to talk about her past. In her eyes, tears started to appear. For weeks she'd been working so hard to just try and get to a point where she could get away and start moving toward a new life. Now it felt hopeless. She was damaged goods. Her mind was no longer her own. She couldn't see how she could possibly undo that.

But in front of her - forcing her to look at him directly so she wouldn't forget who she was with - was a man who didn't appear set on hurting her at all. If he was, he could have done anything to her in the previous few minutes. She was angry within herself, for being someone who couldn't trust any other human being. No-one seemed trustworthy to her - not even someone who only showed her kindness.

"I don't want to talk about those things," she started to say before finding the tears running even more freely. "Please don't make me."

Anthony looked at her in pity.

"*Make* you? I'm not going to *make* you do or say anything you don't want to," he responded. He had no idea how to keep her calm and feeling safe in his home. "How about you grab your bag and I show you to the guest room?"

Alexis nodded and stood up to follow him, not letting her eyes leave him for a moment. That voice was just too similar.

"You can sleep in here," Anthony said as he opened the door to a large bedroom.

In it, Alexis could see a selection of old furniture, including a large brass-framed bed.

"Just across the hallway, there's the bathroom," Anthony continued. "There's no ensuite, I'm afraid, but there is a lock on the inside of the bathroom door, so you'll be quite safe, I assure you."

He watched her as she walked into the bedroom and looked around her, still with tears fresh in her eyes.

"Are you hungry? It's almost lunchtime. At this time of day, I usually cook up something simple. Today I'm feeling like having eggs and bacon. I am more than happy to prepare some for you too," he said. He saw her eyes instantly pick up and look at him like she hadn't eaten in weeks.

Alexis studied him. She was in a bedroom, in a strange house, with a strange man. He could, right at that moment, be forcing her to do *anything* - but he wasn't. Instead, he was standing before her, informing her of the lock on the bathroom door, and offering to cook her lunch.

Thinking about the food that was suddenly on offer, she heard her tummy growl loudly in response. It broke the tension for both of them, making them both laugh.

"I'll take that as a yes to eggs and bacon then, shall I?" he asked in a light-hearted way.

Alexis nodded back at him, grateful.

"Can I help?" she asked.

Anthony felt uncertain of what would be the best response to give her.

"If you want to. I'll make a start. You get settled and come down to the kitchen when you want to. It's down this end of the hallway," he said calmly, pointing in the direction opposite the front door before he started to walk away.

Once on her own again, Alexis put her bag on the bed and sat down. Looking around, she was overwhelmed with the realisation that she was in a real home. That was something she'd never felt a part of. Seeing photos on the mantelpiece over the fireplace, slowly she stood and went over to look at them. Some of them looked so old that she found her curiosity about them intense. Looking from one to the next, she found a more modern one of two parents and two boys. As she studied it, she was sure she could identify Anthony as one of the boys. He was young in it - maybe 12 or 13 years old - but his face was similar enough. Even in that photo, he looked kind. She hoped her gut was right about him. She hoped he really was as nice as he seemed to be.

Emotions flowed through her that made her feel incredibly alone, and incredibly sad. Once again, she fought tears straining in her eyes. She moved from the bedroom to the bathroom and locked the door. Standing at the hand basin, she looked in the mirror. Who was that person staring back at her? She kind of looked like her - like a run down and worn image of who she was as a person - but she didn't feel like her. She'd never been overly confident, or sociable, or any of those positive things she wanted to be deep inside. As she studied the face in the mirror, the person staring back at her seemed like someone else altogether.

Moving to sit on the toilet, Alexis let the emotions break through fully. They didn't come out in a dribble or even a light flow. They let loose like floodgates being opened, and she let them. She'd held back for weeks how she'd been feeling about the track her life seemed to be on. Even over the previous thirty-six hours, she'd held back. Her recent focus had been on keeping it all together so she could get away. Now she sat and held back no more. She had to heal. She knew that. It was up to her to let it happen, or at least to let it *begin.*

Sitting in the bathroom, she openly wept. She didn't move until all the tears that had been threatening were finally released. When she felt them end, she got up, rinsed her face, unlocked the bathroom door, and walked to the kitchen. Already she could smell the alluring scent of bacon cooking. The glorious scent made her salivate in the realisation that it had been a very long time since she'd eaten a proper meal.

Anthony saw Alexis slowly make her way to where he was cooking. He observed the redness in her eyes but said nothing. If she wanted to talk, she would talk. His most pressing desire was simply to make sure she was safe for two nights. He was also determined to make sure that she ate. In his view, she looked like she had forgotten that simple requirement of life, for far too long.

Alexis felt shy, even though she didn't want to. She wanted to feel normal, but what did normal even feel like? She raised her eyes to meet his and found him watching her steadily.

"Do you want your eggs on toast?" he asked. The tone of his voice indicated nothing was out of the ordinary, and they were established friends.

Alexis nodded and mumbled quietly, "Yes, please."

After handing one plate to her, he led her to the dining table in the centre of the large kitchen.

Sitting down, Alexis felt almost desperate to eat the food in front of her. She held back, determined to at least maintain some semblance of manners.

"Dig in," Anthony said, pointing to her plate before starting to eat his meal. "I know it's not entirely nutritious, but it tastes good."

He saw her look at him, watching him take the first few bites of his bacon before she finally looked down again. Slowly he saw her pick up her knife and fork, cut one tiny piece of bacon, and move it to her mouth.

Anthony stopped his eating mid-chew and watched her. It was like watching slow motion as he saw her raise her fork to her mouth and pull the tiny piece of bacon in before closing her mouth and starting to chew slowly. Her eyes were closed. She looked like she was truly in the moment, as if that tiny piece of bacon was the most amazing thing she had ever tasted in her entire life.

Alexis revelled in the flavour, and the freedom to *enjoy* the flavour openly without having to pretend otherwise. She didn't want to monitor every little thing that she put in her mouth, out of fear of what would happen if it was the wrong thing. She chewed and swallowed. Upon noticing the silence, she opened her eyes. She was initially startled by the intense look on the face before her, before she let herself relax and smile sheepishly.

"I haven't had bacon in a long time," she said quietly.

Her voice made Anthony think of a timid mouse. Her speaking broke him out of his gaze, and he smiled back at her.

"Well, then you have some serious making up to do, Missy," he said in a tone that was far more relaxed than he felt at that moment. He was determined to make light of whatever she had been experiencing a moment earlier. "Don't be polite on my account, because I won't be on your account. I love food, and I eat it as I want to."

His speech seemed to activate a different switch inside of her. Straight away, he saw her look down and start to eat - *really* eat. He suspected that not only hadn't she eaten in a very long time, but she also expected she would never again eat *after* that meal.

They sat in silence, each indulging in the food before them. Finally, Alexis put her knife and fork on her plate and sat back in the chair, hand on her belly.

"Thank you," she said. "That really was the best food I've ever had."

Although at first, Anthony thought from the words that she was exaggerating humorously, when he looked at her face, he wondered if indeed she was.

"You are very welcome, Allie," he replied softly, determined not to scare her or put her in any position where she felt threatened.

He saw her look at the clock on the kitchen wall. For a moment, he felt scared as she seemed to be heading into a deep trance again. She had been looking at the clock for so long that he felt the need to speak. He had to make sure she wasn't disappearing into herself again.

"Do you have to be somewhere?" he asked.

There was enough force behind his words to succeed in bringing her gaze back to him.

For a few minutes, Alexis had looked at the clock and suddenly found herself thinking about the time. It was 12.45pm. It was now more than 15 hours past the time that he would have turned his phone on to leave an instruction for her. What had he thought when she hadn't answered her phone, and he'd heard her 'too sick to answer' message? What would he have done? Where would he have gone? What actions would he have taken to get to her? Where was he, right at that exact moment in time?

Suddenly Anthony's voice came through the haze of her mind. She turned back to him and forced a smile, albeit a sad one.

"No, Anthony," she replied. "I have nowhere else I need to be."

CHAPTER 2

The Softening

Anthony watched the young woman on the seat near the sofa he was settled on. It had certainly been an interesting day, to say the least. Now that they'd gotten through the afternoon and into the early evening, the young woman had settled into one of the large armchairs in his lounge. She seemed more at peace since he'd encouraged her to choose a movie for them to watch. To him, it appeared that the concept initially had seemed strange to her. It was like it would never occur to her to watch a movie in the comfort of one's own home. To Anthony, it had always been a good way to escape the realism of life, even if only for a couple of hours. As he looked at her face, he hoped she was falling under that spell too.

Under the guise of watching the movie as well, his view was more focused on her. From the angle of where he was sitting, he could view her face while still broadly facing the television in front of them. He needn't have worried about that. Her attention was well-focused on the screen in front of her. While she was at peace, he took the time to study her. It was something that he hadn't had time to even consider with all that had happened since he'd seen her get off the bus that morning.

There were physical attributes about her that he noticed for the first time. They were the simple and obvious things like her hair being shoulder-length and brownish blond, and her clear, pale skin. She wore no makeup whatsoever, but she suited natural. Her clothing looked like it wasn't new. It also looked like it wasn't from last year or even probably the year before. Looking closely, it seemed like she was wearing clothing that could be a decade old. Perhaps it had been bought from a vintage store, except there was nothing about anything she had on that said 'fashion' so probably not vintage, so much as second hand. It was clothing that had been chosen to be comfortable, but there was something else about it. To him, it appeared that it had also been chosen to give her an air of 'genderlessness'. Wearing those clothes, with her hair hidden under the cap as it had been when he'd first seen her, she could pass as being either a man or a woman.

Age? Status? Perhaps around his age - 23? 24? When it came to status, he couldn't guess. She looked like she had no money, and hadn't come from money. When she'd spoken, she hadn't given any indication of having had no education or at least teaching in good manners, so he didn't think she'd grown up very poor. He was also curious about the way she ate. She'd displayed an extreme level of control during both meals they'd enjoyed together, cutting every piece of food into the smallest size before she ate it. Was that due to the way she'd been raised in childhood, or was it something she'd started to do later in life?

He then remembered her reaction to seeing his house when they had first arrived. It had seemed like an extreme degree to which she'd appeared awestruck by it, even though it was just a normal old house. It was almost as if she'd never *been* in a house before. Anthony wondered how that could be. Even in the biggest cities, he knew there were regular houses - plenty of them. What exactly had intrigued her so much about it?

Suddenly he heard and saw her giggle at something that happened in the movie. He smiled at the sight and sound. What a complex person she was. In one day - and not even a whole day yet - she had taken him on a journey of learning and wonder. Now they sat in his home together, doing the mundane thing of watching a movie together. He realised the degree to which he was somewhat perplexed by the whole situation.

His day had begun as usual. He'd gotten up early in the morning to go into work at the supermarket bakery, and then left once the day's work was complete, still fairly early in the morning. He couldn't remember what he'd intended to do when he left work. It had been only a few minutes after walking out the door of the supermarket that he'd almost run into her.

As he looked at the time on the old clock on the mantelpiece, he knew that soon he would have to go to bed. It was a tempting thought to call in sick and not go to work in the morning, but he wouldn't do that. He couldn't let his boss or work colleagues down. There was never a downtime in that bakery. He looked at the movie and judged that there was probably only another half hour left to go before it finished. With that thought, he settled back, resolved that he would go to bed once it finished.

When the credits started running, Alexis found herself relieved of a wide array of emotions. The movie had made her cry at one point, thoughtful in some moments, but laugh in many. She knew she'd needed that - desperately. She sat up and stretched before turning her head and seeing Anthony sitting quietly. He continued to look at the screen before turning to face her.

"Well, Allie, I am going to leave you now because I need to go to bed," he said quietly.

Alexis looked at the clock and then at him once more, her face full of curiosity.

"It's only 8 o'clock. Why do you go to bed so early?" she asked.

"I have to start work at 3 o'clock so that all the baking is done before the supermarket opens at eight," Anthony replied. "Are you feeling alright?" he asked, still not sure if he should leave her alone or not. In response, he saw her nod at him.

"Yeah," replied Alexis. "Watching a movie was a good idea. I feel much better now, thank you."

Anthony stood up to leave and saw her stand also.

"Do you want me to…" she started to ask.

He could see the same question on her face that she'd asked him when they'd first arrived at the house earlier that day. Before he replied, he made sure to keep his voice quiet and not as forceful as he had responded previously, guessing that the tone he'd used earlier had been what had sent her into a trance.

"Allie, you are a guest in my home," he said. "I invited you here because there's nowhere else for you to stay tonight or tomorrow night. What I want from you - what will give me peace of mind - is simply knowing that you're safe and you're okay. Please don't offer that again. Not only is it not … *required* … but it doesn't sit well with who I am. I don't know you, but I don't believe that you're not worth more than that, so don't offer yourself to me - or anyone else," he said. He watched thoughtfulness pass over her face. It seemed like she understood the individual words but just couldn't quite understand what he'd meant. "You are welcome to put on another movie if you wish."

Alexis looked at him, not knowing what she wanted or how she felt. His not seeming to need anything from her confused her. She shook the confusion aside and focused on the good. The thought of being able to spend a whole night in a bed without any fear appealed to her.

"No, I think I'll go to bed as well. I do feel tired," she said, forcing a smile.

They looked at each other before he started to turn away.

"Anthony," he heard her say. When he turned back, he saw her move forward and tentatively put her arms around him loosely. He responded by putting his arms around her, equally loosely.

"Thank you for helping me," she said. When she pulled back, tears began to flow in her eyes again. "You are a very kind man."

After giving her a soft smile, Anthony turned and walked away. She saw him walk down the corridor to the bathroom. He turned off most of the lights as he went, but left the main hallway one on.

Alexis waited until he was in the bathroom with the door closed before she walked into her bedroom and closed her door. There she sat on the bed and waited until she heard the bathroom door open again, and then another door close further down the hallway. Only then did she open her bag and pull out the new toothbrush and toothpaste she had bought the day before. She made her way into the bathroom for her final activity of the day before returning to her room. Taking off only her jeans and jersey, she climbed into the bed in her t-shirt and underwear to finally let herself drift off.

~~~~~

Sun was streaming through the window even though the curtains were pulled. It took a few minutes for Alexis to remember where she was. The sleep that she'd had was the best she'd had in ages. The bed that she was lying in felt like it had been made just for her. She had an instinct to jump out of bed and start doing things - something - anything. She caught herself in time to not move. Instead, she let herself enjoy a small smile to herself that on that day, she might be able to do not much at all. She grinned at the thought that she'd not have to do anything to a schedule that was set by someone else.

She lay in bed as long as she could before she knew she'd have to jump out to go to the bathroom. When she approached her bedroom door, she stood still and listened carefully. Not hearing anyone around, she remembered Anthony had said he would be at work early. She put on her jeans and jersey just in case, then tentatively tiptoed across the hallway to the bathroom. While in there, she looked at the deep claw-footed bath longingly. She couldn't even remember the last time she'd had a bath - not in privacy by herself anyway. Over the previous forty-eight hours, she had only washed briefly in public bathrooms, from small hand basins. Yes, she thought to herself. She would ask Anthony later about the possibility of having a bath. Maybe he would even expect her to just have one without asking, given how generous he'd already been with her. It was inside of her to not make any assumption like that, and to wait to ask properly … or to be told.

After visiting the bathroom, she walked lightly into the kitchen, still thinking she might be alone in the house. She was startled when she saw him sitting at the dining table.

"Sorry to scare you. Are you alright?" Anthony asked softly. As he looked at her, he could see she was once again wearing the same clothes as the day before.

"I…" she stuttered as she tried to calm down and find words after her initial shock. "I thought you were going to work."

He laughed at her softly.

"I *did* go to work, Allie. It's ten o'clock. I've already done my six hours of work, and have been home for almost an hour," he said. He slowly saw her gain an understanding of what he was saying. "Would you like me to make you some coffee?"

Alexis nodded and then remembered her manners before he could
~~~~~

stand up.

"No! Gosh, no, Anthony, I can make myself a cup of coffee. Would you like another cup?" she asked. Immediately she saw a look of pleasant surprise pass over his face.

"Yes," he said quietly, already seeing a difference in the demeanour of the woman in front of him. "Thank you."

Alexis got to work, finding her way around the large kitchen. She brought the two cups to the table, putting his down in front of him before she sat down opposite him. It felt strange, like it was an intimacy. She knew it felt strange only because she couldn't remember anything so normal in her life for so long.

She fought for words in her head. She was determined to begin working on the biggest regret of her life - her inability to converse easily with people.

"How was your work?" she asked.

Anthony instantly felt like he was under a bit of a spell all of a sudden. Looking at her, he could have considered he was with a completely different person from the day before.

"It was fun. I always love my work. I brought home some unsuccessful cake though - surviving bits of an unfortunate casualty in my baking this morning," he said as he laughed softly. "So I'm sorry, but you might be forced to eat ugly-but-tasty cake later," he continued.

He didn't think about his choice of words. As soon as he'd spoken, he saw a cloud pass over her face. When he played back his wording in his mind and realised his reference to force, he could have slapped himself. He knew he had to quickly think of a way to cover the reference up.

"Sorry. I wouldn't really force you to eat it. In fact, now that I think of it, I don't think I'll even share it. I want to keep it all for myself. Sorry, no cake sharing today," he started to say in a mock thoughtful state. He was relieved to see he did manage to get a smile out of her as she relaxed, making him relax also.

They sat in silence for some time, Alexis finding the view out of the window attractive and enticing. Following her view, Anthony spoke.

"Do you want to see my back yard?" he asked. "I can give you a tour if you like. I'm not much of a gardener, but I do prefer to eat what I grow, when I can."

Alexis nodded and stood up with him, intending to follow behind him. After waiting for him to begin walking, she realised he was purposely making her go first. It flustered her but also pleased her. She knew that was how things were meant to be in polite society - a man should let a woman go first. She wasn't sure how or why she'd let someone convince her in recent years that she deserved otherwise.

Out in the yard, Anthony took his time, showing her all the spoils to be had in his small but sufficient garden. Pointing out his beans, peas, greens, fruit trees and berries, he intermittently looked at her face. He was pleased to see her in awe once again, just as she had been when they'd arrived at the house the day before.

"It isn't much, but it's home, and it's enough for me," he said quietly.

Alexis smiled broadly at him.

"It's perfect," she said, for the first time seeming to be a completely open and easy-going person.

"Thank you," he whispered. The difference in her compared to the day before was immense. He couldn't help but wonder if her confident mood was there to stay, or if he should expect more unexplainable moments ahead. "Allie, do you want to have a shower? Or a bath? If you do, just help yourself. I have a good water system here, and there's usually a decent amount of hot water," he started to say, not wanting to alarm her again at the thought of what he might want from her. "I already had my shower when I came home from work, so you can use the bathroom for as long as you want. There's shampoo and stuff in there. If you want to change your clothes, I'll be doing a laundry wash soon. Anything we hang out soon should dry today if this weather holds, so would be clean and dry for your trip tomorrow."

Alexis looked at him, suddenly feeling the weight of the grime on her. She nodded shyly.

"I will do that. Thank you," she said quietly. "Now?" she then asked.

Anthony was surprised. It sounded like she was asking if *he* wanted her to wash now. It gave him a hint that there was a very good chance that the side of her that had revealed itself so strongly the day before, most definitely was still there. It might be hidden for the moment, but it was there, and it was very likely to come out again.

"Whenever you want to, Allie," he said. "Honestly, if you want to have a bath now, you can. If you want to have a shower now, you can. If you want to have either later, you can."

He watched her face as she seemed to transform again. It was as if she'd needed to get her head around the fact that she was allowed to make the decision herself. Upon realising that, she then seemed to need to take more time to actually make the decision.

"Yes, I will go and have a bath now, if you're sure," she said. She looked at him for confirmation.

Anthony purposely stood still with as much of a blank look on his face that he could produce.

She could see him forcing her to make the decision, and not bow down to him like she seemed to want to do. Understanding that he wasn't going to say anything, she nodded at him and smiled shyly.

"Okay, I'm going to have a bath."

Anthony watched her turn and walk away. He thought to himself, even without any knowledge of psychology, that she had a long way to go to even *start* to undo whatever had been done to her in recent years.

Alexis looked through her bag and found all clean items to throw together a different ensemble. It wouldn't be pretty, but it would feel good to have something different on - *anything* different on. When she went through to the bathroom, she found herself growing steadily excited as she began to run the bath. She sat on the edge of it, watching the water flow. She felt herself starting to become mesmerized by it, but couldn't stop herself.

She roused herself to turn the taps off and undress before climbing in and sinking down into the water. She slid right down so that even her face and hair were submerged. When she came up, she instantly felt more invigorated. Not wanting to get out to have a separate shower, she shampooed and rinsed her hair in the bathwater and massaged in the conditioner. She relaxed back and let the feeling of potential freedom flow over her. Picking up soap from the end of the bath, she grabbed a facecloth and started to wash. She didn't care about the colour the water was turning with two days of travel coming off her.

As she closed her eyes and washed, her mind started to wander back. All of a sudden, she felt like she was transported. She was in her own bath, and *he* had instructed her to clean herself - properly - thoroughly. Then she was to go to him in the bedroom, where he would be waiting for her. She must be thoroughly clean, and she must be hairless where he wanted her to be. There couldn't be the slightest presence of stubble, and there could be no dirt. She had to be scrubbed so clean that there was only fresh skin showing, with no dullness of dead skin cells.

As Alexis thought about all of this, she started unknowingly scrubbing at her skin with the facecloth. She had to shave. Where was her shaver? She was confused, not knowing where it was - not knowing where *she* was. Panic started to set in. What would he do if she wasn't shaven? What would he *do?*

She suddenly got out of the bath and walked to the door, not understanding why there was no shaver in the bathroom. Where else would there be a razor, because she had to shave…

Anthony watched the time on the clock as he sat in the lounge, feeling a little unnerved by knowing she was in the bath. He'd removed his razor and blades. He'd removed *everything* that had given him a bad feeling about her having access to when she had the ability to go into a trance.

When thirty minutes had passed, his nervousness reached a new level. Although he didn't want to intrude on her or cause her any stress, his level of concern surpassed any regard for her privacy. He went to the bathroom with the full intention of just knocking and asking if she was alright.

He stood at the door, uncertain of whether it was right to disturb her or not. As he was about to call out to ask if she was okay, the door opened.

Looking downward when she opened the door, Alexis saw his feet and didn't rightly comprehend who was in front of her. As Anthony watched, he saw her, naked, drop to her knees and sit still with her head down.

"Oh, no, you don't," he said to her. She didn't respond to the tone. He grabbed a large bath towel from the rack and put it around her before putting on a voice of command. "Allie, stand up!"

Immediately she did so, but he still had to hold onto the towel around her. She didn't seem aware of anything going on. When she was at eye level with him again, he saw that her eyes had glazed over. He took in the sight before him. She'd bathed, but she had conditioner thick in her hair. The blankness of her eyes made her look like she was just 'gone'. He waited to see if she would just snap out of it. When she didn't, he cringed inside, not knowing what to do.

He tried the same thing he had done the day before.

"Allie! Look right at me!" he said to her firmly, his voice verging on yelling. She didn't respond as easily as she had the previous day.

Feeling helpless, Anthony looked around him. He was still holding the towel around her. Out of respect, he didn't want to let that go. A distance away from them, he could see her clothes, and her hair was slick with the conditioner. Finally, his frustration got the better of him.

"FUCK!!!" he yelled loudly. He was beyond the point of being able to think straight and decide what was the right thing to do in the weird situation he'd found himself in.

Surprisingly, the level at which he had yelled finally seemed to reach her. He was trying to hold the towel securely around her with one hand. At the same time, he was trying to use his foot to reach out to her pile of clean clothes on the floor, in an attempt to drag them over so he could at least dress her. He had almost gotten them right over when he heard her voice.

"Anthony? What are you doing?!" she exclaimed as she took hold of the towel herself.

Anthony looked at her, relieved but at the same time horrified at what it must have looked like to her. She had every right to be angry and scared at him being in the bathroom with her.

"Allie, are you back? Please tell me that you really are here!" he said more forcefully than he would have preferred.

"What...?" Alexis started to ask. It was at that moment that she realised she'd blacked out again. However long it had been since she'd gotten into the bath, she had no recollection of.

"You lost it again, and you scared the *hell* out of me!" Anthony exclaimed. He took a deep breath to calm down. Finally, he felt his heart rate slow down once more. "I am going to leave the room so you can rinse that out of your hair and then get dressed. If you're not out of the bathroom in ten minutes, I'll assume something is wrong, and I'll come back again."

Alexis looked at him and nodded. It was hard to know which of the many feelings that were running through her, she should focus on and accept as the most important.

Slowly she let the water out of the bath and turned on the separate shower to rinse the conditioner out. What had happened had left her shaken, but it felt good to wash away the soapy feeling on her skin. After she dried off, she finally put on her clean clothing. She scooped up her dirty clothes and, with some reluctance, went to find Anthony. She found him sitting in the lounge on the sofa, leaning forward with his head in his hands.

"Where's the washing machine?" he heard her ask, making him quietly laugh. It wasn't a laugh of happiness. It was a laugh of disbelief. Of all the things that had been running through his mind - all the things she could have come out and said to him - she wanted the washing machine?

He stood up and walked in front of her.

"Follow me," he said firmly.

Alexis followed without hesitation. When they reached the laundry, she put her clothing into the machine, along with the laundry powder. She took her time figuring out how to start it before finally she turned and looked at him. She could see that he was very pale - almost white. She immediately felt guilty and responsible for whatever he was feeling.

"I'm sorry," she said timidly.

Anthony could see tears start to come to her eyes. Not caring about how she would feel about it - perhaps needing it as much for himself, as to comfort her - he moved forward and put his arms around her. He pulled her to him tightly and held her there for a long time. He felt her respond by slowly moving her arms around him, but didn't hug him as tightly as he was doing to her.

As Alexis breathed in, she noticed that he didn't smell the same as *him*. The only similarity at all between the two men who were occupying her mind was the voice. If she could just keep looking at Anthony - and smelling him - that should be enough to stop it from happening again. She was sure of it.

"Allie, you really shouldn't travel like this - not alone," Anthony said softly as he pulled back and away from her. He looked at her closely to make sure she was present and listening, while the washing machine did its magic noisily in the background.

"I know. I *am* worried about it," she admitted. She wanted to hang her head low but was terrified of letting her eyes move away from his face. "But I have to keep moving. I'm not yet far enough away to feel ... safe."

"But you aren't going to *be* safe if you're out in the world and that happens to you again. If you cross paths with the wrong person..." he started to say. A shudder shot through his body at the thought. "Will you please come and sit down with me, and tell me what is going on with you?" he asked softly. After looking into his eyes for a long time, she nodded. "Okay, this washing won't take long, so I'll hang it out, and then I'll make us some coffee. We'll sit in the lounge. Okay?"

Alexis nodded at him again. Despite feeling safe in his presence, she was terrified of the blackout moments that kept happening. She was fearful of what it could mean, and what could happen to her as a result.

A short time later they settled on the sofa together, sitting a comfortable distance from each other. Both turned on an angle so they could face one another. Once comfortable, Alexis took a deep breath and began talking. It was 11am when she started. It was 3pm when she finished.

Anthony looked at her - stared at her - as she talked and told him about all that had happened in her life to date. In her conversation, she touched on where she grew up, and the people she faintly remembered as her parents. For the most part, she talked about what had been happening in her life over the past few years.

As he listened, Anthony was taken on a journey that pulled him through emotions like movies did when he needed escapism. At some points, he felt grave. At other points, he felt frustrated. At other points still, he felt tears come to his eyes. The emotion he found flowed through him mostly as she talked, however, was anger. Everything she said - all the words she used - she said matter-of-factly. There was no emotion whatsoever attached to the words. It was like she had just accepted everything she had done - and everything she'd had to do - over the last few years. She spoke as if it was just normal behaviour and nothing bad, or good, or pleasant, or sad. It looked to him like she just regarded it all simply as ... is. To her, it was what it was, and there was nothing more to it. To her, it seemed almost ... normal.

Alexis found some strength inside of her start to resurrect as she talked. She had planned to never talk to anyone about anything that had happened to her, or that she'd done, over recent years. Finding Anthony kind and generous, his manner worked on her, making her feel safe with him. He made her truly believe he could be trusted, and it felt good to get things out of her head. It was like one secret had been layered on top of another, and another. As she talked, she felt the layers within lifting up and off her.

"I think it's your voice that … does that to me," she said, startling him. "Your voice is almost the same. I know it doesn't explain why I do what I do, but I can see - hear - that it's a similarity you have with him."

"Maybe, Allie, but I wasn't in the bathroom with you when you changed, so it can't be just my voice," Anthony replied. "There must be other triggers, and if you don't know what they are…"

They both went silent. Each wondered how to deal with the strange thing that happened to her at those times, seemingly without any warning that it was going to happen.

"I need cake," Anthony said all of a sudden. He leapt up and walked from the room, leaving Alexis sitting alone. She wondered what he must think of her after all that she'd told him.

Soon he was back with a tray that he put down on the coffee table. He served small broken pieces of his 'suffered' cake on individual plates with forks and handed one to her.

Alexis took the food gratefully, not sure if she had any further conversation left in her. As she ate, she realised that she couldn't remember ever having spoken to anyone for such a long amount of time - ever. When she asked herself why that might be, the reply that came back to her from her mind was simply because no-one else had ever wanted to listen. As she had that thought, she studied the man sitting with her. She considered he must be some kind of saviour for her. No-one like him had ever come into her life before. There had been people who initially seemed kind, generous, and interested in her life. Over a short time, they had proven they weren't the same people they'd initially presented themselves as at all. They had proved they didn't have any real interest in really getting to know her as a person. Always, people just wanted to take. To them, she was someone who could give them what they wanted or what they needed. She was never supposed to need or want anything in return.

Anthony felt her looking at him and raised his eyes to meet her gaze. She looked intent. He had a brief moment of alarm as he thought she was going to 'go' again. She must have seen it, as her face changed as if it woke up and saw his horror.

"This cake is really good. It does look like it had a serious accident today," she said, attempting to laugh softly. "But it still does taste really good."

"It was a painful thing that it went through this morning, but it's a survivor," Anthony said. "It still gets to live its life and give us pleasure in its taste."

The words were delivered half with humour, and half in thinking that

Alexis was also that - a survivor who didn't seem to know it yet. She was a survivor who could give pleasure to others by being the person that she was, if only she could harness how to stay that person consistently.

"Allie, what are you going to do?" he asked. "Are you sure that you need to move on so quickly? You can stay here as long as you want..."

"Thank you, Anthony, but I do need to keep moving. I don't know where I'm going, or where I'll end up, but sitting still like this makes me nervous. This town is too small. If questions get asked, someone will have noticed me. Maybe they wouldn't right now, since I'm inside your house, but I can't hide out here all day, every day," she said and paused before continuing. "No, I need to get somewhere more populated. When I find that, I'll feel more secure, I'm sure."

"Okay, but at least let me go with you through to your next destination. I have to work tomorrow morning, but then I have three days off before I go back to work. I can go and pick up a ticket this afternoon for the train you're on tomorrow. Then I can come with you and help you get set up there, just for the first few days at least. Please - I don't like the thought of you travelling around alone like this."

Alexis looked at him with a mixture of disbelief and gratitude. She felt disbelief that anyone would ever want to provide her with support and care. She felt grateful that he truly did seem to want to do that for her. He really did want to help her, without needing anything from her in return.

Anthony saw her nod her head, even though her face clearly showed her uncertainty. He could read that she truly wanted to believe that he was sincere, but life experience had taught her to be naturally cautious of people who appeared so.

"Alright, I think I would like that. If you're sure..." she said quietly.

Anthony jumped up suddenly, before she could change her mind.

"I'm going to run down to the train station now and get a ticket. While I'm in town, I'll pick up a few things for the trip too. Then, tomorrow, we can walk straight from here to the station and just get on the train," he said and paused. "I'll be back here in about an hour. If you want to, pick out a movie and put it on. It might help you maintain focus."

As he walked down his path and into the small township, Anthony felt a diverse range of emotions inside of him. He was determined to focus on his present tasks.

Inside, Alexis chose a movie and put it on to watch. It was a futuristic action movie that she knew could, in no way, be realistic, so wouldn't play on her mind too much. She felt her sense of freedom growing, not only through the feeling of safety that she felt being in the house, but also from the hours of speaking. Things that had been buried deep inside of her were finally lifting up, out and away from her. It felt like a heavy tumour had been cut out of the centre of her, and her body and mind could now start to shrink back down to normal size once again. Finally, her body and her mind could begin to be hers once more.

Anthony rushed around as quickly as he could, while at the same time trying not to seem like he was. Even having heard her story, he'd started to wonder if she had a real situation to worry about. He wondered if there might be someone coming after her, or if it was just a deep paranoia over nothing. With the careful nature that he had, he chose to act as if she might be right. There might be someone searching for her, and it might be best if that someone didn't find her.

When he walked back into his home, he did so with a small amount of dread over what he might find. He was relieved to find her engrossed in a movie when he walked into the lounge. She looked the most relaxed he had seen her since he'd met her. He saw her turn and smile when she heard him. For that moment, it seemed like the most normal thing in the world for her to do, and for him to see.

He sat down on the sofa and placed his bag of groceries on the coffee table in front of them.

"I got a ticket, and a load of snacks for tomorrow's journey. I'll bring home some freshly baked goodies from work in the morning, too," he said, still looking at her to make sure she was okay.

"Thank you for doing so much for me," she replied quietly.

Anthony turned to look at the screen, directing her eyes back there also for the last half hour of the movie. When it had finished, and the credits started rolling, Alexis picked up the TV remote and switched the movie off. The action made the TV automatically switch over to a regular television channel. As that happened, both Alexis and Anthony let out sounds of disbelief as a photo of her appeared on the screen in front of them. It was a news item. Anthony turned it up, so there was no missing whatever was being said.

'Police in Melbourne are calling for help from the public in what they believe may be a case of abduction. A young woman, Lexi Jane Montgomery, has been missing since Friday night, having been reported as such by an anonymous call to the central Melbourne police station. Entrepreneur business tycoon, Lincoln Kokiri, has put up $50,000 as a reward to anyone who can provide information relating to her disappearance. When Mr. Kokiri was asked why he had ventured to put up such a large amount to find the missing person, he simply said that he abhorred anyone who would snatch someone off the street. He believes it is time for people like him - those who have the money to do so - to step up and contribute to causes such as this,' the reporter said, as the photo of Alexis once again appeared on the screen. 'Anyone who has seen Ms. Montgomery is encouraged to talk to their local police station immediately.'

Anthony turned the television off quickly and then turned to her. In the photo that had been shown, she'd looked different. In it, she had been smiling and really alive. She'd also looked much healthier. The photo had revealed an air about her that said she was much more easy-going, without a care in the world. She had also looked much younger than she did now, but it was definitely her. He didn't doubt that.

When he looked at her closely, he saw that his thinking was right. It was her that the police were calling for sightings of.

"Oh, Allie," he breathed out slowly as he looked at her face.

He saw her go almost white as she also processed what they had just seen. He didn't mention the difference in her name. The news broadcast had said Lexi. She had told him she was Allie. For whatever reason, it had been important to her to use a different name. He respected that, and would make sure he kept calling her that.

Alexis closed her eyes and felt the wall of tears start to break. There was no hope now. *He* had made sure she couldn't get away so easily. She had thought he would try and find her. In that, she had considered the lengths he might go to, but even she hadn't thought he would put her face on television for everyone to see. He'd now made it impossible for her to go anywhere in public. It would be impossible to simply walk down a street. She wouldn't be able to go to a supermarket to buy food without someone recognising her and reporting her location to the police.

As tears flowed freely, another level of emotion washed over her. It was another level of desperation over how she might never again be able to lead a normal life. A small part of her felt like she should remove herself quickly from where she was, and go and cry in peace in the bedroom. A greater part of her was resigned to just not care anymore.

Seeing her start to deflate once again, Anthony moved closer to her and held out his arms. He didn't want to cause stress in her, but did want to ensure she knew he was there for her. He was pleased when he felt her move closer to him and let herself be enclosed.

Alexis embraced the feeling of being so close to someone without them needing anything from her. He was a man, and he was holding her. It was natural for her to assume a man would only touch her in one way - sexually and for pain. She then had to concede that Anthony hadn't done anything in their time together to harm her. He hadn't even done anything to indicate that he recognised she was a woman, let alone that he was going to try to get her to be sexual with him.

Anthony held her firmly but not too tightly. He let her set the closeness, and the time when she would pull away from him. In his head, he kept seeing the news report playing, over and over. He knew now that she wasn't delusional in her paranoia. He'd also found focus on the name of the donor of the reward money - Lincoln Kokiri. Where had he heard that name before? He repeated the name in his head, trying to remember, sure it was filed away in there somewhere. He flicked through the archives in his mind - different places he'd been, different jobs he'd had, different movies and television programs he had watched.

Finally, he remembered. Lincoln Kokiri was the owner of the supermarket that Anthony worked at, but not just the specific supermarket branch. He was the owner of the entire company. He was at the very top of the food chain, and not just the owner of that supermarket chain either. His company had major fast-food brands and department stores under their umbrella as well. If memory served Anthony right, he wasn't a young man - perhaps in his mid-40s. He'd inherited the company from his father when Lincoln had only been in his twenties. Anthony remembered reading that it had been a small company when it had passed hands, but with an entrepreneurial spirit, the son had since grown it into an empire.

Anthony sat still as he held Alexis. He considered quietly to himself that it was generous for someone like that to put up a reward for information about someone he didn't even know. He must be a really nice person…

Unless he did know her…

Unless…

Alexis felt the body wrapped around her tense up and go rigid as Anthony inhaled and held his breath to stop any of his thoughts from being voiced. She hadn't said who the man was that she had spoken of - not even his first name. Anthony had assumed she didn't want to say. He wouldn't ask her. He put that possibility in the back of his mind and just kept quiet.

"Are you alright, Anthony?" Alexis asked, lifting her head to look at him with curiosity.

Anthony placed his hand gently on her hair and guided her head back onto his chest.

"Yep, just relax. We will work all of this out, Allie. Don't worry," Anthony replied. "You're safe."

CHAPTER 3

The Discovery

48 Hours Earlier - 5pm Friday

Lincoln Kokiri sat in the meeting room, trying to focus on the conversation and negotiations going on around him. He knew that deep within, his heart just wasn't in it, but he had an extremely deep-seated work ethic inside of him. That was something that had been literally beaten into him by his father when he was young.

Letting his mind wander from the discussions, he took a moment to think about his father, both as a man and as a father. As a man, he could win the hearts of anyone and everyone. Even as a child, Lincoln had been aware of the many women who'd passed through his father's bed, despite the picture being presented to the world. That picture presented his father being deeply in love with Lincoln's mother. She'd died when Lincoln was too young to have gained an understanding or curiosity about who his mother was as a person - away from being a mother and a wife. Lincoln hadn't been too young to see the pain his father caused her. That had made him determined, from a very early age, to never treat women the way that his father had treated her.

In his child mind, he'd vowed to himself that he would never be disrespectful toward someone he loved. He would never be dishonest or disloyal. When he grew up and found someone to love, he would be completely faithful, and he would be their world - their all. He would do whatever it took to make sure they knew he only wanted to be with them and no-one else. He would shower them in love and, if possible, money and gifts. He would make them see that they had someone who was devoted to them, and them alone. It had been one of his greatest lifelong plans. In his child mind, he would never deviate from it.

He came back to the discussion before him just in time to hear a major issue that needed to be resolved. Instantly he refocused and was in company owner mode once more. He did it every week. He'd stay in that mode until 7pm, when he'd board his flight in Brisbane, to return to Melbourne.

On the plane that evening, he let his mind relax and tune out from everything business. Always at that time, his thoughts turned to the same thing - Lexi. He thought about her often every single day, but Fridays were different. On Friday he would touch down at 9pm, and that was the beginning of the weekend. His staff around the country knew never to contact him on a weekend. Even if a building was on fire, they were to contact the immediate business manager on duty. Nothing that he directly had to deal with couldn't wait until Monday morning.

As he sat back in the expansive business class seat, he already felt excitement growing. It was the same every week. Friday nights meant two hours of anticipation on the plane, followed by an instruction that he would give to her over the phone when he touched down. From that moment on, she would be his to shower his attention on.

It wasn't a usual arrangement, he knew, but inside of him was that same commitment he had made to himself as a child. Any woman he was involved with, he would give all of his attention and dedication to. He would make sure she knew, without any doubt whatsoever, the level of love, and desire - and great respect - he had for her.

He thought back to the night before, when he'd last seen her. Always, after he left his office on a Thursday afternoon, he drove straight to her apartment. It was a small space of extreme luxury that he had put her up in two years earlier. He'd done that when he'd realised the depth of love he had come to feel for her - and the depth of which he knew he could not live without her.

When he'd arrived, she had seemed a little more dishevelled than usual. It wasn't like her, as she was always immaculate when he arrived. Once he was in the apartment and the door was shut, she had become more herself once again. It drove him wild for her. Just kissing her lips, tasting her - that was all it took for him to feel like he was transported into a world where no such thing as business existed. Nothing existed. No-one existed. Just the two of them.

He loved her, and only her. He could never get enough of her. She was, in his eyes, utter perfection. She always had been, from the moment they'd met. It had only been three years since that first encounter, but he knew that he was meant to be with her forever. She was his, and he was hers.

The only glitch in his perfect world plan was his wife of twenty years. That was where his best intention of always being faithful to any woman he was involved with, seemed desperately to fail him. He had been faithful to Diana, for seventeen years. He had devoted himself to her, and desired her, and loved her. The moment he'd first laid eyes on Lexi, something had snapped inside of him, and Diana wasn't forefront in his head any more. Despite his feelings for Lexi, he still had to remain committed to his marriage. He wouldn't hurt Diana. He knew somewhere deep inside of him that he was doing something wrong. Somehow, by keeping his life with Lexi so well hidden away, out of the spotlight of the media and everyone else, he had managed to move successfully into his double life.

Lexi knew he was married, of course. No-one who followed news - particularly business news - could not know that. His wife stood by him at every social gathering, news media broadcast, and public business meeting. Diana was a rock. When he'd tried to get ahead of himself and overreach in things that weren't a strong enough guarantee, she had listened. She'd made the time to listen to him talk about things, and helped him to come to the right decision.

Yes, he did still very much love Diana. He did still look at her and see the beautiful woman that she was. They did still have a perfectly good sex life. She was always eager to encourage him to move into her and to enjoy her body. Over twenty years of marriage, they had perfected their movements together and still both happily indulged in it.

But she wasn't Lexi.

Lexi was different.

Sitting on the plane in the evening on his way home, Lincoln was highly aroused. He always was at that time. In his core, he was excited to a level that was beyond belief sometimes.

At the sound of the captain declaring they were beginning their descent into Melbourne, he felt his nerves come on. It wouldn't be long, and he had already decided what instruction he would give her that night.

Her dedication to giving in to his requests to please him was endless. That was one of the things he loved about her. She had endless enthusiasm and desire to make him feel good. She made him feel normal, no matter what he had decided - and instructed - they would do together.

Finally, he felt the wheels touch the tarmac. He licked his lips, imagining how she would feel tonight, and how she would taste.

Walking into the terminal building, he immediately took out his phone, turned it on, and waited for it to connect. As soon as it showed bars of connectivity, he found a quiet, unpopulated area of the airport. Just as he did every Friday, he dialled her number. He had his instruction rehearsed. Through most of the flight, he had heard it in his head, over and over. He was excited to finally be able to speak it out loud.

The line clicked as if the phone was answered, but before he could speak, he heard her voice.

"Hi, this is Lexi. Sorry, my phone is turned off. I've got a horrid flu, so am going to bed to sleep it off. Leave a message, and I'll call you back tomorrow, unless I'm still feeling this sick, in which case I'll definitely call you back Sunday," said the voice through the receiver. Then followed a long beep, indicating he was welcome to leave a message.

Lincoln hung up. He left no message. His mind was instantly blank. He found himself immediately panicked. Such a thing had never happened. It was new. He didn't know what to do. It confused him, leaving him to wonder what he was supposed to do.

It couldn't happen - it couldn't. They had plans. They always had plans on Friday nights. Sick? She couldn't be sick. It was Friday, and they had plans.

He worked himself up into a state on the inside, even though anyone watching him wouldn't have seen anything different. He always looked calm and composed on the outside, and most of the time he was calm and composed on the inside.

But not with Lexi.

Lexi was different.

"Mr. Kokiri," he vaguely heard a voice behind him say. When he turned, he saw his driver, Toby, standing close to him. "Are you ready to go, Sir?"

Straight away, Toby saw something was different about his employer. Something had rattled him - seriously so.

Lincoln looked at him and nodded, even though his head was full of … nothing. He followed his driver out to the car and sat in the back, as usual.

"To the usual location, Sir?" Toby asked.

Lincoln found himself speechless. For the first time he could ever remember, he didn't know what to say. He did not know how to answer a question that was being asked of him. He knew he had to decide what to do. Should he go to her apartment anyway, knowing that she was too ill to even answer her phone? He could still go. He could prove his love to her by nursing her, giving her support, and showing how much he cared, even if she wasn't well enough to please him.

Those words hit him hard. She wasn't well enough to please him. That struck a chord with him and helped him to finally speak.

"No, Toby. Tonight I shall go directly home," he said, finding his voice of authority once more. He had lost himself temporarily, but now he could think clearly again. That night, he would get on with home life. He would go home. There he would greet, kiss, hug, and talk to his wife. Later, he would make love to her. It wouldn't be the same, because she wasn't Lexi. But it would do.

Until tomorrow.

Tomorrow, Lexi would be well again. He would see her, and she *would* follow his instruction.

~~~~~

Saturday morning, Lincoln woke up early enough to see that it was still dark outside. He was eager to talk to Lexi. He wanted to see her. Most of all, he needed to be inside of her. Glancing at the bedside clock, he could see it was too early to call. He would put the phone call off until a more respectable hour, but he was already thinking about her. The
~~~~~

longer he lay quietly staring outward from his side of the bed toward the dark curtains, and thinking about her, the more aroused he became. He wanted to save that for her.

From behind him, he felt Diana reach out and put her arm over him, finding him hard. He heard her instantly express through her voice that she had plans for him herself.

Devoted to his wife, and not wanting to distress her in any way, he rolled over and on top of her. With her guidance, he sank into her, making both of them groan immediately. She didn't know that being inside her like that, in the early morning dark, her husband wasn't even thinking about her. He was imagining it was someone else he was slipping into, over and over again.

~~~~~

At 10am, Lincoln told Diana that he was going for a run and would be back soon. He put on his running gear and grabbed his key and his mobile before literally running out the door.

He ran until he was in a quiet area of a park, out of sight of the apartment building they lived in. His eyes were wary. He wasn't a television or film star, or a famous musician, but he'd had enough photos and stories printed about him to know that he equally wasn't unknown, and he trusted no-one.

The situation and the unknowing it produced was still too new. He was nervous as he dialled Lexi's number. The instruction was still in his head, ready to be said when she answered.

But she didn't answer.

Once more, it went to voicemail messaging. He heard the same message he'd heard the night before. It wasn't changed. It wasn't deleted. It was still there.

He hung up. He didn't know what to do. Again he felt confused, like there was a problem in front of him that he just didn't know how to solve. His life worked on order. It couldn't work in chaos - and he was in chaos. The inability for him to contact her went against their routine. It wasn't the same as the previous weekend, or the weekend before, or the almost three years worth of weekends before that.

Perhaps she just needed that one call first to be able to hear the phone, and had picked the phone up too late. If he called one more time, she probably already had the phone in her hand, and would immediately answer.

He dialled again, waited, then heard the voicemail message again. He was more than just curious. His heartbeat had increased, and he felt himself become distressed. He could feel his inner self becoming upset. No, he was more than upset. Inside he was becoming irate. He became aware of his breathing deepening and his heart pounding inside his chest.
~~~~~

His mind blurred. His sanity questioned.

He ran. That was something he could control, right there, right then. He ran and ran, needing to keep the frustration under control. He could feel something building in him. It was a feeling that he didn't like.

Yes, he desperately needed to run.

~~~~~

At 4pm, Diana left home to go out for an evening with her friends, leaving Lincoln alone in their apartment. As soon as he knew his wife had left, he dialled Lexi's number again. The response was the same.

He immediately made a decision. Whether she was sick or not, he just had to know what she was doing. It was her scheduled time with him. Her not being with him was unacceptable.

He showered, dressed immaculately, and called Toby to ask him to drive him. All the way there, he found confusion in his mind. He had never turned up at her apartment before without some kind of conversation first - even if it was just an instruction he had left. Always, she had known he was on his way. That was part of his respect for her - his great respect.

Getting out of the car, he told Toby to wait. He walked to the apartment elevator and pressed her floor number. The nerves inside of him once again made his heart pound heavily in his chest. He took deep breaths as he felt the elevator rise. He had to calm down. He felt it, and he knew it.

He approached her apartment front door and waited. Standing silent, he listened to see if he could hear any movement beyond the door. There was nothing.

He knocked quietly and waited.

Nothing.

He knocked harder.

Nothing.

He had a new decision to make. He had a key, but he'd never used it. It went against his self-proclaimed respect for her, to just go into her apartment without talking to her first.

He waited a few more minutes, then waited no more. He inserted the key, turned it, and opened the door.

"Lexi?" he asked quietly, not wanting to stun her at the realisation that he had let himself in. When he heard nothing, he called out with more volume. "Lexi?"

He looked around the space. As always, it was spotless. Nothing was out of place. Nothing was messy. Not even an unwashed coffee cup had been left in the sink.

He walked through the apartment. It was tiny, but it was beautiful. In that way, he likened it to Lexi herself - tiny but beautiful.
~~~~~

He walked past the open bathroom. Just as the kitchen had been, the bathroom was immaculate. Everything was in the place it was meant to be. Everything that should be there, *was* there - toothbrush, toothpaste, moisturizer. Even her body lotion that he loved the smell of was there. That was the smell that was Lexi.

Finally, he came to her bedroom. The door was closed. Under the door, he could see that the room wasn't light, making him think the curtains must be pulled. Of course they would be pulled, he justified. She was sick in bed, and needed to sleep.

Again he stopped, not knowing what to do. Already everything felt wrong. He disregarded his temporary discomfort and knocked on her bedroom door.

"Lexi?" he asked softly.

On hearing nothing, slowly and quietly, he opened the door. The room was dark, but as he opened the door, enough light poured into the room for him to see all that he needed to. The bed was empty. It was perfectly made. There wasn't a sheet out of place. There wasn't even a crease on the top cover.

He walked to the window and opened the curtain just enough to be sure she wasn't in the room. When he was certain, he forcefully opened the curtains fully, illuminating the room completely.

She wasn't there.

But she was sick. That was what the message had said. That was the reason he hadn't been able to see her last night - she was sick.

He grew frantic. His first thought was that she must have gone away and not told him. Going to her drawers and opening them, he saw that they were full. He went to the wardrobe and opened the doors right up. Her clothes were all there. In the top of the wardrobe was the overnight bag that she always used when she went anywhere. It wasn't missing. *Nothing* was missing. She hadn't taken anything. She hadn't gone anywhere.

So where was she?

~~~~~

He pulled his phone out and called her number again. For a moment, he thought that her phone might ring out loud, right there in the apartment. If he called it, it might reveal itself in the situation of mystery. Once again, he only got the voicemail message. This time he hesitated before he hung up.

"Call me," he said simply, before ending the call.

He looked around the bedroom, bewildered. Nothing was amiss. He left the room and walked to the bathroom again. Everything looked normal there too, except for the bath. The bath was completely dry. That told him that she hadn't used it for some time. For however long, she
~~~~~

hadn't had a bath or a shower. That made no sense. She knew how clean she had to be for him. She wouldn't go a day without bathing - not if she'd *been* there.

In a daze, Lincoln walked into the living area. It wasn't a large area, but it was well set out with a small dining area, a small lounge area, and a tiny galley kitchen. It wasn't somewhere he could live, being someone who needed lots of space around him. Lexi, though, had been thrilled with it, he remembered fondly. For her, it was perfect.

As he walked alongside the kitchen bench, he conceded everything was where it always was. He opened the refrigerator. There he saw food, milk and juice, as always. The new jars of different flavoured coffee that she'd started to collect were present on the benchtop. It was now a couple of years since he'd noticed her veering away from the tea she'd always preferred when he'd first met her.

He sat on the sofa and looked out over the view of the city beyond. His insides felt like they were becoming twisted and squeezed. Closing his eyes, he tried to focus and think. Had she said she was going away? Had she needed to visit a friend? Family? He tried to think if he'd just forgotten something she had told him. Nothing came to his mind and, regardless, the voicemail message had said she was sick, not away on holiday.

He visualised in his head the moment he had said goodbye to her and walked out on Thursday night. She had said nothing that had suggested she wouldn't be there Friday night.

He remained still. In some ways, he felt like he was in a state of meditation, except his mind wasn't at rest like it would be if he was meditating. It was racing, as was his heart. He felt completely out of control. That panicked him. He was fighting to maintain calm, to maintain focus, and to maintain some kind of sanity in what he felt was a situation of exactly the opposite.

Knowing there was no point in just sitting there, he stood to leave. As he walked past the refrigerator, he looked at it. For a moment he expected to see a handwritten list of phone numbers of Lexi's friends and family members. Diana had done that in their home, just in case technology ever failed and they had to contact someone but couldn't get the numbers off their phones. On the refrigerator in front of him, there was no such list. As far as he knew, Lexi had no family. She had no friends.

But she did work…

It was already late afternoon on a Saturday. He would go into his office and take some time to investigate before he did anything else. It was time to see and analyse what exactly Lexi had been doing without his knowing.

~~~~~

As he entered his office, he realised it was the first time he'd set foot in there on a weekend for almost three years. Before he had met Lexi, he'd had a period of time where he often went in at all hours on all days. After he met her, he'd found that he no longer wanted to work all hours, on all days. He had found a different focus. He'd found something else that was all-consuming on his mind, and almost as consuming on his body.

When he made his way to his computer and logged on, he felt a deep dread begin to flow over him. What it was a dread of, he wasn't sure, but it was getting deeper by the hour.

Much to his regret, he experienced the same emotion that he always did when he used technology to check up on her. He couldn't pinpoint the emotion. It seemed to be a blend of guilt, combined with curiosity, and mistrust, but at the same time, trust. When he monitored her, he found the emotion to be an indefinable one as there were so many aspects to it. Internally he knew it was wrong to even monitor her as he did. That didn't stop him - not on that day, or on any day previously when he'd done it.

He started with her bank accounts. Nothing had been accessed that day or the day before. The last time she'd used her card had been on Thursday at the supermarket. She hadn't withdrawn any cash from any ATM. Over the past week, she'd visited a café, seen a movie, and bought groceries. That was it. Nothing was out of the ordinary there. On looking closer, however, he did consider that $57.60 seemed a high price for a cup of coffee in a café. Even if she'd ordered a light lunch - and she never ate anything very substantial - it would only have come to maybe $20 at most.

That was the first light bulb moment.

He went back through her purchases. Even the supermarket one was suspicious. He'd just looked in her kitchen, and while there was sufficient food, there was nowhere near the $342.34 worth that the supermarket amount showed as her purchase on Thursday.

Lincoln's suspicion grew as he went on to look closer at the cinema charge. He knew Lexi loved watching movies on the big screen. She went whenever she could, and she loved popcorn. That would come to less than $30 in total. The amount withdrawn by the cinema was $130.

It became obvious to Lincoln - Lexi had been withdrawing cash on her purchases. That meant that there was a possibility that she had, for a long time, already been aware of this very moment. She had already foreseen this very moment when he would be sitting at his computer, in his office, looking at her bank accounts.

The discovery temporarily stunned him, making him feel that emotion
~~~~~

again. It now heavily veered in a lopsided motion toward the side of mistrust.

He went back through her records and looked closer at the amounts. For the past two weeks at least, she had been doing cash withdrawals on purchases. For two whole weeks, the charges were much higher than they should have been, given where she was. Earlier than the two weeks, everything seemed normal. A $28.60 charge at the cinema. A $7.50 charge at a café. A supermarket purchase that totalled $87.50.

So for at least two weeks - two weeks! - she had been doing this. Planning this.

But he had seen her as normal since then. Even just last Thursday…

Now that he remembered back to Thursday, when he'd arrived, she *had* looked a little pale and withdrawn. She had eased back to her usual self, but now that he was thinking and focusing, he realised she hadn't been her usual self to start with. She hadn't been normal at all. She'd simply found her ability to quickly seem normal - to *act*. In his desire and need for her, Lincoln had instantly disregarded it … until now.

He leaned back in his chair. As he let out a deep breath, he turned around till he was facing away from the computer. His view rested out toward the buildings nearby. His mind was working quickly and furiously, trying to figure out what was going on.

Why would she have planned to leave? And like this? No goodbye? No discussion about that being what she wanted to do? It made no sense. All her clothes were in her apartment, so what was she planning to wear?

He turned back to her accounts. No, there was no indication she'd bought any clothing or anything else out of the ordinary.

Travel? No, there were no flights purchased, nor any train tickets bought.

So where was she - and how did she get there?

He logged out of her bank accounts. Nothing more was to be seen there. Next, he logged into her mobile phone account. All he saw there for the past two weeks were calls from him. There was no record of her having had contact with anyone else at all. Standing back and looking at the view, he was surprised at the number of calls he made to her. Did he really contact her that much? Looking at the list, it looked too much - *far* too much. Without any formal analysis, he could see at a glance that he far too frequently contacted her, but she never contacted him. That was how it had to be, of course. She had never been in a position to be able to call him due to his business and being married. If she had ever wanted to see him at any other time - if she truly needed him - she'd never been able to contact him to tell him. That brought into his head one glaring reason she might want to not be with him anymore - he was never there for her. Despite how much she always made sure she was there for him - every single time - perhaps he was never there for her.

Pulling his mind back to the present, he had to think about how he would find her. Her leaving in such a way wasn't acceptable. It wasn't planned, and in his mind, it was chaos. In his head, chaos wasn't right. It wasn't orderly. It had to stop so that things could be put right again. Everything needed to be put back in the right place, and in the right order.

He had to find her. If he could locate her phone, he could see exactly where she was. He'd done that once before when they had first started to be involved. On that occasion, he'd found himself not only desperate to see her but at the same time, desperate to know where she was and what she was doing.

Looking at his watch, he saw it was 8pm. It was quite late, and a Saturday night. He knew who he could call to search for her phone, but should he? He had to take time to think and plan how he would play things out to locate her. If he asked his head IT manager, Nate, once more to track that phone, he would be putting himself out there as someone trying to find her. That might lead to questions later if anything had happened to her. No, he had to find another way where he wouldn't be in full view as being in this situation. He had to find a way to make *her* come back to *him*.

If he could somehow broadcast that she was missing, but there was no evidence that something had happened to her. His gut told him that she had planned and left, all on her own accord.

He knew people in each of the main television stations. It was possible he could pay for a broadcast to be made, but how could he explain his desire to make that happen? He was rich, and he knew people of importance. He had made plenty of speeches about the goodwill he wanted his company to be part of. He just needed to get things in order and work out a way to make it all flow in the right direction. It had to be planned so that eventually wherever she was - and whoever she was with - she would see it. Once a broadcast was out, she would know she needed to come back. She would know that leaving wasn't an option. She would understand that leaving quite simply was not acceptable.

He considered her nature. She would only come back if she thought someone else was at risk or in danger. Always, she put other people first - never herself. He had to create the right scenario where if she stayed away and hidden, someone else was likely to be caught up in it. That was something she'd never want. After such an intense three years together, he knew her very well. He knew exactly which buttons to push with her. He also knew, without any doubt, that she would act if someone else were threatened.

He knew what he had to do.

~~~~~

"Where's the phone?" Lincoln asked his IT manager, early Sunday morning.

He'd already put in place the plan segments that he'd had to, to try and draw her out. Searching for her phone wasn't something that he had particularly wanted to do, but his desperation had grown to a new level. It was unbearable to think that she'd left without telling him. He knew he wasn't thinking straight, but he couldn't seem to stop his actions. He was trying so hard to keep it all together, but the phone search was something he absolutely needed. He needed to know where she was.

"It's nowhere, Sir," Nate replied with a nervous look on his face. He knew his employer well, having worked alongside him for almost twenty years. Although he understood and identified the cool and calm exterior, deep down, he knew not to ever upset Lincoln Kokiri. He also knew it was best generally to *never* tell him that something about technology couldn't be done.

"What do you mean, nowhere? It must be somewhere! It's just turned off, right? You can turn it back on from here…" Lincoln started to say before seeing Nate shake his head.

"That's just it. That is what I thought - that it might not be coming up on GPS as it must be turned off, and all we'd have to do is turn it back on, but it isn't out there. It has just disappeared."

"But…" Lincoln started to say, standing up straight. He lifted his hand to sweep it through his cropped dark hair. It was the weekend, and he wasn't wearing corporate gear, but even to the man before him, he seemed to be an imposing image of immaculate presentation and presence. "Fuck!" Lincoln shouted. He knew it was an unprofessional way to act, especially in front of an employee, but he couldn't care less about that at that moment. He breathed deeply and refocused. "Alright, what else can we try? How else can someone be found?"

Nate looked at his employer carefully. It was the second time Lincoln had wanted that particular phone tracked. Last time it had seemed to be more a matter of curiosity than anything else. This time it looked serious. Nate didn't like the sense of desperation coming off Lincoln at all. He looked like he hadn't slept at all the night before, and he sounded like he wasn't thinking straight. It was uncertain who the phone belonged to, or what the owner of the phone was to his boss. In truth, Nate didn't want to know. If he knew things, questions would come, and he didn't want questions.

"About this phone … nothing," he said. "It isn't out there, Mr. Kokiri. The phone just isn't out there, and neither is the SIM card that was in it. It's my guess that they've both been destroyed. Sorry."

Lincoln looked down at his employee, feeling anger inside of him that
~~~~~

he desperately wanted to vent. He couldn't take it out on Nate. He was a good worker and had always been loyal. He could also be trusted to not tell anyone Lincoln was looking for the owner of the phone.

"Thank you, Nate, for at least trying. Sorry to drag you into work on a Sunday. You can go now," he said.

He watched as Nate stood up, nodded, and left quickly, as if he couldn't wait to get out of there. Lincoln stood where he was for a long time, his mind alternating between thinking too much and not thinking at all. His head felt like it was on overload. He had to think of everything, but he also needed to stop thinking altogether.

Finally, he took a deep breath. He had put in action what he knew he could, and now he had to wait. Before the end of the day, he would know where she was, and she would be coming back.

He jumped as he heard and felt his mobile phone ring in his pocket. Looking at it, he saw it was his wife calling. Purposely he put a smile on his face and answered it.

"Hello, darling," he said suggestively. As always, it was important to him that Diana felt like she was the only woman in the world for him. He needed her to believe that she was the only woman he desired and wanted to ever be with.

Their conversation was quick and to the point, just as it always was. After he hung up, he made ready to leave his workplace once again. There was no more to be done there. Everything was in place. All he had to do was wait.

~~~~~

Back in their home, Diana got ready to go out for a quick run before they were expected to go out for a fundraiser dinner. She had everything she needed in hand - her phone and her apartment keys. Her headphones were clipped to her running t-shirt, ready to put on music when she left the house.

In the living room, Lincoln had his back to the door, facing and standing close to the television. He hardly ever turned the thing on, but today he had to.

He stood still as he watched the news broadcast that was made. He saw the photo of Lexi come up on the screen. The sight of it made his heart leap. It was an old photo, he had realised too late. It was one he had taken of her right at the very start of their relationship. It showed a very youthful young woman with alert eyes and a huge smile on her face. Seeing it on such a big screen, he realised that she hardly ever looked like that anymore. She hardly ever smiled. He hadn't seen her eyes glistening like that in a very long while. She worked so hard to please him - to do what he wanted - that she had become a robot. She'd become a person with no emotion left in her. He had done that. She had been
~~~~~

youthful when he'd met her. She had only been 18. Since then, her youthfulness had shed away. She seemed much, much older now at 21 than she should do.

Diana entered the doorway just as she was ready to leave. She could see Lincoln standing and looking at the screen in front of him. That was something he rarely did. Her curiosity encouraged her to move slightly to one side so she could see what was on the screen. In doing so, she saw the whole broadcast from start to finish. Her heart became numb. She spoke quickly, without thinking about any possible consequence that could result from her words.

"So that's what she looks like. I've always been curious about what the face of your whore would be like," she said, initially feeling strong.

Lincoln stood where he was, firstly only hearing the comment as background noise. When he realised the words that had been spoken, he stood where he was, still facing the screen, frozen. The level of anger inside of him was immense. He channelled the fury down into his fists, not wanting to move. He had to maintain whatever level of control it would take … to … not … move.

Diana watched her husband for only a couple of seconds. Despite having spoken far too soon when she'd seen the screen, she *was* a fast thinker. In that minuscule slice of time, she could see how the scene before her could play out. She could taunt him with the knowledge of her having realised years earlier that he had someone on the side. 'Did you think I didn't know about her? About your little whore?' she could say, rubbing it in. She could wait and see the look on his face as he fully realised that he hadn't been as discrete over the time as he had thought he'd been. She could stand her ground as he would turn and walk right up to her. She could look defiant and taunt him to act on his anger. And she could take the blow…

No, Diana was faster thinking and far more logical than that. From her view of his back, she could see his fists. They were held tightly by his side. She knew perfectly well the level of anger she had just evoked. After twenty years of marriage, she knew every part of his body. She understood every interpretation of what his body said, with how he was feeling.

No, she was more intuitive and faster thinking than that. She wouldn't let that scenario play out. She loved life far more than she had ever loved him. No part of him was worth the pain that would come to her from her taunting him and making things worse.

Without speaking another word, she turned, and she ran.

As she ran for the front door, she grabbed her handbag off the side table it lived on. She needed it because it had her purse in it, but then she was in the elevator and gone. She wouldn't return - not in a hurry anyway. She knew her husband. Whatever was flowing through his mind right then, when he was watching the news, was something that he would have to dwell on. It was best that he was left alone to do just that. She knew he could present to the world what a loving and caring man he was. Although he had never before hurt her physically, she knew there had been times when he had come close to losing his control. She had always believed that anyone who pushed him far enough for him to do that…

The thought caused a shiver to pass through her as she maintained focus on moving forward as fast as she could. He might come after her, but he might not. The woman - the girl, she had to correct herself, now that she realised how young Alexis was - might be so important to him that he wouldn't even give Diana a passing thought until the girl was found. While most wives would want their husband to forget all about the woman their husband was having an affair with, suddenly all Diana could think was that she hoped he would not.

She kept running, with no thought even of taking one of the cars that were parked in the apartment garage. They lived right in the centre of the city, with hotels and ATMs all around. That would have to be her first stop - go to an ATM and withdraw as much money as the machine would let her. Having cash would give her an easier path to get away, even if only for that one night. She needed to get her head together and think. It would also give her the freedom to openly watch the television and any news reports that were yet to come.

Her husband had started the announcement to the world. Now the police and the media were involved. He would have to see it through, and it would all be broadcast openly, for her also to watch how things were about to develop for him.

After running around and visiting several ATMs, withdrawing as much cash as they would allow, she then ran into her bank also. She had to move quickly, while he was caught up in whatever was happening with the girl. When she had what she believed to be enough cash for what she wanted to do, she walked to the hotel in the city that was the tallest and would have the most rooms. If he came after her to confront her and tell her what he thought of her calling his mistress a whore, he might find the building through his GPS checking. If she used a fake name, it might stall the process of him finding her just a bit longer.

Unknowingly, Diana's mind had just moved to the same place as Alexis's had weeks earlier. Lincoln Kokiri might be her husband. He might be the girl's for sex. But the two women had been involved with the same man - and both were, right at that moment, equally intimidated and fearful of him.

~~~~~

Lincoln stood motionless with his back to the door still. He'd heard
~~~~~

the comment and had very quickly acknowledged the degree to which he had instantly felt not just anger rush through him, but an open and eager need to kill. The thought of anyone calling Lexi a whore enraged him.

Even through his intense rage, he had conceded that the deliverer of the comment was Diana. He had made a commitment to her years ago - for better, for worse. He wouldn't give in to his instinct to rush to her and pummel her for saying what she had. He had watched the way his father had treated his mother. The memories were ingrained deeply in his mind, and he wouldn't treat his wife like that. He wouldn't lay a hand on her. He wouldn't swear at her. He wouldn't call her names. He wouldn't even shout at her. And he would definitely not take one step closer to her right at that moment.

So he'd stood still. He'd forced himself to freeze and wait. He'd maintained stillness until the door had opened, and it had closed. Then he knew she was gone. He knew she was safe.

He had no desire to run after her. Even he knew that the way he was feeling wasn't good. It wasn't sane. It was best that she get away from him. He would deal with facing that situation later, when both of them were in a more relaxed state to talk properly.

For the immediate moment, he had to focus on Lexi, and *only* Lexi. The news was out there. The whole country would be keeping an eye out for her. She might be hiding right now, somewhere new. She might even be in the house of *someone* new. Eventually, though, she would have to come out, and by then people would easily recognise her. Not only that but the person she was with - whoever that was - would have to hide and not come out with her. If they did, they would be immediately arrested for abduction.

It wasn't a claim that would stick, of course. If not alone, Lexi would be with someone she wanted to be with. Once she talked to the police, she would simply say that she was with that person willingly. That was okay. Lincoln had purchased the phone with cash long ago in case he ever needed a burner phone for any purpose. He'd destroyed that directly after he had called the police anonymously with the story of her having been abducted.

At one level, he did know that he had acted too rashly. The whole thing was likely going to come back on him, revealing the lengths he had gone to just to find her. The police and media resources he had used for his own selfish purpose, but it was done now. He couldn't undo any of it. All he could do now was sit back and wait. She would come back, and she would see him when she did.

He would see her. He would explain the depth of his love for her. He would even leave Diana for her. He would divorce his wife, and then he would be free to marry Lexi. After that, they could be together every single day without having to hide their love for one another.

Suddenly he sat down on the vast sofa and then lay down on his back along the length of it. He let his mind wander to the pleasant thought of being able to see her every single day. It was easy to visualise being able to go to sleep with her in his arms every night, and wake up and see her face every single morning. They had never actually slept together. They had never spent an entire night together. Once she came back to him, they would be able to.

It was completely unrealistic, he did know in the depth of his mind. Regardless of that reality, for that moment, he was willing to lie still and let the dream flow over him.

Even knowing it was unlikely he would ever see her again, he found himself highly aroused at the possibilities. He didn't think Diana would return anytime soon. He could lie where he was, without any further waiting, and touch himself as he thought about touching Lexi. It was an arousing thought, but he didn't want to risk that. He'd never been so blatant in their home before, and he wouldn't do it then. Instead, he took himself off to the bathroom and ran the shower.

As he undressed, he realised that he hadn't indulged in self-pleasuring for at least a couple of years. Usually, he was highly self-controlled. On the days he didn't see Lexi, Diana was always there. Between the two of them, his needs had been completely catered to over the past three years. There had been no need for anything more. Before he'd met Lexi, Diana had been sufficient for his needs. He had been consumed then by his dedication to working day and night, every day of the week, to grow the company. That had been his obsession then. Lexi had become his obsession since.

He needed release. She was on his mind, and he couldn't get her off it. He didn't *want* to get her off it. He wanted to tune out everything but her. At that moment, he didn't care about his wife, and he didn't care about his company. All of that could wait. It was Sunday. No-one needed him for the business, and his wife certainly didn't need him. For them to be near each other at that time really would be explosive, and not in a good way. No, he needed to grant his mind access to where it wanted to be, not where it *should* be. He needed to indulge.

He stepped under the water and turned the temperature up higher than normal. He needed to feel its heat on him. He took his time, firstly appreciating how it felt on his skin as the hot water hit his head, shoulders, back, buttocks. As he turned, he felt it on his forehead, cheeks, chin. Pushing his head back, he felt it hit his chest and run down onto his belly. At forty-five, he was still well-toned with no sign of a big gut beginning yet.

He ran his fingers lightly over his nipples and squeezed them, remembering how it felt when Lexi sucked on them - pulled them - bit them. The action didn't make him any harder. He was already upright and as hard as he could ever be. He had been even before he had gotten under the water. Squeezing each nipple made his hardness twitch. He didn't want to touch himself there yet. He didn't think it would take long at all to climax if he did, and he didn't want to waste it. Already he could feel the hot water hitting it. He enjoyed the feeling of that. It felt like her fingertips did when they reached out to him and lightly fluttered across him, teasing him as she sometimes had.

The water suddenly didn't feel hot enough, so he turned the temperature up again. He looked down and could see how red his skin was becoming in the heat, but he felt no pain in it. It was a comfort - a satisfaction.

He wanted to touch himself, but he didn't. Instead, he reached up and pulled the showerhead from its cradle and brought it down, using his hand to guide the direction of the water flow. He brought it directly to his nipple with one hand on the showerhead, pointing the flow at it, and the other squeezing the nipple hard. He changed hands so he could give equal attention to the other nipple, starting to hear himself let out a small groan. Even if he was the only one at home, he couldn't bring himself to be as loud as he felt he wanted to be, given how he was feeling. It was different when he was with Lexi. When with her, he let himself be as loud as he needed to be. She had never teased him about it or tried to stop him. In everything, she just accepted him as who he was.

He couldn't stop himself from believing that she must love him to accept so much about him. It didn't even occur to him that she did what he wanted - and let him do what he wanted - out of fear. He didn't consider that she was terrified of what he would do if she *didn't* do what he wanted.

He moved the showerhead around his body, and back to his buttocks. He hadn't considered that area an area of pleasure through most of his adult life - until he had met her. As he stood under the hot water, he thought of his time with Lexi. Reaching one hand back to pull one buttock cheek aside, he directed the hot water directly onto his anus. It wasn't a new feeling. It wasn't something he hadn't tried before, and he liked it. He was close to orgasm, even though his hardness wasn't in any way being stimulated.

He held the water there, not afraid of the feelings the flow was producing in him. Through his parted legs, he could feel the water move further, hitting the underside of his scrotum. The combination of the hot water hitting both areas was almost enough to make his knees buckle.

He knew he was at his limit. He physically couldn't hold back any more. Letting go of the buttock cheek he had been holding, he let the water stream remain where it was. It stimulated his anus and scrotum at the same time, while he moved his free hand around to his front. Instead of putting his hand completely around himself, he closed his eyes and imagined Lexi was in front of him. He imagined her touching him with just the very tip of her tongue, just the way she had looked that very first time. To simulate that, he touched only one individual fingertip to the very head of his erection.

That was all it took. The image in his head of her tongue starting its journey, as it had perfected so well over the time they had known each other, was enough to drive him to a sweet and incredibly intense climax. He dropped the shower head as he reached out with both hands to steady himself after he felt his knees start to go. His eyes were closed. He didn't need to see to know how much semen was being shot out of him at that moment. For several minutes he felt aftershocks - one tiny little squirt, accompanied by another little mini-orgasm - over and over again.

He stayed in the shower for a long time, even after the pleasure of his muscles contracting had subsided. Picking up the showerhead and putting it back in its cradle, he then took time to just stand under the flow. He let himself enjoy feeling the hot water hit his head and flow down his back as he let his head fall forward slightly. Patiently he waited for his thinking to come back to normal. He had needed the sexual release. Now he needed to get his head together.

A part of him didn't want to face anything real. It was tempting to stay where he was. It was safe within the enclosed walls of the shower. While there, no-one from the outside world was able to penetrate his privacy. He didn't want to see anyone. He didn't want to deal with anyone. He just wanted to be alone. All of a sudden, the thought of being a nobody appealed to him greatly.

He could do that, he thought to himself. He didn't need the wealth that came from being the owner of the company. He didn't need to work at all. He could just disappear. *They* could just disappear - together. Once again he let himself indulge in the fantasy of Lexi running away with him and the two of them starting a new life together. It was a nice fantasy about the two of them, as two unknown people in the world. The reality was that he *wasn't* unknown. No matter what he did, there would always be an element of expectation that someone would have something to say about him. That would flow on and affect her life as well. No, it was better to continue keeping it a secret.

If only he didn't have to be out in the world as the face of the company so much. He didn't need all the meetings, the presentations, the dinners…

"Fuck!" he shouted to no-one, thinking momentarily that he had been shouting that a lot over the past day or two.

He suddenly remembered the dinner he and Diana were supposed to be attending. It was a fundraiser. He didn't want to go - not now. It was a tempting thought to not attend, but his work ethic was what it was, and kicked in full force. Once resolved, he found himself being the professional once again, cursing himself for forgetting, even temporarily.

Quickly he left the shower, had a shave, and put on the tuxedo that Diana had already so efficiently hung up on the wardrobe door for him. Also hanging up was the gown that she'd wanted to wear. Now he didn't know if she would go or not. He guessed not, but then if she had known about Lexi all along, and had continued to stand by him at such events, he supposed she might still attend. She had always been passionate about their charity participation. There was no way of knowing what she would do.

He didn't take any more time to think about his wife. Whatever she was doing, he'd still committed to the charity to be there. Quickly he left the apartment with a dedication to reprioritising and refocusing. He would only just make it in time. With the tight time limit, there was no choice but to drive himself rather than wait for the time it would take for Toby to arrive.

Before walking into the event centre, he took a moment in the car to stop, sit quietly, take a deep breath, and look at himself in the mirror. No matter how much his inner self was in turmoil, he had to get a grip on reality. No matter how much of a mess his personal life was about to explode into, he had to get himself together. No matter how much he wished he could climb back into that shower and hide from the world, he was who he was. He needed to be present at the event, not just in body, but also in mind.

He climbed from the car, entered the benefit room, and held his head up high. He then put on his best smile, as if it were any other event on any other day.

CHAPTER 4

The Beginning - Three Years Earlier

Alexis was serving on the front counter near the supermarket checkout. She didn't like being on the customer service counter, but on that day, there was no-one else to do it. Cindy had called in sick and, as always, everyone else had not quite *refused* to fill in, but somehow it had fallen on Alexis. She didn't like it, but she would do it. It was only one day, and how many customers really would require the attention of the service desk attendant anyway? Not anywhere near as many as would walk through checkout, she was sure. Perhaps it would be just a nice, easy, uneventful day where she didn't have to deal with people after all.

The morning passed quickly with very few enquiries. She began to feel like the end of the day would pass just as quickly, with no real stress at all.

As lunchtime approached, she found her stress level take a sharp rise as she saw the supermarket manager walking straight toward her. He wasn't even walking just generally toward the broad area around the desk. No, he was definitely looking directly at *her*. Her heart pounded heavily in her chest at the sight.

As the manager moved closer, Alexis straightened herself, standing taller while at the same time dropping her eyes.

"Young lady," he said to her, reminding Alexis once again that he did not know - nor had ever had any desire to know - her name. "This is Mr. Kokiri. He is travelling around all of the supermarkets under his company name, and today we are blessed with his company."

Alexis felt sick inside with the level of sucking up she could hear in his voice. It was an obvious attempt by her manager to impress the man beside him.

"Right now he would like to talk to you, so I am leaving him in your hands," her manager continued. "I'll be back shortly."

Left standing in the customer service desk with the man she'd just been introduced to, Alexis had no idea what to do or what to say.

Lincoln looked at the young woman in front of him. She looked intimidated and shy. In his view, that was completely justified, given the wording and manner of the manager who had just spoken to her.

When Alexis heard nothing more, she raised her eyes to look at the man who had been delivered to her. He was very well groomed, she noted. She didn't often get to see anyone who wore a suit.

What Lincoln noticed immediately were her eyes. She was young, and yet something in her face said that she had known pain in her life, possibly as a child.

They were both silent in assessing each other until Lincoln realised she was too shy to speak. He would have to be the initiator.

"I'm Lincoln Kokiri," he said, holding his hand out to her. He watched as she slowly but gingerly took it in her own for a handshake. "I would like to ask you some questions about your work here."

Alexis stuttered at first, overwhelmed by the prospect of actually having to have a conversation with anyone.

"I ... I'm sorry, but I don't usually work here at the customer service desk, so I'm probably not the ... right person."

Lincoln studied her, seeing in her a rare mix of innocence and maturity. The mixture and contrast were captivating.

"I just want to ask you some questions about working here in general - in the supermarket," he said. "It doesn't matter where exactly you usually work. I'm interested in any of the work that you have done here."

Alexis looked shyly at him as he spoke, and nodded when he'd finished talking.

"Okay," she forced herself to say in response.

Lincoln smiled at her nervousness. He then saw her look closely at him. She appeared to be studying his face. Although now over 40, and very comfortable in any situation usually, Lincoln suddenly found himself blush. It was a new experience for him. In contrast, after he had smiled at her, she seemed to take on a new level of confidence. It was like a little slice of his self-confidence had jumped from him to her.

Very aware of his age and the obvious age gap between the two of them, he reminded himself silently that to her, he was an old man, and she was just a child. He was also married. He had been for seventeen years, to a woman who he loved deeply.

"Can we go somewhere else and talk?" he asked her, experiencing a strong desire to whisk her away to anywhere other than where they presently stood.

Alexis immediately fell back into shy territory.

"I'm ... I'm not supposed to leave the desk," she said.

She looked around her as if she could already get into trouble, just for talking to him. It made no sense, of course, since she was doing so under the strict instruction of the store manager.

Not wanting to make her uncomfortable, Lincoln disregarded that chain of thought quickly.

"How long have you worked here?" he asked.

Alexis psychologically prepared herself for an onslaught of questions coming her way.

"Four years," she replied, temporarily stunning him.

"But you can't be more than sixteen," he said, almost stuttering in surprise.

He was horrified at the thought that had finally hit him - the woman he was speaking to was young enough to be his daughter.

Alexis gained some strength once more and looked him directly in the eye.

"I'm eighteen, and I've been working here since I was fourteen - only after school at first, and full time over the past year and a half," she informed him.

Lincoln found himself pulled in again to her confidence. It felt like she had some kind of ebb and flow in her, moving from one extreme of self-confidence to the other of no confidence. It was intriguing. *She* was intriguing.

Alexis watched the man before her. She didn't usually look people in the eye, except when she knew that they were going to pass through very quickly and not think about her again. On the checkout counter, she could summon the strength to face them more, knowing each interaction was only a few minutes long. She found that she liked looking at the face before her. She had no concept of age, but he was obviously much older than her, and yet he didn't seem old, either.

For a few minutes, they remained silent as they looked at each other, doing an honest appraisal of each other's faces - lips, eyes…

"How are you getting on?" they both heard a voice say from behind. When each redirected their eyes, they saw the store manager returning. "I hope this little lady has been helpful."

Lincoln silently cursed the man for coming back so soon, but immediately turned fully toward the manager. He quickly plastered on his most polite smile.

"She has indeed. I can see that she is a valued and loyal employee, which is what I like to see in our stores," Lincoln said to bring the attention back to him and away from the girl in front of him.

He saw the store manager look from him to the girl, and back to him again, confused.

"Now I would like to talk to you about…" Lincoln continued, steering the store manager away and leaving Alexis alone again.

The only thought that passed through the busy mind of Alexis was, 'did I even answer any questions about working here?'

~~~~~

That night, in the comfort of his office, Lincoln found himself thinking about the girl he had met that day. It made so sense for him to do so, but he couldn't stop it. He decided to make an excuse to go back to
~~~~~

that store. Perhaps he could arrange a follow-up meeting with the store manager. That would enable him to see the girl again. He would probably dismiss her from his thoughts after seeing her a second time. It was quite possible that he would then identify her as just someone who turned his head briefly but wasn't attractive at all.

The following week, Lincoln formulated an excuse to go back to the supermarket. He was nervous as he talked to the store manager. When he tried to manoeuvre himself to where the girl would be, he found himself distressed at learning that it was her day off.

"I did want to talk to her about something particular. How could I find her?" he found himself asking. He knew it was not only highly unprofessional but also wrong. That didn't stop the question from leaving his lips.

The store manager looked at him, perplexed. He couldn't give out staff details to anyone, but this was his employer. Lincoln Kokiri was the owner of the whole chain. Could he refuse?

As if sensing the dilemma the store manager had been placed in, having had such a question put to him, Lincoln retracted. He could feel a sense of frustration beginning inside of him.

"I am very glad to see that you do not easily give out personal details of your staff," he said. "That puts my mind at ease. I believe staff safety is paramount, above all other considerations."

The store manager instantly looked relieved at not having had to make the difficult decision after all. He was also thankful at not having to say something that could have proven to be the wrong decision.

As if fate itself was suddenly speaking to him, in the background behind the store manager, Lincoln saw Alexis walk into the store, not for work but as a customer. He wanted to rush to her but knew he couldn't do that. No, he would have to be more subtle. As he stood where he was, his eyes moved from the manager who was directly in front of him, to behind the manager and over the store floor.

"Thank you so much. I am delighted with how you are running this store. You are truly a great asset to the company," Lincoln said to the store manager.

He held out his hand for a handshake before turning to leave. He wanted to leave discretely and get outside before Alexis did.

Sitting in his car outside, he watched the front entrance. He didn't know what he was doing. No, that was a lie. He knew *exactly* what he was doing. He just couldn't stop himself from doing it.

When he saw her walk out and start to walk down the road, he panicked. What should he do? Should he approach her? That would be crossing a workplace boundary - or would it? Was he really considered her employer, given how many levels of people stood between him as the head of the overall company, and her as whatever her proper job was?

He sat in his car until she was a short way down the road. Once she was a distance ahead, Lincoln began driving. As he pulled up beside her, he lowered the passenger side window of his car.

"Hello!" he called out.

Straight away, he saw she was startled before she looked around and then, still from a safe distance, looked into the car.

Alexis saw who it was. Although confused by what he was calling out to her for, she felt relaxed with him doing so.

"Hello," she said back without any expression on her face whatsoever.

"I was just in the supermarket and saw you. Can I give you a lift home?" Lincoln asked, feeling inside of him a blend of nervousness, eagerness, a sense of wrongness … and arousal.

Alexis looked at him doubtfully, not sure what to do. He seemed safe enough, but getting into the car with someone she didn't know wasn't something she would usually do. Her boss had explained the man was the owner of the entire supermarket chain. Surely that meant he was responsible.

"Alright," she finally said. Still uncertain if it was right or not, she decided to trust her gut instinct. Her gut was telling her he was okay.

Lincoln opened the door for her and helped her put her supermarket bags in the back seat. Once they were both sitting in the car, he looked at her. She was facing forward like she was frozen in fear. He resolved to at least help her relax.

"Where to?" he asked.

Alexis looked at him, at first not comprehending his question. When she understood what he'd asked, she gave him directions to her home.

Once the car stopped outside of her home, Lincoln waited. He wasn't sure what would be crossing the line. No matter what he felt he wanted, he couldn't bring himself to push himself on her too much.

Alexis turned to look at him before she got out of the car.

"Thank you," she said simply and climbed out.

Lincoln jumped out and immediately came around to the passenger side. He quickly opened the back door and lifted her grocery bags out.

"Let me help you carry these in," he said, feeling that same desperation coming on. He thought she would say no. Instead, he saw her nod and turn to walk inside, seeming to expect him to follow.

Inside her small home, Lincoln saw that she lived very simply. The kitchen and living areas were sparse, to say the least. There was nothing personal about the space. It held no photos or artwork or books. There was nothing about it to make him think that it was really a home.

"Can I make you a cup of tea?" she asked, surprising him.

"Yes, thank you," he responded.

He deplored tea, but he was determined to not have any reason not to stay longer. He watched her as she worked in the kitchen, putting frozen and cold foods away, and then making the cups of tea.

When she walked right up to him and handed him his, she looked into his eyes. Lincoln felt like she was looking right into him, as if she could see exactly who he was and what his intentions were, and she didn't *mind* what his intentions were.

He watched as she moved to sit on a sofa in the room. It was the only real seat that Lincoln could see. There seemed no choice but to sit right beside her.

"You want something from me," Alexis said to him when they were seated.

The comment made Lincoln catch his breath and find himself blushing once again. As he looked at her, he could see stark openness on her face, combined with what looked like an expectation of utter honesty from him.

"Yes," he replied.

"Why?" Alexis asked. She wasn't sure if she wanted to know the answer to the question, but felt like she *had* to know.

"I … I don't know," Lincoln spluttered out.

His body was on fire from nerves and an unexpected level of arousal. The frankness of the conversation that she had begun was fuelling him. There was no fakeness to it, like he had to put up with day after day, no matter who he interacted with. Even after all the years that he'd been married, his wife, Diana, had a fakeness about her that infuriated him at times.

As they sat in silence, drinking their tea, Alexis let thoughts run through her mind. She had been with men before. She wasn't a virgin. She'd learned from a very young age that they wanted sex from women. It was a core part of their souls. She had come to expect that if they ever wanted anything from her, it was usually sex. Sometimes she had wanted it too, but at different times she'd had sex with them just because they wanted it. She found she had no care at all. She didn't care if they did or they didn't have sex - so she had sex. It wasn't unpleasant, but it never felt truly pleasurable either.

The hardest thing that Alexis found with men was that they didn't always *say* exactly what they wanted. That frustrated her. As she looked at the man beside her and could sense his indecision about how to let her know what he wanted, she looked him directly in the eye and told him what she expected.

"Tell me what you want me to do," she said. She immediately saw surprise on his face.

Lincoln was in shock. His head said he was in the wrong time and the wrong place. His body screamed otherwise. He didn't know what he wanted. All he knew was that she'd been on his mind for days. Whatever it was about her, she had incredible power over him. He'd heard her words and could see she was waiting for his response.

"I want you to kiss me ... on my lips," he said quietly, almost in a whisper, almost as a question.

Lincoln watched as she took their cups to the kitchen to put them on the bench. He gulped in anguish. He expected he was about to be asked to leave. Angry at himself, he then saw her coming back toward him. He watched her kneel on the sofa beside him, facing him, never taking her eyes from his. She then placed her lips on his.

It was the first time in twenty years that Lincoln had kissed anyone other than Diana. Even in the three years before they had married, he'd always been faithful. Even when they had both been at the end of their teen years, entering their twenties and studying at college where anything could have happened, he had wanted only to be with her and no-one else.

He sat still, not reaching out his hands, not moving to stand up. He was too surprised to move. A momentary feeling of guilt gave way to the increase in his arousal. He hoped that she couldn't see how much she was affecting him. He wouldn't act any further. He was enjoying the feeling of her young and exploring lips. They were so different from Diana's, but he wouldn't let it go any further. On so many levels, it wasn't right.

Alexis did as he wanted. His request had surprised her. She had been expecting him to ask for sex immediately, but she was enjoying just kissing him. She didn't touch any other part of his body. She could feel his lips moving against hers. He didn't seem keen to want to pull away. Equally, he wasn't trying to pull her against him. He didn't seem to have any desire to, or move in any other way toward anything else. To her, it was very different from any interaction she'd had with men previously.

Finally, Alexis pulled back from him and sat back down on the sofa, as if nothing had happened. Lincoln looked at her, wondering what she thought of him at that moment. He wondered what he should think of *himself* at that moment.

"I should go," he said, feeling overwhelmed by his emotions. It was too raw for him. Everything in his life was calculated, and the current moment conflicted with that. He needed to go and process it before he let anything else happen.

When Alexis saw him stand up, she stood up beside him.

"Will you come and see me again?" she asked, finding that she didn't fear the possibility.

Lincoln was uncertain how he should reply, or if she was inviting him…

"Do you want me to?" he asked tentatively.

"Yes," he heard her answer, with no hesitation. Briefly, he thought of how different his wife was. Everything Diana said was calculated. He'd always known that, but in recent years, he had increasingly felt like he didn't know what was real with her anymore.

"I don't even know your name," he said, suddenly feeling even worse at that realisation.

"Lexi," she blurted out, not wanting to give her formal name. She'd played around with the shortened name in her head for a long time. Because everyone she knew already knew her as Alexis, she had always felt she couldn't change her name. With the man in front of her, it didn't matter. While in her apartment with him, she could be Lexi. She probably wouldn't see him again, so what would it matter?

"Lexi," he seemed to breathe out like it was a foreign name he had never heard before.

They looked at each other intently. He knew it wouldn't be fair for him to hide the most important fact of his life from her.

"Lexi, I am married," he said quietly, looking and feeling like he was the most deceitful person in the world right at that moment.

"I know," he heard her reply. He gave her a look of curiosity. "I looked you up," she continued as if that answered his unspoken question entirely.

"And you would still want me to come back to see you?" he asked. His curiosity was growing, combined with an alertness that came with knowing he was in the media, and his wealth was well known. He'd had women try to seduce him many times in attempts to gain his affection and his money. He'd always felt like he could easily see their intentions, so had moved out of their reach very quickly so that nothing could be misconstrued.

"If you want to," Alexis replied. "I'm always here after six in the evenings, even on days that I work. If you want to visit, I would like that, but not after eight at night, please. I do have to start work quite early some days, so tend to go to bed early."

Lincoln listened. It was the most words he'd heard her use at one time. He couldn't find any suitable words for a response, so just nodded. His eyes followed her as she moved to the door, leading him. She said no more either. Instead, she simply held the door open for him to walk out.

Silently, he did so - before he went home and made love to his wife for the first time in a long while.

~~~~~

Over the next week, Lincoln absorbed himself in his work. He wouldn't think about Lexi during business meetings. He wouldn't think about her in the evenings when he was with Diana. He wouldn't think about her when he was travelling anywhere.
~~~~~

That was what he wanted.

That wasn't exactly how things went.

Alexis didn't give him another thought. She had no expectation there. For whatever reason, she had caught his attention for a moment. She expected that immediately after leaving her home, he would have gone back to being who he really was. He was a husband. He was a business owner. He was a wealthy and mature man who could have any woman he wanted, whenever he wanted.

She was surprised when a week later there a knock on her door. On opening it, she saw Lincoln standing in front of her.

They looked at each other in surprise. Even he seemed to be shocked to have found himself at her home. As much as he'd tried to fight it, he couldn't deny the desperation he felt about her. The need to see her again had been intense and almost all-consuming for him.

What had impacted him as much as anything else, was the memory of her telling him to tell her what he wanted her to do. All through his life with Diana, he'd always needed to be the initiator. He was always the one who had to move first, and who had to try and figure out what it would take to please her. On the rare occasion when he had dared to ask her to do something - to try something different - she had always laughed as if it were a joke. Because of that, things never changed between them in the bedroom. It wasn't bad. He didn't *not* enjoy making love to his wife, but it was always the same.

Alexis moved aside, welcoming him in. After she closed the front door, she moved to the sofa once more and waited for him to speak.

Lincoln felt awkward. That was something he never felt anywhere else, no matter what he was required to do. Despite his uncertainty, he spoke honestly and openly, just as she had so far.

"I liked being kissed by you," he said simply.

When the words had left his mouth, he expected her to laugh at him. Diana certainly would have if he'd said such a thing. From Lexi, he instantly got his reply. It wasn't a laugh.

"Then tell me to do it again," Alexis said. In response, she heard him instantly let out a long, deep breath.

Lincoln was still standing, in one way afraid to sit down beside her.

"Stand up," he said and watched as she did so. "Kiss me, Lexi."

Alexis raised on tiptoe and placed her lips on his. She didn't put her arms around him or even lean into him. She once again did exactly as he told her to. Her actions were nothing more than his request, but also nothing less.

While she kissed him, Lincoln relished the feel and taste of her lips on his. There was something so erotic about just their lips touching, without anything else happening. He liked it. He liked the 'not rushing to sex', that had always been the situation in his sexual life.

Pulling away from her, he studied her face. She was so young, he acknowledged again. It briefly occurred to him that she must have been around the same age that Diana had been when he had met her.

When Alexis sat down again, Lincoln settled beside her. They looked at each other.

"Do you want me to listen to you talk about your work?" she asked.

Lincoln was so surprised that he laughed softly.

"No, thank you, Lexi. I don't want to think about my work right now," he said. His heartbeat finally began to calm as he relaxed.

"Tell me what you want me to do," she said.

With such a raw sound in her voice, Lincoln felt himself stretch to an extreme point of arousal. He had to move to adjust himself in a way that might at least hide his arousal from her. Once comfortable again, he smiled at her.

"Have I mentioned how much I enjoy you kissing me?" he asked, shyly.

Alexis looked at him, already knowing that it was what he wanted her to do. It wasn't enough for her to just perceive what he wanted. In her mind, she needed to be told clearly, without any hesitation. She wanted to have no doubt so she could be sure not to do the wrong thing.

"Tell me what you want me to do," she said again.

Lincoln fell under her spell once more.

"Climb onto my lap," he whispered, not sure where she would regard his request as crossing a line. The words were met with her standing up and then straddling him. "Put your hands on my chest," he ventured to say, feeling bolder with each passing moment. He felt her do as he'd suggested. He knew that there was no way he could hide his arousal from her. She was almost sitting right on it. "Kiss me."

Alexis heard each request and complied. She was happy to do so since she knew it was definitely what he wanted. She could feel how excited he was, and yet he wasn't asking her to have sex with him … yet.

They kissed for a long while. Eventually, he put his arms around her and pulled her close to him. Both indulged in the feeling of their lips getting to know each other. He could feel her moving on him, driving him to an extreme level of desire, but he didn't sense that she was trying to deliberately pleasure him there. She was only doing what he had asked. Her movements, and the effect they were having on him, were just a by-product of that.

He felt her tongue wrapping around his. As if from a great distance, he heard himself groan at the sensation. Even just kissing her was so different. It was intoxicating. He didn't want it to end, but he knew it had to. Firmly he pushed her away from him just enough so that their lips separated.

"Lexi, I have never cheated on my wife," he said with a sound of despair in his voice. His hands remained on her hips. They felt comfortable there. It didn't feel wrong at all. It felt right.

Alexis could see the confusion on his face. She didn't want to contribute to that. Not for him. Not for anybody.

"I'm not asking for anything from you," she said, in her consistent simplicity of conversation. "If you want something from me, then ask me for it. If you don't want anything from me, that's okay too."

Hearing her words, Lincoln could appreciate their age difference. She saw things so differently to how he did.

"There are two kinds of wants," he said, lifting one hand and gently touching her cheek. "We can want physically. That want, you are bringing out in me greatly, as I'm sure you can feel," he continued. He saw her blush softly, making her even more endearing. "But there is also the want for things that are right, and not wrong."

Alexis sat quietly, letting him work through things in his mind.

"That want, I have to let get right inside of me. I'm attracted to you, and I know that I'm physically wanting of you, but I am married, and I am so much older than you. I'm also not an unknown figure out there in the world," he said, raising his other hand to wave, as if pointing to the world outside of her home.

"Do you want to have sex with me?" she asked.

Lincoln groaned heavily before standing up and turning around with her still in his arms. Gently he set her down on the sofa.

"Would I like to? Perhaps later - much later - but not tonight. And before you ask if I will tell you to, no, Lexi, I won't do that," Lincoln said, trying without success to will his arousal to go away. "Not unless you and I get to know each other much, much better … over time."

He knelt on the floor before her.

"Part your legs," he said.

Alexis did as he asked. She was wearing jeans, so Lincoln felt safe asking for that. He gently placed his hands on her knees and slowly and lightly ran his hands up and down over her thighs. Even the texture of the denim of her jeans enticed him. When had he even last touched denim? He seemed to live in suits - suits and running gear. To his immediate regret, his wife would never have been seen in anything she considered so common as jeans.

Alexis watched his face and could see the level of desire on it. She waited, not wanting to push him into anything.

Lincoln leaned in and put his arms around her, pulling her to him again as she perched on the edge of the sofa. They stayed like that, cheek to cheek, for a few minutes, before he recognised what was missing from that position.

"Put your arms around me," he said. He relished the movement of her arms coming up and circling his neck.

Already he had come to see that her way was to wait for commands. She seemed to need requests - instructions. Despite knowing that, he didn't ask for her to kiss him at that moment. Pulling his head back far enough so that he could look at her face, he wanted to indulge in kissing *her*. He was curious to see how she'd react to not being commanded.

Alexis saw his lips moving forward toward hers. She happily let the kiss happen. It wasn't that she couldn't enjoy things happening as a man made it happen. His lips moving onto hers, and the way he was kissing her, was welcome. She had to find a way to find a compromise between needing to be told what he wanted from her, while letting him feel relaxed enough to do what he wanted also.

Lincoln kissed her lips over and over. The taste of her, the fullness of those lips, and her enthusiasm with her tongue, was driving him crazy. It contributed to him straining in his hardness. There was no way she wouldn't be able to feel it as he naturally rubbed against her while nestled between her legs.

When he heard her groan, he almost lost control. It was the first indication that had come from her that she was being as turned on by him, as he was by her. The groan was followed by her kissing him in a way that was almost aggressive. It wasn't just her kissing him because he'd asked her to. At that moment, she was kissing him on another level. It was kissing as was natural to her as she rose in arousal as well.

Alexis forgot where she was, and who she was. Lincoln's style of kissing was nothing like she had experienced before. It wasn't like the boys she had been with. He was kissing her in a way that made her think it wasn't a case of him simply wanting to have sex with someone, and she was just there. It truly felt like he really wanted to kiss *her*. The discovery fuelled her greatly. It pushed her to the point where she forgot everything else and just let herself indulge in it, without any care for control or permission. His lips … his tongue…

They continued like that until Lincoln had to break away from her. He had to. He was suffocating in her arms and her lips. He wanted more of her - so much more - but he couldn't take it. He could not give it.

He stood up abruptly. Upon looking down at her, he knew he'd left her hanging, with a confused look on her face. He was frustrated, not at her but rather, of the situation. It was so right and so wrong at the same time.

"Stand up," Lincoln said, more forcefully than he meant. Regardless of the force behind the words, Alexis complied. When she was in front of him, he kissed her once more, softly, determined to get himself under control. "I need to go, Lexi. Whatever this is, it's powerful, and I need to … go … now."

Alexis nodded, seeing the confusion and conflict in him. She followed him to the door. There he turned and looked at her before kissing her on her forehead and then walking out.

~~~~~

When Lincoln got home that night, it was late. He'd stopped at his office and had a shower there so he could try and find some way to look normal before he went home to Diana. He even sat down and did half an hour of work. He knew there was a chance his wife would ask him when he walked in how his work was. He didn't want to lie to her, so he worked. He did that purely so he could talk about his work, all the while leaving out details of everything else he had been doing that evening.

Lexi was on his mind, of course. She had made him feel like she had woken him from a dream. Her mouth and her eyes invaded his thoughts. He had purposely not looked at her body. He didn't want to venture there in case - he didn't want to think the words, but they were there, in his head - in case he didn't see her again.

Being a business professional, he had to find a way to not let her consume his thoughts. Not seeing her was not an option to him. He'd only been alone with her twice, but already he knew that he had to see her again. That was dependent on whether she wanted him to. He would never pressure anyone into anything unless it was a major business decision. He'd never had any desire to pressure a woman into doing anything she didn't want to do.

Once again, he thought about the enjoyment she'd gained from being told what to do. She wanted to please. She wanted to be told what was required of her. He wasn't sure how healthy that was - or would be if he kept seeing her.

After letting himself into their apartment, Lincoln quietly slipped into bed and instantly felt Diana's hands on him. He had just talked himself down from being aroused, but let himself be coaxed, indulging in letting go of what he'd been holding in since seeing Lexi. As he slid into Diana the only way she liked sex - with him moving on top of her and into her - he found himself wondering how it would feel to slip inside Lexi. With that thought, he quickly climaxed, finding great relief in the well-overdue release.

As a man, he didn't self-pleasure at all. It was something he hadn't done since he was a teenager. He took pride in being in control of all bodily needs, including good nutrition and fitness. Generally, he considered it a waste of precious time to touch and pleasure himself. His view on that was changing. As he relaxed on top of his wife, he found himself wondering if he might not be more honest if he started to. It
~~~~~

might be good to do anything to get rid of the need that Lexi had already evoked in him, even though he'd only visited her two times.

Diana reached up with her hands and pulled his mouth to hers. It was a belated kiss that followed the release. There was no desire in it. Lincoln often felt her kisses were just a token of appreciation on her part. It was an action that was calculated and old, but she was his wife and he had committed to her … and he did love her.

Lincoln dutifully kissed her back before rolling off her, turning over and going to sleep, thinking about another woman entirely.

~~~~~

After two more weeks had passed, Lincoln was almost gone completely from Lexi's mind. She had moved him into the back of her memory. Men came and went. That was a fact of life, and she didn't expect anything different.

One evening there was a knock on her door. On opening the door, she was once again surprised to see him there. He looked flushed, like he wasn't sure he would be welcome. She invited him in, curious to see what he would say, if anything.

Lincoln looked at her, feeling all of a sudden like the visit was a bad idea. He had tried so hard to keep her off his mind. He'd been determined to move on and put their two small intimate moments aside and forget them.

He'd found he just couldn't do it quite so easily. That frustrated him. He worked hard and took pride in putting things in his life in order. Thoughts of her were so *messy*.

He had fantasised about her, especially while and directly after making love to Diana. Sex with his wife had always been mechanical and limited. It had always been her preference to feel him move immediately into her, and then remove himself when he was finished. She didn't want to pleasure him in any other way, and he had long ago given up trying to pleasure her at all. The monotony of their lovemaking had always left a void in Lincoln. There were aspects of sex that he had tried as a teenager before he'd met Diana, that he still thought about on occasion. The present thought of being with someone new brought those memories back to him. He didn't believe that no woman liked a man's attention at the core of her pleasure, as was the case with his wife.

As he stood in the small living room with Lexi, he wasn't sure what to say or do. She had opened a door for him. He so much wanted to walk through it.

"What do you need from me, Lincoln?" she asked.

It was the first time she used his name. That affected him. All day long, almost every day, he was 'Mr. Kokiri'. He didn't want to be that person - not there, not with her.
~~~~~

Alexis saw his confusion and conflict once again. She already felt used to that, even after only two meetings in her home. It was like he had a puzzle that he just could not solve. She wondered if he had some challenge he wanted to face but didn't know how to.

She moved to him, and they stood together in the lounge area in front of the sofa. He seemed frozen on the spot, so she reached out and just used the tips of her fingertips to touch his arms. With him wearing a short-sleeved v-neck t-shirt, she was able to feel the hairs on his arms stand up, and a layer of goosebumps appear. She stroked his arms as he looked into her eyes.

Lincoln felt the light touch and ached inside. He had been married for seventeen years. He still had sex with his wife, sometimes several times a week, but it had been a long time since anyone had truly touched him.

He let the simple feelings of touch flow over him. They'd been greatly missed and long needed. After a period of indulgence, he took one of her hands in his and raised it to his mouth to kiss. He kept his eyes focused on hers. He watched her look at his lips as he kissed her hand.

"I can't stop thinking about you, Lexi," he said, so very quietly. "Come and sit down with me."

Alexis heard the request and instantly sat on the sofa, close to him. Feeling him take her hand in his as they faced each other, she waited patiently for him to find the strength to say whatever he wished to say.

"What do you want from *me*, Lexi? That is something that I need to know, before…" he started to say.

He couldn't find the words for what he wanted to say. He couldn't find what it *was* that he wanted to say.

"Before you have sex with me?" Alexis asked, always so frank and never sugar coating anything.

It sounded raw to Lincoln. At the same time, he did like her straight to the point approach when she spoke and when she asked questions.

When Alexis saw he wouldn't answer, she answered his question.

"What I want from you, is for you to tell me what you want from me," she said.

The answer confounded Lincoln both with its vagueness and with its brilliance. He loved the way she had turned it around to somehow have been directed back on him once again.

"Lexi, do you understand that I could only see you irregularly?" he asked and saw her nod. "I would never be able to be seen with you in public. I have a wife," he continued and saw her nod once again.

"I know. To see you, I would have to be a secret," she replied.

When Lincoln heard the words, his heart felt like it would break. She was absolutely right in her statement. He had no wish to mislead her. She was someone who seemed to prefer honesty - raw and plain without deception. He would continue to be truthful with her. It would be disrespectful not to do so.

"Yes," he said. "I won't pretend things could ever be any different."

"Okay," Alexis replied as if it weren't any great deal to her.

"Okay?"

"Yes. We agree that if you come to see me, you will do so when you can, and it might not be often. I won't tell anyone about us," she said and paused, kissing his hand. "I won't expect anything from you. You'll come and see me on any night that suits you, but only between six and eight, because that is *my* condition."

Lincoln nodded slowly, feeling like something was completely on offer to him. It was a moment he had to think about. At the same time, he knew he didn't need to think about it at all. He'd been fantasising about her too much already.

"Are you a virgin, Lexi?" he asked directly.

Alexis shook her head. "No."

Lincoln was instantly aroused again and full of desire for things his wife wouldn't let him do. His thoughts veered to nothing that he considered 'odd', but normal things that other couples did, that he'd missed so much.

He pulled her close and kissed her. Again and again, he kissed her until she was moaning loudly, her arousal completely audible and apparent to him. He wanted to undress her, but his knowledge that she wanted him to tell her what he wanted finally kicked in as being acceptable.

"Stand up," he said. He watched as she did so, turning to face him as he sat back on the sofa. "Take off your clothes," he continued. His words felt forbidden, like he was indulging in something sinful.

He saw her pull off her sweatshirt, then her t-shirt. She kept her eyes on his. He saw her bra and how it was filled out. She was tiny in stature, and until that moment, he hadn't realised how shapely she was in her chest. He let out a deep breath as she continued to undress.

He saw her undo her jeans and push them down, taking off her socks at the same time. Finally, she stood before him in her bra and panties. She wore nothing pretty or frilly. Lincoln could see only items that didn't match, and would have probably been bought in a plain five-pack from a low budget department store. That didn't matter. To him, she looked incredible. As he reclined backward, looking at her, he could see in his view the bulge showing in his pants. About that, he didn't care.

Alexis moved to put her hands behind her as if to undo her bra. Lincoln didn't want to rush to that.

"Stop," he said. "Don't take any more off yet. Just let me look at you for a moment."

Alexis stood still, waiting for him to say what he wanted next. After a period of silence, she saw him stand up next to her.

Lincoln put his hands on either side of her face and kissed her softly. He dared not touch her in any other way in case he lost control. He was aware that he didn't want to go home with any sign or smell of her on his clothes.

"Undress me," he said, tentatively. It was something no-one had ever done to him. Never.

He watched her as she worked through her assigned task. He felt her hands push his t-shirt up and over his head, revealing his chest. She then began undoing his pants - belt, button, zip. He felt his erection stretch out toward her as if it in itself was desperate for her attention. After she pushed his pants down to the ground, he sat on the edge of the sofa so she could remove them along with his socks. Finally, he wore just his boxers. They hid nothing.

Alexis looked at him for a moment. She observed his chest, which had only a small amount of hair stretching across the area between his nipples. Other than that, his chest was smooth and shapely. His legs were well-toned, making her instantly recognise that he must be very sporty.

Lincoln watched her eyes and felt, for the first time in a very long time, like someone was truly seeing him. There was no ulterior motive behind her attention to him. She wasn't seeing his business power. She wasn't seeing his wealth. She was just seeing *him*.

Alexis knelt before him and placed her hands on the waistband of his boxers. Lincoln held her hands there, not ready to be completely naked yet.

"Climb onto me and kiss me," he said.

He watched as the young body, in its plain and mismatched bra and panties, straddled him. She inadvertently rubbed herself against the length of him. Even through the two thicknesses of fabric, he could feel wetness. That was something he never experienced with his wife. Because Diana would never let him pleasure her, he never felt any moisture on her, even when he slid into her. With Diana, it had always seemed like she didn't *want* to be aroused and moist when they joined.

Alexis found herself starting to be very excited. She was doing what he wanted, but she was also feeling things she hadn't felt before with anyone else. She moved up and down lightly, enjoying the feeling of rubbing herself against the hardness of him. When she leaned in to place her lips on his, his arms moved around her and held her tight as they indulged in kissing again. They both felt the fire of their closeness and were soon breathless.

"Oh Lexi, what you do to me! Please … remove your bra for me," Lincoln said, suddenly desperate to see her.

When she took it off, he knew he was almost at breaking point. He knew he could easily make a mess, even without joining with her. He didn't want to wait for her to do any more. Instead, he pulled her close so he could kiss her breasts. It was like experimentation with him, having not been allowed to indulge in such pleasure for so many years. He sucked on the nipples. Hearing her suck in her breath and groan deeply, he continued to do that. He lovingly caressed one then the other, and then back again. His hands rested on her buttocks. She moved her pelvis slightly, causing a rubbing sensation on him. It was almost unbearable.

"Stand up," Alexis heard him say, his voice so husky it was almost inaudible. She obeyed. "Take them off."

As Lincoln watched, Alexis lowered her underwear and stood in front of him, finally naked. He could feel his heart get heavier in his chest. Everything felt so forbidden.

"Lexi, I want to touch you … there. Can I?" he asked, wanting to be certain if she knew what he wanted from her … really.

She nodded at him. "Yes."

He felt a new sense of arousal in anticipation of being able to touch her intimately. It was something Diana had always prevented him from doing.

He leaned forward and lightly lifted his finger. Just lightly, he touched her around her outer lip region. As he did, Lexi naturally spread her legs enough so that he could run his finger deeper. Lincoln knew the anatomy of women well enough. He just hadn't been allowed full access to indulge in exploring it for an incredibly long time.

As he let his finger find its way around, he was overwhelmed with the moisture he could feel coating it. He had never understood how Diana could always be completely dry during sex, and yet still seem to *want* sex. The wetness he could feel on Lexi, he knew he'd missed. He located her clitoris and lightly touched it. Instantly he heard her moan and saw her eyes close in desire.

"Lie down here beside me," he said, his arousal growing even more. As always, she did as he instructed. "Wait. Do you have a towel?" he asked. She moved as if to get up. Lincoln stopped her. "No, I will get it."

Alexis directed him to the laundry cupboard. She watched him walk there and back. All the while that he was walking, Alexis could see the level of his desire showing through his boxers. It caused a particular hunger to begin in her.

After returning to her, Lincoln asked her to lift her hips so he could put the towel under her. Already he could sense how much the sofa could suffer from her level of arousal.

He guided and moved her so that he could sit between her legs. Once she was in position, he leaned forward in anticipation of a flavour he hadn't tasted since he was in college. At the first touch of the tip of his tongue on her, he felt her hips begin to move in line with her moaning and breathing. He was overwhelmed with her creaminess. It seemed like she'd been extremely aroused for a very long time.

He wanted to stay there. He felt like he could stay there all night, tasting her and listening to her excitement. It seemed like only a few minutes before he heard her call out loudly. At the same time, against his lips, he felt her muscles contracting, as her thighs gripped around his head tightly.

He kept licking and drinking her until he felt her pushing his head away. From a distance, he could hear her begin to giggle. It was the first time he heard that sound, and it invigorated him.

"Stop," she said between giggles. "It tickles now."

Lincoln pulled back, licking his lips. He saw her smiling at him and realised he was smiling broadly himself. He hadn't done that for a couple of decades, and yet she had been so easily pleased by him.

Alexis sat up and kissed him.

"I want to please you. Tell me how," she said.

At the words, Lincoln felt his erection strain again. He wasn't used to being around such a level of forwardness. He wasn't used to being permitted to be honest and direct about what he wanted during sex.

He tentatively stood up in front of her.

"Take these off," he said, hardly hearing his voice come out of his mouth, but she understood.

Alexis gently pulled his boxers down, allowing Lincoln to steady himself against her while he stepped out of them completely.

When she looked up at him, he liked the look in her eyes. It felt sinful, but he continued because she was looking at him, waiting.

"Lick it," he said.

Alexis heard the request and thought nothing of it. She had performed fellatio on the men she had been with, but she didn't want to do what she had done to others. She wanted to do what *he* wanted her to do.

She leaned forward, poked out her tongue, and just lightly placed the very tip of her tongue on the very tip of him. She gave a tiny lick as a start.

Looking down at her, Lincoln could hardly believe he was where he was. The look on her face as she placed her tongue on him was incredible. That first touch - tip on tip - he knew he would always remember, no matter what happened after that moment. That was only the start. She then started to use her whole tongue, licking in long strokes from hilt to tip, up and down, over and over.

"Oh, Lexi, I'll come soon," he said to her, not sure where he should ejaculate. She took that decision out of his hands as she moved her whole mouth over him. He realised that in doing so, she had provided a clean place for him to explode, which he did, while calling her name. He looked down and saw that even as he was still ejaculating, she held her lips over him and didn't flinch in her gaze at him. After a moment, she pulled her mouth away and licked him clean.

Lincoln, after a period of relishing the pleasure flowing throughout his entire body, sat on the sofa and kissed her deeply, not caring about the taste.

"I have not felt that … for a very long time," he said before he kissed her again. The power with which she kissed him back was incredible.

"Neither have I," she said, suddenly timid again with a slight blush on her face.

Lincoln couldn't help but smile at her unexpected shyness, the response to which was that she smiled demurely back at him. As he reclined backward, he told her to straddle him again. Lexi did so, allowing him to pull her against his chest and hold her close. He kissed her lightly now and then, but also looked into her eyes, and at her lips. He felt very content at that moment, but despite his contentment, reality began to set in.

Alexis felt him tense up underneath her.

"I know you have to go soon, Lincoln. It's okay," she said quietly, but not with any sadness.

"Yes, I will always have to run away and leave you after I come and visit. Are you sure you're alright with that?" he asked again.

Alexis kissed him and smiled.

"Yes," she replied. "Come and see me when you want to see me. It doesn't matter how often."

At that moment, Lincoln knew that he was going to become highly addicted to her.

~~~~~

He visited her on the same night - Thursday night - every week for the next month. In that time, he didn't let things go any further. He was enjoying too much the feeling of pleasuring her with his tongue, and feeling her mouth pleasuring him. Sexual intercourse itself - penetration - he got at home. He didn't feel as much need for it when he was with her.

In their second month, Alexis brought the possibility up as they sat on the sofa together, cuddling after mutual oral satisfaction.

"Lincoln, don't you want to be inside of me?" Alexis asked, curious about why he had not wanted them to join yet.

As she straddled him, Lincoln watched her face as she asked that question. It was the first time that he perceived that perhaps she wanted it, and not just as a way to please him. She, for herself, wanted to join with him. The realisation immediately caused him to grow again, and she
~~~~~

felt it. He saw her smile and laugh.

"Oh, I think that might be my answer," she said.

Hearing her giggle made Lincoln smile with what he could feel would be a slight blush on his face.

"I don't have any condoms with me," he said out loud, annoyed at himself silently for not thinking about that.

"I do, in my bedroom," she said, giving him a look of raw desire.

Lincoln stood up while still holding her in his arms, and instructed her to guide him there. Once in her room, he set her on her feet beside the bed and kissed her, holding her close.

"I'm going to lie down on the bed. Stay right here," he said as he crawled right up the bed and lay in his back. For a moment, he just let himself enjoy the view of her. He wasn't as hard as he wanted to be, with it being the second arousal in such a short time.

"Touch yourself," he said.

He watched her hand immediately move to between her legs and lightly move up and down over her clitoris. As he watched her, he moved his hand and began to slowly stroke himself. He never pleasured himself, but for just a moment, he did so to build the hardness up.

"Get a condom out and come to me," he said.

Alexis did as she was instructed. Lincoln was enthralled as she crept along the bed toward him on all fours. He saw her stop and kneel, open the packet, and look to him for confirmation. When he nodded, he watched and felt her roll it down onto him. He almost came in anticipation of what was to come. For weeks, he'd been thinking about how she would feel inside. He was highly excited to think he wasn't going to wait any longer. Even in that, he knew it was going to be different. Diana always had to have him on top of her - always.

"Straddle me, Lexi," he said.

Lincoln watched as she moved over him. She sat upright, stopping still when she hovered above him, waiting. He looked at the sight before him, appreciating how magnificent she looked, kneeling like she was. He could see that part of him standing straight up, as if eager and trying to reach for her.

"Lower … slowly," he said quietly, almost a whisper.

He watched as she moved onto him. Seeing that at the same time as feeling her enclose his tip made him grow the final level of hardness he could before he watched her move down on him. The look she held as he filled her up was enough in itself to push him close to orgasm.

He reached out his hand to her and touched her clit as she started to move. Hearing deep moaning from her in response pleased him. It lasted only a few minutes before he felt her clench her muscles tightly around him and then seem to collapse on him, falling forward in release. He pulled her head to him and kissed her deeply. From there, it was natural for him to thrust up into her. He came quickly after that, for the first time while they were kissing. It felt so intimate to him. It felt so unlike the routine he had with his wife.

As they lay together, they kept kissing and looking into each other's eyes, as Alexis remained on top of him.

"Thank you," she said, smiling at him.

Lincoln laughed, pushing her off him and then nestling between her legs.

"Thank me?" he teased her. "Oh, Lexi. Don't you know what you do to me?"

"I don't know," she responded quietly.

Lincoln felt a strong desire to please her again. Moving backward, he tasted her once more. He didn't stop until he felt her shimmer under his tongue.

Moving up to her face level again, he thought about how much his wife was against him doing that to her. As he thought about Diana, Alexis felt him tense up, as he always did whenever it was almost time to go.

"You have to leave, I know," she said.

Lincoln kissed her and nodded. He pushed out of his mind that he'd just been thinking about his wife, and not at all about leaving.

"I do," he said. "I don't want to, but I do need to."

Alexis watched him as he stood up, looking down at her until she stood up also. She walked to the lounge with him so they could both get dressed.

There, Lincoln kissed her. There was no doubt that he was full of emotion.

"I think about you all the time, Lexi. I know I shouldn't, but I do," he said, with a slight shimmer in his voice. "You are an incredible young woman."

He walked out the door to go to his office. He needed to shower away any trace of Lexi and what he had shared with her. After that, he intended to go home. He hoped his wife didn't have plans for his body that particular night. All he really wanted to do was think about where his newfound friendship with Lexi could possibly go.

CHAPTER 5

The Train to a New Life

Present Day

Alexis woke up on Monday morning feeling refreshed from another good sleep, but also extremely agitated and nervous. She once again lay in bed for as long as she could, enjoying the peace, the warmth, and the sense of safety she felt being in Anthony's house.

'Today is the day I move on,' she thought to herself, in some ways regretting that she had to. But did she have to? She could stay right where she was. She could stay with the man who so far had only been kind to her.

No, of course she had to move on. She wasn't his problem, and now that the news broadcast had been made, it wasn't fair of her to even let him be seen with her. The last thing she wanted was for Anthony to be dragged into her mess.

He was set on catching the train with her to her next destination. Being honest with herself, she selfishly did want him to go with her. The ongoing episodes she kept having, where she would 'zone out', as Anthony described it, were of increasing concern to her. She would see a doctor when she got settled, she'd decided. She had to. Something was wrong. Even she, with no medical knowledge, could sense it. That was one of the reasons she'd had to get away from *him*. Too many things just didn't feel right. Too many things felt wrong.

When she couldn't hold on any more, Alexis used the bathroom and then made her way to the kitchen.

"Good morning," she heard Anthony say as she saw him move to her and put his arms around her. It seemed like the most natural thing in the world, as if they had done it a hundred times before.

"Oh! Good morning, Anthony," Alexis responded, slowly wrapping her arms loosely around him in return. She'd intended to only very briefly hug him. It felt so good and so secure that she didn't immediately pull away, letting him decide when that would happen.

Anthony was careful to not say anything to her when she wasn't looking directly at him. He wasn't convinced that his voice was the trigger for her moments of losing herself. Regardless, he didn't want to take the chance, so just remained quiet while he held her.

He pulled away from her finally, thinking that perhaps they might be getting a bit too comfortable.

"Can I get you some coffee?" he asked and saw her nod. "How are you feeling about today, Allie?"

Alexis moved to stand close to him as he organised their cups.

"I feel uncertain, to be honest," she said. "I feel safe here … with you…"

"Then stay here, with me. You don't have to leave," Anthony reassured her.

"Yes, I do, but I am thankful for all that you've done," she said. She placed a hand on his arm and, in return, received another hug. "It looks nice outside. Could we sit out there with our coffee this morning?" she asked him, pulling away again.

Anthony nodded as he grabbed his cup. Taking hers, Alexis followed him out the back door and into a small spot that was warm in the sunshine.

"I feel relaxed with you. That's a new thing for me," Alexis said. "I've always felt … I don't know … awkward, I guess … with people. Something about you is different. It's new for me, but I really do like it."

"Thank you," Anthony replied quietly. "I like this comfort too."

"You haven't told me much about you," she said and paused. "Will you?"

"Perhaps," he replied as he smiled at her with a sad look on his face. "Maybe when we're on the train."

"Are you sure you still want to come with me?" Alexis asked. "I understand if you've changed your mind, after having the night to think about it…"

"Oh, no, you don't, Missy," Anthony said. "I bought my ticket. I'm all fired up to go on a new journey, so on a new journey, I shall go! Now, what would you like for breakfast? I am thinking I'm in the mood for pancakes. What do you think?"

They stayed in the house, relaxing with each other until it was time to leave the comfort and security of his home. Before they began walking to the train, Alexis reflected on how she hadn't reverted into herself at all so far that day. She held out hope that she might not. She still felt desperately concerned about people identifying her from the television broadcast. She mostly worried that people would then think that Anthony was her 'abductor.

"Are you ready?" she heard Anthony ask as she took one last look at herself in the bathroom mirror. "You don't look like the photo that was on the TV, so don't worry too much. With my clothes and that hat on, you could be a boy," he said, making her smile. He'd lent her a pair of his jeans and a hoodie. It was designed to help her to look even less feminine, but both of them quite liked the look.

Alexis was thankful she had lost so much weight over the past year that her chest size had reduced right down. With the weight loss, it was much easier to disguise her gender than it had been a year or two earlier.

"Okay. Let's go," she said, grabbing her bag. Also being masculine, it only added to the deception.

They walked quickly to the station and immediately got on the train, making sure they caught the attention of as few people as possible. Settling down into seats at the far end of the train, they both felt a sense of excitement, even though the circumstances called for them to be alert.

Alexis looked around her with the same paranoia she had experienced ever since leaving Melbourne. She looked inside and outside the train to make sure she would see anyone who looked like they might be looking for her. When she felt the train start to move out of the station, she let herself take a deep breath to calm her nerves.

"Are you okay?" Anthony asked beside her.

Alexis nodded and smiled at him.

"Yep. I'm fine."

~~~~~

The journey was five hours long and would deliver them to their destination in the evening. During the long ride, Alexis prompted Anthony to talk about himself. Once he relaxed, he found it therapeutic to talk to her.

"But you're not ... attached ... to anyone, Anthony? Why?" Alexis asked. She was curious since he seemed to be such a nice, caring person. Although she didn't look at him in the sense of him being a man, she could see that he wasn't in any way unattractive.

Anthony hadn't wanted to talk about the particular subject because it always hurt when he did. Knowing the woman beside him had revealed so much about her life, it didn't seem fair to not share.

"I was engaged, Allie," he finally began.

"Oh? What happened?" Alexis asked.

"She died, in a car crash, two years ago."

Alexis could hear distress in his voice. She reached out and took his hand in hers.

"She was beautiful," he said, trying to smile but Alexis could see a tear forming in his eye as he did so. "Her name was Cynthia. With her, I could see the whole future ahead - getting married and starting a family. I didn't anticipate her not being there forever..."

They sat silently for a while before Alexis started her real questioning.

"But Anthony, have you been on your own for all of these past two years?" she asked. She saw him nod as he continued to look at her.

"I've had other women approach me, but I can't give myself to anyone
~~~~~

new - not yet. My heart is still too raw." He noticed the quietness of her beside him and wondered what she thought of what he'd said. "What are you thinking?" he asked, quietly. He saw her take a moment to consider the question before she answered.

"I think that … you are … a lovely person," Alexis replied. "You deserve to be loved."

Anthony lifted her hand and kissed it gently before turning away from her, saying nothing more.

Alexis let him have peace to indulge in his thoughts and his memories.

~~~~~

"Tickets, please!" they heard the conductor shout out as he entered their carriage.

Anthony instantly felt Alexis tense up. No-one else in the carriage was looking around so were not noticing any other passengers. When the man moved to where they sat and looked directly at them, he seemed to look directly at her as he punched a hole in each of their tickets.

"Thank you," he said before moving on.

To Alexis, it seemed like he had stood and looked at her for too long, even though she'd tried to not look too directly at him. Beside her, she felt Anthony squeeze her hand.

"It's alright, Allie," he said. "He was just checking tickets."

Alexis nodded at him and took deep breaths until she could feel her heart relax back into a normal rhythm once again.

~~~~~

Finally, the announcement was made that they had reached the right station. Once the train came to a full halt, they climbed down onto the platform. Anthony had been in the town before so had some enough basic knowledge to be able to find his way around.

"Come this way, Allie," he said. "There's a guest house that I stayed in last time I was here. It's quiet, cheap, and out of the way."

At the guest house, Anthony used cash to check in, then called Alexis to join him as they made their way to the room. He had only booked one room so that she could stay in it longer if she wished to after he left. On entering, Alexis saw that he had asked for a room with two queen size beds. Anthony looked at her face to make sure that was okay.

"I thought this way we could present as husband and wife, but not actually sleep together," he said.

On seeing him suddenly look awkward and shy, Alexis smiled at him.

"It's perfect, Anthony," she said. "Thank you for doing this for me."

"Well, I'll try not to snore too loudly, but I can't make any promises," he replied happily to try and help her relax.

Alexis pulled the curtains, turned on the lights, and then sat on one bed. It was late. Nothing more could be done before the morning.

"I think I'd like to take a shower," she said shyly, knowing it might not be a good idea to have a bath. She hadn't wanted to bathe that morning in case anything happened. She hadn't wanted anything to stop her from getting on the train. "Anthony, I'm going to leave the bathroom door open a little, if that's okay with you … just in case," she said to him. She saw him gulp in uncertainty. "Will you please check on me in ten minutes if I'm not out by then? I know … it might be … uncomfortable … but I really would like you to, please."

Anthony looked at her and understood completely her fear and desire for her request.

"It's fine, Allie," he said. "Go and enjoy your shower. I'll poke my head around the corner in ten minutes."

Alexis went into the bathroom and closed the door except for a small gap, so Anthony would hear if anything happened to her while in there. She undressed while running the water until it became warm enough, and then entered. With it being an enclosed shower with a hanging shower curtain, even if he entered the bathroom, he wouldn't immediately see her. She indulged in the feeling of the water flowing over her, as she quickly shampooed and conditioned her hair, and washed as quickly as she could … just in case.

Anthony watched the clock, silently hoping she would get out before the ten minutes was up. He didn't want to enter the privacy of the bathroom while she was in there. He watched time pass … eight minutes … nine minutes … ten minutes.

Reluctantly he stood up and went to the door, opening it a bit more so he could call out to her from there.

"Allie?" he asked. Receiving no reply caused a deep sinking inside of him. He moved further into the bathroom, keeping his eyes on his feet. "Allie!" he called out again. This time he was relieved to hear her voice respond from behind the curtain.

"I'm here. I'm okay," Alexis said, grateful not only to him for checking, but for it seeming like all was well. Showering was okay. It wasn't a trigger of any kind. She silently wondered why that was, but she'd never had any greatly uncomfortable orders placed on her in the shower. Perhaps that was it. She had shared showers with Lincoln, earlier on. Later, he'd seemed more interested only in so many other things, and had fairly quickly lost interest in the closeness of showering together.

For a moment, she thought back to the start of her time with Lincoln. He had seemed nice then. Even though she'd embarked on it, knowing they would never be able to tell the world about their together - she would be his dirty little secret - she had found he was nice to spend time with. At the start, he only told her to do things that were what other people normally did during sex anyway. If he had stayed like that - if *they* had stayed like that - things could have been so different.

When she had first left, and caught that first bus, she had found the word 'evil' running through her mind as she thought about him. Now she was further away, with distance and time away from him, she knew he wasn't evil. He had good qualities. In many ways, he was a great man. He'd just become lost somewhere along the way. At some point in their time together, he had jumped tracks. He'd simply started wanting to go on an entirely different journey from the one she wanted to be on.

Evil? No, she conceded. He wasn't evil. To say so - to *think* so - wasn't accurate at all. She just should have said no. A long time ago, she should have simply started saying 'no'.

~~~~~

Anthony, with growing nervousness, kept watching the clock. It passed twenty minutes she had been in there, so he repeated his action. Thankfully he got the same reply. He did the same at thirty minutes. After that, he heard the shower turn off. Minutes later, she walked back into the bedroom area, clothed and with a towel in her hands, drying off her hair.

"I'm okay," she said, smiling at him. While in the shower, she had let herself get caught up in thoughts about her time with Lincoln. She wondered if it was the next part of her healing process beginning. "Thanks, Anthony."

"For what?" he asked. Suddenly he found himself aware that she was, in fact, a woman. He'd known that before, of course, but at that particular moment, he *felt* her before him as a woman. To stop the thought, he visualised that notion in a bubble, like in a cartoon. In his head, he visualised kicking the bubble clear away, out of his head.

"For checking on me … and for not peaking," she said.

Anthony saw she had a smile on her face - a real smile. Even to him, he could see that today appeared to be a normal day. As far as he knew, she hadn't zoned out at all since the big episode in the bath the day before.

"Well, it was very tempting…" he teased her and heard her giggle. It seemed so out of place on her. It wasn't the first time he'd heard it, but whenever she giggled, it seemed to him that she was supposed to sound like that far more often than she did. Unfortunately, because it was so rare, it did sound like a mismatch to her also.

Despite the effort to push out of his mind that she was a woman, Anthony could feel the thought lingering. He felt it best to do something proactive to get the feeling away from him.

"I'm going to have a shower. No peaking from you now!" he said to her with a smile on his face. The smile hid other thoughts on his mind.
~~~~~

He had to get them away from her as soon as possible.

Standing under the water, he did what he knew he had to, to relieve the pressure that had come on so strong all of a sudden. He grabbed the soap and rubbed his hand on it to get a thick layer over his skin. He then proceeded, as quickly as possible, to stroke himself until he climaxed heavily. He didn't feel the need to release like that very often, but it felt good to do so. With how he had just been feeling, it took an incredibly short amount of time.

He gathered himself together, dried himself off, and dressed before opening the door.

When he entered the bedroom, he saw that she had climbed into one of the beds, wearing what looked to be a t-shirt. She was heavily under the covers. There was nothing to tempt his arousal again, for which he was grateful.

Turning all lights off except for the lamp beside his bed, he felt shy. When he looked at Alexis, he saw her watching with a cheeky grin on her face. The sight made him smile at her in return. He was blushing, he knew, but didn't mind. It was nice just to see her looking happy - and normal.

"Roll over there, Missy, so I can take my pants off and get into bed without giving you an eyeful," he teased her. For the following few minutes, Alexis teased him back with a playful look on her face, insinuating she wasn't going to turn away.

He watched her, enjoying the friendly and open interaction without any stress in it. Finally, he saw her giggle and turn over so her back was to him. Quickly he undressed down to just boxers and t-shirt and climbed into bed.

"Are you in bed now?" he heard her ask. After he confirmed, she turned over again in response. "Now we can have a true sleepover. Tell me all about the girls you've kissed…" she said.

Anthony laughed out loud at her, thinking that when all the rubbish was removed, she really could be a fun and happy person.

~~~~~

After a late night of talking and laughing, Anthony woke up the next morning to find her already up and dressed. For a moment, he said nothing. He watched her standing at the window and peaking out while trying to not open the curtain too wide.

"Hey, chatterbox," he finally called out to her softly. He saw her turn to smile at him. If he hadn't seen her three days earlier, he would hardly have believed she could be the same person.

Alexis moved toward him and sat on the edge of his bed, looking down at him.

"And good morning to you, fellow chatterbox," she said, laughing
~~~~~

lightly. "How was your sleep?" she asked and heard him answer softly and briefly.

Anthony found himself enjoying looking at her face. He was suddenly very aware of the state he had woken up in. He quickly moved onto his side so it wasn't so obvious.

Alexis had been with enough men to know what they were often like in the mornings. She had no desire to make him uncomfortable.

"I'm going to walk over to the curtain and look outside again. It would be a good time for you to do a dash to the bathroom and put on some clothes," she said with a slight tease in her voice before walking to the window.

"No looking!" Anthony said as he gathered up clothes and ran into the bathroom, closing the door quickly. Even through the door, he could hear her giggling before he then heard the sound of the curtains being opened.

~~~~~

When they walked out of their room a short time later, both were hungry and eager to find somewhere to have breakfast. Alexis still wore her no-gender clothing. Not wanting to wear a hat inside a café, she hadn't known what to do about her hair.

"Just tie it back, Allie. Guys wear their hair back too," Anthony had suggested. When Alexis had looked in the mirror, she had to admit she could still pass for a guy … perhaps. "I don't think there's anything for you to worry about here but if you're still concerned, let me order, so no-one hears your voice."

In a back street, they found a quiet café that was open for breakfast service. Being a buffet, it suited them even better since there would be no server to talk to them or even look at them too often.

"What do you want to do today? What was your plan for when you reached a destination?" Anthony asked her as they indulged in the food before them.

Alexis had been wondering the same thing.

"My plan originally had been to find somewhere new to set up a new life," she replied. "I had thought I'd just find work and find somewhere to live. I hadn't even considered my face would be on the news…"

"You couldn't have expected that. From what you've told me, he wanted to keep everything hush-hush. It wasn't likely he would want anything about you out in the world, let alone with his name attached to you," Anthony said, seeing the turmoil on her face. "Don't beat yourself up about that, Allie. There's no way you could have anticipated he would do that."

"But what do I do now, Anthony? Where can I go? How can I begin a new life when my face is out there?"

"Well, what if you go to the police?" he suggested. "Go and tell them
~~~~~

you are you, and that you haven't been abducted at all."

"It's just so risky," she replied after consideration of his idea. "I don't want you to be involved in this. You've already done so much for me. He must have somehow expected that I might be with someone. That's why he's turned it around - so that whoever I'm with could be arrested."

She was still surprised that she hadn't earlier seen the darker side of Lincoln, or the true degree of his desperation. Even with all her previous analysis and desire to get away, she hadn't considered quite the level of depth his thinking and actions could reach when he realised she was gone.

"Okay," Anthony replied. "Well, I will only be staying one more night here with you, and then I need to go back. I don't want to leave you, and I want to come and see you again, but I do need to get back to work when I'm expected. Given that he is also my boss, way up the line…"

"What?" Alexis asked sharply, not having even considered what she was being told.

"I work in the supermarket, Allie," Anthony said. "It's a supermarket that his company owns. If I act in any way suspicious, that could somehow make its way up the line. Well, maybe not, but I do need to get back and act as if everything is completely normal. At least then I can't highlight any possible indication of which town you've been in … or are in."

"Yes," she said vaguely, still thinking, but not wanting to. "What time is your train tomorrow?"

"Nine in the morning," he replied. "I'll have breakfast with you and then go straight to catch it."

"Then let's enjoy today. What do you like to do? We could see a movie, go to a museum…"

Anthony looked at her, surprised and pleased, but also wary.

"Are you sure? I would be happy spending the day with you in the hotel room…" he said. Immediately he saw her eyebrow go up, with a teasing look on her face. "Not like that! Cheeky Missy…"

"Well, let's just go and see a movie then," said Alexis. "In the cinema, we'll be in the dark and no-one will notice us. You can buy the tickets, and I'll discretely sneak in with you."

Later, when she sat back in the seat in front of the big screen, Alexis felt truly relaxed and invisible. It was a feeling that was completely obvious to the man beside her. She had her popcorn, she had what appeared to be a good, kind man beside her, and the movie was a comedy. What more could she want?

~~~~~

After the movie, they walked back to their hotel room. Alexis stayed there for the rest of the day while Anthony went out and bought food for
~~~~~

their dinner.

When they were lying in their beds later that night, Alexis felt a wave of emotion come over her.

"I'm going to miss you, Anthony," she said. "You've been a better friend to me over this past week than anyone else has been … in my entire life! I like how I feel when I'm with you. I feel … normal."

"Allie, you *are* normal. You're amazing!" Anthony replied. "Don't think that because of the things that bastard made you do, *you're* the abnormal one. You are you. You aren't some extension of his sick mind."

"Why don't *you* try and have sex with me?" she asked, the question having been on her mind since the moment she had met him.

Anthony looked at her, feeling a huge depth of sympathy for her. "Allie…"

"Am I ugly? I know I haven't got any makeup, and I'm too skinny now…"

"Stop!" he said, a bit too forcefully.

Straight away, he saw her eyes close and head go down, forcing him to jump out of bed and run to her.

"Allie!" he shouted at her, in a panic about what he'd just done unintentionally. "Allie, open your eyes and look at me!" he yelled, holding her shoulders firmly.

Alexis heard his voice - *his* voice - and waited for a command. Unlike before, somehow her head was a bit clearer. She found that somewhere in the distance of her mind a new logic kicked in, like it was coming to her through a haze in the background. *He* couldn't be there. She was in a hotel room with Anthony. No, it was *Anthony's* voice she could hear, and he didn't want her to act like that. He sounded scared. She had to wake up and tell him she was okay…

Anthony saw her eyes open and then focus on him.

"Anthony," she said, smiling like she was waking up from a long night of sleep. "I thought it was you. I could hear you. I knew it wasn't him."

Anthony looked at her, finding himself tense with fear. He pulled her up and into his arms. She wrapped her arms around him, and they sat like that for a few minutes before he pulled away to look at her face.

"I'm so sorry," he said. "I wasn't thinking about the volume or tone of my voice…"

He felt one of her hands come up to the side of his face and suspected what she was thinking then. He grabbed the hand and kissed her palm.

"Allie, you are beautiful. You are not ugly or too skinny, but I don't want to have sex with you," he said. Seeing her begin to ask another question, he cut her off quickly. "Neither of us is in the right headspace for that. Perhaps you think you can easily do that without any emotional attachment, but I can't. I don't want to have sex with anyone else - not until I get my feelings about Cynthia's death under control." He paused and kissed her forehead. "Please don't ask me that again. It has nothing to do with what you look like. It's because I just don't want to have sex."

Alexis heard the speech and nodded. She didn't know what it must feel like to lose someone so close, so suddenly. She had never loved anyone like that. She let go of him and lay down again as she watched him go back to his bed and climb in. They lay looking at each other until eventually, they were both asleep.

~~~~~

"Please be careful, Allie. Go straight to the police station and talk to them. I'm sure it will all be alright. Don't just keep hiding. You deserve better," Anthony said to her as they held each other in the hotel room the following morning.

Alexis nodded, knowing it might not be a good idea, but she was limited in her choices.

"I'll go straight there after I know the train has left," she said to him, and reached up and kissed his cheek.

Anthony looked at her, filled with worry for her, before kissing her lightly on the lips. It wasn't a prolonged kiss. It was just enough to let her know that she did mean something to him.

"You know where I live. I'm just down the train line. Come to me if you want to - *whenever* you want to," he said and saw her nod in silence.

Anthony then walked out, feeling a deep thud in his heart that made him wonder if he would ever see her again.

~~~~~

Alexis walked into the police station. Once inside, she took off her cap and approached the police officer at the front counter.

"I was told that someone might be looking for me," she said quietly. The officer redirected her to another officer, who took her into a small office.

"You are … Lexi Montgomery?" he asked. She immediately corrected him.

"I am Alexis Montgomery," she said. "Only one person called me Lexi, and he is the man I've been hiding from."

The officer looked at her, trying to identify what she said that would be real, and what wouldn't be.

"The police in Melbourne received a report that you had been abducted," he said and saw her nod and look down. "Did you escape your captor?"

She looked up at him. "There was no captor. I left town to get away from someone. Whoever made that call to you was lying."

"Why would someone do that, do you think?" the officer asked.

"He controls everything, and I ran," she said simply, as if that explained everything to the officer before her. She didn't want the one question to come. She wanted to avoid it but suspected she wouldn't be able to.

"Who controls everything?"

She sat silent, willing to keep his name unknown. He had put her through things she shouldn't have had to do. She knew, though, that the truth was that they were things that she *didn't* have to do. She had only had to say no, but was he an evil person? Now that she was so far away from the situation, she knew he wasn't. He just had different tastes than she did.

"Ms. Montgomery," she heard the officer encourage her. "*Who* controls everything?"

Alexis began to panic. She was never to tell anyone about their time together. She was never to tell anyone that she knew him. It was one of the rules. As she sat in front of a police officer, should she lie to him and possibly get herself in trouble? What would he do to her if she told?

The officer watched the young woman in front of him start to hyperventilate in a panic.

"I can't tell you. It's one of the rules," she started to say out loud, over and over again, while getting more and more anxious. "I don't know what he'll do..."

The officer watched as Alexis moved past the point of being logical. The young woman before him repeated the same words over and over. "I can't tell you. I don't know what he'll do."

Finally, the officer called in another officer - a woman - presumably to be there as a witness. From his years of being in the police force, he suspected that something serious had happened to the young woman in front of him.

"Ms. Montgomery," they both said to her. She didn't respond, just kept saying the same things over and over.

"Lexi!" he said finally, forcefully.

Before both officers, Alexis immediately left her chair and dropped to the floor, on her knees, with her head down.

"Tell me what you want me to do," she then said, as if in a trance.

~~~~~

Alexis felt like she was in a dream. She could hear voices around her, but she couldn't find *his* voice. She kept searching through them in her head, but he didn't seem to be near.

Then her logic seemed to come back to her again, just as it had the night before. She knew she could find a way out of where she was. She just had to stop trying to find *him*.

Both officers saw her eyes open and refocus, while a look of horror
~~~~~

came over her.

"What…?" she started to ask, realising that she was back up in the chair again, even though she had thought she'd been on the ground. Someone must have lifted her up…

"What happened to you just then, Lexi?" she heard the female police officer ask.

"Please don't call me that. Only he calls me that. My name is Alexis."

"Alright, Alexis. Has this happened before?"

Alexis nodded and took her time to find the right words.

"It was happening too often," she said. "That's why I had to leave. It can't be right … right? It isn't normal…"

"Alexis, who is the man that you're talking about? If he has done this to you - if he has hurt you…"

"Please, I just wanted to make sure that you knew I wasn't missing and I wasn't abducted. I just want to start a new life. Can we just leave it at that?"

The officers looked at each other.

"Whatever he has done to you, he might go on and do to other girls. But you could prevent that…"

"No, he won't," Alexis replied, shaking her head. "He's worried. If he wasn't, he wouldn't have associated himself with my name in that broadcast…" she started to say before she considered what she was saying.

"The … news broadcast? About your disappearance?" the male officer asked and saw Alexis nod her head slightly. He turned to the woman officer, whispered something in her ear and then walked out, leaving the two women alone.

~~~~~

After a few minutes, the man came back and sat down again.

"Ms. Montgomery, the news station has told me that the broadcast was initiated by them after they heard of your abduction from the police in Melbourne," he said.

Alexis nodded at him, not wanting to say anything.

"But there is one person - a man - who was mentioned in the broadcast. Do you know who that was?" he asked and she nodded again, her head sinking lower. "Lincoln Kokiri," he said and immediately saw her look away as a tear began to appear in her eye. "Do you know Mr. Kokiri, Ms. Montgomery?"

"He owns the chain of supermarkets I used to work in," Alexis said, avoiding the real question.

"Did you ever see him outside of the supermarket?"

Alexis looked at both officers, her eyes moving from one to the other.

"I can't say," she said. "Don't you understand? I don't know what he'll
~~~~~

do!"

"He won't do anything, Ms. Montgomery," the officer said. "He's presently in custody in the central Melbourne police station."

Alexis thought she must not have heard correctly. "What?"

"Lincoln Kokiri is in custody. He can't hurt you."

"He has people everywhere..."

"Yes, he does, but you don't understand. He is the one who has come forward and confessed to lying to police about your abduction. He has admitted he made it up. He won't get away with that easily."

Alexis looked at the officers again, feeling tears begin to flow freely from her eyes. What had she done? It was all her fault. All she'd had to do was say 'no'.

"Can I please leave? I haven't been abducted, and I'm fine. That's all I wanted to tell you, so I can start a new life. Can I please go?" she asked and was greeted in return by a lengthy string of questions from both officers. They asked everything - how she had met him, how long she had been seeing him, and what they had done together when they were alone. She answered every question honestly, but inside she felt a little piece of her die with every word that she spoke.

~~~~~

"We need to get your contact details, Ms. Montgomery, before we let you leave. What's your mobile number?" the woman officer asked.

"I don't have one," Alexis said, shaking her head. "I destroyed my phone and SIM before I left Melbourne. He knows how to track me by my phone. I had to stop using technology."

~~~~~

After convincing the officers she wasn't in any way fearful for her life, Alexis was permitted to leave the station. She'd made them understand that she'd just needed to be away from Lincoln. If she could just find a home and a job, all would be well.

She walked out of the police station feeling a new sense of freedom, but also a deep ache in her gut. She had never wanted to get him into any trouble. She had never wanted to tell anyone she even knew him. Why did he have to put her face and name out there in public with that broadcast? What had he been thinking, to go and do that? She knew that was precisely the issue. He *hadn't* been thinking when he did that. He hadn't been thinking at all - at least, not clearly, and definitely not like a sane person.

She walked in a daze to her room. When she got there, she felt an overwhelming sense of loneliness again. That led to a strong temptation to use the little cash she had left to buy a train ticket and go to Anthony. She wanted to, but she couldn't. He had done enough. She didn't yet know how things would play out as far as Lincoln was concerned. No, she would have to turn her back on her new friend, at least until life returned to some kind of normality.

Her first step had to be finding work. She couldn't - *wouldn't* - go work in the same supermarket chain, so that left only one supermarket in the city she was in. She showered and changed into the only feminine thing she had with her. It was a dress she had bought at the charity store, for exactly that purpose.

She walked in and asked directly to talk to the human resources manager. She didn't quite beg for work, but after offering to start there and then, and work for two days without pay to prove herself, she found herself in a supermarket uniform and at a checkout once again. She had paid for the room in the guest house for a further three nights. All she had to do was prove herself in the supermarket, and maybe she could get a regular pay, and find somewhere to live.

It felt strange being on checkout again. Something had changed in her in the short time that she had been in hiding. She greeted the customers with enthusiasm and enjoyed smiling at them. She knew who she had to thank for that. Anthony had passed through her life so quickly, but he had made a profound effect on her. He had initiated the healing process in her, and given her the confidence to move forward and try to work toward enjoying her life again. She had to get a full-time job, and she had to find a home. Once she'd done that, she would buy a train ticket and go and see him again.

~~~~~

In another town, Anthony was walking into his home. As he did so, he also felt empty. He hadn't realised when he was with her, quite how much of an effect Allie was having on him. He had started to feel the full effect of that when he was on the train ride home.

He didn't know if he'd done the right thing, leaving her alone in a city she didn't even know, but it was her journey. It was her life that she wanted to start over, and he did believe she had the strength to do that.

He opened up the windows and doors to let the sun and fresh air into the house, and suddenly found himself not knowing what to do. He had been so consumed with her since the moment that he'd met her, that he hadn't had time to just let his mind rest. His mind suddenly didn't know what to do since she wasn't around to think about, to watch and monitor, or to protect.

He decided on a movie, but on turning on the television, caught the news instead. His breath caught in shock.

'Multimillionaire and entrepreneur, Lincoln Kokiri is in custody tonight after confessing to police that he had made a false call to them last week about a young woman, Lexi Montgomery, having been abducted. Police have not yet released any further details about Mr.
~~~~~

Kokiri's intention, or any involvement Mr. Kokiri had with Ms. Montgomery.'

"Shit," Anthony said out loud to nobody. He wondered if Allie had seen the news broadcast or not, and found himself wishing he could call her. He *could* call her, he realised. All he had to do was call that guest house and ask for her. But should he?

Overall it was just a crap situation. It was something messy that probably had never needed to be messy. That man could have just let her go, without creating a situation where she had to run and hide. No, Anthony conceded, she had said she hadn't heavily broached the subject of them parting, with the guy. She had lightly suggested it on occasion, but never really pushed it strongly to him. Perhaps if she had, he might have just let her walk away easily.

In the meantime, Anthony wondered if he should try and call her at the guest house. After contemplation, he decided he would let it rest for a bit. He needed to let her think about what she wanted. By now she would probably have forgotten him anyway. No, he argued with himself again, she would not forget him immediately. He did believe she had liked spending that time with him as much as he'd enjoyed spending it with her.

~~~~~

Over the following two weeks, Alexis found herself in a nice normal routine once again. The supermarket manager liked her and was happy for her to stay working with them. For him, the timing was perfect since one of their staff was due to give birth and take a year of maternity leave.

Alexis found serving people on the counter easier than in the past. She received the odd look from people, like they had seen her before but couldn't place where. When they voiced that to her, she laughed and told them she just had 'one of those faces'.

The previous three years, she tried to keep suppressed from her mind. She didn't look at a television. She had heard nothing from the police so assumed everything was alright in the world, at least for the moment.

She had worked every day over the two weeks, happily signing on for extra shifts to get some money in her pocket again. Now that she wasn't reported as missing, she considered that she could probably start accessing her old bank account again, but she still wanted to have some anonymity from Lincoln. She didn't know what would happen if she revealed her location through withdrawing money from the account she knew he had access to.

It wasn't just herself that she worried about. Anthony had helped her so much. She didn't want to even ponder lightly at what Lincoln might do to him if he found out he had helped her to start a new life.

At the first opportunity that arose when she had cash and two days
~~~~~

off, she decided to catch a train. She wasn't sure if she would be welcome or not, but she decided to try anyway. The train would pass through there in the morning and by that day's schedule, would then come back through once again late in the afternoon. The worst-case scenario was that she went there, found Anthony didn't want to see her, and she could still come back the same day.

On the train, she found herself extremely nervous. Before, she'd had nerves about not being seen and identified. Now she had nerves about whether Anthony would welcome her or not.

As she stepped down onto the train station platform, she realised it was early. She panicked. It went against her nature to approach someone's house without organising the visit first. She knew that when he'd left, he had seemed open to her coming to see him. He had told her straight out to get on a train whenever she wanted to. She fought the instinct to not go, and began walking up to the house.

As she walked up the path, she again took a long look at the house from where she stood, admiring its beauty. Upon moving forward, she saw that the door was open. All down the front side of it, on and around the door handle, was blood. Alexis went into a panic, immediately thinking that Lincoln had found him. He must have learned about Anthony helping her, and sent someone to come after him. Of course Lincoln would want to deal with him, to teach him a lesson and make sure he kept away from her.

Alexis ran into the house, suddenly not caring if it was considered polite or not.

CHAPTER 6

Lexi & Lincoln - The First Year

Lincoln lay on his back and watched her moving up and down on him. He had been going to her home every Thursday night for six months. Often he felt like he was drunk with desire for her.

"Lean forward and bite my nipple," he said and felt her do so.

Alexis didn't really like biting. She didn't feel right doing it, but it was what Lincoln wanted, so she did that for him. He never used pain on her, so she was thankful for that. He had asked her in earlier months about the possibility of pain during sex. When she'd told him that she didn't want it, he had said he would respect that. So far, he had.

Lincoln felt himself harden even more inside of her as the biting was happening. He had never even dreamed that he would like something like that, but as soon as he'd asked her to do it, he had loved it. Now he wanted more of it. In his pleasure of her, he never hurt her. She didn't want it, and he always respected women.

When he was honest with himself, what he most wanted to do to her all the time was use his tongue on her. That, he could never get enough of, with how responsive to it she was. He loved the taste of her and how easily she reached orgasm through his pleasuring. Even that alone was so different from what he had enjoyed - endured - with his wife throughout his marriage.

Six months in and he always looked forward to their evening together every week. He never stayed too long - just a couple of hours at most. Then he would go back to his office, shower, and do some work. He did that all so he could honestly answer his wife's question about the work he had been doing when he got home later that night.

Nothing seemed to have changed for him at home. Diana was there, as she always was. The sex was no different. He was careful to not bring anything from the sex with Lexi back to his home. He didn't try and pleasure Diana. He didn't try and pull her on top of him. He didn't try and get her to pleasure him with her mouth. If he did any of those things, she might have become suspicious. If she became suspicious, she would start watching him. That was what he expected, anyway.

"Harder, Lexi!" he said with a firm authority in his voice.

Alexis bit down as hard as she could, making him instantly explode inside of her. She knew he had a taste for giving orders. She equally knew that was her own doing.

As she pulled away and looked down at him, she watched his face as he moved on from the 'sex Lincoln' to the 'soft Lincoln'. He pulled her to his lips, giving her what always felt like a loving after-sex kiss.

"Lie beside me," he said.

After she pulled off him and lay down on her side next to him, Lincoln turned onto his side so they could face one another.

"I want to see you more often," he said.

"You can come here any evening you want, Lincoln," Alexis replied, surprised.

"I want to move you into an apartment in my building," he continued.

Alexis blinked in surprise.

"You want me to live … near you?"

He smiled at her, seeing her misunderstanding.

"No, the building where my main office is, has apartments over three levels of it," he said. "I want to move you in there. It won't cost you anything. I'll cover the rent and other expenses."

"But Lincoln, I have to be able to walk to work. I know that my job seems small and unimportant to you, but I love it, and I want to keep it."

She saw him look thoughtful, and then slightly unimpressed at her not being more excited at the offer.

"Alright," he finally said. "What if I found another apartment that was still within close distance of your work?"

"Why do you want me to move?"

"I want to be able to see you more, without worrying about people seeing me come and go from your home. This once-a-week isn't enough. I need more of you, but I can't risk coming to this part of town very often. Anyone seeing me would question why I am here."

"Then if you find the right place, I will move so you can visit me more," Alexis said, the first tiny niggle beginning in the back of her mind.

~~~~~

Three months later, she found herself being led through a door while a hand was held over her eyes.

"Open them," she heard Lincoln say.

As she did as she'd been instructed, Alexis saw they were in a small but highly storage-efficient apartment. Instantly, she walked to the large windows.

"Wow, we are high!"

"Walk around, Lexi. Tell me if this might suit your needs," Lincoln said.

Alexis looked at him. He acted as if it were someone giving *him* a gift, not the other way around. As she took her time to walk through the
~~~~~

small apartment, she grew excited at the thought of living there.

When she returned to the living area, Lincoln saw the large smile she had on her face.

"I love it," Alexis said. "Lincoln it's perfect, and so close to my work, too," she said, loving how pleased he seemed to look. "But are you sure? It seems an awful lot…"

Lincoln laughed loudly, always amazed at what she considered a lot, when she lived on so little.

"If you like it, and you think it will work, it's yours," he said. "All I ask is that I can see more of you."

"My hours of being able to see you will be the same, Lincoln…" he heard her say, and he nodded in response.

"I know," he replied. "The times won't change. I just want to be able to see you more than once a week. Thursdays still work for me, though, since I finish work early that day and I can see you right at 6pm."

They agreed to her accepting the apartment, and he was relieved. He didn't tell her he had already rented the apartment for her, knowing in his heart that she would accept it. Despite him thinking she would, the fact that she had accepted it fuelled him greatly.

"Stay here for a while with me now," he said and saw her move to him and stand before him, waiting. "Take your panties off," he continued. He watched as she followed his instruction, pulling them off and then standing up again. "Lift your skirt … right up to your waist."

When she had, Alexis heard him groan heavily.

"Kneel on the edge of the sofa, facing that way," Lincoln continued. "Yes, lean on the back of it."

Alexis did so, feeling aroused from the fresh air surrounding her. She had a moment of panic as she didn't have a condom on her. That was another rule she'd laid down at the very start.

She heard him undo his belt and zip, and let his pants fall to the ground.

"Lincoln, not without a condom," she whispered.

"I'm not going to enter you, Lexi. Don't worry," he reassured her as he enjoyed the view of her before him.

He moved forward and rubbed just the tip of his erection against her, feeling her moistness.

"Hmm, you are so wet," he said. "It feels warm on me. I'm going to coat myself in your juices, Lexi, and then you're going to lick them off."

Alexis felt him rubbing against her. She said nothing, waiting to see what he wanted next.

"Stay still," he said.

At his words, she braced herself. She was surprised when she sensed him sitting down on the floor, his back to the sofa front, and reaching up with his hands.

"Crouch a bit lower so I can taste you," Lincoln said.

Alexis did as she was told, lowering her pelvis until she felt him touch her and start licking. Instantly she was on fire. The combination of how it felt, and knowing that he enjoyed it as much as he did, drove her wild sometimes. Even she felt like she couldn't get enough of it. It took very little time for her to climax on his tongue, making him groan more.

Quickly, before she recovered, Lincoln stood and rubbed himself on her again, coating himself in her.

"Kneel on the ground," he said, full authority in his voice now that he was used to it, and liking it very much.

Alexis knelt on the floor as he positioned himself.

"Suck it, Lexi … suck harder!"

Lincoln let his feelings go. Her mouth was exquisite. He loved it even more than being inside a woman. It never took him long to reach orgasm like that.

Alexis heard him make the sounds he always did when he was about to ejaculate. She braced herself, ready to take it.

"Ohh, fuck! Yes!" he yelled out loudly as he let go, his knees instantly threatening to give way. He moved down to the floor, kneeling before her. When he opened his eyes, he kissed her deeply.

"Lie back with your legs wide. I have to taste you again," he said and proceeded to bring her to orgasm again. Oh, how it felt to be between her legs like that. He could drink her over and over.

Finally, he seemed to have enough. He found her panties and gently helped her back into them before making himself presentable and helping her to stand. Always afterwards, he was gentle and peaceful.

He kissed her gently, standing still with his arms around her.

"I love our time together, Lexi. I'm glad you agree with moving here. I just need to see you more often," he said before she nodded and kissed him back.

~~~~~

Two months later, Alexis was settled in her apartment, and found she enjoyed it with it being so new and modern.

In addition to their ongoing Thursday meets, Lincoln had begun visiting Monday after work as well. He felt like they should always be together, but his life wouldn't allow it. He loved his life too much to even consider risking anything so bold as going to visit Lexi more often.

"Get down on your knees, Lexi," he firmly told her one night and watched her immediately do so. "Close your eyes and be still," he went on and took some time to just look at her.

Alexis followed his command, as she always did. She liked that he had taken from her cues right at the start, that she preferred he simply tell
~~~~~

her what he wanted, rather than leaving it to her to try and guess.

Lincoln had grown in his confidence in giving her commands. He still loved his wife. He had no intention of leaving her, but although the two of them still had sex several times a week, it brought out in him no level of emotion. Diana was like a doll, lying still for him and not wanting anything else.

In contrast, what he shared with Lexi was invigorating. He had found his voice and was loving being able to use it. Whatever he told her to do, she would do. It had felt strange at first to give instructions to her, but in those first few months she'd kept asking him for them, so he'd obliged. It had since grown to be a natural aspect of their time together. He maintained great respect for her, as he did for all women. Months earlier, she had told him she didn't want pain, and he had promised her he wouldn't hurt her physically. So far, he hadn't felt any reason to do so.

He looked at her, kneeling and still, with an intense look of serenity on her face. She was so young and looked so virginal, and yet the way he felt when he was with her was intense. She didn't even seem to put effort into driving him wild, over and over. It was just the way she looked - those eyes, those lips…

"Tell me what you want me to do," Alexis said, testing him to see if he really did want her to be silent. She heard him inhale deeply.

Lincoln felt like he could not hear those words enough. So far, he had indulged in anything he couldn't do with Diana - orally pleasuring Lexi, having Lexi orally pleasure him, and having Lexi on top of him as they joined. Tonight, looking at her, for the first time, he felt the desire to be on top of her. He didn't yet know how it felt to have her underneath him, because he was always so excited to do anything other than that. That night, he needed to feel something different.

"Undress and go lie on your bed, face-up," he said. He watched her as she opened her eyes and stood up, not looking at him. She then walked down to her room, and he saw her disappear inside. For a moment, he sat where he was. He hadn't had release yet, having arrived only minutes before. He took a moment to sit back on the sofa and just get his excitement under control before standing and following her.

When he entered the bedroom, he was greeted with the beautiful sight before him. He walked around the bed, looking at her from all angles.

"Spread your legs wide," he said as he stood right at the end of the bed and started to undress. He looked at her from that angle, knowing he would remember the view for a long time to come.

Alexis waited, looking at him, and seeing the hunger on his face. Always he had such a depth of need about him. Mostly it aroused her, but occasionally she found that she was also nervous about it. In that particular moment, as always, he moved to pleasure her first. Always, he started with that and then ended with that. It was like it was an essential part of their time together for him - like him being satisfied and her not being, just would not be acceptable.

Lincoln moved onto the bed and immediately sunk his face between her legs to taste her and feel her move as she always did until she was close. He then pulled away from her and looked at her face.

"Say my name when you come, Lexi," he said. He waited until she nodded before he resumed his actions.

Keeping the instruction in her head as he was pleasuring her resulted in the pleasure being extended. Determined to not forget what he had said, eventually she reached climax, calling his name out in satisfaction.

Alexis sensed he was different that night. He was always so particular about everything, like their time together consistently had to go a certain way. It never seemed like they were enjoying each other just as it felt right to do so in the moment. Instead, it was if he planned their whole time together well in advance, quite without her.

Lincoln reached to the side table and put a condom on. He liked the feeling of her putting them on, but tonight he was too eager to move into her. He wanted her to lie still, looking exactly as she did at that moment.

Alexis watched him and saw him move between her legs, surprising her slightly as he'd avoided that position the whole time they had been seeing each other. He lay on top of her and kissed her softly. He always kissed her gently at the start and the end. She then felt him slowly slip into her, and heard him groan at the initial contact.

Lincoln remained still, wanting to savour the moment. It wasn't the first time they had joined. It was, however, the first time he had taken full control of it. He wanted to make it last as long as possible. He slowly moved inside her, stopping when he needed to, to prevent himself from climaxing. He could sense her arousal building from the stop and start movements he was making. It drove him on to thrust harder into her, and then stop when he needed to.

Alexis felt the familiar feeling growing and was surprised to realise that she was going to orgasm from the movements he was making. The two of them found such a rhythm together that she put her hands on his back to pull him closer, in the process unknowingly creating scratches and indentations on his skin. Lincoln felt the nails and recognised it as a pleasurable pain, so kept moving in her the same way. He quickly realised he wanted her to keep scratching him.

Finally, Lincoln felt her orgasm all around him. Even for him, it was new. His wife never climaxed at all when he was with her. Alexis's orgasm drove him to start thrusting as hard as he could into her, increasing his level of force with each louder groan that came from her.

He finally reached that place - that sweet place that he loved - and

Alexis felt him slump on her. Lincoln was overwhelmed with his emotion. Even though it was the same position that he regularly indulged in with Diana, it had felt completely different with Lexi. He opened his eyes and kissed her gently, not in any hurry to move.

"Are you alright?" he asked, wondering if he might have been too rough with her. He only saw her smile at him.

"More than alright," she said quietly, before giggling.

Lincoln couldn't help but kiss her again, quite content to lie exactly where he was, nestled inside of her.

~~~~~

After Lincoln had pleasured her again - and again - he left her apartment and went to his office. There he started up the shower and took a moment to look in the mirror. Despite his age, he was an attractive man - so people had always said, anyway. He knew that his high level of physical fitness contributed to him being in good shape for his 42 years, but he was old, compared to her. He didn't know exactly why she wanted to keep seeing him. For just a moment, he had a panicked thought that she wouldn't *always* want him. As soon as some young man showed her attention and could love her openly, she would tell Lincoln she didn't want to see him anymore.

He was usually a confident person, that confidence driven by success that flowed from his business decisions. The idea of her not being there for him anymore made him nervous, with just a hint of desperation edging into the depths of his soul.

Starting to turn to get into the shower, he caught sight of his back in the bathroom mirror. He could see the marks on it. He tried to reach back to touch them but couldn't. He instantly remembered Lexi's hands on his back and the way it had felt when she had driven her nails into him. It hadn't felt bad. It had felt incredibly good to him. He would have to stay in his office and work much later that night, though, in the hope that he would then be able to slip into bed without his wife seeing his skin.

When he moved under the hot water, he truly felt the marks. He was surprised to find that he gained further satisfaction from the feeling of the sting that came from the hot water hitting them. He stood like that for a long time, his back to the hot shower flow. He admitted to himself then that not only did he like the pain that was flowing on from her having scratched him like that, but that he would want her to do that again … and again.

~~~~~

The next day - Tuesday - when he was in his office, he found resolve in forcing himself to push Lexi from his mind. His business was important. Not even she would get in the way of that - not that she ever tried, he had to admit to himself. There wasn't one way in which she'd purposely tried to invade his life outside the walls of her apartment. Even so, he was consumed, and he knew it. Even that morning, when he'd been greeted by one of the managers that he got on well with at a personal level, he had felt a light slap on his shoulder blade, as was normal with them. Instantly he'd felt the sharpness of the slap as it hit several of the marks on him. The sting reminded him of the marks once more. Fortunately, he had been able to immediately sit down at his desk before anyone could see his immediate, strong - and very noticeable - arousal.

The morning had passed, and the day had worn on, but the thought was there. He kept thinking about those marks on his back, and how good they felt when they were touched or when he took a shower.

Yes, he knew she hadn't intended to hurt or mark him. He also knew that if she saw the marks, she might be regretful and sorry. Despite that - despite how much she might not *want* to do it on purpose - he would have to tell her to do that again.

~~~~~

Alexis reclined back against the arm of the sofa beside Lincoln, wondering about his mood. They hadn't gone to her room yet, but he had already tasted her and moved her to orgasm, just as he always did for their first course. She watched him as he began undressing. He had such a determined look on his face that Alexis didn't know what was coming, or what he was thinking. When he was naked and kneeling over her - almost straddling her - he pushed himself up to her face.

"Take it in your mouth, Lexi," he said forcefully. As always, she complied. "Put your hands on my butt," he continued. Once again, she followed the instruction.

Lincoln felt extremely aroused and knew he wouldn't last long. She'd been on his mind all day. He had to have that feeling again, but somewhere different this time.

"Use your nails on me, Lexi," he said. "Yes, scratch my skin ... harder!"

Alexis heard the instructions and followed them even though it went against her nature to hurt anyone. He seemed to need her to do it for him, so she did. As he asked for more, she dug her nails into his skin as deeply as she felt she could, and kept scratching them across the skin surface. It wasn't long before he convulsed in her mouth.

She sat, licking him clean like he liked her to, and looked up at him. In that position, she truly felt his power as a man before her. Sometimes he emanated a level of strength that surprised her and frightened her. She saw him as someone who maintained calm and composure when he could, but she suspected that if he ever lost that, he would not be someone anyone wanted to be near.

Finally Lincoln looked down at her, watching her face as she looked
~~~~~

up at him. He came out of himself again, pulling himself back and kneeling down to her level so he could kiss her deeply. He didn't say anything. He now rarely felt the need to say anything when he was with her. In his head, they were just so perfectly attuned to each other that they didn't need words.

Alexis felt him kiss her and ventured to put her arms around him and pull him to her. She felt him relax against her. Having had him visit her once or twice a week for so long, she found she had settled into his curious ways. She didn't yearn for anything different. When he wasn't with her, she found she could get on with her life without giving him any thought. Her work was as enjoyable as she wished it to be. Seeing faces pass her by day after day, knowing none of them would ever notice her, let alone remember her, was not an unpleasant thought to her. It was how she liked it.

Lincoln lay in her arms and felt himself relax. She didn't often initiate anything, but feeling her arms wrap around him was welcome. She wanted and needed so little from him, it felt like in her arms was the only place he could truly be himself. There, no-one demanded anything from him. No-one needed him to smile and be the perfect gentleman. No-one needed anything from him at all.

He felt one of her hands move up, and her fingertips start idly running through his hair, caressing his scalp. He missed intimacy so much. For so long, he'd longed for the feeling of just being held and touched lovingly. When he was with her, it always seemed like his priorities changed, and it was the sexual release that took over as being most important. Afterwards, being able to be soft with her, he did like.

Alexis felt him pull back only long enough to look into her eyes. She kept her hand in his hair, not sure if it was welcome. Not seeing anything but a blank look on his face, she started to remove her hand.

"Don't stop. It feels nice," he said and leaned in to kiss her gently as he simultaneously felt her hand return. He let himself enjoy it while he could before he would have to leave.

The thought of leaving her affected him again, as it did every time he visited her. The thought drove him to kiss her more passionately, before moving down her body to taste her again. Always when he left, he wanted the taste of her to be the last thing that was present on his lips and tongue.

When he later stood up to get dressed, Alexis saw the marks on him. She gasped. He turned to look at her, forgetting initially what she had done, but then he reached back and touched himself there and enjoyed the feeling of the heated marks.

"It's okay, Lexi," he said, feeling slightly embarrassed. He wasn't embarrassed because he was marked, but because he *liked* so much that he was marked.

He quickly dressed, as did she. Nothing more was said about it. For him, he couldn't get away fast enough. He just wanted to get to his office and turn the hot water on so he could feel pain there all over again.

In contrast, Alexis remembered the sight of the marks. Her nails had indented his skin deeply. The long red streaks showed her scratch trails, and she had done that. She knew that he had asked her to, but it was a form of hurting someone, and she didn't want to hurt anyone.

~~~~~

Two months later, Lincoln began to feel like her nails digging into his skin just wasn't enough. He had been telling her to keep doing it, and she had. Even though he still loved both the feeling of her doing it, and the feeling of intense stinging he got when he showered afterwards, suddenly it didn't feel like enough.

He found his mind wandering more and more when it shouldn't be. He needed to find a way to get that feeling without there being any strong visible marks on him. His mind worked overtime trying to consider different options for how he could grow that nail-scratch feeling.

Eventually, he considered a riding crop. He didn't know how it felt to be slapped. No-one had ever dared do such a thing to him. Lexi was different. She would do it to him - if he told her to.

~~~~~

Alexis looked at the item he had placed in her hand, feeling her gut sink as she realised straight away what he wanted to use it for.

Lincoln looked at her and saw her look at him in confusion. She was timid in many ways, strong in others, but always difficult to read.

"Why do you look so worried?" he asked, trying to smile at her, but feeling like he was asking for something abnormal.

"I don't want to be hurt, Lincoln," she said, almost in a whisper.

Lincoln immediately pulled her into his arms and kissed her softly.

"It isn't for me to use on you, Lexi," he said, seeing her confusion only grow. "It's for *you* to use on *me*."

"I have no wish…" she started to say.

From her confused look, he perceived that she thought he thought she wanted to do it to him. He kissed her again.

"Lexi, I want you to use this on me. Don't ask me why. Even I don't know the answer to that, but I want you to try. Will you?" he asked.

Alexis could hear the doubt in his voice, as if he were deeply afraid she would think him weird for wanting it. Regardless, she nodded slowly, looking into his eyes. She had been finding it hard enough to scratch him, but at least she wouldn't feel his new desired action on her own hands. Perhaps not directly feeling it as something she was doing to him might make it easier than the scratching thing that he'd seemed to enjoy so much.

"Come to the bedroom," he said, his voice thick with desire.

Instead of instructing her to undress in front of him, Lincoln found himself needing to take a softer approach in anticipation of what would come later. He took his time and enjoyed removing her clothing, piece by piece. After softly kissing every area of her skin, he indulged in his usual pleasuring of her before kissing her lips passionately.

After removing his clothing, he lay between her legs. He had already thought about the order of things with his new idea, but lying with her, he found himself letting things happen as they would naturally happen.

He slid into her and brought them both to orgasm with his subtle movements before pulling out and lying in her arms, enjoying her natural move to stroke his hair and scalp. When they had relaxed for a long while, he looked at her.

"Kneel here on the bed, Lexi," he said.

Alexis took a deep breath, only wanting to do what he asked for. She had faith in his promise to never hurt her physically, but still found herself panicking slightly as she moved onto her knees. She watched as he knelt before her, the two of them upright on their knees and facing one another. After he put his arms around her and kissed her gently, she saw him turn around so that he was on all fours and at a 90-degree angle to her, lined up perfectly with her being right-handed.

"Pick up the crop," he said.

Alexis could feel the desire in his voice. She couldn't understand it, but she certainly could hear it. She followed his instruction and picked up the foreign thing into her hand. It felt alien to her. The whole idea of hitting someone with it felt wrong to her, even though he was asking for it.

"Hit me ... on my thigh," Lincoln said, having earlier considered where he wanted to feel the pain.

Alexis hesitated, not even sure how to use the thing in her hand, but resolved to try - for him.

"Now!"

She raised herself high and held her hand and arm well out to the right, before moving it sharply left and letting the end of the crop hit his skin. Inside of her was an automatic brake, she discovered. He felt it too.

"You aren't hurting me, Lexi. Hit me harder. I promise it's okay," Lincoln said to her. He could feel a combination of not wanting to get angry at her, but also needing to feel the pain that he knew could come from her hitting him.

Alexis tried again. She convinced herself that she could master it if she kept trying.

She tried only five times in total before Lincoln moved slightly. He could feel she was getting comfortable with the crop in her hands, and he was excited by it. They both were aware of how aroused he was getting.

"Strike it across my butt cheeks now," he said.

Alexis realigned herself so she could bring the crop down on him.

Not satisfied with the power she was showing, Lincoln moved off the bed and stood up, facing her.

Alexis was astounded by his erection. It was evident just how much he was enjoying the experiment - or at least, the idea of it. Something about the sight of him like that pushed her final resolve to give it her full effort if it was something that he wanted so much. She stood up with him and watched him bend over so his hands were on the bed, instantly giving her much more power by being able to swing her whole body if she needed to.

"Do it," she heard him say.

She used her full strength to deliver a smack with the crop onto him that was much more audible than her previous attempts. The sound startled her, making her jump in surprise at it.

Lincoln seemed to only be fuelled by it. "Again!"

Alexis felt slight nausea inside but pushed it down. It was a strange feeling she was experiencing, having to cause pain in someone who wanted her to, even though it wasn't something she'd ever wanted to do.

She pushed logical thought aside and braced herself to try again and again. After a handful more blows, she heard him as she hadn't expected to, breathing out her name as he climaxed before her, over her bed cover. It was the first time she had seen him ejaculate, with him usually doing so in her mouth or inside of her. The sight was new to her. He hadn't even had any direct stimulation there. He wasn't touching himself at all. It just seemed to happen. She hadn't known till that moment that such a thing *could* happen without direct touching.

Lincoln felt a new high. Having the orgasm without having had any direct touch at all on his erection was completely new to him. Briefly, he found himself wondering if that was normal. He didn't care even if it wasn't. All he knew was that it felt good - *very* good. Everything felt good in his body. He could feel the traces of the crop's strikes on his buttocks and thighs and found himself looking forward to his shower later, when he would *really* feel it.

Lincoln stayed where he was for several minutes, leaning over with his hands on the bed. When he turned his head to look at her, he felt temporarily detached from her. She was there but not a part of what had just happened to him. When he realised he was feeling like that, he immediately stood up, went to her, took the crop out of her hand, and put his arms around her to kiss her passionately. He felt her melt against him before he guided her to sit on the edge of the bed. He then pushed her thighs wide and knelt before her to give her a parting orgasm before he would leave.

~~~~~

Later, after he had left, Alexis lay in her bed, initially wide awake with her mind racing. Later she let herself peacefully drift off to sleep. As always, when he was in her apartment, he was very much in her life, but when he walked out, he just … wasn't.

She didn't want to think about what she had just done. She didn't want to think about the fact that she'd been hitting someone, over and over again. She'd caused pain. She'd left marks. He'd been so aroused by it that he hadn't needed anything sexual from her at all to reach his desired point of orgasm. She'd been there, but knew from the look in his eyes that he hadn't really been there with her. On that particular night, even though they had still earlier joined, and he'd still made it a priority to take time to please her, ultimately she had been his accessory - his tool - and not his lover.

After leaving her apartment, Lincoln eagerly went to his office and into the bathroom. When he turned to look at the marks, he felt a huge satisfaction from them. It had been her first attempt, and he had already felt her grow more confident and strong, just in that first attempt. It was possible she would hurt him more next time. The thought was very arousing to him.

Entering the shower, he turned the water to hot again. He groaned at the glorious sharpness of it hitting each spot of red. The crop had been a good idea, he thought to himself as he smiled inwardly and outwardly. Now he just had to get her to learn to *really* hit him with it.
~~~~~

CHAPTER 7

Lexi & Lincoln - The Second Year

"Harder, Lexi!" Lincoln shouted at her after he felt the chain hit his back. He had bought it earlier that day and was on all fours on the floor in her apartment living room.

Alexis, at his instruction, was standing. She had so far hit him four times with the length of metal that he had brought to her. She could see the marks it was leaving on his back. He kept asking her for more, but she was deeply fearful that she was going to hit his spine with it and do real damage. Already on his skin, she could see bruising starting. She didn't feel good about having made that happen. No matter how much he wanted it - no matter how much he *begged* for it - she never felt good delivering it.

Lincoln kept telling her to hit him, again and again, over and over. He had moved on from the riding crop. Since then he'd brought a wide selection of items into her apartment. Accompanying each item had been a request for her to use it on him, to cause him as much pain as she physically could. He seemed to thrive on it, she understood. He was regularly having orgasms from that, and that alone. She'd started to recognise that she was becoming less and less important to him as a person and as a lover. Instead, she'd begun veering more toward simply being his deliverer of pain.

In some ways, he was still attentive to her. He continued to pleasure her when he arrived, and at least once more before he left. Between his arrival and departure, things had dramatically changed. Sometimes he joined with her, or wanted her to still please him with her mouth, but more and more frequently his choice of pleasure for himself was the pain.

It had started to affect Alexis. At a logical level, she didn't think it should. He had maintained his promise to never hurt her physically, but she couldn't stop the worry when she was with him. It wasn't right, within her, to hurt anyone, even if they begged for it - which he often sounded like he was doing.

As Lincoln received another blow, his body was pushed over that the blissful edge that he could never get enough of. He finally found himself reach that point. He ejaculated as he relished the intense contraction of all of his bodily muscles. He didn't understand how it was all connected, but something about the levels of pain he was receiving, had a direct link to his arousal. He found it increasingly exciting as the months passed.

The only problem was, he acknowledged to himself, that he couldn't seem to find quite the right thing to keep him happy for very long. The crop had lasted a couple of months. After that, he'd gone out and bought a variety of normal things from a sex shop including floggers and whips, and the two of them had tried those. For the first month or so, each item was exciting and brought on a new level of pain, a different kind of sting in the hot water, and a new level of satisfaction. After that initial rush, he needed something more.

At home, he had managed to keep all the marks from Diana by continuing to work later at night if he had to. In doing that, he was able to slip into bed unseen in the darkness of the night. She still pulled him into her arms often. He found he could experience some slight pain again there, too, on occasion when she put her arms around him while he was moving inside of her. The marks were like an addiction. The more of them he had, and the deeper they were, the better.

Ever-increasingly, he still found his thoughts extremely focused on Lexi when they were apart. Even though he knew there now came a point each time when he was with her, that he would almost forget she was there, he was still excited by her. He was obsessed with her, especially on the long, drawn-out days when he didn't see her. She consumed his mind. Somehow he still believed when he was away from her, that it was her consuming him. He couldn't seem to align his obsession as being about the hurt she gave to him, and not her at all.

Even though he'd increased the frequency of his visits to three nights a week, he still just couldn't get enough. It was only his extreme commitment to control and business success that forced him to take a break from her the other four nights of the week. The company was thriving and growing. He found that when he had to, he could still focus for most of the day. It took a degree of effort that he sometimes found extremely taxing on his body and his mind. He had always been physically fit, but was finding more and more that on occasion, he wished he could stop everything and just crawl into bed alone and sleep. The only time he felt truly alive was when he was with Lexi. When he was with her, he felt like he was full of vigour and full of adrenalin. He knew he was addicted.

He was an addict. She was his drug.

In his business, he had recently acquired a new and significant corporate client in another city. The day-long meetings there on Fridays were always intense. To deal with that, he purposely left his phone off and pushed Lexi from his mind all day long. He had to, otherwise he could make an error that would be worth millions. As much as he was driven to think about her whenever and wherever he could, he did believe that his company was much more important to him.

When each Friday's business was concluded, he had taken to instructing her to be ready for him before he arrived at her apartment that night. He had forgotten her 8pm rule and disregarded it completely. Somewhere along the way, she had stopped trying to tell him she didn't want him turning up after 8pm.

As a result, at 9pm on Friday nights, she started to receive instructions that sometimes he delivered via a text message. Sometimes he would ring her and tell her the instruction with his voice over the phone. The how didn't matter. It only mattered that he gave her an instruction - and that she followed it.

As strange as it initially was, Alexis was getting used to the routines that Lincoln seemed to need. She was finding it an odd existence, with the contrast between what happened in her apartment with him, and what happened outside her apartment door the rest of the time.

Just after 9pm on Friday nights, he would knock on her door, and she would open it. Always at that time, she would be topless, only in panties, before moving into the living room, kneeling, and putting her head down to wait.

Lincoln would then take his time. Sometimes he would walk around her. Sometimes he would just take in what she looked like. Sometimes he would sit down in front of her and just look at her face before he even spoke to her. Sometimes he would kneel before her, push down his pants to his knees, and then rub himself over her lips. Always on Fridays, even though he would have only seen her the night before, he couldn't wait to get back to her and see her again.

He was oblivious to the increasing internal distress she was experiencing by having to constantly deal pain to him. He didn't notice how little she spoke as the months passed. He didn't notice how much weight she was losing. He was so caught up in his journey of pain for pleasure that although he believed in his mind and heart that he loved her, he really had stopped truly seeing her, long ago.

~~~~~

"Scrub harder, Lexi," Alexis heard him say one evening as she took a bath. For whatever reason, that evening he had told her that she had to have a bath when he arrived. Not before he arrived, and not a shower - it had to be a bath, and it had to be when he was there with her. "Yes, see how shiny your skin becomes when you scrub it," he continued.

Alexis followed his instruction, almost as if she'd been hypnotised. She watched as Lincoln's fingers entered the water and trailed down to touch her labia.

"Hmm, now I want you to shave. Come and sit up on the edge of the
~~~~~

bath - no, at the end there so I can watch you," he said. He then positioned her so that he was able to see the full view of her.

Alexis continued, as if in a daze. It wasn't the first time he had instructed her to shave in front of him. It was just his latest request, and when she consciously thought about it, she did find it odd. Somehow, even though she didn't believe it was his intention, the act and the order successfully put her into a trance. She sometimes felt like she was dreaming it instead of living it. It was like she was seeing it from a third-person point of view, not first-person as she was.

She picked up the shaver and wet it in the water.

"Spread your legs wider, Lexi," he said and moaned as she did so. "Yes, now rub that soap all over."

Alexis did as she was told, just as she always did. She soaped up her hands and rubbed the suds over her body, down her legs, and all over herself as she sat wide to him.

"Yes, shave your legs first. I want them to be beautifully smooth," she heard him say as she began the methodical and rhythmic movement of the shaver over her skin. It was a slow process. He liked it to be slow, and she knew that he got slowly but extremely aroused by watching her do it.

After she had finished one leg, she moved on to do the other and saw the deep desire on his face. She couldn't see his hand but knew it was there, on him, touching himself through his pants. He always did that now. It was his 'flavour of the month'.

"Hmm … now your armpits," he continued. She could hear his voice changing. It was like he was eager for her to get to the time when he would give in to his feeling of urgency.

When he acknowledged that her legs and armpits were completely free from hair, Alexis widened her legs further and rubbed more soap all over herself, making him groan deeply. Then she picked up the razor and started to shave that area. It wasn't easy to do. She'd had to practice quite a few times to be able to do it well, but as always, when he watched her do that, she saw his eyes glaze over.

She took her time, making it last as long as possible. When she looked at him, she could see his hand moving faster. As she neared the end of the job, she saw him stand up, just as he did each time, and take his clothes off. He finished by ejaculating into the water in the bathtub.

When she put the shaver down, he climbed into the tub, picked up the handheld showerhead and asked her to stand up so he could rinse her off completely, including her genitals. That, she did enjoy. When he pointed the water flow there, he watched her squeal and moan in desire, making him aroused again.

"Now me," he said and handed the shower head to her. She rinsed him all over, but the area that he particularly seemed to enjoy the water shooting into, was his anus. The first time she had done that, he had sounded surprised but then full of force in telling her to keep the water flow there. He'd told her to turn up the power of the flow so it was more forceful. Then he'd turned up the temperature so the water was even hotter.

As he felt the hot water hitting him from behind, Lincoln reached for her head and pushed it down onto him. The first few times, Alexis had found it difficult to coordinate holding the shower head to point it from behind, while at the same time taking him into her mouth. Since that first time, she'd worked to perfect it.

Lincoln didn't wait for Alexis to orgasm during that particular ritual. Her time came later. That time was just for him. Her part was to get exceptionally clean with no dull, dead skin visible. She needed to have no hair in the areas that he said must be hairless, and then help him reach orgasm.

After he did so, he gently pulled her up to face him and put his arms around her, kissing her, before turning off the water and assisting her out of the bath. He took his time, gently and lovingly drying her off with the towel, and letting her do the same to him. He wanted to be gentle with her so she would always know how much he loved her … respected her … needed her.

After the bathroom ritual was complete, Lincoln then found he could focus on her once again. He led her into the bedroom, walking in front of her as he always did. She walked behind him. That had become her place every single time they walked in the same direction. Always.

"Kneel there, Lexi, on the edge of the bed," he said to her. He looked at the view of her from behind before he knelt on the floor near the bed edge, and used his tongue to bring her to orgasm like that. After she had, he needed another fix of that.

"Now turn over and lie down of your back. Spread your legs wide for me," he commanded.

Alexis did as instructed, to then find his tongue on her again, feeling it different from the different angle.

After that, he seemed to be sated, at least for that moment.

"Next time I come here, I want you to go through that cleaning process yourself, while I wait here on the bed for you. Scrub as hard as you can, like you were doing, to get all dead skin off, and then shave every little piece of hair. When you are finished doing that, then come to me here," Lincoln said to her as he held her close, already thinking of his next visit - and every visit thereafter.

CHAPTER 8

Lexi & Lincoln - The Last Six Months

It was Friday night again, and it was approaching 9pm. Always, soon after 9pm, Alexis received a phone call or a text message with a request from Lincoln. He was out of town all day on Fridays, but instead of wanting to rush home to his wife, he always seemed to want to come and see her. On Fridays, he had only seen her the night before, so on a logical level knew he could have had a night away, but inside of his heart, he knew that he couldn't. There was something different about Fridays. It didn't matter that they had been together the night before. He just had to have her with him on that night each week.

Alexis knew that after she would open the door to him, she could be asked to do anything. He could request anything that would cause him pain. She was starting to hate that. She had never felt comfortable with it, but she had endured it. He wanted it, so she would do it. It wasn't hurting her. She tried to tell herself that over and over, but even she knew she was arguing with herself. He might not be hurting her physically, but she was hurting.

Lincoln sat on the plane on its approach to the airport. He'd had a two-hour wait until he would see or talk to her. On his mind was the previous Friday and the weeks before that when he'd approached her and directed her to do to for him whichever 'just one more thing' he had been thinking about. Sometimes now his mind was utterly consumed. He just couldn't stop the thoughts that bombarded his mind, day and night. He knew he was sleeping less too. He stayed up later and later, with the expectation that he would reach a point of exhaustion where he would fall asleep as soon as he got into bed. If it didn't happen when he got into bed, it certainly should after he made love to Diana. Things were changing inside of him and sometimes even after staying up late, even after being in bed and releasing into his wife, his mind was often still too active. It was too full. He sometimes wished he could just find an 'off switch' for it. He wished he could find that thing - that *one thing* - that would be so satisfying to him that he would be blissfully subdued after it.

When Lexi let him into her apartment that night, he stood in front of her and handed her a sex toy - long, metallic, cold, hard. She worried he wanted to use it on her. Again, he reassured her it was for her to use on him.

"Lexi, tonight I want you to put this in me," he said to her. As he spoke the words, he watched her face. He was too far into his own thinking to accurately read her thoughts or feelings.

Alexis immediately felt sick. She knew it wasn't anything unusual, inserting anally, but she found she didn't want to do it. Suddenly she found the strength to mumble that she didn't want to. She said the words over and over, trying to force them out of her so he would hear her.

"Stop!" Lincoln shouted in anger at her saying she wouldn't do it. As soon as the word left his mouth, he saw her fall to her knees and go quiet. He had seen her in that position so often that he no longer thought anything of it. All he could think about was what he wanted her to do to him.

Alexis didn't know she had done it until she felt him shaking her, there on the ground.

"Lexi?" she heard him ask. She could hear his voice in the background, but something wasn't quite right. Then the voice cut through the mist and found her. "Lexi! Wake up!

Lincoln watched her but could only think one thought - 'she isn't doing what I want her to do'. He didn't recognise that it wasn't a normal thing to happen to her. He couldn't see that something was changing in her, and affecting her so much that her body now automatically fell into that position when he yelled at her.

Alexis came around and, for a moment, was confused before remembering where she was.

"Tell me what you want me to do," she said automatically, not remembering what he had told her to do, but knowing that he was waiting and needing her to do something.

With the two of them already being down on their knees, she watched as he simply pulled down his pants in front of her, and got on all fours, waiting. She could see on his face the level of anticipation he had. She couldn't miss noticing and seeing how aroused he was. As she looked at his face, she could see that he was in a completely different zone from her.

"Pick it up and put it in me," he said.

Alexis glanced at what he was looking at and remembered what he had asked her to do. Reluctantly she picked up the object and felt her hand start to shake uncontrollably as she processed what he was wanting from her. She knew it was normal. Many people liked anal stimulation, but something about being on the delivery end of it affected her greatly. In her gut, she felt sick to the point where she wondered if she might pass out.

She looked at his face and could see on him the intense hunger he had. It was almost like he was looking at a meal after having not eaten for weeks. She could almost see the saliva coming off him at the sight of the item she was holding.

She tentatively moved into position, ready to push it into him, feeling increasingly nauseous at the thought. Part of her wanted to shout out, to tell him that she couldn't do it. She wanted to scream that it was too difficult for her, and she wasn't the right person for what he needed…

"Do it!" she heard Lincoln shout at her.

The fear his voice produced in her finally forced her to do as he'd instructed. She could just try it, she told herself. It wasn't hurting her so there was no real reason why she couldn't do it to him.

It wasn't easy. She hated doing it, but she equally was afraid not to do it either. So she did it. He wanted her to do it, so she did.

"Push it in harder, Lexi - oh yes … hmm … harder! Oh yes, in and out, faster," he kept saying to her, wanting more and more. She obliged, trying to hide the dead feeling in her heart.

Once again, it was enough for Lincoln. After a short amount of time, he climaxed then relaxed, turning to her and hugging and kissing her. He didn't move to pleasure her before he left that night. She was glad. She knew with the way she was feeling that she wouldn't have been able to enjoy it, and he would have gotten upset if she didn't climax when he pleasured her. She'd never not been able to climax with his pleasuring, but on that night she knew in the core of her gut that she would not have been able to.

Lincoln left that night feeling another level of ecstasy in the new thing he had experienced. He had her to thank for it. She was wonderful. He loved her for being so accepting of him. He loved her for being so generous to him. He loved her for being so giving.

He was satisfied with giving those instructions for two months. For him, that was a long time. After that, he seemed to change again, needing more. Alexis kept doing what he wanted her to do to him, but she felt like her heart was dying. The stress of hurting someone over the extended period was taking its toll on her. She was thankful he only visited her three times a week. She knew she couldn't have handled seeing him any more than that.

The next month, he came home with something that horrified her - a strap on.

"Put it on, Lexi!" he yelled at her when she had shown on her face that she did not want to.

She did as he asked, and worked out how to get into it and make it fit securely. When she looked at his face, she saw the excitement that was there - and the look of absence. He was in the room with her, but he wasn't really there. He had left her somehow. He was present in his body and mind, but not there with her.

"Yes!" she heard him exclaim. "Oh, yes. Now that you have it on, I want you to come to me and put it into me."

Alexis felt sick to her stomach. She was at the limit of what she could do. Once again she said she didn't want to do it. It didn't matter that other people found it normal and pleasurable. For her, it was the breaking point that she had no desire to pass. She could feel tears threatening, but she knew Lincoln couldn't see her emotion. He could hardly see *her*, he was so eager for what he wanted her to do.

"Do it!" he yelled.

Immediately she fell to the floor, in the same position as always. She again found herself not feeling normal - almost like she was out of her body. Her soul was dying, and what was left of it was somewhere else entirely.

"Lexi! Wake up!" Lincoln said, shaking her. To him, it didn't compute that this was happening more and more. Each time, he was too eager for what he needed her for. All he could see when she went vacant was that she wasn't acting as quickly as he wanted her to.

The force of his voice woke her up again. Her fleeting thought was, 'There's something wrong with me'.

"Lexi, I need you. Put it in me ... please," she could hear him begging.

She told herself she just had to keep him thinking she was fine. She just had to make him think that for a little while longer. She did as he wanted, keeping her eyes closed so she couldn't see what she was doing.

"Fuck me harder, Lexi. Really push it into me!" he yelled at her, pushing her to slam into him as hard as she possibly could. All the while, she kept thinking about how she was going to get out of the situation she was in, and away from him. Something was wrong inside of her. The moments of weirdness were starting to creep in more and more often, and they couldn't be right. Something was wrong!

Lincoln was oblivious to what was going through her mind. He was too focused on the feelings she was evoking in him by moving in him like she was. Every new thing he wanted her to do to him, she did. He told himself that he loved her more and more with every act she performed on him. He was well past seeing what it was doing to her - the pain and the illness she felt in everything she did to him. About her, in any way other than the deliverer of what he needed to feel, he was numb. He just didn't know it.

Afterwards, he pulled her into his arms and told her how much he loved her. He told her how wonderful it was to have her - someone who liked and enjoyed the same things he did.

~~~~

"Go and run the bath," he told her on the phone one Friday night
~~~~

when he arrived at the airport. "Don't put any cold water in. Fill the bath just with water from the hot water tap."

That was his instruction. It wasn't like any previous instruction. As always, Alexis was nervous about what he had planned.

When he arrived, she opened the door, wearing only panties, as he had long ago told her to always be. She had her eyes down, looking at his feet in the doorway.

Lincoln walked in and closed the door behind him. For a moment, he felt tender toward her before he went back into his own headspace, thinking about what he wanted.

"Undress me," he said once they were in the living area.

He watched her face as she complied. When he was naked, he started to walk to the bathroom.

"Walk behind me. Follow me!" he said to her with force in his voice that alarmed her.

Despite her alarm, Alexis fell in step obediently, as she knew she was supposed to. When she walked into the bathroom, she saw him lowering himself into the water. She waited for him to speak further.

"Come closer, Lexi," he said, with a different look in his eyes. It was a look that she couldn't define. She just hadn't seen it before. It was new. It was unrecognisable, and it scared her.

She walked to him and stood beside the side of the bath, looking along the length of his submerged body. Even in her fear, she found herself reacting to looking at his body. There was so much that she did enjoy about him, and could have been happy, if only…

"Kiss me," he said, for a moment briefly seeming to see her before he faded away into his own world again.

When Alexis leaned over the edge of the bath and kissed him, she knew he was different. For a fleeting moment, she thought back to when she had met him. She desperately wished that she had never asked him to tell her what he wanted her to do. It was a lesson learned, and one she would never make the mistake of doing again.

"Leave your panties on," Lincoln said. "Climb in. Straddle me."

She carefully stepped into the bath. It was the first bath they had ever truly had together. She relaxed down on top of him, straddling him over his hips. He was flaccid. It was a state she had hardly seen him in since she had met him.

Lincoln reached out and caressed her breasts for a few minutes. He remembered how much he had loved her body when he'd met her. but somehow it had become not so important when he spent time with her now. In the depth of his mind and his heart, he wanted to be back there, enjoying the sex with her again, but now something else called him.

Vaguely he considered that he was sure when he had first met her, her breasts had filled his hands. Now they were hardly there. That was the limited extent to what he could comprehend about how much weight she had lost since he had come into her life.

"Put your hands on my throat, Lexi," he said, startling her. "Do it!" he then yelled.

Alexis could see his face full of a new anger and a new desperation. It wasn't just fear that dwelled in her as she saw it. At that moment, she knew she couldn't remain with him on his journey anymore. It had to stop. Perhaps he still had further to go on his never-ending quest, but for her, it had to stop.

She put her hands on his throat as he ordered. Already she had a suspicion of the words that would next come out of his mouth, even before he said them.

"Tighten your hands. Grip my throat as hard as you can," he said to her.

When she looked at him, she saw his eyes had changed. It was like he was possessed by something completely different. Regardless, behind her, she felt him grow hard at the thought of what he wanted to happen. That he could get turned on by such a thought was sickening to her. It didn't matter to her what other people found acceptable as far as bodily harm went, even during something as pleasurable as sex. To her, she just couldn't stomach any more.

Alexis calculated her move. She was in a bathtub with a man who once again wanted her to hurt him. She had to think quickly. She wanted desperately to be anywhere but there at that moment. She didn't know for certain, but there was a chance that he would be angered if she got out. If he got angry, she didn't want to be near a bathtub full of water. He had never hurt her physically. He had promised right back at the start that he never would. So far, he had kept that promise, but she had always said yes. For the first time, she was about to gather all the strength she could muster, and effectively - firmly - say 'no'.

The calculation in his time might have only taken a moment, but in her mind, Alexis followed right through her visualisation of how to quickly get out of the bath before he could stop her. She wanted to get out and get away from the bathroom. It would be wise to get ahead of him, just in case he snapped. He might not do so - but he might.

She looked at the sides of the bath. She would need to put her hands there quickly to be able to raise herself up and off him, and then out of the bath.

Lincoln watched her even though he really wasn't seeing her. All the way home on the plane that evening, and then in his car, he had been thinking about his current desire. He didn't know where the thought had come from. He just knew that he had a need. Lexi loved him, as he did her. She would do it without asking, just like she did with everything he asked her to do. She was wonderful like that - so giving, so loving of him, and so eager to please. He loved her so much for being the wonderful, generous person she was. They were meant to be together. Diana might be his wife, but Lexi was his soul mate.

He was heavily caught up in his own mind's chatter. He was so distracted that he didn't immediately register that instead of tightening her hands around his neck, she had moved her hands to each side of the bath, steadied herself, and quickly climbed out. She had left him there. She had left him hanging.

Alexis didn't wait to look at him. She left the bathroom and went to her bedroom to get dressed. She made sure she got fully dressed, not just into clean, dry underwear. She also put on jeans, socks, a t-shirt, and a thick, warm and comfortable hoodie. She wanted to be sexless - genderless. She wanted him to not see her as a woman. She wanted him to not see one tiny piece of her skin. She wanted her life back.

It hadn't seemed like a very wonderful life that she'd had before she had met him, doing a job that she didn't completely love or hate. It had, however, been pleasant enough to pass the time and pay her enough income to live on. She'd lived in a small home that was run down, but it had still been a roof over her head and a way for her to stay warm and dry at night. Back then, she had sometimes dreamed of living differently - having a new home and a man who adored her - perhaps even kids. Now she wanted nothing to do with her current life. She wanted her old life back. She wanted her own home and her own space. She wanted a place that was just hers, which no-one else would invade. More than anything, she wanted to be alone - every single night.

Lincoln sat in the bath and saw her move off him but wasn't quick enough to move his hands and stop her. His mind was somewhere else. He felt like *he* was somewhere else. He knew he was in Lexi's apartment, in the bath, but something was making everything so hazy.

He couldn't remember why they had been having a bath together. They had never bathed together before. He had watched her plenty of times, but he was never sitting like he currently was when that happened. He supposed that he had suggested it. He must have told her to have a bath with him. That was all he could think of, as any reason why he was lying in the bath in her apartment.

He lay there for a while after she left, enjoying the warmth of the water. His mind was hectic, darting from this thought to that, and he couldn't seem to focus at all. Glancing down at his body, he could see that he must have been hard but was now wilting slowly. He must have had sex with her, even though he couldn't remember it. They must have had sex in the bathtub, and she got out after he finished.

Alexis went to the living room and waited, nervous. She had prepared to leave if she had to. She was dressed. She had her shoes on. She'd placed near the door a bag with her wallet and anything else she would immediately need. If she needed to get out of the apartment quickly, she was ready.

For a moment she considered grabbing a knife from the kitchen - just in case. A secondary thought made her wonder if he might get turned on by the sight of it, rather than be scared if she showed it. He might even ask her to use it on him and to mark him with it. After hesitation and consideration, she left the knife where it was.

He had never hurt her. In that, he had kept his promise to her. She couldn't cry self-defence if anything happened. She would just sit and wait and see what was about to happen.

The clock on the wall said 10.20pm. She would wait until 10.35pm. If he wasn't out by then, she would go back into the bathroom. She'd have to. In the state of mind he had been in, she didn't think it was too much of a consideration that he might sink down into the water and not want to come up. Despite how things had turned between them, she couldn't let that happen. Something wasn't right with him now. Since she'd met him, something had changed deeply within him, but she wouldn't let that happen.

Lincoln tried to straighten out his mind, but found he couldn't. Around his body, the water was getting colder. He couldn't stand tepid water. He had to have it hot. For a moment he considered refilling the bath with hot water, but it seemed pointless to stay in there if Lexi had left the room. She was probably in her bedroom, waiting for him.

He then had a stark realisation that the thought of Lexi - his sweet, loving, beautiful Lexi - lying on her bed, naked and waiting for him, wasn't in any way arousing him. Even straight after having sex with her, he often got hard again. At that moment, he couldn't muster the arousal he would need. He reached down and touched himself to see if that would help, but he felt like his mind was fuzzy and dead. His body felt dead too. He wasn't himself. In a distant observation, he conceded that he had known that for a while, but it wasn't important. Only his career was important to him now - and making Lexi happy.

With that thought, he roused himself out of the bath, let out the water, and grabbed a towel to start drying himself off. He had never had a proper bath in her apartment before. He'd watched her do so, and he had used the shower. It felt odd to be in the room by himself, without her beside him, but she would be waiting for him, so he had to hurry. When he was dry, he stopped to look in the mirror.

Sometimes when he looked at himself, he hardly recognised himself. At a top level, he was the same person. For the most part, he looked exactly like he had done for the past ten years at least, except for a slight greying starting on his short sideburns. But sometimes when he looked in the mirror, he felt like he was looking at someone else - a clone of his former self. Something in his eyes was different. At times it scared even him.

He wrapped the towel low around his waist and walked out of the bathroom and toward the bedroom. He was nervous because part of him - an essential part of him - didn't seem to be awake. That was new to him. That never happened to him when he was with Lexi. He desired her all the time. His body *always* wanted her.

As he went to enter the bedroom and stood in the doorway, expecting to see her spread out on the bed, he was stunned. She wasn't on the bed. She wasn't lying naked, spread out, waiting for him at all. He walked into the bedroom and felt himself get confused. His thoughts were hazy, like he could identify something was wrong, but he just didn't know what. He turned slowly and walked down the hallway toward the living area, expecting then to see her naked, kneeling, with her head down, waiting for him.

Alexis heard his soft feet padding down the hallway toward her and braced herself. She had to be strong even though she didn't feel strong. She felt nervous. That nervousness bordered on fearful.

When Lincoln reached the living area, he saw her sitting on the sofa, fully dressed. Seeing her dressed and ready to leave if she had to, Lincoln's confusion reached a new level.

Alexis saw him enter the room and look at her, obviously not sure what was going on.

Lincoln stopped and just looked at her, unknowing of what had transpired, or why she was where she was. He didn't even know why he was where *he* was. He walked toward her and knelt before her. Reaching out with his hands to hug her, he saw her flinch and move backward on the sofa as if to not let him touch her.

Alexis held her breath. She could see that he didn't seem to know anything was wrong. He thought everything was perfectly normal between them. He was so unaware of anything anymore.

"Lexi, why do you seem afraid of me?" he asked serenely and quietly. His tone was so soft that, to Alexis, it was almost as if his earlier request to tighten her hands around his throat had not even happened.

Lincoln waited, but she didn't answer. He then became at least aware enough to sense something was seriously wrong. He pulled his clothes to him and started to get dressed, trying desperately to remember the time before he got in the bath. He fought to remember the time before he got to the apartment. The last thing he could remember clearly was checking in to his flight in Brisbane, and getting on the plane. Why was there a chunk of time missing in his memory?

When fully dressed, he looked at her again, not sure how to act or what to say to her. He sat beside her and reached out and took her hand in his. He wanted to act normal to not let her sense how worried he was at that moment. He saw her reluctantly let him take and hold her hand.

Alexis looked at his face. She could see his vagueness. At that moment, he seemed safe and normal.

"Lincoln, we can't keep doing this," she started and immediately saw him start to speak. She found her voice - probably far too late - and cut him off. "Things have changed, and I'm not the right person for … your needs."

"Lexi, don't say such a thing. I love you, and you are *exactly* the right person for me," Lincoln said, trying to maintain calm in what felt like extreme chaos right at his core.

"I don't want to do this anymore," she continued and saw his increasing confusion. "I can't keep doing to you what you want me to. It hurts me."

"I have never hurt you!" Lincoln replied forcefully, as if she had accused him of hitting her. "I promised you when I first met you that I would never lay a hand on you, and I haven't! Why would you say such a thing?"

Lincoln felt a pain in his heart. He couldn't remember part of the evening. Had he struck her? No, he couldn't have. He *wouldn't*.

Alexis stood up, their hands still together. Lincoln stood up with her.

"Lincoln, please," she said, starting to cry softly. She was sad, fearful, and regretful. So many emotions were running through her. All she knew was that she had reached a point where she couldn't go on with things like they were.

Lincoln, too, felt fear flowing through him. The fear combined with worry, and frustration … and anger…

"Stop!" he yelled at her, surprising both of them.

Alexis immediately and naturally dropped to her knees in extreme fear, putting her head down and not looking at him. Lincoln couldn't see the fear. To him, she had changed her mind and was back to wanting to please him.

He knelt in front of her and kissed her softly with tenderness seeping out from him. Initially, she was tense, resistant to it, but the more he kissed her, the more she melted. He was kissing her - *really* kissing her - like he could finally see her again. For a moment, he seemed like his old self. Inside, she knew it could be a fleeting moment, but she let herself enjoy the feeling of his soft kisses. It had been a long time since he'd kissed her like that, and she lapped it up.

Lincoln kept himself aware of what was happening. Whatever had happened earlier had to be disregarded and forgotten. His Lexi was talking about leaving him and not seeing him anymore. He couldn't let that happen. He had to stay in the moment and make sure she knew - make sure he could *show* her - how much she meant to him.

He kissed her softly until he felt her fully respond and heard her groan. Standing up, he held out his hands to her, guiding her up to stand with him once more. He pulled her into his arms, still kissing her softly while feeling her lean into him.

Alexis saw him hold out his hand to hers, and let him guide her into the bedroom. For the first time in a long while, he kept her beside him as an equal instead of making sure she was behind him. While walking alongside him, she kept watching his eyes to see if he had changed again.

Once in the room, he became tender Lincoln again. He undressed her slowly, kissing each part of her skin as it was revealed. He undressed himself and guided the two of them to lie back together. There he kissed her everywhere. He made love to her as he hadn't done in months, before settling in for the taste of her.

Lincoln had always loved the taste of her, and yet he couldn't remember when he'd last pleasured her. He took his time, bringing her close and then easing off so that it would last longer. He didn't want to leave her. He needed to expand the time out so she wouldn't ask him to leave.

Alexis knew it might be the last time she could enjoy his attentions like that, so lay back and let the feelings and the need flow through her. When he was like that, she did love being with him.

She felt it coming. It was building. He'd been trying to stop it from happening so she wouldn't climax soon, but the need to release was increasing, and then she was feeling it. Finally, she was on that slope toward complete letting go.

Just as he'd taught her to, Lincoln heard her call his name as she climaxed heavily against his mouth. He could have stopped there but instead kept going, softly at first and then, once her sensitivity had lessened, more intensely. He was determined to bring her to that point as many times as he could. He couldn't lose her. He couldn't.

After the second orgasm, Alexis had to stop him. She could sense his determination, but had no need herself to have orgasm after orgasm.

"Lincoln," she said to him softly - sadly - to gain his attention.

Lincoln raised his head, not eager to move. Seeing her face, he pulled himself up to lie between her legs and kiss her. He wasn't aroused himself. Both of them could feel that, and he felt a sense of loss and a hint of sadness because of it.

Alexis pulled him close and kissed him passionately without any immediate desire to stop. She caressed his lips and tongue with her own.

Finally, she felt him connect with her and start to work with her, kissing and caressing her also with his mouth. She felt him grow, as she heard him groaning against her mouth. For that moment, it seemed like his hunger was back, and she wanted to seize it. She wanted to capture it and hold it like it was a solid thing she could grip in her hand before it was lost again … before *he* was lost again.

Lincoln felt himself melt against her. They were only kissing, with their bodies rubbing together, but he was waking up to it. He hadn't done that for so long and, for a moment, realised how much he'd missed such closeness. He wasn't sure why it was something they'd not shared for so long.

When Alexis took a condom from the bedside table, Lincoln positioned himself to let her put in on him. He watched her face - her lovely face. He had to kiss her again. Once ready, he nestled back where he had been, between her legs, and resumed kissing her as he slowly edged into her.

The feeling caused them to both moan out loud. It felt like such an incredibly long time since that feeling had been experienced. It was a unique feeling for her, feeling like she was being filled up. For him, it felt like he was sliding into a warm enclosed space that was welcoming like a glove.

Lincoln didn't rush, instead taking his time and indulging in the feelings he was experiencing, which he found that he had missed. At home, he still had sex with his wife, but it was always mechanical. Diana's way was for him to roll on top, put it in her, orgasm, roll off her, then turn over to go to sleep. For her, he could always perform as she wanted him to. It was just a routine and a habit. He didn't even know if she enjoyed or truly wanted it, or if it was just something the two of them did because they should do it as husband and wife. Sex was different with Lexi. It had *always* been different with Lexi.

Although Alexis enjoyed her time with him, she made sure to not touch him, for fear of scratching him. She didn't like the thought of him sinking again into that dark place of what seemed to be, to her, pain worship. Instead, she put her arms back over her head and held them there, giving him full control of what was happening. She was determined to not play into any of the darker desires he seemed to have developed.

As Lincoln moved inside of her, he alternated between kissing her lips and looking into her eyes. For the first time in so long, Alexis felt like he was really there with her, and truly aware of her. It conflicted her because such a short time earlier she had resolved to end it all with him. She had intended to tell him she didn't want him coming to see her anymore, but now he was back to his gentle self - his *nice* self.

Lincoln took his time, not wanting to end the pleasure. If it ended, the time might come when the conversation would start up again. Lying on top of her like he was, moving inside of her, he didn't want to talk about them going their separate ways. He loved her too much.

No, she couldn't end things…

She couldn't.

Finally, that time was reached, and Alexis heard and felt him climax heavily inside her. He didn't rush to move afterwards, as he usually did. He lay inside of her for a long time, looking at her and kissing her, before he eventually pulled away.

They both dressed in silence, not knowing what to say.

"I will see you on Monday?" he asked tentatively before he moved to leave, and saw her nod.

~~~~~

In the two months that followed, Alexis started putting together her plan. She liked her job, and she did love the apartment that Lincoln had her set up in. Her conflict was that she knew for sure she wasn't made for delivering physical pain, or hurtful pleasure - or whatever it was that she was giving him. She felt like she was slowly dying inside from having to give it, over and over again. Even though he'd had a slight respite where they'd shared simple pleasure again, Lincoln had ventured back to wanting her to hurt him relatively soon after.

There hadn't been any mention of the bath again, or her putting her hands on his throat. She wasn't even sure he remembered it, he seemed so vague about it. Still, she knew what she had to do to save herself, and find herself some form of a normal life again.

She had to make a break.

She had to get away from him.

It wouldn't be easy. A month earlier - around the time the whip had resurfaced in his needs, she remembered - she had suggested to him that he find someone else. She'd hinted that he could find someone who would enjoy doing the things he needed. Perhaps even a man might have been more suited, being able to offer more force … and other things.

Lincoln's reaction hadn't been good. He had responded firstly by telling her that he couldn't be with anyone else. He loved her too much, and she was the one he was meant to be with. She was the only one he trusted to keep secret the time - the things - that they did together. She was the only one who would enjoy those things with him.

Then he had turned mean, telling her that he knew where she was at every minute of every day. He had recited to her where she had been that week, including the very coffee shop she'd bought a coffee and a muffin for lunch one day. He'd told her how much money she had spent on groceries that week. He'd accurately said how many texts she had
~~~~~

received on her phone and how many she had sent.

He told her enough to make sure she understood that no matter what she did, he would know. In his own way, he'd drummed into her that leaving was not an option. It was a degree of information that shocked her and made her realise the depth of which she had let herself become entwined with him.

Immediately after that conversation, she had resolved to try harder to please him. She'd decided then to never again bring up the subject of them not seeing each other anymore.

She knew it was too late to fix anything. Too many things had happened, and it was easy to see that the two of them were toxic together. No matter how much he begged or how mean he got, she knew she had to find a way to extract herself from him. It would mean walking away from her apartment. If she really wanted to get far away, she would have to leave her job as well.

He had become too unpredictable. After one time of her mentioning them going their separate ways, he was gentle. After another time, he was mean. In between those times, he didn't seem to want to acknowledge she had even brought the subject up. He appeared to want the possibility of them ending their time together, to simply not exist.

Despite all of his efforts, Alexis didn't lose sight of what she had to do for herself. She had to get away. She had to leave. She had to escape. She had to move on and start a new life. She had to find a way to put it all behind her and simply forget. They would never be able to go back and start over. His desires had moved too far away from hers. He had already proven that although he could have a small respite from it, he would always want to go back there.

No, his needs were too different from hers now. No matter how much planning it would take, no matter how far she would have to go to hide from him, no matter what he would do or how he would act when he realised things had changed permanently … it was time for her to go.

CHAPTER 9

Lincoln - The Confession

Present Day

In the initial days that followed the police report on television that Sunday afternoon, Lincoln acted in desperation. He had staff around the country looking for 'Lexi Montgomery'. The question on everyone's lips was why he was willing to go so far for the girl. He had ensured every supermarket, fast food outlet, and department store under the umbrella of his company, had vast numbers of flyers on their staff and public notice boards, showing her face. Over a busy highway in one part of Melbourne, he had a large billboard changed, so her name and face were on it. There was no way that drivers passing under it would be able to miss it.

He offered money to the public for any sightings of her. He offered money to any staff member who saw her and reported her location to him. His head was full of thoughts on how to get her to come back to him. He was so consumed by that thinking that it didn't even occur to him that something serious could have happened to her. She could have suffered a bad accident, or worse. That kind of thinking, his mind never ventured to. In his head, all he cared about was that she wasn't there with him. She wasn't there *for* him.

He managed to get through the following workdays, from morning till night. Always she was there, in the back of his mind. His obsession over her disappearance resulted in even him starting to question his stability where she was concerned. When he'd called the police, he had thought it a good idea. He'd thought it would be an easy way to bring her out of hiding and ensure she came back to him. As reality set in over the following forty-eight hours after he'd made that call, he knew he'd made a stupid mistake, making it seem like she had been abducted. Even worse, he'd associated his own name with it. There was going to be damage. He cursed himself profusely at the level of desperation he had let build up in himself.

In his home life, Diana hadn't come back. He could see through their bank statements that she was already purchasing lots of new things. It seemed obvious that she had left him completely and was already starting to set up a home somewhere. She hadn't tried to contact him, and he hadn't gone after her. He had been disloyal and disrespectful toward her, and that went against everything he'd thought he stood for in a marriage. He was sure she would be filing for divorce. If she did, he would let her go, wish her well, and generously reimburse her. As a wife, she had done everything perfectly. She had played her role with dedication and utter professionalism.

With time away from Lexi, admitting things had not been as perfect in recent times as he'd believed them to be, Lincoln took time to think over their three years together. He still knew that he loved her. He still believed that she loved him, but away from her, he could see that he had asked her for everything but given her so little. Yes, there was the apartment, but even that was his idea - what *he* wanted, to suit his wishes and desires.

In hindsight, there was a small part of him that knew he should never have gone near her. He was an old man, and she was a beautiful young woman. She'd been a young girl when he'd met her. She'd only been 18 then. In his head, she had inspired him to be who he really was inside, and had let him try so many new things. In reality, it had always been about him, never her. When he thought about it, he couldn't remember her even once saying to him 'try new things, Lincoln', or even 'I want to do that for you'. He wanted it all to have been driven by her … her ideas … her initiative … but it was never her. She just went along with it … to please him.

He did regret that. If only he could see her and tell her how sorry he was. If only he could get her to listen to him. She would then understand. She would know he wasn't angry at her. She would feel safe with him again. She would forgive him for his stupidity. She would want to be with him again. She would again remember how much she loved him. She would want them to start again, in a new life together.

From his resources and research via various kinds of technology, he knew the lengths she had gone to, to plan and work toward getting away from him. He vaguely remembered her saying more than once that she had wanted things to end between them, but he hadn't accepted that. He had tried to make sure she could never leave because that hadn't been what he'd wanted. Always, it was what he wanted that had mattered most, never what she wanted.

He felt ashamed all of a sudden, and sick. His emotions swayed from feeling regretful and remorseful, to then feeling anger at her for thinking she could walk away from him. After all the hours he had put aside for her - all the attention he had given her, and generosity - an apartment, clothing … love. And she had the nerve to just walk away from him? No, that wasn't on. That was not okay. He had invested too much time into her, and she had no right to walk away from him. No right!

He felt like he couldn't get his thinking straight. Too often he was in a constant state of confusion, not able to focus. That wasn't good, especially for his business. He needed to get her off his mind so he could resume normal living, but how could he do that? He needed to talk, openly and honestly about her, but who could he even talk to? No-one knew about her…

Except that wasn't quite right. Three people knew about her.

Although he hated to admit the truth of it, Diana knew about Lexi. She shouldn't have known. If he hadn't put that broadcast on the television, and stood and watched it in their apartment when he knew she was there, she wouldn't have known. No, that wasn't quite true. Diana had told him the last time he saw her that she had already known he was seeing someone else over those three years. She'd implied that she had always known. In thinking about that, Lincoln cringed. He had been certain that he'd been discrete, saving his wife from knowing what he was doing, and who he was doing it with. He had honestly thought that he'd saved her any possibility of humiliation that might come from people knowing her husband was being unfaithful. He would never have wanted to hurt Diana by the world finding out about Lexi. Despite telling himself that, now he had gone and associated his name with Lexi's after all. He'd openly associated himself with the women he'd been having sex with for three years, to the entire country. Even he knew it had been an act of sheer stupidity on his part.

Ironically, Lincoln thought to himself, Diana would have been a good person to talk to about the situation. She had always been open to listening to him talk about anything. His world - his company - was not her world, but she was a committed wife. She'd been dedicated to the perfect wife role she was expected to play, especially in front of the outside world. She had always encouraged him to talk to her about his work, even though she didn't truly understand the nature of business.

Yes, he thought sadly, he wouldn't have minded talking to her about everything if he hadn't known it would hurt her so much. Not that she was talking to him now, of course. The fact that she had run when she did on that afternoon, proved her high level of intelligence and sense of self-preservation. If the possibility had been there, though, perhaps she would have been the right person to listen and to advise. In addition to her many other strengths, she had always been good at providing him with advice. Even things he didn't think she completely understood, she seemed to easily grasp and see the best solution to.

It was a fleeting series of thoughts. Diana was no longer around, and she wasn't available to him. She was scared of him, and understandably so.

Second on his list of possibilities was Nate - his IT manager and long time employee of twenty years or so. Nate had helped him with the first and second attempts to locate Lexi through her phone. Even though Lincoln hadn't told Nate who she was, he would have suspected. Of course he would. The very reason Lincoln considered him so important to the company was his high level of intelligence, forward-thinking, and forward speaking. The fact that the information hadn't leaked out into the public meant that Nate hadn't told anyone. He could be relied upon to keep quiet, but he was a staff member. It wouldn't be professional for Lincoln to talk to him about something so personal. No, Nate also wasn't the right person to talk to about all of this. He could be trusted, but he wasn't the right person.

That left one other person - Toby. He hadn't been a staff member of Lincoln's for very long, but he was fully aware of Lexi. He, too, had proven he could be trusted.

But what could Lincoln talk to Toby about? He was his driver, and fairly new since it wasn't so very long ago that Lincoln had stopped driving himself everywhere. That had been mainly so that he could be dropped off at Lexi's apartment and the car could move on and not be parked outside. Toby had always returned later to pick him up when he was ready to leave, rather than the car sitting outside the building every time Lincoln had visited her.

Could he trust his driver? He'd had to, of course, to a certain degree. If he didn't trust him, he wouldn't have let Toby see where he was going or who he was visiting.

Lincoln felt like his head was going to explode. He had to take a chance. He had to talk to someone. His choices were to choose a professional counsellor he didn't know, or choose someone he knew. He suspected a counsellor wouldn't provide him with any advice. Their job would be to listen but not advise, and he needed advice. Every day at work, he made decisions that were worth millions of dollars and sometimes affected thousands of people, but now he needed advice - desperately.

He sat quietly and considered all options. He had to be sure of what he was doing. He knew he hadn't been thinking clearly for some time, and he couldn't keep making mistakes as he had been. No, he had to be certain, without any possible doubts. Once he started talking, he would never be able to undo that. It would be out there for anyone to know, if he started to talk about it. If he made a bad decision about who to trust with the information, the whole world could know about everything.

He made his choice. He had to talk. There was no denying the need. He had already let himself become too self-absorbed into the mess of the all-encompassing existence he'd been living in for the previous year or two. He needed help, advice, and support. Those things Lexi would have given him, if only she were still close by…

~~~~~

Twenty minutes after calling his driver, Lincoln saw him walk into the apartment. He couldn't miss Toby's look of great apprehension on his face, even though he was never anything but professional.

"Toby, thank you for coming at such short notice. Please come in and sit down," Lincoln said, trying to welcome the man into his living area.

Since receiving the call, Toby had considered he might have done something wrong and was going to lose his job. Being invited inside the apartment of his boss wasn't normal. He was surprised when he heard the words his employer next spoke.

"I need your advice," he saw the powerful man sitting beside him say. The words temporarily stunned Toby. He had been in the service industry for decades, including extensive time as a chauffeur to many wealthy business owners. In his career, he'd been asked for many things and many favours. Not once had he been asked by an employer for advice.

"Of course, Sir. What can I help you with?"

Lincoln looked at his driver. Toby was older than him, and Lincoln found something so ironic about that. He was forty-five years old with a driver who earned only a fraction of the money he did. That driver had no recognition in the world at all, even though he had worked much longer and much harder than Lincoln had in his lifetime.

"Toby, you know about … the young woman I … visit," he started to say, feeling incredibly awkward all of a sudden.

"Yes, Sir. Of course," Toby replied quietly, intrigued by what his employer was going to say. Although his employer had never said why he visited the young lady, of course it had been the assumption Toby had made, that they were seeing each other intimately. Lincoln Kokiri was wealthy and attractive to everyone. Even if he hadn't been who he was in the business world, he had an air about him - a level of self-confidence, handsomeness and poise - that made him attractive. It would have surprised Toby more if his boss *didn't* have a mistress.

"I need … I need someone I can trust, to talk to about some things that are going on with her … and I trust you."

Lincoln looked at Toby's face and waited to see if there was any discomfort, but the older man only looked kind, yet professional.

"Thank you, Sir. I am happy to help in any way that I can."

Lincoln stood up and paced. His driver could immediately see how stressed he was. Toby knew the level of stress had started on Friday night at the airport. He had thought then that something had upset his employer. Whatever it was, it was still going on.

It was difficult for Lincoln to find words. He had worked so hard to keep Lexi a secret for so long. To openly talk about her wasn't a natural thing for him to do. At his core and in his heart, he didn't know if he
~~~~~

should talk about her. Did he have the right to share information about the two of them? It wasn't only him who would be exposed. He didn't want to hurt Lexi. He loved Lexi.

"I can't think. My head is overflowing," he started to say as he paced back and forth across the living room floor.

The older man waited, not sure what to do or what to say.

"Are you in some kind of trouble, Sir?" Toby eventually ventured to ask in an attempt to get the conversation flowing. After he'd seen the TV news report on Sunday, he'd wondered if Lincoln was involved in anything to do with the disappearance of the young woman. Toby wasn't sure he was brave enough to mention that he had seen the report, or had considered those thoughts.

Lincoln heard the question and came back to sit down beside the older man once again before looking him directly in the eye.

"I lied to the police," he said. "Lexi has gone and I know - I believe - inside of me, that she's just left. I don't think anything bad has happened to her. I do think that wherever she's gone, she has gone willingly, but I told them that she'd been abducted. I don't even know what made me do it. I was just so desperate to get her back, and I wanted a way to bring her out of hiding. But why is she hiding from me anyway? I don't understand. I put her up in the apartment and looked after her. I never hurt her. I just don't understand. Why did she leave?"

Toby listened and kept quiet, his mind rushing. His employer was sitting beside him, and he was rambling. Words were spilling out of his mouth at an alarming rate, as if he was talking almost as quickly as he was thinking. That wasn't like him at all. Always, Mr. Kokiri was very much in control and could articulate anything with grace and patience.

"What do I do?" Lincoln asked. "I shouldn't have lied to the police, and now people will be looking out for her. She won't be able to move without someone identifying her, which is what I wanted, of course. That was why I did it, I think, but it isn't fair. It isn't right. I need to put it right. I need to put *everything* right."

"Do you need to go to the police then, Sir?" Toby asked tentatively, not sure if he really was welcome to speak and provide advice or not.

Lincoln looked at him, having already considered that option but not knowing if it was wise or not.

"Should I? That is exactly what I'm uncertain about," he replied. "I know I'll get in some kind of trouble for it, and rightly so. I just don't want everything coming out in the open about her."

"It's likely they'll find out everything that has happened between you, and formulate their own story of events and information about who she is to you," said Toby. "Wouldn't it be better to control everything that they learn, by telling them directly?"

Lincoln considered the words. He did have to step up and take control. Always he could handle things as long as there was order. Everything seemed to be in chaos, and chaos he did not handle well at all.

"Yes, I think you are right. Will you drive me to the police station, please?" he asked. He still wasn't entirely sure it was the most intelligent thing to do, but it was probably the right thing to do.

Toby nodded and stood up.

"Of course, Sir," he said. "Whenever you are ready."

Lincoln stood up also and nodded at his driver.

"Let's go now. I need to put a stop to all of this. I need to put things right."

~~~~~

"Are you sure this is what you want to do, Sir?" Toby asked his employer as they sat outside the police station in central Melbourne.

For a fleeting moment, Lincoln considered not going in to see them. He still had the option to see how it would all pan out naturally without him admitting what he'd done. Despite a darker side of his nature having shown and grown in recent times, he did pride himself on his honesty. What he'd done wasn't good. Everything he had done - particularly every way he had acted since Friday night - went against everything that he had always felt he stood for. Professionalism. Trust. Honesty. Integrity. He felt like he had turned his back on each of those things, and he didn't like feeling that at all.

"Yes," he replied. "This needs to be done. I've wasted police resources already, having told them the lie that I did. Now I need to put it right."

~~~~~

Lincoln walked in and approached the front counter. He didn't know who to talk to, so considered that since he would likely be in news in coming days, he may as well start exactly where he was - at the front counter.

"Can I help you, Sir?" the officer asked.

Lincoln chose his reply carefully.

"I would like to talk to someone about Lexi Montgomery," he said. Instantly he was directed to another officer, who led him into a small room.

"You have some information about Ms. Montgomery?"

"I called you. I'm the person who called the police. It was me who reported her missing," Lincoln started to say, finally feeling a calm come over him. "And I shouldn't have."

The officer looked carefully at the man before him. He knew who he was. Lincoln Kokiri was photographed enough to be familiar to the police.

"Why is that, Mr. Kokiri?"

"She wasn't abducted," Lincoln said and put his head down, letting so many memories flow over him. "She went away, I think … I think to get away from me. I misled the police because, in the moment, I panicked and thought a report on television would force her to come back … to me."

The officer wrote notes as Lincoln talked and talked, telling why he had felt it was a good idea - at the time - to do what he had done.

"She might be afraid of me, and I don't want her to be," Lincoln said. "She's safe from me, but she wasn't abducted."

It seemed like, from that moment, he was there for hours, answering questions of different officers and detectives. Finally, they informed him that they would require him to stay there while they checked out different aspects of his story.

It was right about that time that Alexis was walking into a different police station. She was in a different part of Australia, telling her side of the same story. She was also demonstrating to the police there, the extent to which something had gone seriously wrong somewhere, and made her fall into trance-like states when someone yelled at her.

CHAPTER 10

The Final Chapter

The door to Anthony's home was wide open. All down the front side of it, on and around the door handle, was blood. Alexis went into a panic, immediately thinking that *he* had found him. Lincoln must have learned about Anthony helping her, and had sent someone to come after him. She ran into the house, not caring if it was considered polite or not.

"Anthony?" she yelled while making her way into his home. She looked into every room from the front of the house to the rear as she ran down the hallway.

When she finally approached the kitchen, suddenly he was right there. He stood at the end of the hallway in front of her, looking at her.

"Allie?" Anthony asked, wondering if he wasn't seeing things.

Alexis saw he was using one of his hands to hold the other hand, which was wrapped in a towel. There was dark red blood all over both of his wrists. She rushed forward and took his hands in hers.

"What happened?" she asked. She could tell Anthony was in slight shock at the sight of her. "Where is all the blood coming from?"

"You came back," he said.

Alexis noticed he was extremely pale. He didn't seem to be thinking straight. She realised that for once she needed to be strong so he could lean on her.

"Anthony, you're bleeding … a lot! Come and sit down at the table," she said. He followed her instruction. Immediately she unwrapped the hand and saw a long knife cut across the palm. "What happened to your hand?"

Anthony felt like he was in a dream at first, but then seemed to finally return to normal and look down at his hand.

"I just cut myself when I was trying to cut back the rose bushes out front. It isn't too bad. It looks worse than it is," he said, looking at her again. He remained seated as she stood beside him, leaning over him to look closer at his hand.

Alexis sensed him looking at her and turned her head to look at him. At the same time, she leaned in to touch her lips to his before pulling away just as quickly.

Anthony watched her as she took the towel and rinsed it in the kitchen sink, then brought it back and started to wash both of his hands clean of the blood. He sat quietly as his eyes moved back and forth between her face and what she was doing to his hand. He could smell her. He didn't know what gave her that scent - perhaps her deodorant - but it was a smell he liked.

It had only been a couple of weeks since he had last seen her. As she stood over him, he thought about how much he'd missed her. She had blown through his home so briefly. Despite it having been only two nights that she'd stayed, the length of time didn't matter. As soon as he had returned home after their nights away together, his home had felt empty without her. In some part of his mind, he knew that she was meant to be in his house with him. She belonged there.

He thought about the many things she had going on. There were so many stresses she had to deal with. It wouldn't be fair to put any pressure on her. He resolved that he wouldn't even do anything that she could simply *perceive* to be pressure.

Although his mind was racing with thoughts, he sat silently, not wanting to say anything.

"There. The cut's clean, but do you have some kind of disinfectant cream?" Alexis asked him, not certain whether he needed medical treatment or not.

"Yes," he said softly, hardly without any voice, he was so speechless at her being there with him. "In the cabinet in the bathroom."

Alexis walked into the bathroom, unaware of how at home she felt in the house. Her mind was consumed with worry for him. She could still visualise the moment she'd seen the blood on the front door. She shuddered at the horrific thoughts that had immediately crossed her mind.

Looking in the cabinet, she spotted the cream and grabbed some gauze squares she saw there also, along with medical tape. Quickly she walked back into the kitchen.

Straight away, Anthony saw her walk efficiently and confidently to him and pull up a chair beside him. She was unbearably close to him. He watched as she went to work, holding his hand firmly while caressing the cream into the cut, before placing the gauze over it and securing it firmly with the tape.

All the while, he became aware of her leg touching his under the table. He could feel the warmth coming through their jeans, from her to him. Although he didn't want to acknowledge it, he could feel arousal from her closeness. He closed his eyes and thought of anything else that he could, to stop his body reacting. He didn't want to go there. He didn't want *them* to go there. He especially didn't want her to *think* that he wanted them to go there.

Alexis looked at her handiwork and hoped it would suffice. When she was fairly certain the cut wasn't actively bleeding anymore, she took a moment to catch her breath and look closely at him.

When she looked at his face, she saw him looking right back at her, his eyes looking directly into hers. She had felt confident in her decision about travelling to see him. Now she felt nervous, wondering if she was welcome.

Anthony looked at her and found himself not just pleased that she had come back to visit him, but almost ecstatic. His heart was beating loudly in his chest, but he couldn't think of anything to say to her.

"Perhaps I can make us both a cup of coffee. Would you like one?" she asked him.

She saw him nod slowly, not taking his eyes off her. She smiled at him before standing up and moving over to the bench once more. The two of them said nothing to each other as she prepared the coffee. Instead, they silently watched one another in and around her doing what she had to do with the cups.

When she sat down again and pushed his cup toward him, she realised she had surprised him - a *lot.*

"Is it okay for me to be here?" she asked timidly, snapping him out of his trance.

"Yes!" Anthony said forcefully. When he realised how he'd spoken, he looked at her and changed his tone. "Allie, yes! I am so glad you're here," he said more quietly. He waited to see if the sound of his voice had triggered anything. "Are you alright?"

Alexis laughed at him softly as she reached out to take his good hand in hers.

"I am. I actually feel really good. I haven't 'zoned' since you left, Anthony. I think I'm okay," she said, the instance at the police station discarded from her memory.

Anthony hoped that she was right. He also didn't want to be complacent about that, especially if it was his voice that triggered the periods where her mind seemed to take her elsewhere.

"How have you been?" she asked him tentatively, blushing at the intensity of his stare.

Anthony saw her nervousness and purposely looked down, pulling his hand back so he could lift his cup.

"I've been fine, except for this," he said, holding up the injured hand. "I just wanted to cut those rose bushes back, but I wasn't concentrating on what I was doing, and I let the saw slip."

Alexis watched his face. She could see him clearly as a man now - not that he wasn't a man before; she just hadn't wanted to see him in that way previously. She still wasn't ready to think about intimacy - not with anyone - but she could acknowledge, at least, that he was a man … an attractive man … a *good* man.

"Are you staying?" Anthony asked quietly, trying to find the balance between letting her know he would like her to, but at the same time not sounding like he was pressuring her to.

"I would like to … if I can," Alexis replied, nodding. "If that's not okay, I think today the train goes back this afternoon…"

"No!" he said, again more forcefully than he meant. Immediately he looked closely at her to see if it had affected her, but relaxed when he saw that it hadn't. "No, Allie, please stay. The house has seemed so empty without you here."

The words were welcome to Alexis. She was safe with him, not only because he was a good person who wouldn't abuse her in any way, but also because she knew he had things to work through before he would get involved with someone. There was safety in that for her. It was a warm promise of security.

"Alright," she said, smiling at him. "Thank you. Can we sit in the lounge, to talk more comfortably?" she asked him. She didn't miss the surprise on his face before he stuttered a reply.

"Yeah … of course."

Anthony saw her stand up and start walking without waiting for him to go first. He smiled to himself. It was a good sign that she was well on her way to healing.

They settled on the sofa together, facing each other. Both felt the mixture of excitement, eagerness, and nervousness.

"Tell me what has been happening with you," he said to her.

Alexis happily began talking. She had never been very conversational, but was finding that she didn't mind it so much as time passed. It wasn't as hard as she had always thought it must be.

"After you left, I went to the police station and talked to them. I had to tell them his name, which I hadn't wanted to do," she started and paused before continuing. "They'd already guessed anyway, but it felt wrong for me to talk about him. I gave them as little information as I could to satisfy their questions. But then, before I left, they told me that he'd gone to them himself, and told them he lied about me having been taken by force."

Anthony nodded at her, remembering that day.

"I saw the news that night, reporting he'd done that," he said.

Alexis looked at him, wondering what he thought of her for having gone through what she had, and staying in that situation for so long. She disregarded the consideration. She knew Anthony didn't judge her.

"After that, I was lucky to find a job, which I do really like," Alexis continued. "The people there are nice."

"You look different, Allie," Anthony said. Reaching his hand out, he took hers in his, not feeling awkward or wrong about doing so. "You look ... different ... happy."

Alexis looked at their two hands entwined. There was no discomfort in sitting like that.

"I do feel happy, and I feel very different, Anthony. I think I have you to thank for that," she said, looking up into his face. She saw him look directly into her eyes once again.

Anthony pushed aside a natural desire that was creeping up on him - a natural pull to kiss her. It was there, but he didn't want it. Instead, he held out his arms and welcomed her into them. He was glad to see and feel her move against him and just relax in his arms.

The feeling was one of comfort and companionship. Alexis loved that she could feel that way with him. It was so different from what she'd had with Lincoln. Even at the start of her relationship with him, when he'd been far more relaxed, there had been little of anything so simple as just cuddling.

"I've really missed you," she said to him, not afraid to admit it. "I hope that's okay."

Anthony sat quietly and didn't say anything, even though he felt his heart happy at the words.

Alexis didn't prompt him in any way to say anything. Instead, she just cuddled more against him and rested. It was enough that she was with him, and that he knew how happy she was to be.

~~~~~

"Your room is still made up," Anthony said to her as the evening arrived. They were settled on the sofa again after having eaten dinner and watched a movie together.

He saw her turn and look at him. He wasn't sure, but he thought it might be a look of expectation on her face. In response, he said nothing.

Alexis smiled at him. There was a natural desire growing in her for him, but she would respect his need to take the time that he wanted, to recover from the grief of losing Cynthia. One thing she had determined, having spent the previous two weeks alone, was that she wouldn't rush into anything with any man again. When she was next in a relationship, it wouldn't all be one way. She wouldn't bow down to the next person who caught her eye. Whoever came into her life next, would have to be as set on a 50/50 relationship as she was. She would work harder at giving and receiving. She would always say no when it was something she didn't want.

"Thank you. I think I will turn in now," she said, pulling away from him. "Are you working in the morning?" she asked and saw him shake his head.

"No, I am all yours tomorrow. Do with me what you will," he said,
~~~~~

feeling relaxed enough to tease her. He saw her laugh in understanding that he wasn't seriously suggesting anything sexual.

~~~~~

As she lay in bed, Alexis felt happy. It was a strange sensation in her. She hadn't always been unhappy, but the unique feelings of happiness and true contentment had somehow eluded her for most of her life.

She was in Anthony's home for two nights. That was the time she'd have before she had to get back to work. She liked the way it felt to be in his home again. She'd also liked the way it had felt being in his arms, talking to him, knowing that when she spoke, he intently listened and was interested in what she had to say.

It was easy to go to sleep with that peace of mind.

~~~~~

Down the hallway, Anthony lay in his bed, very aware that she was in his home once again. He could almost feel her presence two doors down, but he wouldn't act, no matter what his body was trying to tell him to do. He did believe they could build a great friendship over time. She would become a valued part of his life if he let her, but he couldn't yet think beyond friendship. He knew two years was, in some people's eyes, too long to grieve after someone died, but he would take as long as it took.

He felt tears begin as he remembered Cynthia again. As time passed, he thought about her less often, but when he did, he brought himself to tears. It still felt unbearable thinking about how much he had loved her, and how much he missed her.

No, he wasn't over her yet, and until he was, he wouldn't be moving forward - not with anyone. It just wouldn't be fair to him or her.

~~~~~

Waking up with the sunlight trying to make its way through the curtain, Alexis felt like she was home. She hadn't yet found a permanent home in the city where she was working. The landlady of the guest house had offered her a good rate if she stayed longer-term so she had stayed there for the meantime. It was convenient to her work, and it was easy.

In Anthony's home, she did enjoy the feeling of homeliness. It was nice waking up in the bed she was in, in the room she was in, in his house.

As she lay in bed, contemplating getting up, she heard a door down the hallway open, and then Anthony's voice as he walked down and into the bathroom. Alexis smiled to herself as she realised that he was kind of humming and kind of singing. After she heard the shower start up, he began *really* singing. It lasted only a few minutes before the bathroom door opened once more and the humming passed by her door again. It made Alexis giggle. She couldn't help it.

"Is that you laughing at me, Missy?" she heard him call out to her as
~~~~~

his voice moved down the hallway further. "Pancakes for breakfast if you hurry, but only if you tell me what a good singer I am!"

Alexis jumped out of bed and ran into the bathroom to have a quick shower. To her relief, there was no instance of a trance. So far it seemed to have left her. She refused to take it for granted that it was completely gone. She did still expect that something might trigger it. For the moment, however, she tried not to dwell on it, and only felt like she was building in confidence and developing as a person.

~~~~~

Anthony was already cooking the pancakes when he saw her walk into the kitchen. As much as he didn't want to, he enjoyed the sight when she entered. She seemed to have ditched the old second-hand clothing, and now wore new clothes. Not only that but they were feminine clothes, designed to show off her figure. When she had arrived the previous day, she'd had jeans and a jersey on, and he hadn't thought about it. Now that she wore a sundress and a cardigan, she looked so different from when he'd first met her that she almost could have been a completely different person.

Alexis saw the look on his face. For a fleeting moment, she couldn't decide if she liked him looking at her like that or not. She knew there was no reason to fear Anthony looking at her with desire. A part of her had thought she *wanted* him to look at her like that, but seeing the look was different than just thinking about it. Suddenly she became aware that perhaps she also wasn't ready to move on with someone into physical intimacy after all.

It was a period of quiet for both as they each made their own observations. After a long while, Anthony broke the silence. It was something he felt had to be done.

"Were you laughing at my singing, Allie?" he asked with a light-hearted tone in his voice as he pointed a large wooden spoon toward her. "Think carefully before you answer because I hold the batter to your pancakes."

Alexis laughed at him, pleased he could use humour when it was needed to break an awkward or serious moment.

"Hmm, perhaps I'll keep quiet and just get us some plates and some coffee, shall I?" she teased him back. The grin she received in return was magnificent.

~~~~~

"When do you think you'll head back?" Anthony asked her as they started eating their breakfast. "You can stay as long as you want to. You know that, right?"

Alexis looked at him, thankful that of all the people who could have approached her when she was so vulnerable that day, he was the one who had.

"I have to go back on the train tomorrow afternoon, to go back to work the morning after that." As she said it, she saw a moment of seriousness cast over his face. The sight touched her. "What do you usually do on your days off? Other than rescuing damsels in distress, I mean."

Anthony smiled at her, the serious moment past.

"I begin wars with rose bushes, can't you tell?" he said and laughed. "Usually there is a bit to do around here with the garden, and there's always maintenance to be done. That stuff keeps me busy enough on my days off."

He paused for a while, looking at her and watching her while she ate. As he looked at her, he remembered how difficult it had been to watch her eat when he'd first met her. The way she would cut everything into tiny little pieces had seemed strange. It was easy to see she'd relaxed and was now a much better eater, with a healthy appetite. That showed in her face and body. She had been too slender when he had first met her. The dress she currently wore showed that her body and face were both starting to fill out with a more healthy shape - and more curves.

"Although, if we have the same days off, I could be tempted to catch a train five hours up the line," he said, watching her face to see how she would react to the idea.

Alexis stopped and looked at him.

"Really?" she asked, feeling timid all of a sudden. "You would want to do that?"

"Yeah, of course I would," Anthony replied, grinning. "I miss our sleepovers. Do you still have the same room, with the two beds?"

She nodded, smiling broadly. "I do."

"And would you still promise not to peak?"

Alexis laughed out loud.

"Well, I can't promise that … but I do promise to *try*," she said.

"That sounds acceptable," Anthony said. "Now, what would you like to do today?"

~~~~~

They spent the day together, pottering in the garden and then watching movies in the evening. Alexis felt nervous as bedtime got closer. Anthony hadn't said anything to make her nervous, but throughout the day, now and then she remembered the way he'd looked at her when she had entered the kitchen that morning.

Thinking about it through the whole day, she knew she didn't want to be sexual with anyone yet. She possibly wouldn't want that for a long while. Studying him as he watched a movie with her, she knew inside of her that he wasn't going to try that - not for a long while, anyway.
~~~~~

Primarily he was her friend, and she wanted to be just as good a friend to him. That was enough.

"I'm going to head off to bed, Allie," Anthony said as he hugged her. "I'll see you in the morning."

Alexis watched him walk off to his room before she made her way to hers. She smiled to herself. Being in Anthony's house was okay. Spending time with a man and not sharing her body with him was okay. It was *more* than okay. It was nice.

~~~~~

Alexis was in her guest house room twenty-four hours later. As she closed her door, she felt a sliver of loneliness at being on her own again. At the same time, she appreciated that she *could* be alone without someone invading her space.

The next day at work, she felt invigorated. She felt alive, compared to how she had been in the years before. In five days, Anthony was going to jump on a train and visit her on her next days off. She felt excited in anticipation of that.

When she was almost finished work for the day, a woman came through checkout and shocked Alexis when she said, "You are her. You are the one I shared my husband with for three years."

Alexis didn't have to look up from the scanning she was doing of the woman's items, to know who was standing in front of her. She took her time and kept scanning. She tried hard to not look up, but after a period of silence, found herself curious.

When she raised her eyes, she saw before her an extremely wealthy woman. Everything about her oozed money and power. She was like a female version of *him*, Alexis thought to herself.

"I must thank you," the woman continued. "After you disappeared, and the police became involved, I learned a lot, not only about you but also about the things he made you do to him. You must be a strong woman. I couldn't have done anything like that, but I know how intimidating he can be. You doing it for him, saved me from being asked to, I suppose, so I don't harbour any resentment toward you, Lexi. In a way, you saved me, but I am sorry that you went through what you did," the woman said.

As Alexis looked into the woman's eyes, she was surprised to find herself believing her sincerity.

"I hope that you have now found happiness," the woman said. "I've moved on from him too. He and I both agreed that he obviously needs something … different. Keep happy, Lexi, and stay strong. There is life beyond Lincoln Kokiri … for both of us."

The woman then walked out. That was the first and last time Alexis ever met Diana Kokiri.
~~~~~

~~~~~

"Really?" Anthony asked her as they lay in their beds in the guest house on his next visit to see her.

Alexis had just relayed to him what Diana had said to her. He was enjoying listening to her speak. It hadn't escaped his attention that she now spoke with animation, like she was a completely different person from when he had met her.

"How incredible, and unexpected," he continued. "Were you afraid when you realised who she was, though?"

"I was frozen," Alexis replied. "I didn't know what she might do there in the store. I mean, it's my workplace. I don't know if she was sincere. I have doubts that she could be, really, but it doesn't matter. That chapter is over with now."

"But why do you think she happened to be in your supermarket?" Anthony asked. "Of all cities and all supermarkets. Do you think that she knew you were there and came to find you?"

Alexis had thought about that also. Anthony saw a worried look cross over her face.

"I don't know," Alexis said. "It does seem a huge coincidence that she would walk into the supermarket I'm working in. It isn't even in her city."

They both lay silent, similar thoughts going through each of their heads.

"But what if you saw *him* again, Allie? What do you think you would do then?"

Alexis took time to think about that, just as she had done many times in recent weeks.

"I would hope I'm a stronger person now, but I guess I'll never know."

No more was said after that, but Alexis lay awake long into the night, even after she heard Anthony's breathing change, indicating he had found sleep. She didn't want to be, but she was worried about whether Diana would tell Lincoln where she was - and whether he would come after her. She found reassurance that at least now the police would believe her if something happened - probably.

~~~~~

The next morning, Anthony prepared to catch the train back to his hometown. Regret was heavy in his heart. He had spent two nights with Alexis again, doing their established 'sleepover' thing, which he did enjoy. They'd seen a movie together, eaten out together, and talked a lot.

Now that they could be open about being together, and didn't have to hide from the outside world, Alexis openly walked with him to the train station to see him off right at the train, rather than him leaving her in the guest house.

She walked beside him in the approach to the train, trying to will her mind to not think sad thoughts. He was a good friend. That was something to celebrate, not be upset about in any way.

When they reached the platform, Anthony turned to her and put his arms around her, before kissing her on her forehead, as he always did. He held her just a bit longer and a bit tighter than he had previously.

Alexis relished the feeling. She would never push him to do what he didn't want to, but she openly admitted to both of them how much she liked being in his arms. She didn't want to hide that.

"I have to go, Allie, but I'll see you in a couple of weeks, right? You'll still come down and stay with me?" he asked, looking into her face and seeing her nod. He didn't miss the sad smile on her face.

"I will. Definitely," Alexis replied.

When Anthony looked closely at her at that moment, he knew his heart was finally mending from Cynthia's death. With that realisation, he reached up to touch her cheek before leaning in to softly kiss her lips. He wasn't quite there yet, but he knew he was close to being ready to move on. He knew Alexis was ready too. He would never push her, but he knew how she felt. She hadn't been in any way demanding toward him, but she had gently let him know how she felt, and what she would like.

As he pulled away, he saw the surprise on her face. He could also see determination. She had the look of determination to accept the kiss for what it was, and not react or overreact to it.

Alexis pulled right back and smiled at him.

"Have a safe trip home, Anthony," she said. "I will see you again soon."

~~~~~

Two weeks later, Alexis was on the train herself, looking forward to seeing him, but also apprehensive as she didn't know what the kiss had meant - if anything. She resolved to let him lead. If nothing immediately happened, before she left to again, she would ask him directly if he wanted things to change. She wouldn't go on forever, wishing he would just tell her. She would never again want any man to tell her what he wanted her to do.

Anthony was waiting on the platform of the train station when she stepped down from the carriage. It surprised her as he hadn't done that before. Previously she'd walked up to his home before seeing him.

Immediately upon seeing her, Anthony walked up to her and put his arms around her. He kissed her lightly and quickly on the lips before pulling away and guiding her in their walking.

"I want to take you somewhere new," he said softly.

Alexis nodded and let him lead the way. Half an hour later, she found herself being guided into a cemetery. In her gut, she understood where they might be going.
~~~~~

"Allie, this is Cynthia," Anthony said as he pointed to a young gravestone. "Cynthia, this is Allie," he continued.

Alexis laughed inwardly although she didn't want to do so outwardly. She didn't want any action to seem disrespectful for the love he had lost.

"Cynthia, I've brought Allie here today so you can meet her, because I still love you and I know I'll never forget our time together," he said. He looked intently at Alexis even though his words were directed at his lost love. "But now the time has come for me to move on, and I want to do that with this beautiful woman - Allie."

Alexis felt tears come to her eyes. The way he was speaking, and the way he was talking to her and Cynthia, seemed too beautiful to her. She felt like she shouldn't be a part of it, but remained quiet as he continued.

"Allie, please tell me you feel the same way I do," Anthony said. "If you don't, that's okay. I love ... having you as a friend. Nothing will change."

Anthony saw her break down and begin to weep. Briefly, he considered he might have misread her feelings. Although she didn't speak, he finally saw her nodding at him while she turned away and tried to hide her tears. Instinctively he pulled her close and held her against him.

They stood together quietly, drawing strength from each other before finally pulling apart.

"I'm still not ready for sexual intimacy, Allie," he said and saw her nod in reply, confirming she might not be there yet either. "But I would really like to keep trying the kissing thing."

Alexis laughed at him. It was such an Anthony thing to say. She nodded again, still speechless. He held her in his arms again before taking her hand in his and guiding her out of the cemetery. They said nothing on the journey back to his home, both feeling nervousness inside of them.

Once in his home, Anthony felt normal and relaxed again. Nothing more was said of a serious nature. It was good for Alexis. She needed to know she wouldn't be forced or pressured into doing something she might not want to, and Anthony was aware of it. It made things easy between them, both working so hard to not pressure the other.

After an afternoon of talking, eating, and spending time in the garden, they settled down on the sofa and watched a movie together. When it finished, Anthony turned it off and they sat together, looking at one another.

"I meant it when I said I can't share that kind of intimacy yet, Allie," Anthony said one more time. He needed to be certain she didn't assume they would sleep together that night.

"I know," Alexis replied, nodding. "I feel the same, Anthony. I don't want to rush. There's no need to…"

Anthony, despite best intentions, could hold back from kissing her no longer. He leaned in and kissed her lips softly again, and again. Slowly he felt her move and change in the intensity of her kissing.

Alexis became aware of it and eased off, desperate to move it back a notch, so they were just beginning their kissing exploration again.

When they pulled apart, she saw from the clock that they had been kissing for an hour. For a whole hour, she had enjoyed his lips on hers, and he hadn't asked her for anything. He hadn't touched her in any other way.

Anthony looked at her during her revelation and saw her smile at him, and then blush. He knew he was going to enjoy moving through that initial phase of their relationship. She was right. There was no need to rush.

"I'm going to go to bed. Your room is made up and ready for you," he said, standing up and kissing her on her forehead before leaving her.

Alexis sat in the living room for a while longer, processing the feeling of having been kissed for so long, before making her way to her bedroom and drifting off to sleep.

~~~~~

Over the following two days, they did much of the same - watched movies, kissed, ate, kissed, gardened … kissed. It was freeing for both of them. Anthony eased into feeling it was alright for him to move on from Cynthia. Alexis felt happy in knowing she could move into another relationship without having to indulge in things she didn't want to. She could take her time and move at a speed that was easy on her.

"I'll come up to see you week after next," Anthony said to her as they stood at the station, ready for her to get on the train that would take her back to her home.

"I look forward to it," Alexis replied. For the first time, she initiated a kiss herself. Looking at his face, she knew it was okay for her to reach up with her hands and pull his face down to hers. She kissed him, openly and without any hiding.

Anthony smiled inwardly at her doing it. He knew it was a big step for her, to be able to be the initiator. He felt a slight sense of pride toward her for starting to move into another level of confidence with him.

They stood together, kissing and holding each other until the conductor announced all passengers needed to be on the train.

After the train was out of sight, Anthony painfully looked forward to the following week and a half passing.

~~~~~

Over the next two months, the routine was established with Anthony travelling to see Alexis for two nights, and then her doing the same.

During that time, they still only kissed, but it felt incredibly safe and right.

On the second night of one of his visits, Anthony walked out of the bathroom after his shower, to find her standing at the window. Alexis had all of the lights off, but the curtains open, allowing the lights of the city to flow into the room. Slowly Anthony walked up behind her, placed his hands on her hips, and moved so his chest was touching her back. Instantly he felt her lean back against him.

Alexis felt his presence and warmth. She'd finally allowed herself to accept that she was calm and safe in his presence. She had nothing to worry about with him. He was a good man. He wouldn't hurt her. He wouldn't ask her to hurt him.

She reached back, took his hands in hers and pulled his arms around her so they rested over her belly. Together they stood like that, looking out over the city.

Anthony knew he was at the point he had needed to reach. He didn't know if she was, and he was afraid of pushing.

Alexis was in the same position. It felt safe and calming with his arms around her like they were. Naturally, she tilted her head, making her hair fall away to one side.

Anthony couldn't help but kiss her neck where it was bare. The kiss was light, but it was enough for him to sense her feelings. He kept kissing her while holding her tight, his mouth moving all over the area of her neck that was exposed skin.

Alexis remained still except for the natural swaying that was happening in her body. Her focus was on the feelings of his lips on her skin. She made no move to get away from that. She wanted him to do that for however long he wanted to. She had no desire to stop him.

Anthony felt himself longing for her. He'd reached the point of wanting and acceptance. He was also very aware of her body and how it was reacting to him kissing her as he was. After a long while, he felt her turn around and face him. He looked at her and waited to see if she really wanted their possible intimacy herself, or if she just wanted to please him. If the latter, he didn't want to move things forward.

He saw her look up at him, then reach up to kiss him on his lips. At that moment, he knew in the depth of his gut that she wasn't doing it to please him. He felt sure that she was kissing him purely because it was something she truly wanted for herself.

Alexis kissed him and indulged in the glorious feelings being produced from having the freedom to kiss him how she wanted.

Together - neither one nor the other pushing more than the other - they both moved back to the bed and lay down. Lying side by side, they kept kissing, letting go of worries and inhibitions. It was time to let the urgency flow over them.

Anthony forced his senses to come back to him. Abruptly he broke away from the kiss, while still holding her as he was.

"I don't have any condoms with me, Allie," he said. "I didn't think … I'm not prepared," he said.

In hearing him say that, Alexis felt happy. It meant he hadn't been presuming anything would happen. She laughed in the happiness of that.

"Neither am I, Anthony," she said. "I'll be prepared next time I see you. For now, can we please just keep kissing?"

Anthony blissfully did as she asked.

A long time later, their kissing eased off, and they lay on top of the bed. Still fully clothed, they looked at each other and held one another tightly.

"Are you sure you're ready?" he asked her, not needing to voice the rest of the words for the question.

"Yes. Are you?" she asked in return.

Anthony nodded and kissed her softly. "I am."

~~~~~

Two weeks later, Allie walked with him into his home and could sense his nervousness as he led her into the kitchen to make coffee. He seemed to be set on doing anything but seeming eager. That made her smile since she also didn't want to appear pushy, regardless of how hungry and desperate she felt to be closer to him.

They sat in the lounge on the sofa, talking while she let her legs rest softly on his. When they had relaxed completely, Anthony pulled her closer.

"How do you feel now?" he asked, again knowing he didn't need to find words for all that he was asking.

Alexis leaned in and kissed him. Together they melted into the kiss, indulging in its pleasurable simplicity for a long time. After they pulled away from each other and could see the honest desire in each other's eyes, she saw Anthony stand up and hold his hand out to her. Alexis gladly took it and let him lead her into his bedroom. She had never seen his bedroom before, and found herself curious as she looked around. It was nice to have a slight distraction, so they could both regain their thoughts without bounding ahead too quickly.

Anthony stood still and watched her looking at different things. He didn't move. In his nervousness, he was happy to just watch and wait. When she had seemingly seen enough, she walked up to him and put her arms around him. He kissed her softly at first, before they moved to the bed once more, kissing heavily.

The equality of it felt different to Alexis. She could feel the power of them both wanting and working toward the same thing together, instead
~~~~~

of one person taking it from the other.

It all flowed naturally, the undressing and lying down together, not rushing. Anthony pulled the covers over them both as he kept kissing her, neither of them moving to touch the other in their most erotic places. That could wait. For the present time, it was a new kind of bliss to simply have the closeness.

Finally, he felt ready for it to move forward. He asked her to kneel over him. When she moved to straddle him to join, he guided her to turn around and kneel over his face. She found herself in a place she'd never been before, feeling his tongue start to explore her, while she could similarly explore him with hers.

Alexis revelled in the feelings. It had been so long since she had felt that pleasure. She hadn't touched herself at all in the time since she'd last been sexual with Lincoln. As she found joy in caressing Anthony with her mouth, she felt a very quick and intense development of feelings inside of her as she felt his tongue exploring and tasting.

Anthony was lost. It had been two years since he'd been physically close to anyone. To be as close as he was, it was like how he imagined heaven to be, nestled under her, experiencing her shimmering against his mouth as he felt and heard her orgasm. He could feel himself simultaneously reaching a point he also hadn't been to in a long while. He remained still after she climaxed, focusing on the feelings she was producing in him. Soon he found himself reaching and going over the final point of no return, letting himself release into her mouth.

They lay like that for a while, neither in a hurry to move. Eventually, Alexis pulled off him. She turned around to look at him and kiss his lips.

Anthony kissed her passionately. His desire had been let loose after two years of confinement. His body was screaming to keep going. It wanted and needed to do more.

Alexis felt like she couldn't get enough of his kissing. The depth of it, and the way his lips and tongue moved against her, were erotic and sensual. His hands were all over her as he moved with her, their bodies not joined but still somehow in sync, moving against each other.

Finally, she pulled away from him, just to look at his face. She had to make sure there wasn't anything dark there. All she saw was a man who was enjoying her company, exactly as she was enjoying his.

"Are you alright?" Anthony asked, glad to take a moment of respite in what felt like a huge urgency inside of him.

Alexis gave him a brilliant smile and nodded before kissing him again. They kept doing that for a long time until he was highly aroused not only in mind, but in body too. She watched him as he put a condom on, and then leaning down to kiss her, asked her one more time if she was alright.

"I am, Anthony - very much so," she replied before she felt him kiss her and slowly slide inside her, making them both gasp at the feeling.

Anthony let himself go. He didn't need to keep wondering if it was what she wanted. Without any doubt, he knew that it was. He let himself go into his own world for a moment, concentrating on how it felt to be joined with her, before he felt his body convulse and release. When he opened his eyes and saw her studying his face, he smiled at her.

He pulled out and discarded the condom before lying down beside her and putting his arms around her. Leaning in and kissing her, his fingers trailed down and started caressing her clitoris while he explored her mouth with his tongue. A short time later she exploded once again, this time against his hand.

Their two nights together were spent in the same way. He let her choose where she wanted to sleep. On both nights, she chose to sleep with him, not having slept beside anyone all night for so many years. It was a comfortable way to spend the nights, with his body wrapped around hers all night long.

Anthony loved the warmth that came from her.

When it was time for her to leave to venture home, he kissed her deeply on the station platform.

"I'll see you soon, Allie," he said to her.

Alexis could vividly sense the sadness coming off him.

"You will," she replied and kissed him as deeply back before turning and climbing up into the train carriage.

She thought about him all the way home, considering where they could go as a couple. She also wondered if he would have any regrets between then and the next time they were due to see each other.

In the core of her gut, she also sadly wondered if she would ever see him again.

~~~~~

The next morning, Alexis made her way to work and got herself set up at the checkout counter. She served a woman with a small toddler. Alexis smiled at the little boy sitting up on the shopping trolley. She was getting good at talking to people, she was thinking to herself as she engaged in conversation with the mother and the child. When all groceries were packed into the shopping trolley and the payment processed, she followed them with her eyes as they were leaving. She didn't hesitate in giving the little boy a big wave and smile as they walked out. Her focus was on that way - to the left - to the exit. She wasn't watching the direction customers approached the checkout counters from - the right.

All of a sudden, she felt the hairs on her arms and the back of her neck stand up on end as she heard the familiar voice. The voice. *His*
~~~~~

voice. It was spoken at a normal volume. It wasn't a whisper. It wasn't a shout. Regardless of volume, it directly linked into her brain, like an electric shock passing through her.

"Lexi."

She remembered briefly that when she'd first met Anthony, she had thought his voice was similar. Now she could easily hear the difference. Even if she hadn't noticed the slight difference, in her gut she would have known that the owner of the voice wasn't Anthony. Even though she wasn't looking at him - not even looking in his direction - she could feel him.

For a moment, Alexis stood still, not moving her body, not moving her head. She could feel her body willing itself to do as it had always done - drop down to the floor and wait for an instruction. It was a pull inside of her, like an automated response. She could feel it deep within her, even without having heard that voice for so long.

But something had changed inside of her. It seemed easier to find the strength and determination to fight it. She slowly pulled her body even more upright, raised and turned her head, and looked directly at him.

She noted briefly that he was still immaculately dressed. Although it hadn't been that long since she'd last seen him, he looked slightly greyer around his temples. He also had dark areas under his eyes, as if he hadn't had a good sleep in a very long time. Even so, he still had the same overpowering presence and a strong aura of power emanating from him. To Alexis, the look on his face and in his eyes could not have possibly been any more intense or intimidating.

She stood her ground, determined to look confident even though that was exactly the opposite of how she was feeling. Her legs felt like jelly, desiring to give in and fall to the ground - trying to encourage her to do so. She could feel her heart more than beating inside her chest. It was thumping heavily. She wondered silently if anyone in the immediate area would be able to hear it.

But what she saw most clearly as she looked directly at him, was that by doing so, she had startled him. For a moment, he seemed confused, like he didn't understand how she could stand so tall and look at him in such a way.

Alexis gathered further strength and finally spoke, not faltering in her stare directly into his eyes. It was a bold move as she made a very solid point to him that she would not now - nor ever again - call him by the name he had always instructed her to.

"Mr. Kokiri..."

~~~~~~~~~~~~~~~~

The End
~~~~~~~~~~~~~~~~

DARKNESS OF HEART

~~ Book Two ~~

CHAPTER 1

The Reunion

Lincoln Kokiri saw her from far away as he partially hid himself behind the end of the grocery aisle, down the far end of the supermarket. In direct view of the checkout area, it was his first glimpse of her in more than three months. The discovery made his heart pound heavily in his chest.

From where he hid, he watched her and saw her greet a mother and a child. Even from where he stood, he could clearly see her facial expressions. His attention was captivated as he watched her smile and laugh at something the mother said. He saw her wave and smile at the small child. She looked relaxed. She looked happy. He remembered her being like that when he'd first started to pursue her. He couldn't remember her looking like that in more recent times.

She looked like she was chatting as she packed groceries for the woman in front of her. He could hardly remember her talking to him in such an easy-going manner at all. During their three years together, had she even *had* the ability to talk so easily?

He took a moment to rejoice in the revelation that at last, he had found her. Finally, she was no longer just some figure from his past. She wasn't just a dream that he recently had found himself wondering was real or imaginary in his head. Lately, he'd noticed there was so much haziness inside of his mind. Now and then he'd found himself wondering what was real in his memory, and what was only perception - what he *wanted* to be true.

But now there she was, directly in front of him. She was within reach. She was almost within his grasp. He licked his lips at the possibilities that he realised had become available to him once again.

He saw her finish packing the groceries into the woman's shopping trolley, and then start to process the payment. He looked around to see how many other customers might be making their way to checkout. It pleased him to see that due to it being early in the morning, there were few people in the store at all.

He watched as the woman started to walk away. He saw Lexi turn her head turn toward the exit and give the young child another wave. She was focused on them still. There was no-one else in line.

It was time.

~~~~~

He walked briskly from the end of the supermarket he had been concealed in, up to the checkout area. He could see Alexis continue to watch and wave to the young child. As he swiftly moved toward her, he could sense the level of happiness she had inside of her. She had put on weight, too, he noticed as he moved closer still. Even in the dull, shapeless supermarket uniform that she had on, he could see that her body had taken on more shape since the last time he had seen her. Her face was rounder and, overall, she looked far healthier.

She hadn't yet turned back to his direction when he finally reached her checkout counter. He watched her face as he moved closer. On it, he could almost see her *sense* that he was there. She had stopped smiling, but she stood still, with a look of determination to keep watching the direction the mother and child had gone. To her left. Through the exit.

Lincoln almost lost his nerve. He almost turned and walked back the way he had come. She hadn't seen him yet. It wasn't too late to pretend he'd never been there. He knew he was fooling himself in that. Deep inside of him, he suspected that she did already know he was right there, within reach of her.

Finally, he found the courage to speak.

"Lexi," he said. He was desperate to keep his voice steady and not betray how nervous he was, or how *aroused* he was.

He held his breath, desperate for her to turn and look at him. He needed her to show him how much she had missed him. How much she loved him. How happy she was to see him. How much she regretted having run away from him.

For a moment, he thought she was going to faint. It looked as if her legs tried to buckle underneath her. He felt panic stream through his veins, like he understood the effect he had on her. He didn't want to put her through that.

As he focused on her, he saw her body do the opposite of what it had looked like it wanted to do. She became more upright as her back straightened. When she turned to face him, he saw her eyes connect directly with his.

There were many things he had dreamed he would see on her face when he finally found her, and she saw him again. None of them was what he saw on her face at that moment. The look she was giving him was completely *unfathomable*.

He saw her eyes move over his face, up to his hair, down to his neck, but then settle on his eyes once again. He felt like he was undergoing an important appraisal. Whatever test he was being subjected to, he desperately wanted to pass. He had been searching for her for what seemed like far too long. He was frantic with the need for her to want
~~~~~

him again.

Looking deeply into her eyes, he saw something so different from what he had seen before. It was like a new confidence - almost a rebellion. She oozed a determination inside of her to stand her ground and show him how strong she was - to show what strength she had recently discovered inside of her, without *him* in her life.

Lincoln felt confused. It wasn't the reaction and greeting he had expected. She wasn't falling at his feet, wanting to do whatever he wanted her to do. She wasn't falling at his feet, wanting to *please* him. It flustered him. That was a feeling he wasn't used to. He was always confident and self-assured, and even when he wasn't, he could always present himself as being so.

It must have only been seconds since he'd approached, but it felt to him like things were moving in slow motion. He saw every little reaction in her body to knowing he was there. He thought he could almost see every thought that passed through her mind. It didn't feel like seconds. It felt like a lifetime.

Seeing her start to speak, he hung on for hearing her say his name again. She was one of the few people who had ever had the confidence to call him by his first name. That in itself had long ago separated her from so many other people he had to deal with every single day. He loved how she said his first name. He had never wanted her to call him by anything else. It was like his first name had always been meant to be used by her, and her alone.

In slow motion, he saw her lips part. He waited with joy to hear the name escape her lips. It wasn't what he heard at all.

"Mr. Kokiri."

He had to take a moment to process what he had just heard. She wouldn't call him *that.* She had *never* called him that. That name was what everyone else used to address him - his business associates, his employees, the media. No, that wasn't the name she was supposed to use, and she knew it. She *knew* it.

They stared at each other for a long while before Lincoln became aware that someone else had appeared in line behind him. Even with it being a competitor supermarket to the businesses he owned, he would never intentionally create havoc in a competing company. He wouldn't hold up the queue for no reason, and at that moment, he presented no reason at all to be in the checkout area. Having no groceries, he felt like a time-waster. He was standing in the line when other people needed to buy their groceries and then move on with all the other things they would have to do in their day.

Quickly he grabbed a handful of items that were on display at the checkout counter. He didn't even look at them. He didn't care what they were. Their only purpose was to pretend that he was going through checkout for a reason - for *any* reason other than why he really was there.

He handed the items to Alexis. As he pulled out his wallet, he watched her immediately move on in her checkout operator duties, as if he were any other customer, on any other day.

~~~~~

Alexis pulled herself together quickly, seeing there was someone else in line. She had no desire to cause any kind of scene or any delay to their day.

She saw Lincoln grab a handful of chocolate bars and hand them to her. It made her silently laugh inside at the absurdity of that. He was a professional, not only in his work, but also in the ongoing and in-depth maintenance of his body. There was no way he would ever eat a bar of chocolate.

As she scanned the items, she kept her eyes lowered, as she would do if he were any other customer. She could have stood there, maintaining eye contact, but it wasn't a natural action to take when scanning groceries. She had to appear normal. She just wanted the moment to be over.

She rang the process through the cash register and said out loud the total sum required from him. She watched as he reached into his wallet and pulled out a $50 note. His hand extended out toward her with the note inside of it.

For a brief moment, she felt herself pulling back away from his hand. It was a natural reaction for her to have, but she had to do her job. At that moment, he was a customer who needed to pay for their grocery items. She knew that *wasn't* what he was, but it was what they both had to *pretend* he was.

She reached out and took the cash, being careful not to let her hand or fingers touch his. She had played through different versions of such a moment in her head many times. She had considered how she would feel if she ever saw him again - what she would *do*. She knew now that, in some ways, she hadn't really prepared for the moment at all. It wasn't how she had imagined it would be if she once again came face to face with him. It wasn't what she had wanted to *believe* things would be like if they saw each other again.

And yet, she did feel an inner strength that she might not have had before. Perhaps the preparation in her mind had worked somewhat, after all.

She moved on with the transaction, processing the payment and assembling the change in her hand. She kept her eyes on his hand as she counted the change back to him and gave him his receipt. In her mind, she had to keep trying to deceive herself, just to get through the
~~~~~

transaction. The hand was not his. The hand was not *him*. The hand before her belonged to just another customer, passing by her as so many did every single day that she was at work in the supermarket.

~~~~~

Lincoln watched her hand move toward his. He held his hand still, even though he could feel his body trembling all over. As she voiced the counting of the change into his hand, he raised his eyes and studied her face. He listened to her voice. He'd missed her voice. She had never said a great deal in their times together, but it was still a voice that he loved and missed.

When she had put the change and the receipt into his hand, he saw her raise her eyes to him.

"Would you like a bag, Mr. Kokiri?" she asked.

Lincoln found himself trying to think of ways to delay having to leave. He wanted to think of a way of extending the moment right out, so that they could stay right there, together, and not be apart again.

He sensed she was waiting. Once again, he considered the person who was waiting behind him. He could see the line was growing longer with more people in it.

"No, thank you," he said as he put his cash away in his wallet. His hands were shaking visibly. He gathered up the purchased items into his hand and looked at Alexis one more time before he knew he would have to leave. "It's good to see you again."

He'd hoped to hear her voice one more time, but she didn't reply. In her eyes, he didn't see any kind of recognition or enthusiasm for him being there in front of her. He stayed another couple of seconds to give her the chance to let him know that she wanted to see him again. That she wanted to spend time with him. That she wanted to hear about how he had been. That she *wanted* him.

Instead, she stood still, already moving her eyes to the next customer in line. Lincoln saw her smile broadly at that person. She hadn't smiled like that at him. She had been polite, and she had been professional, but she hadn't smiled.

Resigned to the failure of his first meeting with her since she'd left Melbourne - since she'd run away from *him* - Lincoln finally walked out of the supermarket and headed to his rental car.

~~~~~

On his journey, Lincoln hadn't brought his driver with him, or any other staff member. He had flown in to the small airport nearby, hired a rental car, and was driving himself around. The city had limited accommodation, but he had located a small 3-star motel that would serve his purpose while he was here. He didn't need luxury. He just needed privacy and peace, to think … to plan … to prepare.

When he had flown in, he had already known where she was, of course. His efforts to keep trying to find her had already paid off. For more than a month, he had known which city she was living in, and where she worked. He hadn't acted immediately when he'd heard the news. He had forced himself to take time to think and to assess. He'd needed time to consider all the different ways things could go, depending on all the different ways he could act in those first few minutes of the two of them meeting again.

He had thought it would be best to approach her in her work. By doing that, she wouldn't be able to run away at first sight of him. She possibly wouldn't even be able to ignore him, or say anything negative to him. It was still in his mind that she had run away from Melbourne to get away from him. He had thought it best that, at the moment that she first saw him again, she not be in a situation where she could easily run and hide.

~~~~~

In the carpark outside the supermarket, Lincoln sat in his rental car. He had travelled there to find her. To see her. To make sure she saw *him*. Yes, he had considered it best to see her at her work so she couldn't run away from him, but he hadn't thought hard enough about that situation. She couldn't walk out with him. She couldn't take him to a private area of the supermarket to talk. She couldn't even go out to his car with him. No, the plan he'd formulated hadn't been a sufficient one to result in success.

It made him flustered. He made business decisions every week that were worth millions of dollars. That took dedicated skills in analysis and problem-solving. He was a professional at it, and he never failed at it. As always, when it came to Lexi, with her it was different. Always when it came to her, he just couldn't think straight. Always he felt like he was looking at a puzzle that he couldn't solve, or a decision that he couldn't make. It had been that way since the day he had met her. He did not know why he kept forgetting it.

The question running around in his head was what to do next. He had put so many hours in to tracking her down. He had put so much time into finding her. The least she could do was talk to him. Listen to him. Hear what he wanted to say to her. What he *needed* to say to her. What he needed her to *hear*.

He sat in the car for a long time, not starting it up or moving. He felt a sense of déjà vu and knew why. He had done the same thing before, that day more than three years earlier. But things were different now, he argued with himself silently. At that time, he'd just had to meet her, to start to get to know her. Now he loved her. He was meant to be with her. She was meant to be with him. There was no uncertainty. That was just how it was meant to be.
~~~~~

He looked at his watch. It was mid-morning. As the owner of a supermarket chain, he knew that people were changing shifts all the time. There was no such thing as a *standard* morning tea, lunch, or afternoon tea break. She could have started work at any time that morning. She could finish at any time, and she could have a break at any time. So what would he do? Sit there all day, hoping to see her come outside? And then what?

It was mid-morning, he reminded himself once more. He would sit and wait a while, and continue to weigh up options. One thing he excelled at was working out what was best. In business, he would take time to assess what would be most effective for the goal he wanted to reach. Then he would play out different scenarios in his head, visualising the end result at the very end of each scenario. Only after all of that would he make a sound decision based on the most likely outcome. It was that simple, even when there were millions of dollars involved. He just had to apply the same logic to figure out the best path to take in his current situation. It really shouldn't be so difficult - not for him.

~~~~~

Alexis served customer after customer, appreciative that the supermarket was finally becoming busy. The rush meant that she was forced to keep smiling and keep chatting throughout the morning. Lincoln continued to keep entering her mind, but she kept pushing down thoughts of him. She didn't want to dwell on the fact that he had finally found her and knew where she was. Not only that, but he had approached her, making sure she *knew* he had found her and knew where she was.

"Are you that girl who was on the news? That girl who was missing?" she heard an elderly woman ask her. Alexis smiled at her and shook her head.

"No, but you aren't the first person to ask that. I must just look like her," she said. She had answered the same question many times in recent weeks, always the same way - always untruthfully. She didn't like to lie. She never had. With that question, she had lied over and over, and would continue to lie. She didn't want to be 'that missing girl'. She just wanted to be herself, but a better version of herself than she had been before.

So much had happened since the news broadcast, she found herself always surprised when someone asked that same question. It made her think that people, in general, must be very observant, to see a random face on a news bulletin and then remember so well what that face was like. She was becoming more and more aware all the time of how other people acted and reacted to things that happened. She had been feeling like she was on a new journey of self-enrichment, learning how to be a better person. Seeing Lincoln in her workplace seemed to have drained her of some of her newly gained self-confidence. She didn't like that - not
~~~~~

one bit. She didn't want to go backwards. She only wanted to go forwards.

The elderly woman seemed to accept her answer, and moved on. Alexis smiled and chatted to customer after customer until finally her supervisor came and told her to go and have her half-hour lunch break.

Alexis smiled at him and walked away. Usually, on her breaks, she walked around the large block the supermarket resided on. It wasn't far, but it was enough in the middle of the day to help her re-energise and prepare for the coming afternoon of more smiling and chitchat. Not that she minded the smiling and friendly conversation. Since she had begun her new life, she had found herself able to do it far more easily than she had been able to previously.

She knew that part of that was due to having gone through what she did with Lincoln, and then getting away from him. A greater part of her growing self-confidence was due to her having met Anthony. He was a good man, and he was good for her. She was consistently thankful that when she'd stepped off that bus in his town, he was the person who had approached her and asked if she needed help.

She stopped at the outer doors to the supermarket exterior. It had grown into a habit, going through them and walking around the block, whenever she had a break. At that moment, before stepping through, she felt utter fear flow through her. She remembered how Lincoln had sat in his car, waiting for her, in another time, in another supermarket carpark. He'd waited so that once she left the building, he could follow her and then approach her.

She halted her footsteps before opening the door. She believed she was stronger now. She did believe she could summon the strength to simply say 'no'. Regardless, a large part of her still didn't want to *test* those theories. She didn't want to step outside of those doors and find herself approached by him again. She didn't want to have to look at him, and she certainly didn't want to sense him following her. If she made an error and he followed her, he would know where she lived. If he knew where she lived, he would try and get inside. If he got inside, alone with her…

Alexis shuddered at the thought. She knew she had to be more alert and aware than to let that happen.

She considered that perhaps he wouldn't have any intention of following her, or learning where she lived. Perhaps he had already left, immediately after he had walked out of the exit of the supermarket after she served him. Perhaps she wasn't even on his mind.

But he *had* gone to her workplace, and it wasn't anywhere near his home. It wasn't even in his city. With that in mind, she considered it best to assume and believe that he *had* sought her out to try to re-establish contact with her.

Alexis turned and walked toward the staffroom. That day wasn't a good day for a midday walk. It was, however, a very good day to stay inside.

~~~~~

After her morning and lunchtime breaks, Alexis started to watch the clock on the wall near the supermarket checkout. She had one more hour of work to get through, and then she could go home. In one way, she wanted to go home. She'd been on her feet for hours, and they were certainly crying out for some decent rest. Despite that, she was also concerned about going home. If she did go home, she might be alone there. She might not be, but she *might* be. Her landlady and other tenants might be there, but they might not. That thought did not appeal if Lincoln was nearby and watching her. She felt limited in her options.

If only Anthony lived closer, but that would never have worked anyway. She didn't want him to get messed up with Lincoln. She didn't want Lincoln to know who Anthony was, or what part he had played in her setting up a new life.

She hadn't yet moved out of the guest house she and Anthony had gone to when he'd first escorted her to the city. It was comfortable, and she was reluctant to find a whole apartment just for herself. The guest house was close to her work, and the landlady was appreciative of Alexis living there, being the good tenant that she was proving to be. Plus she could afford it.

She still hadn't accessed the bank accounts that she knew Lincoln had earlier proven he had access to. Now that she'd seen him, she suspected his investigations would have delved deeper to find the new bank account she'd had to open since beginning work in the supermarket. Perhaps that was even how he'd found her. Thinking about that, she decided that she may as well withdraw the money that was in the original accounts. She had left most of her money in there on purpose on the day she had left Melbourne. She hadn't wanted to alert him to her leaving, by making any large cash withdrawal. Now he knew where she was anyway, she may as well have the money for herself, and close those accounts completely.

Soon enough, it was time to leave work. She found herself trembling at the thought of walking out the door. In the supermarket, she got on well enough with all of the staff but didn't have one particular friend she would lean on if she needed to. She didn't know what to do. She wanted to stay inside the building and not walk out at all. That wasn't an option.

"Where are you heading now, Alexis?" she heard a male voice beside her ask. The deepness of the voice made her jump. She turned and saw her checkout supervisor, Tom, smiling at her.
~~~~~

"Oh, I was thinking that I need to get to the bank, actually," she said shyly, not wanting to seem as stressed as she felt.

"Well, I'm finished for the day and heading over to the mall. I can give you a lift if you like," he said, still grinning.

Alexis looked at his face. She had always had so many strong beliefs ingrained in her about men. It was still taking her time to undo some of that thinking. She had to concede that the man before her had never shown her any interest of a romantic or sexual kind. He was as respectful toward her as he was toward all of the checkout staff. She didn't think he was asking her into his car for any reason other than what he had offered - to give her a ride.

"Thank you, Tom," she said, nodding and smiling. "I would greatly appreciate that."

Tom smiled again and held out his arm to indicate he was letting her go first. Even in that, Alexis was still working through her thoughts and reactions to such gestures, given how strongly it had been drummed into her that she must not ever lead, and she must always *follow*.

When they reached the outer doors, he opened the door and held it open for her to pass through before him. Tentatively, Alexis walked out into the sunshine. Tom wasn't much older than her, although he seemed to have been in the supermarket forever. He was someone who appeared to be much liked by everyone. She didn't have any real fear of getting in a car with him. She would be okay with him. She would be *fine*.

"My car's over here," she heard him say.

The two of them walked beside one another in comfortable companionship. Tom thought nothing of the gesture. He would offer a ride to any of his staff needing it at the same time as he was leaving work. Alexis thought it a very big deal. To her, he was offering her a safe passage. The ride he offered was a way for her to be sure no-one *else* would stop and try to approach her.

~~~~~

Lincoln was still sitting in his car, thinking, when he saw her walk across the carpark with a man. He was unaware of how long he had been sitting there. When he saw the man beside her, he didn't *care* how long it had been. All he saw was his Lexi with another man. He didn't like that. She may not have been near him over the preceding months, but the thought of another man having her attention, spending time with her - *touching* her - made Lincoln see red. He felt inside of him the rage growing. He'd only felt that level of anger once before, and he had controlled it. He had, on that day, controlled the need he felt to *kill*. He didn't know if he would be able to control it at that moment, knowing what he was seeing.

He watched them walk over to a car and get into it, smiling at each
~~~~~

other in a friendly way. He felt his mood change. He felt his blood start to heat up drastically inside of him. He felt his heart beating loudly, and his breathing deepen. He had to calm down, and he knew it. It had to be done. Knowing he had to do it, and being able to do it, were two very different things.

He started his car with the intention of following them. He wanted to see if she was going home with that man. He needed to *know* what was happening between them. He just *had* to *know*.

Before they pulled out of the carpark, and before *he* had pulled out, his mobile phone rang. His first reaction was to ignore it, but he was more of a professional than that. He looked at the screen and saw it was one of his major clients from Brisbane. Quietly to himself, he admitted that it was a timely phone call because he needed to think before he acted on what he had just wanted to do.

He turned off his car and answered the phone to take the call. When he listened to the client speak, he automatically fitted back into his role of business owner.

When he finished his phone call, he knew that Lexi was long gone. He wouldn't be able to find out where she went with that man … not that day anyway.

But definitely the next day.

~~~~~

Alexis sat quietly in the car with her supervisor. She had a huge tendency to mistrust people. As much as she hated that, it was so entrenched in her nature that she knew that of all the things she wanted to change about herself, that would most likely be the last thing she could succeed in changing.

"Which bank are you at, Alexis?" Tom asked, startling her in her thoughts. She forced herself to smile at him and answer his question. "Alright. I might drop you off just up here, if that works for you. I need to go on to the hardware store, but I think just up here will be closer to your bank, right?"

Alexis nodded and agreed with him, not seeing anything about Tom to make her think that he had any intention of any kind as far as she was concerned. She sat quietly until he pulled the car over to the side of the road and she began to get out.

"Thank you, Tom. I appreciate this," she said. In response, she saw him smile and wave at her before turning his attention back to the road.

Alexis closed the door and watched him drive away. She felt the sunlight on her face for the first time all day, and wanted to stand there and let it wash over her. Soon enough, though, fear entered her head. She began to walk quickly into her bank.

~~~~~

"I would like to close my bank accounts, please," she said to the young woman at the customer service desk of her bank.

"Of course. Please come with me, and I'll take you to see Sharon. She'll be able to help you with that," the young woman said before she moved around to the front of the counter and then led Alexis away to another area further away.

Once seated, Alexis found it a relatively quick process, having her accounts closed. The woman before her went away for a few minutes and then came back and handed her a cheque.

"Here are the funds from your combined accounts, Ms. Montgomery," she said.

Alexis looked at the amount on the small piece of paper in front of her.

"Oh no, there must be some mistake, Sharon. There is no way I had that much in my account. It should have been maybe $400 at most," Alexis stuttered. The woman looked confused.

"Oh, I see. Alright, let's take a look. Yes, you are right - you did have a combined account balance of $389.56 until three weeks ago. Then a deposit was made for $15,000."

The bank staff member looked at the woman in front of her and watched her go pale while appearing very nervous.

"Who was the deposit made by?" Alexis dared to ask, dreading the answer that would come back.

"It was made by … Sunshine Supermarkets Limited."

Alexis looked at the woman, wondering what to do. The deposit had been made by the supermarket she used to work in - the company anyway, although not likely the branch. Lincoln owned the supermarket chain. It was most likely his doing. The question was, what to do about it.

She took a moment to put her head in her hands and just think. Why would he do that? Why would he deposit such a large sum of money into her account? Had he wanted her to withdraw it so she would deposit it into another account? Could he see her deposit a cheque she took now? And if that was the case, was that why it was such a large, round amount?

She didn't want his money, but she *could* use it. She took a few moments to think. One thing she knew was that she didn't want one large cheque to deposit.

Finally. Sharon saw Alexis raise her head once more.

"I know you just prepared this cheque for me, but would it be possible for you to rip that up, and instead give me the same amount in individual cheques of no more than $300 each?"

"You want me to give you fifty cheques, each for $300?"

"Yes - well they don't all have to be exactly $300. A mix of different amounts, but no very large cheques, would be ideal. Is that possible? Sorry. I know I'm asking a lot..."

"No, not at all. There will be a higher processing fee for that though. Are you sure?" Sharon asked and saw Alexis nod. "Alright," she continued, ripping up the cheque in front of Alexis. "I won't be long, Ms. Montgomery. Please wait here. I'll be back shortly."

Alexis sat where she was, hoping that she was doing something that made some sense. In truth, she didn't know if her request did make *any* sense, but the thought of having one cheque for more than $15,000 seemed ludicrous. With individual cheques, she could deposit small parts of the amount over a long period of time. She could even deposit one cheque each week over almost a year.

She knew she was being overly paranoid. Lincoln already knew where she was, so it didn't matter what she did anymore. He had always made sure he knew where she was and what she was doing. He had been watching her for so long, and had never hidden the fact. She had to suspect he had made the deposit only as a way to try and find out where she was. He wouldn't even need to notice the deposit now that he'd found and seen her.

She didn't like the thought of using money from him - but she would.

~~~~~

Lincoln returned to his motel room. It was a depressing place, but it would have to do. He hated being confined in such small spaces. It was bad enough in Lexi's apartment...

He caught himself in that thought. He hadn't touched her apartment at all since she'd left. He had decided, instead, to leave it just as it was when she had gone, in case she wanted to go back to it. In his heart, he knew that she wouldn't, but he couldn't bring himself to accept that, or to get rid of it, just yet.

He thought back to the day he had taken her to that apartment to show it to her. It hadn't been the first one he'd shown her, but she'd needed to be much closer to her work than the previous ones she had seen.

When she had opened her eyes that day, he had seen such joy in them. On that day she *had* been truly happy. What had happened since then that had stopped her being that happy? When had she stopped smiling so much?

He felt angry all of a sudden, and highly aroused. It was a blend of combined feelings that he had come to know all too well. He undressed, turned on the shower to the hottest temperature, and waited for the water to heat up.

While he waited, he looked in the mirror. He stood, fully naked. In that particular mirror, he could see from his head right down to his thighs. He looked front-on first and then stood sideways. He wasn't vain,
~~~~~

but he knew he was in good shape for his age. That wasn't surprising. He should have been in incredible shape, given how much effort he put into his fitness, especially since she had left. He had gone through two pairs of running shoes since then, having felt so much the need to run … the need to maintain *control.*

As he turned further, he remembered how much he missed Lexi and the pain she had always loved giving to him. Now his back was too bare and too pale.

He walked into the bedroom area and removed his belt from his pants. He tried, not for the first time, to hit himself with the leather end. It was something, but it wasn't enough. He turned the belt around in his hand so that it was the buckle that was free, and he repeated the action. He felt the cold metal strike his skin. It still wasn't enough, but it was the best he would be able to do at that moment.

He hit himself, again and again, eventually finding it easier to swing the belt around him and plunge against his back with some force. When he'd had enough, he looked in the mirror and looked at the red marks the belt buckle had produced.

He moved to the shower and stood under the hot water, feeling the heat hit the marks he had created. He felt highly aroused at the sensation, but he didn't indulge in self-pleasuring. He hadn't had an orgasm since he had last been with her. His ongoing level of arousal hadn't gone away, but he wanted to save it … for her.

He focused more on just the feeling of the hot water hitting the marks. It was a simple pleasure, but something that he knew he was not easily satisfied with. Always he felt like he needed so much *more.*

No, it wasn't enough, but for now, it would do.

Until he got her back, it would do.

~~~~~

After a nervous walk, constantly looking around her, Alexis finally got back to the guest house and into the safety of her room. Immediately she sat down on the bed she slept in, and lay down. She needed to get out of her uniform and hang it up in the bathroom so the creases would lessen and smooth out when she had a shower. She only had two changes of uniform, and one was still wet from having been washed the day before.

For that moment, she just wanted to lie still, in the peace and calm of her room, and not do anything. Her emotions had been in turmoil for hours. She needed to let her mind rest.

When she had arrived at the guest house earlier, she had stayed around the front door for a while, discretely looking out the front windows to see if she had been followed. No-one had appeared. She'd not seen any suspicious car or any suspicious person.
~~~~~

"Are you alright, Alexis?" her landlady had asked her, and she'd nodded in response.

"Yes, thank you," she'd replied to the older woman, before leaving to go to her room.

Now she just wanted to take a minute.

In her handbag, she had more than $15,300 worth of cheques. She had to put them somewhere safe, first of all.

She sat up and looked around the room. She had no reason not to trust her landlady, but in all honesty, she wouldn't know if the woman ever entered her room when she was at work. She decided to put them in an envelope and then used a safety pin to discretely attach the envelope to the back side of the edge of one of the curtains. She would deposit some of the cash into her new account at a different bank the following day - at least the money that was her own. The rest she didn't care about. She would use it if she could, but if it disappeared, it didn't really matter.

~~~~~

The next morning, Alexis woke and showered quickly before putting two of her cheques into her purse and heading off to work. It was only 7am so it was still slightly dark outside. That did make her nervous, but she still had to walk to work. She always did. Knowing that Lincoln had been in the city the previous day was no reason to be any more cautious than she usually was on her way to work.

She walked quickly. It was only a ten-minute walk between the two buildings, and it was along a fairly busy main road. There was always sufficient traffic to make her feel like she wasn't completely alone.

With each car that drove past, she wondered if *he* was in one of them. He would know she must live somewhere near the supermarket, just as she had needed to do in Melbourne. He could be in any one of the cars driving past her right now, watching … waiting.

Finally, she rushed inside the supermarket staff entrance and closed the door behind her, at last feeling safe once again. She just had to get through another day, and then get to her new bank to make the deposit. That was all she had to do. That was all she had to think about and all she had to *worry* about.

As she set up her checkout counter for the day, she felt herself start to shake. There was no reason for it, she knew. It was an involuntary reaction to something, but what? Stress? Worry? Fear?

Would he come to her again today? Would he come *every* day until she acknowledged him in some way? Would he keep following her and wanting to see her, until she told him she wanted to go back to Melbourne with him? What more did he *want* from her?

"Are you alright, Alexis?" she heard Tom's voice ask her from behind. "You seem a bit concerned about something."
~~~~~

She looked at him, fearing that if she gave away her level of fear, he would take her off checkout and she would lose income.

She smiled at him in response.

"No, I am good. Thanks, Tom."

He looked at her for another moment and then smiled at her before moving on to the next checkout counter.

~~~~~

Once the customers started filing past her, Alexis found she could relax more and put Lincoln out of her mind. If she could just keep smiling and talking…

"Can I help you, Sir?" Alexis heard Tom's voice ask from near where she was working. She raised her head and instantly wished she hadn't.

She saw Lincoln walking directly up to Tom, with a look of anger on his face. In her mind, she could see what *could* happen in that instant, so stepped out from behind her desk. She quickly moved between the two men.

"Tom, I have this," she said to her supervisor, trying to smile at him while coaxing Lincoln to look directly at her instead of at the man in front of him.

Lincoln finally looked at her, upon hearing her voice - that sweet voice. He noticed she was looking right at him. He looked briefly at the man he had been intending to confront, but stepped back and let his attention fall to Alexis instead.

"Mr. Kokiri, please…" she started to say in an effort to defuse him. Her choice of name only angered him once more.

"Don't *call* me that, Lexi!"

Alexis looked at him, and then at Tom, who seemed to have a look of uncertainty and nervousness on his face.

"Tom, can I please take my fifteen-minute break now?" she asked.

Tom nodded, sensing the usually-quiet worker who never asked for anything, really did need it.

"Thank you," Alexis replied.

Lincoln quietly watched her face and hated the way she had gotten her supervisor - her *supervisor* - to do what she wanted. She had told him what she wanted, and he had given it to her. That wasn't right. That wasn't how things were meant to be.

"Come with me," he heard her voice say quietly as she spoke to him - *only* to him. She still didn't use his first name, but at least she was talking to *him*.

Lincoln nodded at her, unable to speak for the moment. He had dreamed of having such an opportunity again. He had yearned to be close to her again, but now felt overwhelmed with feelings that were arising from it.
~~~~~

Alexis led him out the front exit, determined to get him away from where she worked. When they were clear of the exterior doors, she turned to him.

For the first time ever, Lincoln saw anger looking at him from her face.

"Don't you *ever* come anywhere near my workplace again," she said, in a terrifyingly controlled and low voice.

Lincoln was initially surprised and stunned, before he found his thinking and his voice again.

"You let him touch you?" he asked, referring to Tom.

Alexis had no idea who he meant, thinking that surely he didn't know about Anthony.

"What? Who?" she asked.

"That guy in there!" he exclaimed.

He saw a look of confusion come over her face, and had to admit to himself that it didn't look as if it was an act.

"That guy in there - Tom - is the checkout supervisor!" Alexis said.

"He gave you a ride yesterday. I *saw* you with him."

Alexis looked at him in horror, but then relief. She hadn't been too paranoid the day before, after all. He *had* been there, in the carpark, waiting for her.

"You *were* watching me yesterday…" she said quietly, in almost a whisper.

"I'm trying to keep you safe…"

"Safe?!" she exclaimed. "The only person I need to be kept safe from is you! You are the one who follows me, who watches my every movement. It has to stop - right now! If you keep watching me, I *will* have you arrested."

Lincoln heard the words but could not believe them. That wasn't how it was meant to go when he got her to talk to him again. She wasn't supposed to be so forward in talking to him like she was. She *always* wanted to please *him*. That was the power of their relationship. He groaned as he realised that he had miscalculated *again*.

"You don't mean that, Lexi," he said. "I *love* you…"

"This isn't love," Alexis replied. "This is obsession. I don't love you, Lincoln. I have *never* loved you."

Lincoln heard the sentence, but when he next spoke, Alexis knew he didn't actually comprehend what she had said.

"You used my name … thank you."

She turned away from him to head back into the store but then turned back.

"Keep away from me, and keep away from this supermarket," she said. "I am not a part of your life anymore, and you are certainly not any part of mine. Go back to Melbourne, and please just forget all about me. I don't want to see your face again. *Ever.*"

Lincoln heard her words and finally understood something she was saying to him. Before he could reply - before he could tell her again how much he loved her - she had gone. But some of her words had sunk in this time, and he would not go into her workplace again. For now…

He couldn't believe that she didn't love him. If she didn't love him, she wouldn't have done all those wonderful things for him - all of those wonderful things *with* him.

No, they were meant to be together. There was no-one else he was meant to be with. There was no-one else *she* was meant to be with.

He would go away, but he certainly wouldn't forget her. Of that, he had absolutely no doubt - and absolutely no intention.

~~~~~

Alexis walked into the supermarket and immediately went to approach Tom, who had been filling in on her counter. As soon as there was a gap between customers, she stepped in and took over once again.

"I'm sorry, Tom," she said quietly to him, hoping she wouldn't get into trouble. She really did need the job.

Tom looked closely at her. They got on well enough, but not at any personal level. He realised then that he actually knew nothing at all about her personal life.

"Was that the guy who owns all those companies? Lincoln Kokiri?" he asked and saw her nod. "He looked like he was coming at me … to *fight* me," he said. Alexis cringed in the knowledge that he was probably right. She waited for the present customer to leave, and there to be no more in line before she spoke freely to him.

"I think he saw me get in your car yesterday, and got the wrong idea," she said. "Sorry. I hope I've convinced him now that he'd made a completely wrong assumption there."

Tom looked at her still, wondering how his most timid checkout operator knew such a powerful man.

"He called you by a different name though - Lexi. I suppose that is short for Alexis," he said and saw her nod in acknowledgement. "Is he … a … *friend* of yours?"

Alexis laughed at the terminology and found herself speechless as to how to answer the question. She could see Tom's curiosity, but really didn't know what to say.

"I wouldn't use the term *friend*, no," she said and decided to leave it at that.

Tom heard and immediately understood the avoidance of his question so resolved to not ask any more. It was intriguing. Suddenly *she* was intriguing, but he respected boundaries. He wouldn't ask any further
~~~~~

questions.

"Well, if you ever need a friend to talk to about anything, I have good solid shoulders," he said and smiled at her before walking away, leaving her to get on with her job.

~~~~~

After her work for the day was done, Alexis tentatively left the supermarket and began the walk to her new bank to deposit the cheques she had grabbed that morning.

As she walked along the road, she was wary but hopeful that Lincoln wouldn't be anywhere to be seen. She couldn't have been any more forward with him. She had to trust he'd now finally believe that she did not want to see him.

But then, he must have known that before, and yet he still came all that way to seek her out.

Suddenly she felt lonely and eager to talk to Anthony. She had another four days of work before she would get some time off, but he had already told her he would come up and stay with her on those days off. She welcomed that greatly, and only wished it could be sooner. She also conceded that four more days would give her a better indication of whether Lincoln was really gone or not. If he wasn't, he would have made it known by then. He wanted her attention desperately. He wouldn't sit in wait for too long before making another attempt at getting it, if he still desired to do so.
~~~~~

CHAPTER 2

The Options

"What?" Anthony asked, thinking he must have heard incorrectly. He and Alexis were standing in her room in the guest house she resided in. They had just arrived from the train station, where she had met him upon his arrival. She had only originally intended for the room to be temporary accommodation for the first few days after she had initially arrived in the city several months earlier. It suited her so well that she'd found she was in no hurry to move.

Alexis instantly felt some regret at having mentioned the interaction with Lincoln. She and Anthony had only just arrived in her room. They had much more pleasant things to do, and more pleasurable ways to catch up with each other after having spent the past week apart. She'd spoken because she did want to talk to him about it. She hadn't seen Lincoln at all over the previous four days, so either he had left the city she lived in, or he was still sitting in wait - waiting and watching.

That thought had almost made Alexis book a ticket to go and see Anthony, rather than let him come to her. She knew that whichever way they did things, if Lincoln wanted to watch her and follow her, he would find out about Anthony. That, to her, was even more terrifying than Lincoln Kokiri finding *her*.

"He was here," she repeated. "He came into my work earlier this week … twice."

Anthony looked at Alexis in disbelief. He had thought that episode of her life was over and she was finally safe. The knowledge that Lincoln had found her, and might now be determined to push himself back into her life again, infuriated Anthony and scared him.

"Allie," he said, the name coming out of his mouth like it was a breath rather than a spoken word. He knew her proper name but still continued to use the name she'd introduced herself as when they had met. He liked it, and she seemed to naturally have taken to him calling her by it. Between the two of them, they had silently accepted that he would always call her that, no matter what anyone else called her.

Alexis could see the fear on his face so reached out to put her arms around him.

"I'm fine, Anthony," she said. "He didn't hurt me in any way."

"But how did he find you?" he asked as he responded to her hug, wrapping his arms around her and pulling her body tight against his.

Alexis shrugged her shoulders and saw his facial expression change from fear to anger, and back to horror once more.

"I don't know, but I had to open a bank account when I first got here, for my pay to go into," she replied. "Maybe it was through that. It doesn't really matter now. There was always a good chance he would find me. It just isn't possible for me to live without some kind of electronic record being out there about me. It's just the kind of world that we all live in."

Anthony found his mind working quickly, with far too many thoughts. There were too many worries flowing for him to be able to clearly focus on any one of them. He had only just let someone into his life after two years of grieving for his past love. The thought of losing Alexis as well was a devastating thought to him.

Alexis felt his arms tighten even more around her, and let him hold her for as long as he needed to.

They stayed like that for a long time, each in their own thoughts. After she felt his hold ease off, he stood back from her and looked intently into her eyes.

"I don't want to lose you," Anthony said, knowing he couldn't again go through anything like he had when Cynthia had died in the car accident. He knew it was a selfish thought, thinking about how something happening to her would impact *him*, but he couldn't stop the thought entering his mind.

Alexis looked into his eyes and felt a tear threaten in her own. It was difficult for her to consider what he must have gone through with his previous partner. One minute, he'd been thinking he and Cynthia had a long future ahead of marriage and children. Then he'd been told that she was gone forever and none of that could happen. She reached up and kissed him, softly at first, just as a comfort.

The movement caught with Anthony and he pulled her close again, indulging in the kiss. The emotions flowing through him from the news that Lincoln Kokiri had found her and approached her, made him feel even closer to her. He also felt an extremely strong sense of protectiveness flow over him. He indulged in kissing her, feeling himself start to get carried away in her lips.

Alexis revelled in the discovery that she was being walked backwards toward the bed. It was a move she welcomed. In their intimacy, she found so much equality with Anthony. Even as he pulled her down to lie with him, he kissed her and moved *with* her, letting things happen in a natural way - not in a planned way, and certainly not in a controlled way.

They undressed each other slowly, mixing the process up with caresses of lips and hands. Alexis felt herself sinking into the blissful feelings that came from that. She was eager to be closer to him.

Eventually, she pushed him onto his back and positioned herself on top of him. As she lay there, she looked into his eyes, subconsciously checking that her taking the initiative wasn't something that was upsetting him. All she saw was a mirror image of her own arousal and eagerness on his face.

Anthony relished the feelings. Prior to when the two of them had finally let themselves move to physical closeness, it had been two years since he had been sexual with anyone. At that moment, he was carried away in the pleasure he had missed for so long. He felt her kissing him, and he couldn't seem to get enough of those kisses. Her lips, her tongue … they moved so easily with his, resulting in a deep moaning from him in his hunger for more, and his desperation for it not to stop.

While her lips maintained the attention of his, he felt her start to move against his hardness, like she was stroking it. He could feel her arousal. The level of moisture and wetness was heavenly to him. It was proof that she wasn't doing it just because she felt she *should* pleasure him, but because she wanted to share the sensations and the moment with him. She truly wanted it for herself. The thought and understanding that she could share something equally with him, rather than just do what she was told, as she had done for so long with *him*, fuelled Anthony to not indulge so much in thought. Instead, he switched his mind off and focused purely on the feeling of their two bodies intertwining.

Alexis felt like she was on fire. They had taken so long to get to that point. Even though it wasn't their first time joining, it was still new enough that it felt like it was a brand new form of discovery, getting to know each other's bodies. She could feel his hunger for her through his lips, and hear him moaning in pleasure. The feeling inside of her that was coming from her rubbing against him was magical to her. He wasn't telling her to do this or to do that. She knew she could stay where she was and indulge in the blissful feeling of pleasure for as long as she wanted, and he wouldn't force her to do anything differently. He wouldn't force her to do something that was focused solely on pleasing *him*.

Finally, when she couldn't wait any longer, she reached for a condom and rolled it down onto him. As she did so, she looked up at him to see if he had any objection, but only saw raw desire in his eyes.

She leaned down and kissed him again for a long time, not quite yet rushing. She wanted to let them relax back to where they were a moment ago, indulging in lips and tongues enjoying each other.

Anthony felt it happen, ever so slowly. He focused on feeling being moved against and then enclosed. She did it with incredible control, given how aroused he knew she was. She didn't stop kissing him as she moved so slowly down onto him until he was fully inside of her. Both of them let out a groan at the same time, as they reached the point of being fully joined. Once there, she lay still, just kissing him, feeling full of him, while he felt like he had slipped into a tight-fitting and warm glove. To Anthony, it felt like he was home.

Alexis relished the feeling before starting to move up and down slowly on top of him. She kissed his lips and felt her arousal grow as she moved her pelvis back and forth over his, causing rubbing on her clitoris.

Anthony could feel what she was doing. The act of her moving for her own pleasure *and* his pushed his own arousal even higher. He determined to hold back and not climax until he finally felt her squeeze him tightly and almost flop down onto him in release. Then he let himself go. She heard his breathing change and felt his muscles twitching inside of her as he also reached orgasm.

They lay together, silent but restful, kissing softly and looking at one another, neither in any rush to move. They had taken their time in getting to know one another enough for physical connection to finally feel comfortable between them. Now there was no rush for anything more.

~~~~~

"Were you scared when you saw him, Allie?" Anthony asked after they separated and moved under the bed covers to cuddle together.

Alexis gathered her words and felt a shudder go through her as she remembered that moment when she had just *known* Lincoln was close by.

"I think that, for a moment, my body felt like it went into shock. But Anthony, I didn't feel intimidated by him at all. If anything, I felt empowered to be able to stand up to him. Something has changed in me. Knowing *you* has changed something in me. I don't know how or why. I just feel *different* now."

"You seem different too. You're far more relaxed and happy now than what you were the day I met you," he replied. They both were silent for a few moments before he continued. "You didn't react to him, though? His voice didn't make you zone out?"

"No. At first, my body felt like it wanted to, but then something else kicked in, and I just *knew* that he no longer had any control over me."

"Wow, that must have been a surprise to him. A disappointment? How did he react to that?"

Alexis took some time to think about that, before turning slightly to look into Anthony's eyes, and speaking once more.

"He ... didn't," she replied. "He didn't react to it at all. He pretended to purchase something, just like a normal customer, and then he left. I didn't see him again until the next morning, when he came into the store again." Looking closely into Anthony's eyes, she saw his concern. "I wouldn't have acknowledged him that second time, except that I saw him walking toward my supervisor. He looked like he was going to hit him..."
~~~~~

"Why would he hit your supervisor?"

"The day before, I got a ride with Tom - my supervisor - to the bank after work," Alexis said. "Lincoln must have read something into it, and gotten his head twisted around it. I think he was going to confront him about me."

Anthony listened with dread in his heart. Everything about the whole situation made him feel ill at ease.

Alexis found herself worried that Anthony might also read something into her having gotten into a car with another man. When she looked into his face, she saw no trace of any kind of jealousy or concern there - not about Tom anyway. With that discovery, she relaxed, pleased with the knowledge.

"Anyway, I coaxed him away from Tom and led him out of the supermarket. Then I told him to forget me and never come near my workplace again. He left after that, and I haven't seen him since. I assume he went back to Melbourne, but I have no way of knowing if he has. I do think if he was still here, he would have made himself known to me again by now."

She felt Anthony's arms tighten around her, and revelled in the feeling of safety she felt with him. She had always dreamed of being normal. It seemed like such a simple thing to wish for, but she'd consistently felt different to everyone else throughout her life. She'd always felt like she didn't belong, or like she didn't know how to feel true humanity inside of her. Lying with Anthony so close to her, she knew her humanity had started to not only return, but also grow. She was starting to finally feel - for the first time in her life - *normal.*

"Do you think you should stay here, Allie?" she heard Anthony ask. "Now that he knows where you are?"

Alexis looked into the face before her, saddened but at the same time glad that he was worrying about her so much.

"Anthony, wherever I go, he'll find me if he wants to. He didn't do anything to me the other day, so I might not have anything to worry about. It might now be all over. And if it isn't, the police here are already familiar with my situation because of the time I spent with them when I was on the run from him. They know me, and they know not only the lengths I went through to get away from him, but also the lengths *he* went to, to try and bring me back to him," she said and paused before continuing. "Where would I go that he would never find me if he wanted to? There's nowhere..."

"You could come and live with me!"

"I know, and when I saw him last week, believe me, I *was* tempted to go and jump straight on a train..."

"Well, why didn't you? You know you're always welcome," Anthony said.

"I know, but I don't want to bring him to your town," Alexis replied. "Not if I can help it. Here, there are always people around, and the police are nearby. Your town is small, and it would be easier for him to find you. No, I have to stay here, at least for now."

They looked at each other for a long time before he kissed her, needing his mind to be clear again. Once the kissing began, it was.

~~~~~

Through their time together over the following two nights, Alexis and Anthony both tried hard to keep Lincoln from their minds. Anthony could feel a deep thud in his heart, driven, he knew, by his constant concern for her, but he wouldn't try and pressure her into moving away. Her life was her own, and it *needed* to be her own. She had been controlled for too long already by someone else. No, Anthony thought to himself, he would not try and make her do anything. She had to follow her own path and make her own decisions.

During their day together, they escaped into the cinema, knowing it was a sound method for them both to tune out their minds from anything real. Alexis found her strength building further with every hour she spent with him. He was like her battery charger. When something happened, and she felt a slight touch of uncertainty, she leaned on him and instantly felt strong again. She knew she had her own inner strength. She just sometimes forgot about it.

On their second evening together, they went out to a restaurant for dinner. Alexis took her time and dressed up for their outing, for the first time working hard to make herself look like a sexy woman for him. As she got ready, Anthony joked with her through the bathroom door about what was taking her so long, making her giggle.

"You know I'm going home tomorrow, right, Missy? So we have to go to dinner *tonight*, not *tomorrow* night!" "Are you painting a self-portrait in there? Is that what's taking so long?" "Should I call the restaurant and change the reservation to next week? Would you be ready by *then*?"

Alexis kept laughing at him, loving the ease of his nature. Despite how worried she knew he was about her, one thing she had always seen in Anthony was his ability to use humour to make things easy. It was one of the traits that had immediately drawn her to him.

Finally, Anthony saw the bathroom door open. As it did, he had cheeky words on the tip of his tongue, ready to fly in an affectionate dig at her. On first glance at her, he found himself completely silent.

She was wearing a red halter neck dress made of some kind of shiny fabric - maybe silk, or satin. She had her hair up, tousled but secured on top of her head. Her ears were adorned with long dangly earrings that
~~~~~

looked like diamonds even though he knew they wouldn't be. Circling her throat was a choker that matched, made up of several rows of the same diamond-looking pieces. From the centre of that hung one large gem, positioned perfectly between the two halter sides over her chest.

He cast his eyes from the top of her head, downward. The dress flared out from her petite waist and stopped just on her knees. Further down, he could see mid-height heels, red and shiny.

Raising his eyes again, they settled on her face. Although she rarely used makeup, and he loved how she looked without it, he noticed that she'd applied some subtly. He could see how it accentuated the beautiful colour of her eyes and the shape of her lips.

Alexis could see him looking at her, and felt herself blush deeply.

"Allie…" Anthony breathed out and then fell silent as his eyes made their top to toe journey once more.

Alexis watched him and took note of her feelings about the way he was looking at her. She remembered when she'd put on a plain sundress. His face then had revealed that he viewed her in a different light when she had that dress on. At the time, she hadn't been able to ascertain if she liked him looking her like that or not. It seemed like so long ago. In the present moment, she loved the way he was looking at her. There was no concern over him looking at her like that. There was no *threat*.

"We don't *have* to go out for dinner," he said and saw her laugh out loud at him, making him smile shyly and then laugh also. "Okay, we'll go," he said, moving closer to her.

Alexis felt his hands reach out to her hips as he moved until he was almost touching her, chest to chest.

"You look so beautiful," she heard him say softly while smiling at her. Alexis thought she would melt with the way her heart felt. Almost instantaneously, he was pulling back from her. "Come on. If we don't leave now, I'm afraid you definitely won't be eating tonight," he continued with a suggestive but humorous look on his face. His easy-going suggestiveness made her relax and laugh with him as they grabbed their coats and began their evening walk.

~~~~~

It was a twenty-minute walk to the restaurant, along a pathway that wove down the edge of a small waterway. Dotted along the path were wooden benches, set along the length of the path in a way that enabled people to sit and look out over the water.

Alexis had never spent any time walking that way through the city, but thought it would be nice to sometimes, when she wasn't in a hurry. It would also be a great place to sit and think.

As she walked alongside him, she felt Anthony's eyes move back to her now and then. For the most part, the two of them remained silent in
~~~~~

their walking. When they were almost at the restaurant doors, Anthony stopped suddenly and faced her again.

"Sorry, Allie, but I have to do this," he said, instantly alarming her before she felt him move closer to her, pull her into his arms, and kiss her deeply.

Automatically, she wrapped her arms around him and indulged in the kiss, feeling her arousal begin and then deepen. They clung to each other as if they hadn't made love only hours earlier, or early that morning, or the night before. Alexis indulged in the feelings and realised how much she had grown to love the feeling of his arms around her, and his lips on hers. It had been right for them both to wait as long as they did before they had become intimate with each other. He had needed time to work through his ongoing grief over Cynthia's death. She had needed time to get over what she had gone through with Lincoln. Now nothing felt more right than being in each other's arms.

Anthony had tried to not interrupt their plans, but with each step they had taken since leaving her room in the guest house, he had felt his arousal grow more and more. He needed her like he couldn't remember needing any woman. She looked beautiful, sexy, desirable, and alluring. The stark contrast to her compared to that day when he had met her - when she had been wearing old jeans and an old jersey in an attempt to not look like a woman - overwhelmed him. He had just *had* to kiss her.

He pulled away from her, a little ashamed at almost losing his self-control. When he looked at her face, he didn't see any look of alarm in her expression at all. All he saw was desire and a deep level of arousal in her too.

"Sorry, I really didn't want to upset your lipstick," he said and heard her giggle at him, relaxing them both.

Alexis held out her hand to him and he took it, both of them smiling as they took deep breaths to relax their bodies, and finally entered the restaurant.

~~~~~

"Oh my gosh, this is amazing," Alexis said as she indulged in her meal of roast chicken, roast vegetables, and stuffing. She knew they were in an expensive restaurant, where a certain level of decorum was expected, but she didn't hold back in enjoying her meal.

Anthony remembered the first time he had seen her eat. That day, she had cut the food up into the tiniest of pieces and slowly eaten one small piece at a time. Now he watched her with amusement, enjoying the way she ate wholeheartedly. Even looking like she did - to him as the most beautiful and sexy woman in the room - she still ate with relish. She was making no secret of how much she was enjoying the food in front of her.

Alexis laughed at the expression on his face. It wasn't her intention to
~~~~~

arouse him in any way, but she knew that in addition to his obvious amusement, he was, and she liked it. She liked that he was turned on by her being just who she was. She liked that he was turned on by what she looked like. She liked that, for him to be turned on by her, he didn't need her to do anything to him. She just had to be herself. The result wasn't conditional on whether she did what he told her to do. It wasn't conditional on her being able to do what he wanted her to do, well and with force.

There was a small part of her still that wanted to hide as a woman and appear genderless, as she had tried so hard to do when she'd first left Melbourne. A greater part of her now enjoyed looking and feeling like a confident woman. Yes, the result would probably be the same at the end of the night - he would want to make love to her. But it would be an equal desire and something they both wanted. It was how things were meant to be. That was normal, and she had needed normal for so long.

They enjoyed their restaurant time for two hours, relaxing more and more with each other and talking to each other about the more mundane aspects of their lives.

As they talked, Alexis grew increasingly aware that it was something that she and Lincoln had never really done at all. He had told her at the very beginning that he would never want to talk about his work, and that was what took up most of his life. And of course he would not want to talk to her about his marriage to Diana. Alexis would never have expected that. So, all in all, they had just never really spoken. She hadn't given it any thought over those three years. It was just the way they had been together. She much preferred what she'd found with Anthony. With him, everything was easy, and everything was relaxed. Nothing needed to be a drama, or even serious.

"What is happening there, Missy? You haven't touched that there dessert for quite a few minutes," Alexis heard Anthony asking. She could hear the teasing in his voice as he was smiling at her.

She looked down at her plate. The meringue nest of whipped cream and fresh berries had sounded delectable, but her tummy was arguing that it simply could not hold any more food in it. She laughed softly.

"I can't eat it," she said and saw him raise his eyebrows, teasing her more. "I know, I ordered far too much. It all sounded just so good, though!"

Anthony laughed at her, finding her utterly cute at that moment. It wasn't a word he would often use for a woman, but at that moment, it described her perfectly.

"Do you want it?" she asked him.

He laughed out loud at her, making her giggle softly in return. It was a blissful sound that he was still getting used to but always gained great joy from hearing.

"No. It looks good, but I'm full as well. Shall we go?" he asked and saw her nod in reply.

When the waiter brought their bill, he offered to put the dessert into a box for them to take it away with them, making Anthony laugh again.

"Yes, I think that might be a good idea. Thank you."

Finally, they were on their way. Anthony enjoyed slipping her coat on over her dress slowly to make sure she wouldn't get cold when they left the warmth of the restaurant.

Alexis watched his face as she turned to face him once again. He was watching her in such a way that made her blush and eager to get him back to the guest house.

~~~~~

Walking along the waterfront again, Alexis found a level of peace in her mind that was relatively new to her.

"Would you mind if we sat here for a while, Anthony?" she asked as they approached one of the wooden benches.

Anthony nodded. Inwardly, he was pleased with another question from her that indicated her acceptance that her mind was her own. He was pleased that she was realising she had as much right as anyone else to do what she wanted, and not just always give and do to others what they wanted her to do. He sat down and immediately felt her sit down close beside him.

Alexis nudged herself against him and felt him put his arm around her. As she rested her head on his shoulder and let herself enjoy the moment, her eyes looked out over the water. Even though it was evening, lights from all around the edges shone over the water, creating a magical effect in front of them.

"I love being with you," she said quietly, almost unable to be heard. "Thank you for giving so much to me."

Anthony pulled away and twisted his body so he could properly face her and then kiss her. He only meant to give her a slight kiss to reassure her that he had heard her. As their lips touched, something ignited in both of them, and soon they were kissing passionately. They didn't reach for anything more. They kept their arms wrapped around each other tightly. Each of them could feel the other melting and diving deeper into the kiss and into the desire.

Alexis groaned as she felt her body wake up and reach that fulfilling state where everything was tingling, especially the core of her sexual being, which was throbbing heavily. She wanted him so much, but she couldn't pull away for the moment. It felt simply too good to be in his arms.

Anthony also let himself go in the moment, purposely keeping his
~~~~~

hands off her even though he wanted to touch her everywhere. He held his arms tight around her but fought to keep his hands where they were and not let them wander.

When he finally pulled away from her, he could tell she was as breathless as he was. He looked into her eyes as she leaned in and kissed him again. Alexis needed to let him know she wanted so much more from him right then, which he indulged her in for a few minutes more until he pulled away again.

"Allie, what I want to do to you right now, we can't do here," he said shyly.

Instantly he relaxed her, making her laugh softly at him before kissing him gently and quickly, and nodding.

"Let's go," she replied.

They walked the remaining distance holding hands but not saying or doing anything more to fuel each other. The only interaction was the occasional look and smile at one another, the smiles revealing the knowing of what was to come.

Any normal outsider who saw them right at that moment would have seen a young couple in love. They would have seen a couple who were in the prime of happiness together.

But in a car nearby, there was no happiness at what had just been witnessed. There was only deep seething - and an increasingly strong desire to cause pain.

CHAPTER 3

The Finding

Two Months Earlier

Lincoln knew that everything was a mess in his life. Somewhere, he'd taken a wrong turn. He should never have called the police and told them Lexi had been abducted. He should never have put his name out there at all, in association with her. Knowing that he'd done that caused frustration and anger in him. Both of those feelings were growing intensely inside of him.

What affected him even more greatly though - the one thing that could cut through everything messy in his personal life - was his company. Even though much of every day he felt like his mind was misty, somehow he was maintaining professionalism as far as his clients and his business decisions were going. Regardless, he worried that he was losing focus, and he was going to make a mistake that would affect people - *lots* of people. He desperately did not want that to happen.

He had to find a way to move forward. He needed to find a way to return to who he used to be. He couldn't understand what had happened to him. Always he was focused and in control of everything. How did everything get so messed up? How did everything get so messy?

He had been using resources to keep trying to find Lexi but had to concede that it was getting nowhere. She didn't want to be found. She didn't want to see him again. He had known that right from the moment he'd realised she'd left, but he hadn't wanted to acknowledge it. He still didn't want to acknowledge it.

It wasn't how things were meant to be. He and Lexi were supposed to be together. He loved her, and she loved him.

He took a deep breath and declared to himself that he would search for another week or two, and then he would stop. Just another week or two.

~~~~

"There you are," he said to himself as he finally found the information he needed. Over the previous two weeks, since his self-declaration of almost defeat, he had been monitoring transactions of all kinds. Just before he was going to stop looking, her name had finally appeared next to a new bank account opening.

Instantly he felt himself become heavily aroused. He was in his office,
~~~~

and it was during general office hours. He couldn't - wouldn't - act on it. Instead, he made sure to stay right where he was, behind his desk, until he could get his arousal under control.

He made a note of the town the bank account had been opened in. It was well outside of Melbourne, but not inaccessible. He could easily take a flight to an airport nearby and then hire a car to get to her.

Instead of reacting quickly, he forced himself to think carefully. He had made so many mistakes since she'd left, due to him not taking enough time to assess and consider all possible outcomes of his actions.

He resolved that he would do nothing that day. It was enough that he had learned where she was. He would take one month to consider his options before he did anything. To remember, he set an alarm in his watch so he wouldn't keep counting days. Once that month was up, then he would decide how to act.

He knew she was out there, and he knew where she was - or at least, where she had been in the past week. All he had to do was get in front of her. As soon as she could see him, all would be well again. As soon as she could see him, she would remember how much they loved each other. How important it was that the two of them were together. How they were meant to be together.

"Mr. Kokiri," a voice said as his office door opened. "Mr. Grace is here for his 10 o'clock appointment with you."

Lincoln nodded and smiled at his personal assistant - a gracious woman only four years older than him. She had stood by his side, organising almost everything in his life ever since he had taken over the business.

"Thank you, Hannah. Please show him in," he said, immediately making sure that his arousal had gone before he stood up and held out his hand to the client before him.

There would be no more thinking about Lexi that day, but he would see her soon. Very, very soon.

~~~~~

Later that evening, he made his way home to his apartment. He had been living there alone for over a month, but he found he didn't mind the solitude. It gave him more time to concentrate on finding her, formulating different things to try to locate her.

When he walked into the apartment that evening, he instantly felt something was different. Things were out of place - not messy, but simply not there.

He walked over to the side table, where he always placed his keys and wallet when he arrived home. There sat a note.

'I came in and took everything that was mine. I want us to talk. Call me with a time and suggestion of a public place where other people will
~~~~~

be in at the time, so we can talk. D.'

Diana. She had finally found the courage to step foot inside their apartment. He hadn't seen or heard from her since that day when the news broadcast had shown on the television, reporting Lexi as missing. He had needed to control his anger that day. He could remember so clearly the level of rage that had instantly flashed through his blood when Diana had called Lexi a whore. Even thinking about that at the present moment, he felt some residual anger at the comment.

But he couldn't be angry at Diana. As far as he knew, she had never done anything wrong in their marriage. She had smiled when she had needed to smile, and she had supported him when he had needed support. She had played the part of the perfect wife.

He knew that he had loved her. He didn't know when that feeling had changed so much that he could so easily be unfaithful to her, but it must have changed. He told himself that surely he wouldn't have been driven to see someone else if he still loved her as much as he thought he did.

She wanted to see him. He would give her that. She wanted it to be in a public place. He understood that. She had possessed the intuition to know that the last time they saw each other, he was restraining himself from acting out of anger. She knew the level of rage she had evoked. Of course she wouldn't want to be alone with him.

He walked into the living area and sat down on the sofa. He was still in his work suit, although he had loosened his tie, as he always did when he left work at the end of each day.

He wanted to have a shower, under water that was as hot as possible. He wanted to feel pain. He could have the hot shower, but he couldn't have the pain. For that, he would wait until he saw Lexi again. She was the one who was meant to deliver him the level of painful satisfaction that he needed.

For the moment, he had to think about Diana. He owed her so much. He wouldn't mess her around. He picked up his mobile and called her number.

"Hello," he heard her voice say. She sounded quiet and tentative, as if uncertain about what kind of response she was going to get after having gone into the apartment without him knowing. Not that she had to let him know, of course, since she was half owner of it.

"Diana. Tell me where to meet you, and what time suits you," he said to her. He suddenly found himself eager to see her, not due to love, and not due to sexual attraction, but simply to be able to talk to her. Yes, he felt an undeniable need, all of a sudden, to be able to talk to someone.

"Two hours. Revolution Café."

He agreed and heard her hang up on him. Always straight to the point with no embellishment, that was Diana. For many years, he had loved her for that directness, but in recent years, he had begun to recognise a certain level of fakeness in her conversation. It was if she had started to more often say what she thought he wanted to hear, rather than what she wanted to say.

He took a few minutes to sit back on the sofa and just close his eyes. Two big things in one day: re-establishing contact with his wife, and finding Lexi. It was the latter that made him smile.

At last. At last, he had found his Lexi.

~~~~~

Diana took her time showering and preparing to meet Lincoln at the arranged time and place. Even with so much time having passed, she felt hugely apprehensive. In the weeks following the day that she'd seen the news report about the girl's disappearance, she hadn't dared return to their apartment, or even make contact with Lincoln. She had been prepared to turn her back on her entire life, just to get away from him. She'd thought it best to get away from any possibility of feeling the depth of his anger toward her after that one remark.

"So that is what she looks like. I've always been curious what the face of your whore would be like", she remembered clearly having said to him when the girl's face had appeared on the television that afternoon. She also remembered the extreme level of anger that, even from where she had stood, she could so easily sense rushing through his entire body.

In that instant, he could have been in front of her, yelling at her, or worse, but he hadn't moved. He had maintained control at least long enough for her to go. She'd been quick-thinking enough to know it was best that she leave the apartment. At that moment, she'd needed to get somewhere safe, away from him.

Since that day, he hadn't come after her. She had thought - hoped - on that day, that he wouldn't, if he was as messed up about that girl as he seemed to be. Seemingly, that had proven to be the case.

Now that a month had passed without her seeing him, she knew her feelings toward him had changed. She thought she would be happy starting over. In many ways, she was, but she had also started to miss him.

They had always had a strange marriage, with him having had to take over the family business when he was only twenty. That was only a relatively short time after the two of them had wed. The order of how things had panned out for them had meant that right from the very start, they had experienced a distance between them. He had needed to focus on learning the business, first of all, and that had taken almost every waking hour of every day. But that was only the start. After that, he'd started to fit into the role and begin building on the business, planning takeovers to grow the company further by taking on more and more
~~~~~

businesses under the umbrella company. That had taken time and commitment. All through that, Diana had supported him. It was what she wanted to do. It was a life that she wanted to live.

With that life came wealth and a sense of independence, although looking back, Diana could see that she'd never been truly independent. Lincoln had never told her she had to give up ideas of having a career. She knew deep down that he would have supported her in anything that she wanted to do, but she had wanted to be his wife. That wasn't just a status that she had wanted and enjoyed. It was also the activity that she wanted to do every day. She would have liked to have become a mother, too, she reflected, but that had never happened. Again, Lincoln had never said that he didn't want to have children, and he had never tried to control her body in any way. She had tried to conceive by not using contraception, in the hope that a child would come into the world. It never had. Diana had asked Lincoln once if he would consider getting tested so they could identify why she wasn't getting pregnant. He had dismissed that, and she had stopped asking.

It wasn't the life she'd anticipated for herself, but the wealth and status had enabled her to mix with the kind of people she wanted to be around. She did love the charity aspect of it once the company had begun to grow so much. Standing beside Lincoln at events where he gave away literally millions of dollars was something she took pride in - pride for having a husband who was so generous and so successful.

Never once in all the years they had been together, had her head been turned by anyone else. She wondered if she could ever have been tempted if the right person had come along. She had particularly been thinking about it since the day it was confirmed that he'd been seeing that girl. Diana still couldn't understand what it would have been about that girl that had attracted him so much. She looked so young on the television screen when Diana had seen her photo. Why did he want to be with someone so young? As far as Diana was aware, he had never been unfaithful to her in their years together - until that girl had crossed his path. She hoped that one day he would explain it to her so she could understand. She knew their sex life hadn't been great, of course, but he seemed to accept it for what it was. Until that day a month ago, they had still had sex together a few times each week, which she'd believed was doing pretty good for a couple that had been together for twenty years. She had never said no when he had wanted sex. She didn't think she had ever given him a reason to go elsewhere. She still didn't understand that - she didn't understand the *why*.

~~~~~

When she arrived at the café, she saw him waiting for her. She didn't immediately move toward him, finding inside of herself a reluctance to
~~~~~

get too close to him yet. In reality, if he wanted to hurt her in any way, he could have approached her in preceding months and done so. He hadn't. He hadn't hurt her in any way at all. He hadn't searched for her physically, he hadn't cut off her money supply, and he hadn't changed the locks on the apartment door. He just seemed to have forgotten about her. That realisation resulted in her feeling a mixture of sadness at how little she must have meant to him, but also happiness that she could so easily be free and start a new life if she wanted to. But that was the big question - did she want to?

Lincoln sat quietly, waiting for his wife to arrive. Before he'd left the apartment, he had spent an hour in meditation, working hard to refocus his mind. As much as his emotion had been focused on Lexi, he didn't want to be thinking about her when he met with his wife. Diana deserved better than that. That horrible comment aside, she was a good wife. His name might be on all the documents out there about the business, but she had done her bit as his support person. She'd been there for him for the past twenty years - almost half of his life.

He looked toward the door, wondering why she was late, and if she was going to turn up. When he did so, he saw her standing there, not moving. She was just standing still and watching him.

Diana took a deep breath and felt her nervousness deepen even further when she realised he was looking right at her. His visual attention prompted her into action. She made her way through the café to the rear, where they always had a table put aside, being major benefactors to the business. It was then that she actually started to feel like they were on their first date.

As Lincoln watched his wife walk toward him, he took the few moments to really look at her. It was the first time in their entire life together that they had not seen each other for such a long time. Having let the day to day ritualistic lack of notice drift away, he immediately saw her as simply the woman she was. He was instantly reminded of how confident, immaculately groomed, physically toned, incredibly poised and beautiful Diana really was.

She moved closer, to within reach of their special table. Lincoln stood up to let her set the pace and style of their greeting, not wanting to alarm her at all. Diana approached him and forced herself to kiss him on the cheek, breathing in the smell of him. She inhaled the blend of men's moisturiser and aftershave that she knew so well.

After she sat down, Lincoln followed and sat opposite her, not yet certain why she had wanted to meet him.

"You look beautiful," he said to her, truly feeling that, as he looked at her after all their time apart. He immediately saw her blush. The blush took his memory back to when he had first met her at university. He smiled at the thought.

"What?" she asked him when she saw the smile.

"I was just remembering the night I met you, at that party at David's mother's house," he said, laughing softly. The memory didn't take any further explanation as he could see on her face that she also remembered their moment of meeting.

"David was chasing me relentlessly, and you came to my rescue. My knight in shining armour," Diana replied, remembering how she had felt toward him that night. How handsome she had thought he was - so handsome that he was also probably completely inaccessible.

"We spent the evening arguing because you didn't believe that I wasn't involved with anyone," Lincoln said, grinning.

"You were too handsome to not be involved with someone," replied Diana as she nodded and smiled sadly.

They looked at each other. While he could see her beauty and healthy vitality, what she could see was that he was aging too quickly. It seemed to her that his hair had actually changed over the time they'd been apart. There were more grey hairs around his temples, and his face looked worn. Tired. Strung out.

"How have you been, Lincoln? You look ... tired," she said with hesitation that he heard in her voice.

"I..." he started to say, before finding it difficult to know what he could even start to think to say to her. "I am sorry, Diana."

While she welcomed his apology, a part of her wanted him to expand on it. She wanted to be certain which aspect of their current situation he was apologising for.

"What exactly are you sorry about?" she asked.

Lincoln looked at her for a long time, wondering what could have tempted him away from her, when she was such a beautiful woman who had never done anything wrong to him.

"Every week for three years I visited a young woman..."

"Let us talk frankly to each other, Lincoln," said Diana. "You had *sex* with a young woman."

Lincoln cringed at the terminology. In his opinion, what he and Lexi had together wasn't just sex. Despite the thought entering his head, he didn't want to say that to Diana. He didn't want to hurt her any more, so he agreed.

"Yes."

Diana looked at him. She could see remorse on his face, and yet at the same time, there was something different. She considered that he might honestly hold remorse for hurting her and for hurting their marriage, but he didn't seem to hold any remorse for seeing the girl.

Right then, a waitress approached them, and they automatically ordered the same things they always had on their visits to the eatery. It was natural and easy. When the waitress left, Lincoln saw Diana look at him once more.

"Why, Lincoln?" she asked. "What was missing in our marriage that someone so young could give to you?"

"Diana, I don't want to hurt you any more than I have…"

"No!" she exclaimed. "You don't get to choose what bits you reveal to me and which bits you keep hidden away. We are in this marriage together - for better and for worse. Stop being a coward and talk to me. Tell me everything that happened between the two of you, without leaving anything out."

Lincoln looked closely at her. She wasn't usually so forthcoming in saying what she wanted, but on her, he didn't mind it.

"Have you given up on our marriage completely?" she asked.

Lincoln felt panicked. He didn't know how to answer. It was a perfectly reasonable question, but what did he want? He had no idea, and he wouldn't lie.

"Diana, my head is a muddle right now," he said. "I'm not in the right headspace to be able to think clearly about anything."

"*Have* you completely given up on our marriage, Lincoln? I'm not asking where you want me to be in your life. I just want to know if you have already reached that point, where you know you do not want to ever be a part of my life again."

As Lincoln looked at her, he tried to imagine never seeing her again. He knew he had needed the previous month to focus on only one thing. But as he sat in front of her, and considered her not being around at all, he did start to feel a sadness and a sense of panic.

"No," he replied. "I'm screwed up, but no, I haven't reached a point where I don't want you in my life, Diana. Do you want me in your life?"

Diana had already pondered that question earlier, as she had prepared to see him. He had made a huge mistake. If being honest with herself, he had made a long run of mistakes back to back recently. As if that weren't enough, he seemed to be getting himself deeper and deeper wrapped up in whatever it was about that girl that had him so captivated.

"You are my husband," she said. "I have needed this time away from you, and I don't know how we can move forward from all of this, but I am not ready to give up on us yet. But Lincoln, you need to talk to me. Now. Tonight. Hold nothing back. Show me that courtesy."

With such a speech, he was coaxed to start speaking.

~~~~~

"There are aspects of being with her that I found … addictive," he began. "During the three years that I was visiting her, I came to realise things about me that I didn't know about before, and I became … excited
~~~~~

... about them."

"Such as?" Diana asked, and saw him gather the courage to speak on.

"The first thing was scratching and using her nails on me to create marks. I don't know what it was about, but when I felt marks on me, I ... liked it. So I told her to keep doing that to me."

Lincoln looked at his wife to see how she was handling the information he'd provided so far. On seeing her nod, not seeming judgemental at all, he continued.

"After that, I think I bought something else - a whip or a riding crop. I can't remember the order."

"You used these things on her?" she asked.

"No," Lincoln replied, shaking his head. "I needed her to use them on me - to *hurt* me. Over our time together, I gave her many things to use on me ... and in me..." he admitted.

Diana found a strong dislike growing for what he was saying.

"All that time, you were getting that young girl to hurt you, over and over ... and then you would come home to me, for what? 'Normal' sex?" she asked.

Lincoln wanted to be able to deny it, but couldn't.

"I never stopped wanting to have sex with you. With her, I don't even know if it was a sexual thing, especially in our last year together. All I know is that I wanted that pain. I want that pain, and she can give it to me."

They sat silent for a long time.

"Say something," he begged her, hating to see the hurt he was delivering to her.

"I ... don't know what to say. I had always suspected you were having an affair, Lincoln. I haven't been oblivious to your patterns of going out on those nights, week after week..."

"Why didn't you ever say anything to me? Why didn't you ask?"

He saw her face change, taking on a look of extreme weariness all of a sudden.

"Because you are you," she replied. "I married you with full understanding of the way you attract people, Lincoln. I always expected that as your wife, I would probably have to share you with other people..."

"Diana, I never have seen anyone other than her. Never. Not during our marriage. Not even when we were dating. I was always faithful to you..."

"Until three years ago."

He nodded at her in acknowledgement.

"Yes, until three years ago."

After a long silence as their meals were presented to them, she spoke once more.

"But Lincoln, she has now gone…"

"She'll come back," he said automatically, for a moment having let his guard down. He had spoken naturally without any regard for the way he'd wanted to control the conversation and not hurt her.

"Why did she leave, Lincoln, if the two of you were so happy?" she asked and saw a disappointed look on his face.

"I don't know," he said. "I have to find her and ask her so that I *do* know."

At that point, Diana Kokiri saw how much her husband had been affected by the young woman - and not in a good way. The situation wasn't what she had assumed it was. It wasn't an affair between two people who had fallen in love. It ran deeper, further into the desires he had spoken of - his obsession with having someone hurt him.

"Are you still looking for her?" she asked, disbelieving he could be so stupid, after all the bad decisions he had already made.

"I have now found out where she is," Lincoln replied. "When the time is right, I'll go and approach her, and I know she'll want to be with me again."

Diana looked at him, feeling quite sorry for him. He truly believes she wants to be with him, she thought to herself. He cannot comprehend that she may have left *because* of him, and to get away from him.

She sat quiet, feeling she had heard quite enough to determine how things had been in the 'relationship' between her husband and that girl. It wasn't any great two-way love affair, as she'd always imagined it was. To her, it seemed to be more of a one-sided obsession - and an obsession that didn't seem welcome by the girl in question.

They ate in silence, but Lincoln kept looking at her. He could see that she was processing what he'd told her. He would rather have not told her but had to admit to himself that it felt good to be talking about everything so openly to her. He remembered the day he had gone to the police, and his brief thought then that Diana would be the perfect person to talk to about everything if only he could do it without hurting her so much. Looking at her in the present moment, he understood her saying that she had always expected him to be with other women, so wasn't so shocked by his revelations after all.

The longer they sat, each in their own thoughts, the more he started to look at her more as his wife once again. It had been more than a month since he had been sexual in any way. He hadn't even indulged in self-pleasure since Diana and Lexi had both stepped out of his life.

Diana caught his look and accurately perceived it. He had always been fairly sexual, she knew, with a high sex drive. She studied him, purposely not making any suggestion herself.

Eventually, he spoke.

"I don't want to deceive you anymore, Diana," he said. "I don't know where my head is, or where I am at. Right now, I can't promise you a happy ever after. I can't promise you *anything*, but I would like your company … tonight."

He left his speech at that. There was no romantic wording or grand gesture to try and get her to want to be with him sexually. He had put it to her plain and simple. He wanted to have her body on that one night, and nothing more than that. It was there for the taking, laid out in front of her. She could take it or leave it.

"Alright," Diana replied and heard him let out a sigh of relief. "One night."

As Lincoln nodded at her, she saw a hunger start to grow in his eyes.

"One night."

~~~~~

After making their way back to the apartment, he led her directly into the bedroom. Diana was curious to see how things would play out, given that they usually had sex when they just both happened to be in bed at the same time and it was a matter of reaching out one's arms to the other. It had been a very long time since they'd made love outside of the bed.

They didn't say anything more to one another. All words seemed to have already been spoken for the time being. Instead, he stood with her, put his arms around her, and kissed her passionately. Diana hadn't been kissed like that literally for years. It felt foreign to her, but she let herself indulge in it, curious about what her husband had been sharing with someone else.

He pulled away from her and directed her to turn around. Diana felt his hand lightly push her hair out of the way as he kissed her neck. It was an area she couldn't remember having been explored before … ever. As he kissed her there he unzipped her dress and let it fall to the floor. She was a long time fitness lover and didn't need to wear a bra, given her petite breast size. She felt vulnerable as she stood wearing only panties.

Lincoln indulged in kissing her. Never before had his wife been so receptive to such simple attentions, and he had given up trying to truly please her years ago. From standing behind her, he reached around her body and let one hand caress a nipple, while the other he slipped downward and into her remaining underwear. As always, she was dry. He would change that. On that night, he wouldn't just accept that, like she'd always seemed to want him to. That night, he would get her aroused, and then he would slip inside her and feel her moisture enclose him as he did.

Diana let him touch her. She wasn't used to it. To her, it was a foreign feeling that she'd never warmed to, but she allowed it. As he continued to
~~~~~

kiss her neck and caress her with his hands, she closed her eyes and concentrated on the feelings beginning to flow through her.

She felt him stop his attentions and push down her underwear, leaving her naked. He didn't turn her around yet, instead taking a moment to leave her like that. She sensed him removing all of his own clothing. When he had finished, he turned her to face him. She looked at him in wonder that she had forgotten how toned he kept his body. He held her tight, both of them naked, and started to kiss her passionately again, eventually feeling her arms come around him and hold him also.

After a long while, he let his finger fall down once more. On first touch, he felt for the first time that he could remember, at least a slight amount of wetness. The realisation drove him on. He nudged her back onto the bed and guided her to move up so she could lie down fully.

Diana watched him, unaware of what was happening. When he moved between her legs, she prepared for their usual routine - him slide into her, orgasm, and then slide out, turn over, and go to sleep.

He didn't do that. She realised too late that he was bending his head down. Knowing that she had always pushed him away so he couldn't kiss her there, he clamped his arms and hands down on her thighs to keep her still, before moving his tongue onto her.

Diana had always stopped him, but resolved that she would let him do it. She had never felt comfortable about oral sex, but she wanted to, so she lay back and let him do it. After a while, she relaxed. After a while longer, she started to feel the pleasure in it. After longer still, Diana Kokiri had the first orgasm she had experienced literally in decades.

Lincoln felt like he was in heaven when she climaxed against his tongue. He should have persisted with oral pleasure in their earlier years, but he still couldn't come to terms with forcing a woman to do something she didn't want to do. That was what he told himself, anyway.

He raised his head and moved his body up to kiss her. The thought initially sickened Diana. She didn't want to taste herself. Keeping quiet, she forced herself to forget her fears and let him do it. Once he was kissing her passionately again, she forgot about it altogether.

Lincoln enjoyed the taste of her lips and kept kissing her as he slid inside of her. Even though they were in their usual position - her on the bottom, him on top - it felt different because they were kissing. The lights were on, and they were coming at it from a different place than they usually did.

Diana felt the difference too. Even him entering her felt different, she supposed because of the orgasm she'd had. Again she let herself go with the feelings she was experiencing, finding that she was relishing being in bed with her husband once again. It felt good. It gave her hope that she could look past his indiscretion, and they could start over again with things different between them.

Lincoln was thinking no such thoughts. His focus was solely on how it felt to be having sex again. It had been so long since he'd had release, and it felt like a new experience to be moving inside of his wife, with her being so aroused and wet for him. He followed the signals of his body, increasing in the tempo of his thrusts as he needed to. Finally, he reached that place - that blissful place - as he went over the edge, collapsing heavily onto her.

When he lifted his head and looked at her, he immediately felt overwhelmed. Under him, enclosing him, was Diana - his wife. He had just made her orgasm. She had been wet when he'd entered her. It was different, and he could see on her face that she thought so too. He pulled out of her but continued to lie on her and kiss her until he felt the room cool down.

Gently he guided her to get under the covers, as he did the same and pulled her close to him. They generally never cuddled anymore. It wasn't something they had done for many years, but neither pulled away from it.

"Will you stay?" he asked her.

Overwhelmed, Diana responded in barely a whisper.

"Yes."

~~~~~

The next morning, Diana woke up, not sure what she would find with her husband, or how he would react to her. When she turned her head, she saw he was no longer in their bed. She got out, put on her dress once more, and after using the bathroom, walked out to the living room to find him.

He wasn't there. He was gone. Looking at the clock, she saw it was only 9am. He'd left early without even saying good morning to her. She didn't know how she should feel about that, but in her heart, she knew it wasn't acceptable to her for him to shrug her off quite so easily. It might have only been one night, but walking out without any kind of greeting was beyond belief to her. It spoke volumes about how little he regarded her.

She didn't want to wait around any longer. Instead, she made herself presentable and took a few minutes to look through all the storage areas in the apartment one more time - cupboards, drawers, wardrobes. She wanted to make certain that nothing of hers was left behind before she walked out of there for the very last time.

The previous day, she'd grabbed her things from obvious places, much like a snatch and grab, to get in there and out of there as quickly as possible. This time, she explored everywhere. When she opened his drawers, one by one, she saw things she'd never seen before.

In the first drawer of his stack of long drawers, she saw the whip. She
~~~~~

tentatively put her hand onto it and felt the rawness of the leather. It was an earthy feel that she realized she never felt these days. She considered taking the whip out, but resisted the temptation. She was too interested in seeing what else he had in the drawers that she had never ventured to go near before.

The second drawer held a chain - heavy and thick. She didn't want to think about what he needed that for. It wasn't some thin, weak chain. It was an industrial-strength chain that had weight behind it. Shuddering, she closed the drawer and continued her exploration.

In the next drawer down, she found a riding crop. That, she did pull out, looking at it with curiosity. Another level of inquisitiveness made her slap the end of it down onto her hand. She didn't like the feeling.

It caused in her a small amount of distress that the items had all been there throughout the night. He could have used any of them on her, or made her use them on him. They were the tools he had talked about during their dinner - the things he had made that girl use on him. But why? Where did that desire come from? She had never even known he had that side to him, and she had known him for twenty years. The sad thought flowed through her mind - had she ever really known him?

Having seen enough, she closed the drawers and made sure that everything was as it should be, in preparation for letting herself out. She took the apartment key off her keyring and put it on the side table in the entranceway, on top of the note she had left the day before. It didn't escape her attention that the note remained unmoved - disregarded, just like she had been.

The night had been better than she had been imagining her first meeting with him would be, but the apartment wasn't where she wanted to be anymore. That life wasn't how she wanted to live her life. She wanted much more from a husband than he could give her. It was time for her to move on too.

Before she walked out, she remembered that she hadn't checked the drawer of the side table when she'd removed her belongings the day before. After she opened it, her sight was captivated by a piece of paper on top of the varied items in the drawer. She pulled it out and looked closely at it.

There was a date on it - yesterday's date. In Lincoln's handwriting was the name of a town, and the name of a supermarket. Below those two items, was one more thing written - 'Lexi'.

Diana breathed out heavily in the realisation. He had told her during dinner that he had finally located the girl and now wanted to speak to her. The piece of paper indicated where he would go to see her - but not before Diana spoke to her herself.

Later that day, she made her travel plans and headed off to another small town, where she walked into the supermarket and immediately saw the girl she was looking for. Upon seeing Lexi in person, Diana noticed that she was no longer a girl. She no longer looked as alive and fresh as she had in the photo that had been broadcast for all to see. She almost seemed to have undergone the same level of stress that Lincoln had - a stress that had contributed to a slight increase in ageing.

Diana approached the checkout, said what she wanted to say to the young girl she had shared her husband with for three years, and then walked out. She did not harbour any resentment toward the girl. If Lexi had helped Lincoln with things that Diana knew she wouldn't have been able to do, she shouldn't be condemned. She should, if anything, be thanked.

~~~~~

After the evening and night with his wife, Lincoln resumed work the next morning feeling refreshed and more alert than he had in over a month. He pondered again that he now knew where Lexi was, but he would hold onto that information. He would wait at least another month - maybe even two. She might come back to him in that time by herself, and then he would hold all the power when she asked to return to his life.

His wife was already forgotten.

~~~~~

He let the month pass, forcing himself to focus and indulge in his work. He hadn't given Diana another thought. She was completely gone from his mind, as if their night together had never happened.

One evening, his watch sounded, and he looked at it, not sure why the alarm was going off. He was surprised to see that it was time. One whole month had passed by, and it was time.

Yes, it was time for him to assess if he wanted to go and see her or not. He didn't want to panic. He wouldn't boldly and blindly rush at her without thinking first. As he considered and visualised seeing her again, he felt too desperate still, and he didn't want to make any more mistakes.

He used his resources to do another check of her accounts. From that, he could see that she still had wages being paid by the same supermarket, and was still withdrawing money in the same town. She was staying still, and would probably continue to do so if she thought he hadn't found her yet, or didn't think he was still looking for her.

He decided he would wait another few weeks, and then he would go and see her. He would make her see him. Once she saw him, all would be well again. He was sure of it.

~~~~~

Finally, four weeks later, he believed he had the strength to go to Lexi and convince her to return home with him. He flew into the closest airport to where she was, hired a rental car, and booked into a three-star
~~~~~

motel. The next morning, he went to the supermarket as soon as it opened, and waited.

After their interaction that first day - with her treating him like a common customer - a customer! - he had lost sight of her as she had gotten into a man's car.

The next morning, he had gone to the supermarket again, having let such anger build up in him that he knew he would hurt that man in the supermarket. The thought of anyone else touching her infuriated him, and he had to deal to that.

Lexi had stopped him from hurting that man - her supervisor, who she said she had no romantic or sexual entanglement with. At first, Lincoln hadn't believed her, but then he had. She had spoken to him so harshly, and with so much passion and forwardness. She was so different from the Lexi he knew. He had found himself quite stunned at the different person she was - so much so that he'd vowed to not go near her workplace again, and he hadn't.

But he hadn't left town.

~~~~~

For the following days since their last interaction, he had watched her. He wouldn't approach her yet, as he didn't want her to bolt again. For the moment, he could see her, even if only from a great distance. That was better than not seeing her at all.

During that time, he still managed his company. Remotely, with his laptop and mobile phone at the ready, his staff didn't need to know where he was or what he was doing.

He was just about to consider approaching her one more time, certain that by now she would be wanting to see him. In his mind, she would have gone away and had those few days, and that would have been enough for her to realize how much she missed him and wanted to be with him again.

Then he saw something he hadn't wanted to see - a man, and this time there was no mistaking that they were involved. He watched them walking along the waterfront. He saw them kiss. It wasn't a friendly kiss. It was a kiss with great passion and desire. He could see it on her face, even from the distance he was from them. He didn't act. He was scared to let himself get out of the car. He felt his head go fuzzy again, into a different space, but he was determined to maintain control. Everything about her was chaos, and he could hardly stand that, but at the same time, he just couldn't let her go.

Inside of him, he felt the rage building. It was a level of fury that even he didn't like the feeling of.

He had to talk to someone urgently before he did something…

"Diana," he said into his phone after dialling her number.
~~~~~

"Lincoln? Are you alright?" she responded and heard him take a deep breath.

"I found her. I can see her right now," he said vaguely, as if he were talking to himself rather than to her.

Diana heard the words. Although she wished she could just tell him to leave her alone so she could start a new life, she took a deep breath and formulated the best words that she could. She knew she had to at least try and stop him from making any more mistakes. Their marriage might be over, but she wouldn't let him do any more stupid things that could affect his future.

"Lincoln, where are you?" she asked. "Are you in a hotel somewhere?"

"I'm in my car. I can see her."

"Lincoln, please listen to me. You have to stop what you are doing. Start your car and drive away. She is terrified of you…"

"No, you're wrong," he said vaguely. "She loves me…"

"Lincoln! Listen to me!" he heard Diana scream down the phone at him, in a tone that finally seemed to reach him. "Lexi left Melbourne to get away from you. She does not want to see you. You scare her. *Stop scaring her!*"

"I would never hurt her, Diana," Lincoln replied, his mind full of confusion and fogginess. "You don't understand…"

"No, *you* don't understand, Lincoln. You can't see the situation as it is. Think! Why would she leave if she loved you? Why would she go to such lengths to hide from you? Lincoln, please listen and think about this. You are going to be arrested if you keep harassing her," Diana pleaded to him, hoping something she said would make him see what a mess he was making of his life. "Do you want to go to jail?"

"No, of course I don't…"

"Then leave her alone," Diana continued. "She wants a new life, without you in it."

Lincoln heard the words and the mist began to clear … partially.

"She's with someone," he said. "I can see them together right now. He's kissing her. He's kissing my Lexi."

"She isn't yours, Lincoln," Diana said. "You have to wake up and see that, or something very bad is going to happen in this situation. Please don't let anything bad happen. You are my husband, and I have known you forever. Even if our marriage can't be repaired, please … *please* don't throw away the rest of your life by doing something you are going to deeply regret."

They were both silent for a while as Lincoln watched Alexis and Anthony indulging in their kissing and then standing up. Both looked happy, even though Lincoln didn't want to believe it.

He couldn't remember the last time she had looked happy when she was with him. He could remember how she looked when they had first met. She hadn't looked like that for a long time.

"Please come home, Lincoln," Diana laid one final plea to him. That one, he heard.

"Yes. I will come home, Diana," he said as her words finally sunk in and he began to believe. "I'm going to leave now. I'll be back in Melbourne tomorrow night. Will you meet me at the apartment then? Can I see you?"

Diana held back the sigh that so much wanted to escape her right then. She had just resolved to be free again - free to start a new chapter in her life - and she still would. First, though, she would make sure that her husband got away from that girl so he could not do any more harm than he already had.

"I will," she said. "Call me when you're back in Melbourne, and I will come to the apartment."

"Thank you," he said and hung up.

He sat a while longer, watching Alexis and Anthony make their way back along the long waterfront path. He would not follow her again. That night, he would stay in the shabby three-star motel. The next morning, he would go home and start to salvage something from his marriage.

CHAPTER 4

The Enlightenment

Alexis ventured back to work two days later, having enjoyed every minute she had been able to spend with Anthony. Everything was always so easy with him, like nothing needed to be a drama, and nothing had to be so serious.

"Good morning, Alexis," she heard Tom call out to her as she started to set up her counter for the morning. She returned the sentiment before she saw him move down the line of checkout counters, stopping at each one and delighting staff with his cheerful greetings.

The day passed as any other day did in the supermarket - any other day when Lincoln Kokiri was not around, anyway. Alexis hadn't seen him for five days, and found that he had mostly left her mind. Her time with Anthony was so limited when they saw each other, in the alternation of him coming to see her on their same days off, and then her going to see him on their next same days off. During those times together, she only wanted to concentrate on him. Lincoln was her past, and he had to stay there. Hopefully, he had listened to her when he'd seen her, and he was now back in Melbourne, moving on with his life also.

She gave a brief thought to his wife, Diana. When she had approached Alexis in the supermarket, she had indicated that she had left Lincoln and was starting a new life too. It made Alexis wonder how he was dealing with his life, with both of his women having walked away from him. It must be extremely lonely to have two women you are seeing, and then suddenly they are both gone, she pondered to herself.

She then kicked all thoughts about Lincoln Kokiri out of her head once again.

~~~~~

"Do you need a ride anywhere, Alexis? I'm off to the hardware store again," Tom said to her as she was walking toward the exterior doors at the end of her day.

"Oh, thanks, Tom. Actually, I do need to get to the bank," she answered, remembering she had another two cheques in her wallet to deposit.

"Great! I can drop you off there. Let's go," he said genially, holding the door open for her to pass through.

As Alexis opened the passenger side door of his car, something in the
~~~~~

back seat caught her eye and made her halt abruptly.

"Are you okay?" Tom asked her, seeing the change in her immediately.

When she didn't speak, he followed her eyes to the back seat of his car.

"Oh," he said, laughing softly. "You can see my secret life."

Alexis looked up at him, suddenly wary of getting in the car with him. The items on the seat were things she had seen before - floggers, a whip, and a riding crop. The sight made her feel almost faint.

Tom watched her face, confused at why the things in his car were upsetting her so much. No matter why, there was no doubting that she was upset - very visibly so. He walked around to her side of the car and stood close to her.

"Alexis, this is something I wouldn't share with any staff members usually, but I am part of a local BDSM club. Those things are props and tools that my partner and I use when we go to demonstrations."

Alexis heard the words and was confounded.

"You go to a club?" she asked. "To use those? On your partner??"

She saw Tom smile at her softly, not like anyone who would want to inflict pain on her, or want her to inflict pain on him.

"Jump in the car, and I'll give you a ride to the bank. Don't worry, those things will stay in the back of my car, I promise. Don't give them another thought. All I ask is that you don't mention this to anyone else in there," he said, indicating to the supermarket behind them. "I trust you, so I don't mind that you know, but I don't want *everyone* to know."

Alexis looked at his face and nodded softly. Trusting people was so difficult for her, but she was changing as a person. That was the next obstacle she had to overcome. Tom had only ever been nice to her. He had never, in any way, shown any interest in her, other than as a friendly work colleague and supervisor. She also knew now that he had a partner. Not that such a situation had stopped Lincoln, of course…

~~~~~

"Has that stuff really affected you so much, Alexis?" Tom asked her before she opened the door to get out. She had always been a quiet person since she had started work in the supermarket. During their car ride, since seeing his gear, she had been particularly subdued and silent.

Alexis looked at him, feeling herself yearn to be more relaxed about things.

"You are open about it. You're not trying to hide it," she said, with a sound of curiosity in her voice, like it was a question rather than a statement.

Tom looked at her in wonder. Had she lived such a closed-off life that she was unaware of such activities?
~~~~~

"Alexis, I'm part of a large club where hundreds of people take part in using this kind of stuff. I don't want everyone to know about that side of my life, but it isn't something to be ashamed of," he said to her. On her face, he could see her confusion only intensify, not relax.

"I don't … I'm sorry, Tom, I have to go. Thank you for the ride. I'll see you at work tomorrow," she said and gave him a sad smile before climbing out of the car, leaving him in a vast state of curiosity himself.

~~~~~

The next morning, she was setting up her checkout counter when he approached her. She saw him look around them as if making sure no-one could hear before he spoke.

"Were you okay yesterday?" he asked, concerned for her. "I'm sorry if the stuff in my car freaked you out."

Alexis smiled at him in a desperate attempt to have the subject done and finished with.

"Yes," she said. "I'm sorry about how I reacted. It's no big deal, and don't worry, I won't mention it to anyone."

"I know I don't have to worry about that, Alexis," Tom replied. "I trust you, and hadn't thought you would tell anyone. I was more worried about *you*, and your reaction to it."

"I'm fine," she said, purposely putting on a larger smile to hide how seeing the stuff had made her feel. "There really is nothing to worry about."

Tom looked at her face. He wouldn't pressure her, but he was intuitive enough to know that there was something worrying about her reaction.

"Okay. If you want to talk about it, I'm here," he said. He then walked off, leaving her to serve the first customer of the day.

~~~~~

Two days later, Alexis found herself curious again. No more had been said about the matter, but it was on her mind. She found herself increasingly wanting to talk to Tom about the club thing he had mentioned. It seemed impossible to her that people would get together in large groups and do things like that to one another. It just didn't seem right.

When she was about to leave work for the day, she saw Tom getting ready to leave.

"Are you okay, Alexis?" he asked in his usual cheerful voice as he started veering toward the exterior doors, to also finish for the day.

"Tom, can I ask you questions about … you know?"

Tom looked at her and instantly did know what she was referring to. He smiled at her, but with great care to make sure she did not think he was suggesting anything to her.

"You can, but not here," he said. "Let's find somewhere quieter.

Where would you like to go?"

"There are seats down by the waterfront…"

He nodded at her.

"I know the ones. Let's go," he said.

They talked no more as he drove them to a parking spot close to the water. Once there, they walked down to the waterside and sat on one of the benches close to where she'd sat with Anthony only a few nights before. It was also where she'd been watched by another set of eyes, even though she didn't know it.

"Ask me anything, Alexis," said Tom. "I'm an open book, but first, can I ask you why those things freaked you out so much? Has someone used that kind of thing on you before?" he asked her, very curious as she was of such a quiet nature, although through the club he had met many different kinds of people who he wouldn't have suspected were into such activities.

He saw her shake her head and look down for a long time before she brought her eyes back up to meet his.

"No, quite the opposite," she said and watched his face as he tried to process what she meant by that.

"You've used things like that on other people?" he asked.

Alexis felt a blush appear on her face. It was an intense blush that came from the shame she still felt inside of herself because of the things she had done to Lincoln.

"I have," she began and took another deep breath before continuing her wording. "But I didn't want to."

"I don't understand. Usually, there's a mutual gain from BDSM. A person who likes to be in control, matches in sync with someone who wants to be controlled. There should never be any aspect of someone doing - or having done to them - something they don't want. That isn't what it's about," he said. "Was it as part of a club?"

Alexis shook her head again.

"No, and I don't think it was a 'BDSM' situation like you talk about," she said. "He was just someone who wanted me to … hurt him."

"This is a boyfriend of yours?" Tom asked, his curiosity growing by the minute.

He saw her give a smile that was unfathomable in terms of what kind of smile it was.

"Not a boyfriend, but…"

"But he wasn't a formal play partner, as such."

"I don't know what you mean by formal play partner, Tom," Alexis replied. "I don't know anything about this BDSM world you're talking about. I'd never even heard the term until you said it the other day."

Tom remained quiet for a few minutes, trying to process what she was saying. He had only gotten into the club through a friend of his, and as far as he knew, that was the only kind of scene where people used things like whips and floggers.

"It wasn't in a club situation that you used that gear?"

"No," Alexis replied quietly, feeling some of the residual guilt and bad feelings about her time with Lincoln start to evaporate as she talked more. "He wanted me to hurt him, so I did, but I never enjoyed it. I never should have done it. I should have said no, but I didn't have the strength to," she said and paused before continuing. "But are you saying that people *like* this kind of thing? I know that he liked being on the receiving end of the pain, but you know people who like to *deliver* that pain?"

"Yes! Well, not precisely," Tom began to explain. "My partner - that is my play partner, I mean. I'm not in a relationship, Alexis, just to be clear. Samantha has been a good friend of mine through our entire lives. We went to kindergarten together! Anyway, about a year ago she mentioned to me that she had joined a club. She'd been introduced to it by her then-boyfriend. I think, to her, it was a new thing, but she was loving it. Then she asked me if I wanted to try it, so I did, and I liked it well enough. Then she split with that guy, and she suggested that she and I become play partners in the club, so we did."

"So you *hit* her?"

Tom hated the way that sounded but understood the question. He answered as best as he could to try and bring her thinking around to a different angle.

"Okay, let me explain that Samantha mostly likes to be in control of everything in her life. For the duration she was with her boyfriend, he wanted her to be aggressive with him. He wanted her to be dominant, but in reality, he was controlling that, which caused a strange dynamic for her, I think. Like he wanted her to be in charge, but he was in charge of her being in charge. It was really weird, the way she explained it to me.

"Anyway, when she ended her relationship with him, and asked me about being her club partner, she wanted to trade places. She wanted to see things from the other side, so to speak. With him, she'd had to hit him and do to him the things he wanted her to do to him - all the while telling her she was in control - so weird, I find that. Then she asked me if I would consider being a dominant, with her as my submissive. We had long talks about that one, I can tell you!

"But in the end, we found our groove. So generally, when we're at the club, she goes into the role of being the person who just wants to be controlled - and with her, that means she wants to be hurt.

"So yes, to answer your question, I do hit her ... spank, slap, whip - whatever terminology you want to use - with a few different things that she likes the feel of."

Alexis had been listening closely and was trying to get her head around what she was being told. Until that moment, she had never heard of anyone doing the things that Lincoln had made her do to him. She had thought it wasn't a normal request, or a normal thing to deliver to others.

"But how do you feel when you hurt her like that, Tom? I used to feel sick sometimes…"

"Well, I suppose everyone is different. Samantha asks me to use different things at different times," said Tom. "In that, we agreed that she would have to tell me what she wanted me to use. I don't want to just try different things on her. It is her body, after all, that's on the receiving end of it. I think that might go against the traditional role of a dominant - to let her choose how things will go - but we don't care. So with us, she sometimes gives me a new thing and asks me to use it on her, and if she likes the feeling of it, I'll keep using it. If she doesn't like the feeling - and there have been some things she's wanted to try but then didn't want to try a second time - then we discard that and don't go back to it. But she seems to get a real sense of pleasure from the use of those things on her. I don't think it is pain to her…"

"Have you been on the receiving end of the pain?" Alexis asked.

"I have - only a little though," said Tom, nodding. "When she first took me to the club, part of the introduction was feeling a few different tools used on me. I didn't mind the small amount that I got that night, but I didn't feel any kind of pleasure from it either. I didn't feel any kind of need for it. I do think Samantha experiences it completely differently. She says it's just pleasure to her, and I believe her. I worried for a while that she was doing it because, for whatever reason, she might think that I wanted her to feel pleasure in it, but over time, she has convinced me that it is what she wants."

Alexis sat quietly again, processing all of the information that was being shared with her.

"Do you get…" she started to ask, feeling her face blush slightly before she continued. "Do you get … aroused … from it? From hitting her?"

Tom laughed softly at her, feeling only a slight embarrassment at the question.

"If I answer that question, you have to promise not to tell Samantha, if you ever meet her!" he said and paused before speaking again. "When I was at the club for the introduction, and *I* was experiencing being struck, I didn't, no. To me, it really did just feel like I was being hit, and I couldn't enjoy that. Even now, being the one who delivers the pain to Samantha, and knowing how it affects her, I don't understand the why or the how it somehow gets perceived as pleasure. But!

"When I'm with Samantha and she is in full BDSM mode, I do get aroused from it, yes," he finished and looked at Alexis, wondering what she would make of him for admitting that.

"But you aren't … involved with each other?" asked Alexis.

"No," he said, laughing slightly to cover his own confusion over that question. "I know it probably sounds like a strange situation to be in. We are close friends, and we do this thing together, and I do get turned on by it … but we have never crossed that line."

"But she must know that you get aroused…"

Tom felt his face go deep red but didn't mind the conversation. In truth, he was finding it quite refreshing to be able to talk to someone about it.

"Oh yeah, she's caught me out a few times when I couldn't hide it, but we find a way to laugh it off and keep our distance from each other sexually. It isn't that way for everyone in the club. There are nights when I wonder if I'm not in the middle of one big orgy!" he said and laughed out loud, making Alexis smile. "But that isn't the focus for most people, I don't think. I expect some people go there and then do go home and … go at it … but then other people never go near sex in it at all. I think for some people, it is all about control, and they don't associate it with sex in any way at all. Everyone is different, but at the club, although there are very strict rules in place to ensure everyone's safety, the people are nice, and everyone is fairly relaxed about things too. We all respect each other, and the differences in what we like, and what we do."

Tom looked at her face and tried to read how she was feeling about everything he had told her. He found, though, that he had many questions emerging in him about her.

"But Alexis, did the person you were with *make* you do things to him?"

"Oh, I should have said no, Tom," she replied. "He didn't threaten me or do anything like that. At the time, it felt like I had no choice, but since I left, I have finally been able to see that I always had a choice. I just couldn't see that when I was in the situation."

"What things did you do?"

Alexis looked at him and wondered how much she would want to mention. But at least the few things she had seen in his car, he would think were okay, so perhaps restricting the list to those would be okay.

"I used the same things that I saw in your car, plus a few different things. It seemed to be progressive, in terms of pain levels. Like he would find something, and it would be exciting and arousing to him, but then one day it just wouldn't be enough, and he would have to go out and find something else … something more. It started to feel like there might be no end to it, and I became worried about the level of pain he was starting to seem to need. That's when I left."

"But you were partners - in a relationship?"

Alexis took a deep breath and wondered where she should stop talking. It was hard to end the conversation with the openness of it being so therapeutic. She had been open with Anthony, but the current conversation was different because Tom lived the whole pain-giving thing in reality. He was opening her eyes to a different side of it, which she did need to be able to put that whole chapter of her life behind her.

"Tom, the man I was with, was married, and he would come and visit me a few times a week."

"Just for pain?"

"No, we were sexual as well," Alexis replied. "In the beginning, it was all sexual. I think the reason he wanted to keep coming to see me was for sex, but then things started to change slowly. Toward the end, he was … reaching his point of arousal … *just* from my delivery of pain to him. At that point, I stopped really being a sexual partner to him, I think." She paused and then spoke again, seeing Tom's intent attention on what she was saying. "I think at the end, I wasn't a lover anymore. I was just a deliverer of pain. That was my role."

"So you ended it. Did he accept that?"

"No," she said. "Well, he hadn't a short time ago, anyway. He might have now. I hope he has. He isn't a bad person. For a while, when I first got away, I thought he was evil - like he had something dark inside of him - but I know now that was never the case. We were just too … different."

Alexis stopped herself before she said too much. It felt so good talking about everything, but she didn't want to keep talking about Lincoln. She didn't want to risk mentioning his name.

Tom looked intently at her face, intrigued by the things they had talked about. She was such a timid little thing in their workplace. He would never have guessed that she had such things in her past.

"Did you move on, Alexis?" he asked. "With someone new, I mean?"

"Yes! I am involved with someone - Anthony. He is wonderful. No pain in sight so far," she said, letting out a small laugh before she looked closely at him again. "It feels good to be able to talk like this. I felt so … oh, I don't even know really … just so different from everyone else, for so long. Anthony has helped with that, but he hasn't lived some of the things that I've done. It feels good to be able to talk about this with you. Thank you."

Tom took note of his feelings. He hadn't known she had a boyfriend, although he had wondered about Lincoln Kokiri that day that he had walked into the supermarket. But obviously, he wasn't her boyfriend.

At that moment, Tom realised that he might have unconsciously been starting to have some design on her - perhaps unknowingly starting to assess her as a possible girlfriend. He shook his head to get that thinking out of his mind. Even if she hadn't been involved, he had never been involved with someone he worked with, and he didn't want to be. Generally, he had always gotten on well with everyone he worked with - and he wanted it to stay that way.

"What was that thought that you just discarded?" Alexis asked with a smile on her face, knowing that she did the same thing sometimes. She saw Tom blush slightly and smile sheepishly at her.

"I was just thinking…" he started, trying to think of anything to say other than what he had been really thinking. "That you and Samantha would probably get on really well. Would you like to meet her? She could provide a different insight again, being a woman, and she's been on both sides of the pain thing."

Alexis was surprised - pleasantly so.

"Oh, but Tom, should you have talked to me about her so much? Would it be better that she didn't know…"

"No, Samantha is the most open person I know," Tom said, smiling. "Honestly, she would tell the whole world private things if she thought everyone would listen, but I appreciate you considering that. I'll talk to her about you, if you are okay with that?"

"Yeah, of course," Alexis replied. "I don't have … I've never had … women as friends. It would be nice if I could get to know more people."

The two of them sat and looked at each other for a long time before turning to each look out over the water.

"But what of this 'Anthony', Alexis?" asked Tom. "Where is he and what does he do?"

It was an innocent question, but immediately Alexis felt her nervousness kick in. She didn't want anything about Anthony to get back to Lincoln. Perhaps Lincoln had left town and was back in Melbourne, quietly getting on with his life even as she and Tom sat on the bench, but the risk was too great.

"He works in a supermarket too, but he doesn't live here, so we only see each other every few weeks," Alexis said. "It is slow, getting to know each other, but that's good for me, I think. That previous person I was seeing - that whole scenario - it played with my head a lot. It's taken a while for me to start to relax and feel like it's okay to enjoy my life."

Alexis felt Tom look at her intently. She could almost see the curiosity oozing from him, but believed that she had gotten to know him at least enough to be certain that whatever he wanted to ask her, he would ask her.

"Of course it's okay to enjoy your life, Alexis. It's more than okay. It's your *right* to fully enjoy your life. Nobody should be trying to force you to not enjoy it - or even just *imply* to you that you shouldn't enjoy it. Life is short. It can be so very short for some people. You have to make the most of every day. Don't do the things you don't want to do," he said, making her thoughtful with his words.

He watched her face. It seemed like she was completely absorbing what he had said, not only about the simple things he was saying, but also the concept of having full control of her life.

"Why do you think it was so easy for him - that man - to control you so easily, Alexis?"

Alexis took her time to consider the question and found herself taken aback.

"I … hmm … Tom, I don't know. I have never thought about that before," she said and paused before continuing. "It all happened so slowly at first, I suppose, so I didn't really consider the level of control he was having over me." Silence again. "When I first met him, I had it in my head that the only way that I could be happy with someone was if I was certain that what I was doing for them, truly was making them happy. So in a way, I started everything that happened between us - the way that it happened. I encouraged him to be forthcoming and simply tell me what he wanted from me, rather than leave it to me to try and guess or … perceive … what he wanted."

Tom listened to what she was saying. He could sense in her a type of reluctance to believe that the things she had done - the things she said she'd been encouraged to do to that man, whoever he was - might be solely things that the man had wanted. She didn't seem to want to believe that she had not been responsible for the happenings at all.

"It sounds to me like you want to take all the blame…" he started to say. His words were quickly cut off by her speaking with an insistence in her voice.

"No, not at all, but I did *start* it," she said. "I didn't mean for it to go where it did. I didn't mean for him to go *where* he did, but it was me who initiated him having control over everything that happened between us. I can now see that was my mistake. Giving full control to another person was a mistake. I think that's why I can't quite understand this BDSM thing you've talked about, and the idea that so many people like it. It isn't a small thing to hand control over to another person."

"But that is where some people perceive it to be the exact opposite of what it is," Tom said. "Some people think that the person delivering the pain - the dominant person standing up, leaning over their submissive - is the one in control. In actual fact, it's the other way around. It's the submissive who controls, as they're the one who can simply say no."

"But what about all the things they have to put up with before they say no?" Alexis asked. "What if you didn't know what was too much before it was done to you? It's all very well that you can then say no, but what if some damage was already done in that moment? That can't be undone, can it..."

Tom heard what she was saying and considered how differently she saw things that he had never even considered before. His mind drifted back to Samantha. There had been things that they had done together, that afterwards she'd said honestly and forcefully that she would not do again. He had respected that and had never crossed a boundary of doing something she didn't want. But Alexis was right in her thinking that, in some ways, it was too late if someone consented to something and then found out they didn't like it. That it was too painful to try again. That it was too painful to bear. There was no undoing the pain that was already delivered if it was then realised that it was too painful to keep going - but what about the pain that was already experienced by that person?

"Hmm," he muttered with thoughtfulness in his tone. He looked closely at her, and then smiled softly. "Okay, now I really want you to meet Samantha. You can be my liaison, doing a check of whether she really does enjoy these things, or if she's doing it for the wrong reasons..."

Alexis laughed at him.

"Oh, Tom! I'm sure you know and accurately understand Samantha!" she exclaimed. "You two have known each other all of your lives, so how could you not? No, don't let my situation flow into your thoughts about your own situation. They're not the same thing. The man that I talk about - he and I didn't know each other before. We didn't already know what each other was like, or what we really wanted from each other," she said to him with more force than she intended before continuing. "No, the thing you have with Samantha - however you want to describe it - is based on a long-term friendship. She must know that she doesn't have to do any of that to keep you in her life. And *she* was the one who instigated it..."

"But so did you, you said..."

"Yes, but that is different," Alexis said. "I instigated him guiding me in what he wanted, and when I did that, I didn't even know he liked pain, let alone would want me to deliver it to him. I instigated giving him control, yes, but in your situation, Samantha is the one who instigated the pain aspect of your friendship."

Tom nodded at her and could see the difference as she explained it.

"Alright, I concede that you might be right there," he said. "But it would still be good to have someone neutral between me and Samantha, to tell me if she's not acting as she really wants to."

Alexis smiled at him. She found it increasingly interesting that her own story was having such an effect on him, since he was fully into the whole 'BDSM' thing that he kept speaking of, and she had never even known about it, let alone been interested in it.

"If you want me to meet Samantha, I will, gladly. But!" she said to him, smiling but making sure he knew she was serious in the sentence to follow. "If she tells me anything and specifically informs me that she doesn't want me to tell you about it, I will respect her wish and keep it to myself. That is how it will be, no matter how much you try and get me to tell you about it."

Tom heard the words and felt them to be a condition that he was reluctant about but agreed to.

"Okay."

~~~~~

Two days later, Tom approached her on her checkout counter when she was an hour from finishing for the day.

"Alexis, Samantha's coming to my place for dinner tonight," he said. "Would you like to come along with me and meet her?"

Alexis looked at him, silent for a long while, before answering.

"Does she know…"

He nodded at her.

"She knows that I've spoken to you about the things that we do, yes," he said. "I didn't want to tell her about *your* situation. I thought you should be the one to do that, but she knows that you're curious about the whole BDSM thing, in particular her experiences and thoughts about it."

Tom saw Alexis nod at him in understanding.

"Thank you," she said. "I know I don't need to hide anything that I've done but…" she said and found herself quite emotional all of a sudden, still finding it so hard to be accepting of her own past actions.

Tom reached out his arm and touched her shoulder lightly with his hand, as an old friend would.

"It's okay. I don't think you should feel bad about anything that has happened to you, or anything that you've done, but I know that you do, and you can trust me. I won't talk about it to anyone," he said and paused. "Now about tonight?"

Alexis smiled at him and nodded.

"Yeah, of course. Where shall I go, and at what time?"

"It's probably easiest if I pick you up, I think. My place is on the outskirts of town and not at all within walking distance. Are you okay with me coming to your home?" he asked, curious about what her actual level of trust in him was, but she only nodded.

"Of course. Thank you," she responded and wrote down the address of the guest house for him.

"Awesome, I'll let Samantha know. She's looking forward to meeting you," he said and strode off, leaving Alexis slightly nervous about the evening to come. Making friends was something she had never really
~~~~~

invested any time into in her life, but she was enjoying getting to know Tom. She had to put trust in the assumption that anyone who was a good friend of his, must also be likely to be a good person.

~~~~~

Alexis was giggling - hard. She was at Tom's house, and while he cooked their meal in the kitchen that was open to the living area, she was sitting down with Samantha. Being told was one of many stories Samantha had so far shared about her and Tom growing up.

It was the first time in such a long time that Alexis felt like she was truly letting go. She couldn't remember the last time she had laughed for so long, continuously.

She'd instantly warmed to Samantha, who had invited her into her arms and hugged her with a huge smile on her face when the two women had met.

"Come on now, Samantha, you're stretching the truth a bit there," Tom threw into the conversation, making Alexis laugh even more at the facial expressions the two people before her gave to each other.

"Don't believe him, Alexis. I'm the one you can trust in these stories," Samantha quipped back quickly, showing her fondness for him on her face.

~~~~~

Sitting and eating the food Tom had prepared, Alexis felt so at ease that she once again found herself pondering the situation between Tom and Samantha. They got on so well. She could see the way that Tom looked at Samantha, and yet they had never crossed the sexual line, Tom had told her.

Alexis listened patiently and with great interest to Samantha talking about her journey through studying to be a clothing designer, and her small, slow start in the industry since her course had finished. It seemed like such a contrast to her own life. The glamour of becoming a known clothing designer was a far cry from being a supermarket checkout operator. Alexis could hear in Samantha's voice the degree of dedication to how far she had to go, and how hard she would have to work, to become a true success in a way that she could support herself comfortably from that kind of earnings.

"You are incredible, Samantha," Alexis said, in awe.

Samantha laughed loudly at her.

"I don't think so! But thank you for saying that, Alexis. It might take some time, but I will get there."

~~~~~

As they finished their meal, Alexis jumped up to show her appreciation.

"What are you doing, Alexis?" Tom asked as he saw her making
~~~~~

moves in his kitchen.

"I'm going to wash the dishes..." she started to say. Immediately she heard Samantha laughed out loud.

Tom was surprised but didn't object, instead taking the stance of being grateful.

"Thank you, Alexis," he said, looking pointedly at Samantha. "That is very kind of you."

Alexis watched the two of them as she set to work. Eventually, Samantha stood up and came to join her.

"Alright, you're making me feel guilty. Move over and I'll wash if you dry," she said, making Tom laugh out loud in response.

"Oh, my God!" he exclaimed. "Alexis, you have to come and have dinner more often when this one is here."

~~~~~

"Right, how about you and I leave this one here in his now-pristine home, and I give you a ride home?" Samantha asked Alexis whilst joking with Tom.

"Are you sure? I can catch a taxi..."

"No, you will not catch a taxi! I have to drive past the area you live in anyway, so it's no bother," Samantha replied, moving in to give Tom a hug and a kiss on his cheek. "Thank you for a lovely dinner, Tom. I'll see you Thursday night."

Alexis saw Tom return the hug and kiss before turning to her.

"Thanks for coming, Alexis. It's good for this one to be able to talk to someone about so many things to do with me!" he said, with a humorous sound to his voice.

Alexis leaned up and kissed him on the cheek softly.

"I have enjoyed this greatly, Tom. Thank you for inviting me."

~~~~~

Soon Alexis and Samantha were sitting in a car, slowly leaving Tom's driveway. It was the first time the two women had been alone all evening.

As she reversed down the driveway, Samantha caught Alexis looking at her.

"I see what you're thinking, Alexis," Samantha said, grinning. "I've seen that look hundreds of times, believe me! You are wondering why Tom and I are only friends, right?" she asked and saw Alexis nod in response. "I know. People ask that question all the time. They have for years. I don't know why."

Alexis laughed.

"Really?" she asked. "You don't know why?"

Samantha laughed softly with her while maintaining a friendly but confused look on her face.

"He is a good friend," she said. "He's *always* been a good friend to me. I've just never regarded him … like that."

Alexis saw a slight level of tiredness appear on Samantha's face. It was as if she were tired of having to answer the same question over and over, so Alexis stopped talking.

"Tom said you might want to ask me some questions about the club he and I go to," Samantha said after a long silence.

"No, not really. I mean, I found it interesting, what he was talking about, but I think the part of my life that was centred around delivering pain to someone is now over. I don't want to go anywhere near that again."

Samantha looked at her, briefly removing her eyes from the road to try and see what was showing on the face of the woman beside her at that moment.

"I sense there's quite a story there," she said and saw Alexis smile.

"Maybe," Alexis said and then paused before continuing. "No, not really. I just … some things I just want to move on from and forget."

They sat quietly, each in their own thoughts before Samantha spoke again.

"Okay, but if you want to talk to me, just ring me and let's arrange to meet up another time. Just the two of us, okay?"

Alexis nodded and smiled. She knew that Tom would want that as well. He was eager to hear how Samantha felt about him in so many ways, she was sure.

~~~~~

"Here's my phone number," Samantha said as she wrote it down on a pad that she kept in the car. "I mean it. Ring me and let's arrange for a girls-only catch up sometime soon. I love Tom to death, but some things, a girl has to talk about just with another girl!"

Alexis laughed at her and took the piece of paper, nodding, before she got out of the car.

"Thank you for the ride home, Samantha. I will call you next week."

~~~~~

Lying in bed that night, Alexis thought about Tom and Samantha, and the way they had interacted together and looked at one another. She was still learning so much about human interaction, after so many years of not wanting to be a willing participant in socialising. She was still learning to read people, but where those two were concerned, she did feel at a loss for words.

But then, what did she really know about people? So far, she didn't have the best track record of accurately interpreting who they were, or what they were really like.

CHAPTER 5

The Matrimonial Discussion

Lincoln had a restless night in the motel, finding his thoughts veering between two extremes of beliefs, and his confusion great.

On the one hand, he didn't want to let Lexi go. He didn't want to let go of his belief that she loved him, and the two of them were meant to be together. The two of them were soul mates.

At the other extreme, he had finally found the insight to be able to stand back and view the whole situation with her. In his head, he could visualise the entire three years they had known each other, just as if it was a movie playing in front of him. He knew things could have been so different. At the start, he had enjoyed the simple pleasure of being with her. He didn't know when that had stopped being enough for him, and he'd started to need so much more from her.

He knew he had to get himself together. He needed to get his life back together. For more than three years, he had been making the wrong things a priority. Even though he knew he was a great businessman, he also had to concede that there must have been a certain level of luck involved in his personal chaos not having flowed over to affect the company.

It was time, he knew. It was time to go home and forget all about Lexi. He had pushed her too far in his ongoing quest to keep finding more and more ways for her to satisfy him, and now she was gone. She had moved on, and he couldn't deny the level of happiness he had seen on her face when she was with that man. He'd seen the way they had kissed, the hunger on their faces, and the healthiness of Lexi. When she'd left Melbourne, she hadn't been so healthy. He couldn't see it then. He could see it now.

No, enough was enough. He stayed in the motel that night, and the following morning drove to the airport and was soon back in Melbourne.

~~~~~

Walking into his apartment, the first thing Lincoln did was have a long shower. He felt unclean. He wanted to get himself back to being the person he had always been before he'd met Lexi. Too much time had been invested in the wrong thing. It was time to put everything back in order. Always he had needed order, but since the day he had met her, his life had been in chaos. It was a chaos he just couldn't control, no matter
~~~~~

how hard he tried. The chaos had to stop. Order needed to be regained once more.

He took his time under the water, thinking about so many different things. The first thing he needed to do when he got out of the shower, and was presentable once again, was call Diana. She had taken the time to talk to him on the phone the night before. When he had needed someone to guide him in his moment of being uncertain what was the right thing to do - the right way to act - he had called her, and she had been there. She had been there for *him*. She could have hung up on him, if not when she first answered and heard his voice, definitely when she realised he was talking about Lexi again. But she hadn't. She'd talked to him and done what she had to, to make him see that it was time for him to wake up and start living life again.

Diana. She had always been the perfect wife, in so many ways. She had supported him right through from when he was at university, and through him taking over and building the company to what it was today. She had never said anything about the long hours he worked. She'd never mentioned anything about their lack of having a family. She'd always stood beside him at every charity event, at every company promotion, at every media event. Always she had smiled when she needed to smile, and she'd put great effort into looking and sounding the part that she needed to, to be by his side.

He sat on his sofa and pulled out his phone. Before he dialled her number, he took a moment to think about the last time he had seen her. That had been a wonderful night for them. It was the first time that he could remember, where she had relaxed and let him enjoy her so much, including letting him pleasure her. At the start of their relationship, she had always stopped him when he had tried that. Eventually, he had stopped trying. But that night, she let him, and it had worked. She had gotten aroused. For the very first time, he had felt her get wet. He'd then felt her climax. Thinking about that, he felt a slight sense of arousal beginning in him. He pushed it down. He didn't want to focus on anything sexual when he spoke to her.

"Lincoln," he heard her say when she answered the call. There was no question in it at all, just a confirmation that she was there, ready to talk and listen if he needed to.

"Will you come over?" he asked her simply, not bothering with any of the gushing that people so often did to him. That was something that he had always avoided with his wife, although on occasion she did it to him.

"Yes. When?"

"I'm home now, so whenever suits you is fine."

"I am on my way," she said and he heard the call end.

~~~~~
~~~~~

Diana looked in the mirror one more time, nervous about going to the apartment and seeing Lincoln. She was worried about him. It was beyond the fact that he'd had sex with another woman. There was something about him that had her on edge. The same question kept going through her mind - did she know her husband at all?

Finally, she left and made her way there. Part of her wanted to still call their apartment home, but she didn't think that would ever happen again. She didn't think she *wanted* it to happen again, and yet it was a twenty-year bond that they shared. Perhaps that wasn't such an easy thing to walk away from.

~~~~~

Lincoln heard the apartment buzzer and remembered that he had briefly noticed she'd left her key the last time she was there.

Jumping up from the sofa, he made his way to the door, finding it very strange to be opening the door for her when they had lived together for so many years. He was surprised when he saw her. It felt as if he hadn't seen her for so long, even though it was only a short time earlier they had spent that night together.

He welcomed her in and found himself feeling nervous.

"Wine?" he asked but was already heading into the kitchen because that was something that they often did - they drank wine together and talked about things.

"No, thank you. I don't need anything except to know that you are okay," she said.

Lincoln looked at her, stopping still on his journey to the kitchen. Finally hearing that she didn't want to have a drink - it seemed to be some kind of delayed response on his part - he came back and sat on the sofa, and welcomed her to sit beside him.

"I'm fine," he reassured her.

"Are you, Lincoln? Because you don't look fine, and you didn't sound fine on the phone last night," she said to him, seeing him cringe silently before he responded.

"I…" he started to say.

Suddenly he felt tears threatening. It was a weird sensation. He couldn't remember feeling like he needed to cry since he had been a boy.

He wiped his eyes, in that moment seeming extremely vulnerable to the woman in front of him. She'd known him for more than twenty years, and not once in that time had ever seen that kind of emotion in him.

"I don't feel like myself, Diana," Lincoln admitted. "I don't think I've felt like myself for a very long time. I know that I have to fix that. Too many things have become less of a priority when they shouldn't have."

Diana watched him, silent, forcing him to continue to be the one speaking.
~~~~~

"I have been so consumed by this woman," he said. "I'm so sorry if that hurts you..."

"No, please just keep talking, no matter what you need to say," he heard her say. He then felt her hand come out and take his, holding it tightly.

He looked at her, feeling so much pain inside of him because of the pain he would have caused her, no matter how strong and composed she looked right at that moment.

"At first, it was just about sex, I think. I had given up on trying to do things differently in our bed, and when she came along, I was driven by her ... eagerness ... to please me, and to let me do whatever I wanted with her. And then the sex changed. I just kept needing different things. And she still let me do - have - whatever I wanted. I think I became addicted to it. It was like a ... euphoria. I didn't want to hurt you. I thought I had kept it from you so you wouldn't be hurt."

"That does not matter now, Lincoln," Diana said.

"Yes, it does! Don't say that! It matters a great deal," he said, suddenly feeling impassioned about her implying she was not worth more than to have a husband who was unfaithful to her.

Diana saw him look deeply at her before he moved in to kiss her. She didn't stop him, expecting it was going to be his way of stopping the talking. She was wrong. After kissing her deeply, he pulled away and looked at her before continuing.

"You have been by my side for all of these years, and I have stood in my own world and just accepted how much you have given up..."

"I never gave anything up, Lincoln."

She saw him look at her with a knowing face.

"Yes, you did," he argued. "When we met at university, you had plans. You wanted a career. You dreamed of being an architect. And then my father died, and the company was handed over to me, and you stopped talking about the career you had been working toward."

Diana looked down at their hands, still joined, and felt a little overwhelmed with emotion. She had thought he'd forgotten that she had wanted to work - that she'd wanted to do so many things for herself in her life. He had never said anything, and she had been thinking for two decades that he hadn't noticed what she had stopped wishing for.

"I stopped encouraging you, I know, and I am sorry for that," he said. "I should have been reminding you to keep moving forward with your self-development, rather than letting you work alongside me solely on mine."

Suddenly he saw her break down in front of him. His words finally - after twenty years - hit a raw nerve inside of her. They made her feel emotion. That was something she had tried to keep under control so that she could be the perfect wife to him.

Lincoln watched her face. He saw her tears and heard her start to sob, even though it was clear to him that she was fighting with herself to not let her feelings show. He pulled her closer and kissed her again, feeling a great need to stop her hurting and start to put things right with her.

Diana felt the movement and was confused. Having spent that one night together was one thing, but did she want to encourage it to happen again? Should she kiss him back, like everything was just normal for them, and nothing had happened?

She pulled back, not wanting to let them drift back to where they had been.

"Lincoln, I am here for you," she said. "I will listen to you. I will stand beside you at any public events you need me to. I will be here in almost any way that you need me to be."

Even though she had stopped talking, Lincoln knew there was another half to that sentence.

"But?" he asked.

Diana took a deep breath, finally understanding her own resolve.

"But you have so many things to work through. I can't … enable … you by just having sex with you when you need it. I need more than that."

He took a moment to hear and understand what she had said. It produced an overwhelming wave of sadness that flowed through him.

"It has never been about sex with you," he said. "That was never the basis of our relationship."

"I know," she agreed. "But right now, you have to get your focus back, and you need to do that for yourself, and *by* yourself. You and I meeting now and then for sexual satisfaction would only be a sticking plaster fix to something much deeper that needs to be sorted. When you called me last night, your voice told me that you do have things you need to work out - not with that girl, but within *you.* You have to get it sorted, Lincoln, because if you don't, I meant what I said - you will end up being arrested. Please don't let that happen."

He nodded at her.

"I know," he agreed. I have already accepted that I have to move on and forget about her."

"Have you?"

She saw him look deeply at her, and for a moment wanted so much to believe what he was saying.

"Yes! I have been lucky that my … consumption … of thoughts about her hasn't lost me the company, with the level of obsession I've been feeling. I do know that I need to move on, Diana. And I can do that."

"Then I hope you are right because, regardless of this whole mess, I do love you," Diana said. "I don't have any regrets about the life we have had together."

Lincoln listened and was suddenly horrified at the tone of her voice.

"You talk as if we are … over … forever," he said.

"I have to get on with my life too, Lincoln," Diana said. "I'm still young enough to start over. I can update my architecture qualification, and I can still go out and find work…"

"I wouldn't stop you from doing that…"

"You wouldn't *intend* to stop me from doing that," she continued. "I do believe that, but being your wife would prevent it. You know it's true."

"What do you want to happen with us then?" he asked.

Diana could hear strong emotion in his voice as he pulled back from her completely.

When Lincoln received no reply, he ventured to the question that he had not wanted to ask.

"Do you want a divorce?"

Diana hadn't considered how that question would sound if it were voiced. There was something just so final about it - so much so that she didn't want to answer right then.

"I want you to get back to being you, Lincoln," she said. "And if that happens - *once* that happens - if you want to make a go of our marriage again … if you are willing then to put the effort in and work with me to get past all of this, then maybe we don't need a divorce. I'm not suggesting it right now, but of course it's a possibility. You were unfaithful to me. Right now, I can see past that because I'm worried about you, but I still have concern. Even if you get yourself sorted and you get back to who you always were before, it won't change the fact that you stepped outside of our marriage."

She saw another burst of tears attempt to erupt in his eyes. The sight resulted in the same happening to her.

"Alright. But what about right now?" he asked, just needing one small piece of confirmation from her that she wasn't going to completely turn away from him.

He heard a long sigh escape from her lips before she spoke.

"I am here," she said. "What do you need from me?"

"Please stay."

Diana weighed up the request. It was obvious he hadn't fully heard or understood that she'd said she didn't want to just be there for him when he wanted sex. On the other hand, she *was* there with him, and she *had* enjoyed the last time they were together. He had slightly opened a box that had been held tightly shut for a very long time. She was curious about that. Spending another night with him would be to satisfy him, but she would make sure it was more so to satisfy her.

"Yes, I will stay with you tonight, if you wish," she said.

Lincoln heard the words and vowed to himself that he would make sure he treated her the way he needed to, to make her stay for much longer than that one night.

He kissed her deeply and then let that slowly progress to a passionate kiss, not rushing for more. He wanted her to want him at a degree that she had never wanted him before.

Diana felt the kiss and forced herself to turn off her mind. She wanted to feel what other people felt when they had sex. To her, it had never been a bad thing. But from the last time she had been there, she had gained a slight understanding of how it could be more than what she had shared with her husband through all of their years together.

Lincoln indulged in her mouth for a long time. He was heavily aroused and knew from the change in her breathing that she was warming up to him as well. It drove him forward in his efforts, determined to not lose focus on who he was with.

Diana watched his face as he pulled away from the kiss and looked at her breasts, lifting one hand and touching one nipple lightly through the thin fabric of her dress. He sat like that for a long time, just focused on using that one finger on that one nipple, stroking lightly, up and down. Diana felt it start to affect her, making her heart beat faster and more deeply.

When he had done that for several minutes, he changed breasts, making the second one as pronounced as the first one was. He was in no hurry. He just wanted to make sure that she was heavily aroused. He felt like he was desperate for that.

He looked at her face and saw that her eyes had changed, before he resumed kissing her again, doing so while both of his hands ever so lightly moved over both of her nipples.

Diana felt new sensations as she focused on the feeling of his hands on her breasts, stroking through the fabric. As his lips left hers and trailed down to her neckline, she felt his tongue caressing her skin in small circles, like it was lightly dancing on the surface of her body.

She felt him slowly slide down her dress straps. When she studied his face, she saw his hunger as his eyes watched the fabric drift down, so it was resting on her lap, leaving her chest bare. It was a partial nakedness that she wasn't used to. Her first instinct was to lift her arms and cover herself. She felt particularly vulnerable. Even though they had been married for as long as they had been, the living area had never been a place they had made love in.

Lincoln saw the movement and looked into her eyes, kissing her to relax her while his hands resumed their delivery of pleasure. He gently nudged her arms out of the way before he lowered his head and used his tongue to enjoy the taste and feel of her nipples. He loved her body. He'd *always* loved her body. She treated it like a temple, as he did his own. Through her efforts, she had a toned and well-balanced sense of proportion due to the high level of physical fitness she indulged in. To him, she had always seemed like a beautiful, pale panther, with an intense level of grace and litheness about her.

Diana automatically lifted her hands into his hair and caressed his scalp as she indulged in the new feelings occurring in her. Although he wasn't touching her 'down below' she could feel that part of her throbbing, like it was alive and awake. All of the feelings flowing through her body were new for her. Why hadn't they enjoyed time like that together before? Why had it taken a third person to jump into their marriage before he would persist in forcing her to accept his pleasuring?

Lincoln couldn't hold back any longer from where he wanted to be. He pulled his kiss away from her breasts and returned to her lips, all the while gently sliding up the skirt of her dress. He pulled away from her, knelt on the floor and reached up, holding eye contact with her as he guided her to lift her hips so he could remove her underwear. On her face, he could see a deep blush, but she did as he indicated. She shyly let him pull her panties down and remove them completely. From where he knelt, he looked at her and enjoyed the sight. Her dress had bunched around her waist. She was bare-breasted and bare on her lower half as well. He couldn't remember ever seeing his wife like that. It was an exquisite sight for him to see.

Lincoln kissed her on the mouth once more while gently pushing her knees apart and moving one finger to gently caress her clitoris. He was in no rush, even though he was stretched tightly inside of his trousers. He kept having brief revisits in his mind to her indicating that their marriage might be over. He wasn't ready to let that happen yet. He just had to focus on her and make her see how much she really did mean to him.

Diana focused on the alertness through her body. It was still new to her, but she had the same determination as he did to try and make the effort. He was her husband, and he wanted to pleasure her. She couldn't even remember why she had stopped him from doing that so many times in their early years. Why had it always felt uncomfortable for her?

When he could feel moisture forming on her, Lincoln revelled in that realisation. Without even thinking, he pulled back and knelt lower to start lapping at her with his tongue. When he heard her moan, he almost climaxed, it was such a joyous sound to hear from her. He persisted and eventually felt and heard her reach orgasm. Two times in a row they had been together, she had reached orgasm. They were the first two times in their twenty-year marriage it had happened.

Diana felt her muscles contracting all around her body. She was in her forties, but she was new to orgasms. She found them strange sensations, but she conceded she could be more accepting of them. She looked at the man in front of her, saw the look on his face, and sat forward to kiss him. It was a bold move for her, but he had finally woken something up inside of her, and she only wanted to keep moving forward. She heard him groan deeply at her kissing him, and she pulled at his t-shirt to indicate her desire for him to be without it. Instead of just taking it off, she saw him stand up and undress completely, making her see at eye level exactly how aroused he was.

Lincoln was desiring then to feel her mouth on him. It was something she had never done, and despite how tempting the thought was, he wouldn't put his desires ahead of her wishes then. Instead, he knelt down again and moved forward.

Diana sensed his movement even though they had never had sex in that position before. Silently she waited and then felt him ease into her slowly.

It was different from the position they had always used. She felt open to him and exposed, but it felt good too. It was long overdue. They should have been doing that before he found someone else, she heard her mind quietly whisper to her in her head.

Lincoln started slowly, letting both of them get used to the feeling. Even for him, it was new as he'd never been in that position with her. There seemed no choice for him but to let himself go. He moved with an increasing pace, while periodically leaning forward and kissing his wife's lips and looking into her eyes to ensure he wasn't in any way making her uncomfortable.

Finally, Diana felt and heard him climax, and saw him crumple slightly with the feeling. It was an odd thing for her to see, given that every other time she'd had sex with him, they had been lying on a bed with him on top of her. Despite having been together for almost all of their adult lives so far, they had never before tried a different position … until now.

Lincoln looked at her when he had caught his breath. He pulled her closer to him so he could kiss her deeply. Before him was a new Diana, letting him move into her in a different location and in a different way. Right at that moment, it was easy for him to see them back together, moving forward on that track, trying new things sexually.

At that moment, Diana wasn't thinking about moving forward with him. Yes, she was enjoying it. Yes, she was in wonder that they had found such pleasure together after so many years of not doing so. Regardless, she absolutely was not thinking about moving forward with him still in her life.

~~~~~

Diana woke the next morning, expecting to again be alone. When they had gone to bed the night before, she had expected him to get up and go to work early, just as he had done the last time she had stayed.

They had made love in their bed before going to sleep. Once again, she had relaxed with the flow of it and not tried to stop it. She had enjoyed their evening together. She found it was a strange place to be - finding sexual pleasure and satisfaction at the very end of a twenty-year relationship.

She turned her head slowly, thinking about what she would get on with that day. It surprised her to see him not only still in bed, but wide awake and looking intently at her.

"Good morning," he said, surprising her further. Even throughout their long marriage, he had rarely been in bed when she woke late.

For a long while, Lincoln saw her just look at him, without saying anything. He had been looking at her for over an hour, his head working overtime in trying to figure out what he was supposed to do in his marriage. Should he fight for it? Should he fight for *her*?

He had never been sure of what Diana was thinking, he suddenly realised. No matter how long they had been together, or how much their lives had become entwined, he had never taken enough time to focus on her.

"Good morning," Diana responded, feeling the strangeness of the situation. All of a sudden, it felt like they were strangers who had met in a bar and gone home drunk together, and were now waking up and realising what they had done.

He moved closer to her, and she felt his arm move around her body before he leaned in and kissed her softly. She let him, but suddenly felt a sense of suffocation beginning inside of her. It made her question what she wanted to happen between them.

"Will you shower with me?" he asked, surprising her, but she nodded.

~~~~~

Diana felt shy entering the water with him, but she also felt in her heart that she would walk out of the apartment that day, and she would not be back. The least she could do was enjoy the morning with him if that was what he wanted.

Once under the water, Lincoln was incredibly gentle with her. Even though she could see that he was highly aroused, he took his time. He lathered up her body and rinsed her off. When he was done, she automatically repeated the process on his body, finding she enjoyed being able to touch him like that, all over, not just 'there'. The feeling of his arms, legs and back, combined with the tightness of his muscles and the smoothness of his skin, enthralled her. It also saddened her that little bit more that she had never really known her husband. For more than twenty years, they'd been together. So many things could have been different.

~~~~~

After their shower, they went out for breakfast, at Lincoln's suggestion to do so. He was tentative to let her go, and to let her out of his sight. Although he didn't want to admit it, he did feel in his heart that he had lost her. They were only delaying the inevitable.

"Lincoln, please get yourself together," she said to him when they had finished eating their meals.

He looked at her as she put her arm out and placed her hand on his. Looking down at her hand sitting there resulted in him turning his hand so that he could hold hers firmly, interlacing his fingers with hers.

"Please don't walk away," he said to her.

The tone of his voice affected Diana greatly.

"We can work together, and we can make our marriage even stronger," he continued.

"I know," Diana replied, nodding. "Perhaps we can, but first, you need to get yourself sorted. Get your focus back on the business, and on your charity work. Get your head in the right space."

"And you?"

Lincoln saw her smile sadly at him, not moving to remove her hand from his.

"I want to take some time to figure out where I need to be too," she said. "I want some time on my own while you're getting yourself together, and then we can see where we're at after that, if you still want to work on us."

Lincoln nodded sadly and pulled away, ready to get on with overdue work in his office.

"Where can I walk you to?" he asked her as he stood to leave.

"I'm going to stay here a little longer," Diana said as she stood up.

He looked at her and saw her move toward him, pulling him into a loving embrace that was rare for them to do in public. She was in no hurry to let him go. They both enjoyed the moment before he finally smiled at her and walked off.

Diana sat down and let herself just take a deep breath and let him go. It was time to let him leave her life. She sat there for some time before, through a haze of thoughts, she realised someone was calling out to her.

"Diana?"

She looked up and was surprised to see before her a face that she thought could be of an old friend from her university days.

"David?" she asked tentatively.

When he smiled and laughed at her, she knew it was him, even though
~~~~~

twenty years had passed. When she stood up, he hugged her lightly and kissed her on the cheek. With the motion of her hand, she invited him to sit down with her.

"I saw you earlier, but you looked like you were in a serious conversation, so I didn't want to intrude," David said. "Was that Lincoln that you were with?"

"Yes, it was. But how are you? What have you been doing all these years?" she asked, wanting more than anything right then to sideswipe any questions involving her husband.

They talked for a long time as two old friends who had not seen each other for half of their life. When they left the restaurant, David hugged her tight.

"Oh, it has been so good seeing you again. I am going to give you my number," he said, pulling out a card and giving it to her. "I hope you'll call me and I can see you again, Diana."

Watching him walk away, Diana was left alone, oblivious to the size of the smile that graced her face.

CHAPTER 6

The Taste for It

Over the following month, Lincoln worked hard to get his focus back on the right things. Lexi was pushed from his mind. He had screwed up, and she'd moved on. He couldn't keep kidding himself forever that things were going to change there. As a result, his company reaped the benefits from the newfound energy he used to start reprioritising once more.

During the month, he didn't see or hear from Diana, choosing to respect her wishes also, including her wish to have time away from him. He found himself yearning for company sometimes, and had to stop himself from picking up the phone to call her.

With regard to Diana, he found himself drifting between two extremes. Sometimes he determined to let her go. He wanted to encourage her to have her own life and do what she wanted, without any consideration toward him. At other times, he wanted to go to her, grab her, and hold her tight. In those moments, he desired to tell her that they should keep working on their marriage, no matter how difficult or useless it might have seemed.

Despite his extremes of thought, he kept quiet and gave her the space even he felt she deserved.

~~~~~

Diana seemed to have found herself spending more and more time with David - the old friend from her past. It was only dating, with the occasional end of night kiss, and she was happy with that. He had recently divorced and knew Diana and Lincoln were only recently separated. Because of that, no lines were crossed between them. Feeling the distance she did from Lincoln, Diana found comfort in being able to talk to, and spend time with, a man who she knew and trusted.

When they had gone out a few times and were starting to be regularly seen, people started to take notice. It wasn't long before a photograph of them appeared in a media article about a fundraising event they had attended together as ticket holders.

Lincoln saw the page and the photo. The article produced in him a range of strong emotions. He didn't want to be angry at her, or disappointed, or accusatory, because he wasn't her husband at that moment. And yet, it fuelled him greatly toward anger. They weren't divorced yet. She had no right to be seeing someone else - and especially
~~~~~

so publicly.

The fact that it was David only fuelled Lincoln's anger. David was the very man Lincoln had pulled Diana away from when they'd first met. Something about that infuriated him even further.

He felt confused about boundaries. He knew he had gone outside of their marriage and been intimate with someone else, but at least he'd tried to hide that. Diana's dating life being in the public eye was something else. Putting it out there, to be reported about by the media, made it seem like a whole other level of deceit.

"Lincoln," he heard Diana say when he called her, feeling his emotions on a very high alert. "What can I do for you?"

"We need to talk," he said. Straight away, he heard her sigh heavily.

"Of course," she replied. "Where and when?"

"The apartment? Tonight?"

"Alright."

The line went dead. It was that simple. That night, he would confront her and ask her to explain herself.

~~~~~

Diana approached the apartment entry with a deep feeling of dread inside of her. She hadn't known from the tone of his voice which aspect of their marriage they were going to have to talk about, but she suspected it was about her having been seen out with David.

She took a deep breath before pressing the buzzer to request admission. While waiting for Lincoln to respond, she hoped he wasn't going to have anger inside of him. He hadn't expressed that emotion many times during their life together, but the day they'd both seen the missing person's report on television about that girl … and the comment Diana had made, calling the girl a whore … Diana had been able to clearly sense just how enraged he had been. That had been the moment when she knew she was best to run and not look back. She never wanted to face that rage again, but she couldn't keep away from her husband forever.

In their recent times together, everything had been good, but she knew her being seen with David was something that might upset him. And perhaps in some small way, she wanted to hurt him, just as he had hurt her through his infidelity.

Soon enough, she was facing him as he opened the door and welcomed her in. He said nothing at first, closing the door behind her and silently offering to take her coat. She followed him through to the living area and finally had to speak since he didn't appear to want to.

"Why am I here, Lincoln?"

He took a deep breath and looked at her, wanting the two of them to sit down, but sensing she might not be as receptive at that moment.
~~~~~

"I want to talk about … the photos … of you and David," he said.

"What about them?"

Her tone surprised him. He realised then that he'd expected her to be defensive. He'd thought she might even try to deny that anything was going on between them. Her lack of attempt to cover it up or apologise for it added to his frustration.

"Why are you seeing him? And so publicly? We aren't divorced yet…"

Diana felt her concern for how he'd react, quickly replaced with an anger of her own beginning to erupt. Throughout their marriage, she had held in many emotions as they had occurred. She'd always been determined to present herself as the perfect wife, dedicated to just being there to support her husband. At that moment, she wouldn't so easily give in to his needs and reassure him she was still there for him.

"You're not seriously going to throw that card at me - the 'we are still married' card?? After your affair that lasted three years?!"

"That was different, and you know it," Lincoln replied.

"Yes, I do know it!" Diana exclaimed, her anger building to another level still. "It was underhand and deceitful. You had sex with another woman - a young girl at that - for three years, without having given me any indication that you were so unhappy in our marriage. You did far worse than I am doing, Lincoln. I'm dating someone who I enjoy the company of. We're not hiding, we're not lying about what we are doing…"

"You're still my wife…"

"Only in name, and you know it." Diana replied. "We are not husband and wife. We haven't been for a long time."

"We spent those nights together…"

"Yes, we spent two nights together, when you needed it. When *you* needed to be close to someone. When *you* needed sex."

Diana saw his face changing, and the anger growing on it. A part of her feared him if he got angered, but she found strength. Suddenly another part of her was ready to start fighting back.

They remained standing, facing each other, both with a look of passion and intense infuriation with the other on their faces.

"No!" she saw him yell at her. "When we last talked, you said you would wait for me to change. You said you would be there for me when I got myself together. You didn't tell me you would go out and start seeing other people!"

"I'm not seeing other people!" Diana yelled back. "I ran into David after you and I last spoke, and we've been spending some time together. I'm not having sex with him, or spending nights with him. I haven't had sex with anyone in my entire life apart from *you*. So don't get all high and mighty with me, insinuating that I'm doing something wrong and you've been an angel..."

"We aren't talking about me!"

Diana moved close to him with what looked like a snarl on her face, surprising him and making him actually feel intimidated with the strength flowing from her.

"Of course we aren't talking about you. Because everything *you* do is perfect and should be in the public eye - except for all those times where you've been not perfect, Lincoln. And *those* times need to be hidden away ... as if they don't exist."

"You will stop seeing him..." Lincoln said.

"Oh no. You don't get to tell me..."

"You are my wife and you will not see him!"

Diana felt the anger inside of her reach boiling point. She didn't stop to check it before she raised her hand and slapped him across his face - hard.

Not only was Lincoln surprised by the action, but on her face, he could see that she was just as surprised as he was. That was nothing compared to the intimidation she delivered to him as she spoke deeply but clearly.

"You will not interfere in my life, Lincoln. You made your choice to be unfaithful to me, and now you have to live with that decision."

"No!" he said, resulting in her hand making another round against his cheek. He rubbed the site she had now hit him twice on, and felt a familiar feeling occurring inside of him.

Diana watched him and saw it too. His eyes were alight and shining. She hadn't seen him like that before, but she knew what it was, a deep understanding flowing over her. She knew she should back away and leave, but at that moment, she wanted to taunt him. At that moment, she was driven to give him a taste of what he gave to others. At that moment, she wanted to hurt him.

"Are you getting turned on by that, Lincoln? I can see that you are. You liked it when I slapped you..." she said and gave him another blow. Incredible power started to surge through her. "Look at you. With every strike, your eyes are changing a bit more, and I can see you're hard," she said, purposely lowering her eyes to his track pants. They hid nothing.

"I am angry at you, Lincoln, for every little moment of our marriage that I smiled and gave all of myself to you, while you lapped it up and gave nothing to me..."

"That's not true!" he yelled at her and received another blow.

It didn't even occur to him to stop her or to somehow restrain her.

"There's something you need right now, and I think that I definitely have the anger in me to give it to you. Go into the bedroom, Lincoln, and bring me that riding crop you have in there."

Lincoln looked at her, confused.

"How…?"

"Now!"

Instantly he walked quickly into the bedroom and pulled the item out. The feeling of it in his hands instantly reminded him of a different person, in a different place and time.

"Give it to me," Diana commanded and enjoyed the look on his face. It wasn't quite a look of fear - but almost, like he was finally seeing something in her that he might need to be worried about. "Where do you want it?" she asked. The question seemed to confuse him, like he couldn't comprehend what she'd said.

"Where do you want it?!" Diana asked again, her voice rising.

Lincoln felt himself start to panic. Everything was so out of the ordinary and so unexpected. But when he looked at her and saw the crop in her hand, he also felt himself lick his lips before he pulled down and took off his track pants and underwear. He turned himself away from her and presented his backside to her.

"Is this where you want me to hit you?" she asked, a different voice coming out of her.

In his confusion, he didn't answer quickly enough.

"IS THIS WHERE YOU WANT ME TO HIT YOU?!" she screamed at him. Finally, she saw him nod.

"Yes!" Lincoln called out, his heart pounding as he did so.

Instantly Diana found an incredible surge of power flow through her to her arm. She naturally brought the crop out to the side before bringing it back to him with a force that almost made him topple forward.

"Brace yourself on something," she said forcefully.

Lincoln looked around for the best position and put his hands on a sideboard that was secured at the wall.

Straight away, he felt another blow come at him, making him grow harder. Diana saw it and was surprised, but it drove her on even more.

"I am going to keep seeing David, Lincoln…" she taunted him, feeling her body awaken to a level she didn't think it had ever been.

"No!" he responded and immediately felt another blow hit him.

He was quiet, revelling in the feelings his wife was bringing out in him.

"Yes! I am going to have my own life, without you."

"NO!!" he yelled out, feeling an odd mixture of emotions - fear of losing her, but also the arousal that was only getting stronger. He didn't want to be so aroused while she was saying what she was. He couldn't help it, however, and with the final blow that she delivered, he felt himself finally reach the point of no return.

Diana watched him as she delivered that final blow. Even from her angle, she knew what was happening. She had never seen anything like it. She had never even *heard* of anything like that happening. His ejaculation had such power behind it. She didn't even comprehend the fact that it was so messy, him having done so down the front of the sideboard. She didn't even care about that mess, so didn't make any move toward wanting to clean it up. What she was focused on was his body convulsing, and his face.

But she wasn't finished with him yet. No, it was not alright with her that he should have an orgasm in pleasure when he had tried to be so controlling about who she could and couldn't see.

Turning around, Lincoln saw her walk right up to him. He raised his eyes to hers.

"I'm not finished yet," Diana said in a deathly low voice. "Don't even think I am close to being done with making sure you know how many emotions I have suppressed over our years together. Stand up!" she yelled at him.

Lincoln pushed himself upright, still feeling like he was in some kind of shock, even after the release. He watched her move toward the sofa. There she stood and pulled down the dress trousers she was wearing, discarding them abruptly before reclining back.

"Get down on your knees here in front of me, and do to me what you did last time," she said.

Lincoln heard the instruction and blinked at it. In his vision, she looked spectacular, wearing only a blouse, and otherwise completely bare.

"Now!"

He immediately walked to kneel in front of the sofa and leaned in to taste her. As he pleasured her, he felt her hand move onto the back of his head and grip his hair, forcefully pushing his face harder against her. He felt like he was suffocating but didn't dare try and pull back. In the surprise of the situation, he found himself becoming aroused again.

Diana revelled in the feelings, using her hand to control him being more forceful, or easing off so she could feel a little less pressure when she needed to.

Finally, Lincoln felt her convulse against his mouth. Regardless, she didn't let up her hold on him.

"Keep going!" she said with power behind her words, curious to see if that could be repeated. She was a woman in her forties and only just beginning to discover different things about her body. He was there. She would use him as she wanted. For the first time since they had met, she was going to take from him and not give any thought to what he needed from her.

Lincoln continued, feeling himself once more very hard at her request for him to bring her to orgasm again. He reached down with one hand to touch himself, but she saw the movement.

"No, Lincoln, you don't get to touch yourself. This is *my* time," Diana said. Immediately she saw his hand move back up to her thigh.

The effect was even more arousing to him. He could feel himself threatening to climax even without stimulation.

"You won't orgasm yet," Diana said. "When I say the time is right, *then* you can orgasm. Right now, you will concentrate only on me."

She heard him groan deeply. The vibration of that sound emanating through his mouth sent her over the edge.

Lincoln held his mouth still, her hand still clamped on the back of his head. After a few minutes, he felt her take her hand away. When he looked up at her, he saw a look he had never seen before - not once in their long marriage. He didn't know what it was, or how to read it.

"Now you can release. How do you want to?" she asked.

At that moment, Lincoln realised he was well past the point of being surprised. It was like he was with a completely different person.

"Answer me!" she yelled at him.

He felt small, like he was someone unimportant, there only to please her. After a moment of confusion, he finally found his voice, although spoke softly to her.

"Inside of you."

Diana sat up a bit and moved to the edge of the sofa, where he had positioned her last time. She braced herself by leaning back on her hands.

Lincoln looked at her, not sure if she was offering herself or not, and found himself actually afraid to use his initiative and make any assumption.

"Do it!" she yelled at him now, with a voice that was almost demeaning.

He didn't know why, but the tone of it drove him on. He immediately moved forward and slid inside of her. In that, she let him take control - initially.

She watched his face as he moved in her gently and slowly, like he wanted to make it last. Not wanting him to have control, she quickly took the control back.

"Harder, Lincoln!" he heard her yell at him. He immediately started thrusting into her with more force than he would have expected her to want. He let go and was moving with faster and faster movements, and deeper movements. Finally, he exploded inside of her, groaning loudly as the release came.

Diana continued to watch him as he went through his recovery, and then felt him pull out of her. She was surprised by the evening's events.

When she'd gone to the apartment, she had been worried about his anger. She had never anticipated she could feel such things herself, or that she could *do* such things herself. When his eyes met hers, she suspected he was also wondering where such actions and anger in her had come from.

Lincoln felt confused, like he wasn't sure what to do. He had lost control completely. He didn't know how to get it back, or if he *wanted* to get it back. He continued to kneel before her, wondering if she would make the next move. Soon he saw her lean toward him and kiss him on the lips. She kissed softly at first, as if finding her way to him, and then more aggressively.

No, she hadn't finished with him yet, they both realised at the same time. She was far from finished.

~~~~~

"I'm going to stay here tonight," she said to him. It wasn't a question, and she didn't want an answer. It was just the way it was going to be.

Lincoln nodded at her, speechless.

"And then, tomorrow, I am going to walk out of here and I am going to resume getting to know David."

Lincoln didn't reply, instead studying her as if he had no idea who the woman in front of him was. He'd thought he knew her utterly and completely. She now seemed like a complete stranger.

They sat on the sofa, dressed again after both feeling absurd at being dressed only on their top halves, with lower halves completely bare. For the first time since his father had died, Lincoln felt intimidated by someone. He had never seen anything before in Diana, like she had been so far that night. It confounded him greatly.

He remained speechless as he watched her stand up and walk to the bedroom, saying nothing to him and not even looking at him. He sat a moment longer, uncertain what he was supposed to do, before he followed her.

When he walked into the bedroom, she was standing by the bed, waiting. As he entered, she turned to look directly at him. When he moved closer, she pushed herself against him and kissed him passionately, yet more aggression showing itself. She didn't let up for some time. Lincoln could feel her pushing her body hard against him, rubbing against him, making him hard again.

Discretely she manoeuvred him so he was standing at the edge of the bed with the back of his knees touching it. Suddenly she pulled away from him and shoved him so that he fell back onto the bed. Since she had last been with him, she had forced herself to do research into sex. She had allowed herself to watch porn for the first time in her life - not to get off and climax herself, but rather to see other things that people did in the bedroom. He was in front of her. She was going to use him for practice.
~~~~~

"Move up the bed more," she said forcefully and saw him oblige, doing exactly as she'd said.

After she'd climbed over him and straddled him, Lincoln watched as she removed her blouse, revealing her breasts. She then leaned forward over him, positioning herself so that he had to take one in his mouth.

Diana felt so empowered for the first time in her life. She made no rush to move from where she was, feeling his tongue and lips pleasuring one nipple, and then his fingers start to caress the other. She could feel his hardness under her and rubbed herself against it, causing a sweet friction between their bodies and their clothing. The feelings that resulted from her being stimulated equally on her clitoris and her nipples soon had her feeling the feeling she was now starting to get used to. She felt herself tip over in climax.

Lincoln was in awe of her. He was in awe of his wife, for whatever change had come over her. He watched her as she pulled off him and removed her pants, becoming completely naked.

"Take your clothes off," she said to him, her voice void of any emotion at all.

Lincoln reacted straight away, undressing as he continued to lie on the bed.

Diana wasn't sure if she could do it. She wanted to be confident and in control, but a little bit of her self-confidence was trying to ease away from her and dissipate. She pushed her self-doubt down and climbed back onto the bed to straddle him and slowly find her way to being able to lower down onto him.

Lincoln watched his wife as she moved herself, finding the comfortable way to move as she seemed to want to. He was highly excited at watching her. Underneath him, he could feel the red marks from where she had used the riding crop on him. The feeling was welcome and contributed to the arousal he also felt from watching her.

Finally, Diana seemed to find a way to ease down onto him, and slowly move up and down. Her face was incredible for him to watch, making him reach out and touch her as she moved. With one hand on her breast and the other on her clitoris, he saw her face change again, into another level of arousal.

He watched his wife as if she was a completely new person - someone he had never met before. It was also like she was a virgin, feeling every little change in her position for the very first time. It pushed him on in his level of desire for her, but he remained focused on helping her get to where she wanted to be.

Diana embraced the new feelings inside of her. She found herself enjoying being the one in control, instead of just lying back and letting sex be something that he simply did to her. In addition to how it felt to move on him as she was, she could feel him working with his hands to increase her pleasure. The combination resulted in her feeling it coming, and then she felt a different feeling as her muscles gripped hard around him.

As soon as she felt herself climax, she became aware that he was also having his orgasm. He'd held on but finally let go, her muscles gripping him so forcefully that it was the last thing he could stand before he had to release.

After focusing on the intensity of physical pleasure, Diana opened her eyes and looked down into his. His look was so intense that she could do nothing but lean down and kiss him deeply.

Lincoln reached his hands around her and pulled on her hair lightly as he indulged in her kisses. Even those seemed different from how she normally kissed him. He didn't understand where this new person came from, but he liked it!

She climbed off him and lay down next to him as they moved under the covers. Neither said anything, both in that moment speechless at the change that had come over them after having been married for so long.

Diana let her husband hold her as she drifted off to sleep, thinking in her head that the following day she would go out of her way to see David and begin moving on with her life.

Meanwhile, her husband next to her silently vowed that he would not let her walk out of their marriage, especially now - especially now that he knew what she could do … for him.

~~~~~

"I have to go," Diana said as she dressed the next morning. She still felt empowered from the night before, but instead of it all making her want to stay with him and work on their marriage, it had only fuelled her on in her belief that she could go and start living her own life finally.

"But last night…" Lincoln started to say, feeling a sense of desperation flow over him at the realisation that she still wanted to leave.

"What about it?"

"I thought…" he started, feeling confused at how things were so reversed all of a sudden. "I thought we were good together, Diana. I thought you enjoyed being here."

"Lincoln, I have to go," she said simply, leaning close to him and kissing him lightly on the cheek. "Take care of yourself."

Then he saw her simply walk out. It did not escape his attention that she didn't even look back at him as he stood in the doorway and watched her leave.

Not. Even. One. Glance.
~~~~~

CHAPTER 7

The Loss

Diana embarked on her new journey with David, her old friend from university days. Neither was in any hurry to move forward to sex, and it made things easy between them. They took their time at a pleasurably slow pace, their only intimate contact being holding hands, hugging, and lightly kissing.

She had thought about Lincoln since their last night together, but still enjoyed the thought of starting over. Although she did believe that they could formulate some kind of new relationship from the old one, she at least wanted the opportunity to try to be with someone new. Lincoln had been her love for her entire adult life to date. Perhaps he would continue to be in the future, but for the moment, she was enjoying the companionable attention of someone new.

She and David had been seeing each other for two months, during which time the media had taken photos of them now and then, but nothing was ever reported on. She considered what Lincoln might think of it all. Having not heard from him again, she hoped that was an indication that he was moving on also.

~~~~~

Lincoln monitored the papers and had seen every photo that had shown his wife with her new 'date'. No-one questioned him about it at all. It was as if everyone was too afraid to ask the question, even though he believed people must want to know what was happening between them.

He had turned his focus heavily into the company. He still thought about Lexi now and then, but he was aware that she was drifting further and further from his mind too. More and more, he found it was his wife who frequented his thoughts, but he would not move forward toward her. He would wait and see how things panned out with Diana and David. Perhaps David was a better man for her, and she deserved a good man beside her.

~~~~~

Diana sat in her GP's office for her annual check-up. The news she had just received had put her into a state of shock.

"I don't understand. What did you say?" she asked.

The doctor looked at her, understanding why her client might be so surprised. Having been her GP for so many years, and knowing the extent that Diana had silently wished to get pregnant, it was indeed - even for the doctor - a surprise.

"There's no doubt, Diana," she said. "The blood tests you just had done confirm it. You are pregnant."

Diana thought back over recent months. She knew she hadn't had a period since she was last with Lincoln, but her periods had been few and far between since she'd turned forty so she had thought nothing of it. There was no way she could possibly have anticipated that she would fall pregnant, after they were not even technically together anymore as husband and wife.

"Oh, God," she moaned, feeling the magnitude of what she was being told. "I'm forty-four years old!"

"Many women have babies at your age, but you do have choices, Diana," the doctor said.

Diana looked at the doctor in front of her. She had seen Diana through adolescence. She had been her GP through the early years of her marriage, when Diana had wanted to get pregnant, and through every illness that had passed Diana by. Her current situation was something she knew the doctor couldn't advise her on.

"I won't have an abortion, if that is one of the choices you mean," she said, certain in that thought.

Her GP nodded at her. "Another option is adoption."

"No, if I am meant to be pregnant now, then I will have the baby," said Diana. "I can do that on my own. Plenty of women do that on their own, right?"

"They do indeed. There are plenty of single mothers out there who are incredible mothers, as I am sure you will be too."

~~~~~

After a long discussion about options, Diana left the medical practice premises in shock. She had to think about different things and different *people*. She was seeing David, she was married to Lincoln, and she was having Lincoln's baby. Of that, there was no doubt since he was still the only man she'd ever had sex with in her life.

But what of David? She owed him an explanation. She made that the priority over telling Lincoln the news. It probably wasn't the right order of things, but that was what she would do.

She arranged to meet David for lunch. As soon as they sat down, he knew she was extremely nervous.

"What is it?" he asked, feeling the dread of expectation that she was about to bring their new relationship to a grinding halt.

"David, I have something I need to tell you," she started to say. Finding the words difficult to express in any soft way, she went on to blurt out the news to him. "I have been to see my GP this morning. and
~~~~~

she told me … it's confirmed … that I'm pregnant."

David looked at her, wondering how that had happened since they had started seeing each other.

"I don't understand. How can that be?"

Diana took a deep breath and could already anticipate the amount of hurt she might be about to deliver to him.

"It's Lincoln's child."

"But you and I have been seeing each other for months, Diana…" he said and saw the acknowledgement in her eyes. "You've been with him since we started dating? You've *slept* with him?"

Diana put her head down but nodded confirmation to him.

"But he's your husband, and you're sleeping with him," David said in disbelief. "Why are you dating *me*? What sick part have I played in whatever you are doing in your marriage?"

She brought her eyes up to meet his.

"No, David, it's nothing like that! I was with him on three occasions. I haven't been with him right through *our* time together!"

"I thought the two of you were separated," David said. "That's the only reason I've been okay with seeing you even though you aren't divorced. I wouldn't have come near you if I had thought you were still so *actively* married to him."

Diana remained quiet as she watched his face. She could feel tears coming to her eyes. There had been so much potential in a relationship with him, but he was hurt, and rightfully so. She suspected he would walk away from her. That possibility saddened her immensely.

As if reading that exact thought, David stood up.

"I can't … sorry, Diana, but I can't talk to you right now…" he said before simply turning and walking out.

Diana sat alone in the restaurant, feeling a sense of grief for what could have been. She knew she could have kept quiet about the baby. She could have been deceitful and slept with him that very night and then pretended it was his. She could have just kept quiet and hoped that the baby might naturally be lost.

No, she had done the right thing. She would raise a baby alone, and that would be okay. She was in a fortunate place in life, and they would be fine, the two of them, alone.

She took a deep breath and readjusted her thinking. She had one more thing to do before she could move forward with planning a new life for her and her child.

Now she had to tell Lincoln.

~~~~~

"Can I see you?" she asked Lincoln when he answered his phone.

"Of course. At the apartment tonight?" he asked, with a glimmer of
~~~~~

hope in his heart, an excitement at the possibility…

"No," Diana replied. "Please, Lincoln, I need to see you immediately. Can I come to your office?"

Lincoln was surprised. Diana never came to his office.

"Yes, I am free right now, until my next appointment at three," he said.

"Thanks. I'm leaving now, so will be there shortly."

Lincoln heard the phone call end and wondered what the urgency was. He found himself thinking that it was probably that time - time for the divorce papers to be served to him, so she could move on with David. He took some time to think about how he felt about that, and could only feel deep regret inside of him. But as she had told him, he had made a decision that had resulted in their marriage breaking down. Now he had to live with the consequence of that.

~~~~~

He watched the time go by, eager to hear what his wife had to tell him. At 2pm, he called her to ask where she was. Someone unknown answered her phone.

"Who is this?" the person at the end of the phone demanded, with a sense of urgency in their voice.

"Who is *this*? You seem to have my wife's phone."

"Oh Sir, this is Central Melbourne Hospital. Your wife has been brought in from a car accident. You need to come down here immediately. It isn't good," Lincoln heard the random voice say. He felt himself go into shock. "Do you have someone who can drive you, Sir?"

Lincoln woke up again and acknowledged before hanging up

"Toby, can you please pick me up urgently? Diana has been in an accident. I have to get to the hospital."

~~~~~

Fifteen minutes later, he was running into the accident and emergency department.

"My wife was in a car accident…" he said to the receptionist, who immediately called a doctor and asked him to come out.

"Mr. Kokiri! Please come this way," the doctor said as Lincoln fell into step beside him. "She's in a bad way. You need to prepare yourself."

Lincoln felt a shadow of dread come over him.

Soon they were walking into a room where she was lying with numerous things attached to her body. Lincoln rushed to her side and looked at her, then looked at the doctor in horror.

"She had intensive internal bleeding, which we have stopped, but she is still in danger. Sit and talk to her, if you like. Sometimes it helps."

"Thank you," Lincoln said to the doctor, feeling like anything else would just be inadequate.

He sat in the chair beside Diana's bed and took her hand in his. She wasn't awake and didn't seem responsive at all. He took his time to think back over their life together. How much he had loved her when he had first seen her, and how easy it had been to see them having a full and happy life together. Somewhere along the way, they had both stopped working on their marriage. He should never have given up, he realised, perhaps too late.

As if sensing his thoughts, Diana opened her eyes and looked at him. Lincoln saw a sliver of smile attempt to grace her face. It faded almost instantly.

"Lincoln," she whispered as if in pain, and he felt himself start to cry. "I was rushing to see you. I wasn't watching…"

"Shh, Darling. Everything will be alright," he said running his other hand over her forehead.

"No, Lincoln, I wanted you to know … I wanted you to know that the news was happy news. He or she - I don't know which it will be yet - will be like you, I am sure. So handsome. You have always been so handsome."

Lincoln felt confused at her words. Assuming she must be rambling from some kind of drugs she had in her system, he didn't say anything, just let her speak.

"I love you, Lincoln. I have always loved you. And I forgive you for … her. That doesn't matter. I know I wasn't what you really needed…"

"No, Diana, please don't say such a thing!" Lincoln exclaimed, feeling tears flowing. "I have always loved you, my darling. I didn't do those things because I don't love you. You are the great love of my life, and I'm so sorry for the hurt I've caused you."

Diana smiled at him softly, but he could see her drifting further away from him.

"You don't have to be part of my life," Diana said. "I can raise it on my own. It isn't David's, Lincoln. It's yours. You are the only man I ever wanted to be with like that. No matter what, you've always been a good man. And a good husband. And now you will be a good father too…" she said.

As Lincoln saw her head flop sideways, he heard the monitor's continuous beeping replaced with one non-stop sound.

"Mr. Kokiri, move!" someone was shouting at him.

Lincoln watched in horror as efforts were made to resuscitate her, but he knew she was gone. In his heart, he felt the depth of loss. He'd woken up to her far too late. There would be no more opportunity to show her how much he had actually loved her and appreciated her.

It was much later, as he sat quietly beside her, that he really thought about the words she had said. Those words were confirmed by the doctor coming into the room.

"I'm so sorry for the loss of your wife, Mr. Kokiri. And your baby."

"She was pregnant?" Lincoln asked, not believing that the news could be right. She must have been just rambling, he had thought.

"Yes, only a couple of months so there was no way we could save it. I'm so sorry. Please stay here as long as you need to."

Lincoln sat beside her bed until finally someone came in to see him.

"Here are your wife's belongings that were given to us by the ambulance crew, Mr. Kokiri."

He took the handbag, suddenly remembering David. A part of him wanted to not tell him - wanted to keep her to himself - but as a last kindness to her, knew that it was the right thing to do. He reached into the bag and pulled out her phone.

"David, it's Lincoln. There's been an accident…"

~~~~~

Soon David was in the room, first behind him, and then walking up to the bed, with a look of incredible sadness on his face.

"I only saw her this morning. She told me about … the baby … *your* baby."

Lincoln looked at him and felt his loss too. The man before him had only just begun to understand and know what a wonderful woman she was. Lincoln had been able to spend time with her for more than twenty years, but hadn't always appreciated what a gift that had been.

With that thought, he stood, shook David's hand, and just walked out. Another chapter of his life was over, he thought as he broke down and cried.

Toby saw him and immediately guided him to the car. Driving his employer back to the apartment, he didn't know who to call to provide comfort to Lincoln. His wife had been his sole supporter all of these years, he believed. Except for…

Toby took a few minutes to think. No, he decided, that was not a good idea. The girl had left for a reason. Everyone believed she had left to get away from him. Even if she *was* gracious and willing to come and provide support to him, there was a chance that history could repeat itself, and Toby wouldn't encourage that happening.

He helped Lincoln settle into his bed, surprising Toby in how easy it was to get his employer to follow his instruction and guidance. After closing the bedroom door and making himself comfortable in the living area, he called Lincoln's personal assistant, Hannah, and asked her to inform the people at the top level of the company, of the death of Diana Kokiri.

"But Hannah?" he asked her before he hung up. "Would you be able to come over here, to his apartment? I'm here, but I don't know who else
~~~~~

there is to *be* here for him…"

"Yes, of course Toby. I will do what I have to here, but will be there within an hour."

He thanked her and hung up to wait for her - anyone - to arrive and provide some guidance about what to do to provide support to one of the most influential businessmen in the country. A great man who seemingly had no family left, and an unknowing number of people who he would consider real friends. In the time Toby had worked for him, he had only seen Lincoln really interact with his wife, the girl he had been seeing, and clients. He couldn't remember seeing anyone who fitted into the middle ground of those extremes.

'What a lonely life,' he thought to himself, wondering why anyone would want to live a life like that.

CHAPTER 8

The News

Alexis was at Anthony's house. The two of them had enjoyed time out in his garden together since she had arrived that morning. In reality, she was eager to be inside the house, entwined around him, but she knew she could be patient. She could also see the look of amusement on his face, in the knowledge that she felt that way.

No more had been seen or heard of Lincoln since she had last seen him in the supermarket that morning. Anthony and Alexis were both fairly certain that she had absolutely nothing to worry about anymore.

Anthony watched her face as they weeded around the vegetables. It was a face he never tired of looking at, especially now that she was so happy all the time.

As the day started to grow cold, he stood up and pulled her to her feet.

"Now, Missy, how about you and I go and get clean, after all this playing in the mud?"

"A bath?" she asked.

Anthony laughed at her. No matter the level of maturity he knew was instilled in her nature, there was still another aspect to it, where she was like a small child, eager to get on and experience things.

"Hmm ... I like that idea," he said, putting his arms around her and kissing her, immediately feeling her melt - and rub - against him. "Ahem! Bath time!"

It had taken him a while to accept that her episodes of 'zoning out' had stopped, and they had only started venturing to having baths together once he was certain she was alright.

He ran the water and took his time undressing her, while she, in turn, removed his clothing. For the moment, both of them ignored his obvious arousal as they climbed into the bath. He lay back with his back to the bath wall and watched as she straddled him so she could kiss him and lie with her chest against his.

After a long time of relaxing in the warm water, holding each other, he spoke.

"I miss you when we're apart, Allie," she heard him say as his hand started to caress her hair.

"I know," Alexis replied, looking into his eyes. "So do I."

Pulling her even closer to him, he kissed her lips softly, then more passionately. She felt his hand edge down until it found her sweet spot. Anthony heard her breath catch as his finger began its magical caress.

Alexis didn't move from the spot, instead revelling in the feelings his touch produced in her. When he edged her upwards and began to lick her nipples, she quickly climaxed, making him almost burst with his own arousal.

"Sit up on the edge of the bath," she said.

Anthony immediately complied. He watched her move between his legs and start pleasuring him with her lips and tongue. The result was almost instantaneous.

~~~~~

As Alexis dried off and went to get some clean clothes, she heard Anthony call out with urgency from the living room.

"Allie, quick!"

She ran down the hallway, wondering what had happened. When she got there, she saw him looking at the television, turning the volume up.

"Diana Kokiri, wife of entrepreneur, Lincoln Kokiri, died this afternoon, after being involved in a horrific car accident. Sources say Mrs. Kokiri was transported to the hospital after being removed from the wreckage, but died in hospital shortly afterward."

Anthony looked at Alexis and saw her go white, but at the same time, the image that entered his head was that of the car accident. Alexis, in turn, saw him start to look pale.

"Anthony, sit down," she said, understanding why the article would have affected him so much. It was more than two years since his previous love, Cynthia, had been killed in a car accident. For the most part, he seemed to live his days no longer thinking about her - not thinking about *it*. "Are you alright?"

Anthony looked at her and nodded.

"Yes, I just … shit, the thought of anyone dying in a car crash … it always affects me," he said. "I'm fine. I just need a minute."

He sat quietly and refocused his mind back to her.

"He'll be going through hell, Allie," he said.

Alexis knew he was talking about Lincoln, so she nodded in reply.

"Do you think you should go to him?" Anthony went on to ask.

Alexis looked at him with a horrific look on her face.

"No!" she exclaimed. "Anthony, that would *not* be a helpful thing for me to do for him!"

Anthony looked at her and conceded that it seemed a stupid idea, given how much the man had pursued her over the months since Anthony had met her.

"Yeah, you're right. Sorry, I wasn't thinking…"

Alexis relaxed back on the sofa and pulled him into her arms. They
~~~~~

sat together, both in their towels, having not yet dressed. Their minds individually worked hard, processing what they'd just heard on the television.

"It is horrible news, though, isn't it," Alexis said, remembering the day that Diana had come into the supermarket to confront her. "I think she must have been a nice person. If she wasn't, she would have treated me differently when she saw me, I am sure."

Anthony heard the sadness in her voice and turned to her. He needed to kiss her. The news of the death brought out emotion in him, making him stand and hold out his hand to her, to lead her to his bed. There he took his time making love to her, culminating in him reaching orgasm while deep inside of her.

They lay together, neither in any hurry to move even though it was early evening and their bodies were hungry and ready for an evening meal.

"Are you sure you're alright?" Alexis asked tentatively, still not able to fully comprehend how he must feel when he thought about Cynthia and her death.

Anthony turned so that they were lying facing each other in the bed, warm under the covers.

"I don't want to waste any time, Allie," he said. "I'd like us to see more of each other. I could move and get a job near where you live…"

"No, Anthony, you can't move away from *here*."

"Why not?"

"Because this is your *home* - your *family* home," said Alexis. "And it's so beautiful. How can you even think it?"

"I can think it because I want to be closer to *you*," he said, stroking her cheek softly with his hand.

"Then we'll think of another way. I can swap the days that I work. You can come up on your days off, and I'll come down on my days off…"

"But then whenever we see each other, one of us will be working."

"We'll still have evenings together," she said, admitting to herself that such a plan did not seem a good plan at all.

Suddenly her stomach growled loudly, making Anthony laugh.

"Come on, hungry Missy," he said. "I had better feed you first, and then we can talk about ways I can get you by my side more often."

CHAPTER 9

The Farewell

Anthony and Alexis stepped off the train in central Melbourne train station, having decided to do their first trip together. Months had passed since their brief discussion about changing their relationship. So far, they hadn't changed anything, deciding to keep things slow.

As far as Alexis knew, the trip was a 'get away from everything' trip - a way for the two of them to forget about everything that was normality to them on a daily basis.

Anthony had other intentions, but he didn't let her know that.

They'd booked into the Grand Hyatt Hotel - a building far grander than Alexis had ever been past, let alone inside of. Anthony watched her face as they walked into their room. He wasn't from money or the kind of lifestyle that would normally enable him to stay in such a place himself. From her expressions, he assumed he had seen better than her in many ways.

"Oh, Anthony!" she exclaimed, in awe of the beauty in front of her.

Her facial expression and the tone of her voice reminded Anthony of the first day she'd seen his home. That was until she ran and jumped on the large bed in the middle of the room. He laughed loudly at her as she seemed to fly through the air and fall on her back, legs and arms wide, as if she had jumped onto a soft white cloud.

Alexis moved onto her side, looked at him, and patted the bed beside her with a suggestive look on her face, making him laugh louder.

"It's so soft, Anthony. Come over here and see," she teased him.

Anthony gladly walked to the bed and lay down beside her. When he rolled onto his side to face her, they looked at each other for a long time, just smiling and not speaking. Then she seemed to become full of energy again and was jumping up.

"What do you think the bathroom's like?" he heard her say as her voice rounded the corner from the bedroom area to the bathroom. "Oh, it's got a huge spa bath!" she said, popping her head around the corner and giving him an even more suggestive smile. "I've never been in a spa bath before."

Anthony felt like he was on fire. He couldn't wait any longer. His body needed hers. He jumped off the bed, walked to her, picked her up, and threw her affectionately on the bed again.

Alexis watched his face as he started to undress her, and then himself, pulling a condom from his pocket and making sure she saw it on the bedside table. She welcomed him into her arms and let the passion flow, loving still how much everything was so equal between them. As she moved on top of him, she looked into his eyes and knew she was in a good thing with a good man. He had never done anything to hurt her, and in some ways, he was the first person in her life who had treated her as well as he did.

~~~~~

After sated and resting, he stood up.

"Come on, Missy. We are heading out on the town," he said mysteriously, making her giggle.

"On the town? Oh, Anthony, I didn't bring any clothes for anything flash…"

She watched him, enjoying what appeared to be a special smile on his face.

"You don't need anything flash, Allie. I want to take you to visit an art gallery that's holding an exhibition of a photographer who specialises in food and kitchen photography," he said excitedly and then looked at her. "Do you mind? I think it will be amazing to see. It costs nothing to get in. I guess they're hoping to make money from the sale of the photos. Tomorrow we can do whatever you want to do," he continued, knowing already at least part of the following day's plans.

"An art gallery sounds perfect," Alexis said as she smiled at him, thankful that he had found something to enjoy that would cost no money.

~~~~~

As they walked into the gallery, Alexis was overwhelmed with awe at the photographs. They were giant-sized and diverse. One room featured food itself - meals mainly, with a baking section off to one side of that. Another featured kitchens themselves, with the equipment having been creatively presented in such large images. But the room that caught her attention most of all was one with photos of people who worked in kitchens. In those photographs, she saw chefs of all kinds and … bakers.

Anthony watched her face as she glanced from one face to another, and then saw her look at him with a look of amazement. Although she had grown increasingly expressive and conversational in the time since he'd met her, for the first time in a long time, she seemed speechless.

"How…" she started to say, a look of intense curiosity on her face.

Anthony laughed softly at her.

"That's you," she continued.

The comment made Anthony laugh louder still before settling down to a quiet but charming grin that was definitely meant only for her.

"Yes, these photos were all taken in the chain of supermarkets that I work in, Allie," he said.

She looked back at the photo and then back at him, a broad smile on her face.

"You are so sneaky!" she laughed as she launched herself against him and into his welcoming arms.

As she held him tight, her sight fell over his shoulder. A familiar pair of eyes met with hers. For a moment, she felt a slight panic. She didn't know what to do, but when she saw him only smile at her - a friendly smile, and somewhat of a shy smile - she relaxed and decided to not bring it to the attention of Anthony, who was so happy in that moment.

They continued walking around the exhibition, which appeared to be a winding exhibition that wove upwards in a progressive flow over several floors. When they were walking past restrooms, Anthony excused himself. Alexis made her way to a large window that was nearby to wait for him.

"You look happy," she heard that voice say.

On hearing it, Alexis noted that inside of her, there was no reaction to it. When she turned around, she saw Lincoln standing close to her.

"Lincoln," she breathed out heavily.

Lincoln also noticed the change. He'd always loved her using his name. It had been like an arousal drug to him. Now there was no response within his body at all. He was relieved at the discovery.

"I was so sorry to hear about your wife," Alexis said as she studied his face.

Lincoln looked at her. She was more youthful since she'd become healthy again, and he was glad.

"Thank you, Lexi."

"Please ... please call me Alexis, Lincoln. I don't want to be Lexi anymore," she said.

Lincoln comprehended what she was saying, and nodded in acknowledgement.

"Alexis."

As Anthony exited the restroom, he looked around to locate her. He was shocked and stunned to see her standing with ... *him.* Well, he *thought* it was him. He had never seen the man in the flesh, only in photos, so couldn't be entirely certain. Regardless, his natural response was to run over and get between them. As if sensing his intention to do just that, he heard a female voice beside him.

"Don't."

He turned to the woman who was standing nearby, looking at him. She was an older woman, although still beautiful.

"You are Lexi's partner, are you not?" she asked.

Anthony nodded at her, hating anyone using that name for his Allie.

"Don't interrupt them," the woman continued. "They are alright. He recently lost his wife, and he now needs to apologize to *her*. Please let him do it. She'll be safe, don't worry."

He looked from her back to the pair in question and decided to put faith in the mystery woman who was speaking. When he returned his gaze to her once again, he saw she was looking at him curiously.

"You are in one of the photos…?" she asked.

Anthony nodded at her but couldn't bring himself to speak, his eyes diverting right back to the pair on the other side of the room.

"I'm Hannah, Lincoln's personal assistant," she said in an effort to distract him once again.

When he turned to her, he saw she had her hand extended out to him.

"Anthony," he said as he shook her hand, wanting to be polite but finding it difficult.

"Anthony, come and sit with me over here for a moment. They will be in view of us, so you don't need to worry. Let them heal each other," she said.

The words made him look at her sharply.

"Heal each other … how?" he asked.

"You know, Anthony. You know how things were between them…" she said and saw him nod. "He needs to make sure she knows he is sorry, and I'm sure she equally needs to know that he *is* sorry. Let us let them do it and be done with it."

~~~~~

On the other side of the room, Alexis was studying Lincoln's face.

"What do you see?" he asked her, as if reading her thoughts.

Together they automatically made their way to a seat that was nearby and sat on it, without any speaking at all about the move. Neither considered the fact that it was the first time they had ever been in the presence of each other in public, for all to see.

"I see a man who is a great man, who I should have said no to about so many things," she said and felt tears come to her eyes.

"Yes, the things I asked you to do to me, I wish you had found the strength to say no to, Alexis," he started to say, making a point of using her real name. "But I equally wish that I had never asked you to do those things. I didn't know it was in me to need something like that. I'm so sorry for everything I've put you through."

Alexis watched his face, mesmerized by it, as he continued to speak.

"I didn't recognise the true extent of how much Diana meant to me," he continued. "I knew I loved her, but if I had looked as closely at her as I did you…"

Lincoln felt a wave of extreme sadness flow over him once more. He fought to hold back the tears that desperately wanted to burst forth.
~~~~~

"I made so many mistakes, Alexis. Now it's too late for me to make things right with Diana," he said, now holding back a sob. "Please let me make things right with you."

"Everything *is* right with me, Lincoln. I went away because I needed to start over … to start a new life. And I have. I have a new home, and a new job - as you know," she said and saw him nod as he listened to her with such an intent look on his face.

"And you have a good man in your life, I know," Lincoln added.

"Yes," Alexis agreed, not daring to ask *how* he knew. It didn't matter now. "With him, I feel balanced. I didn't feel that way with you. I don't think we had something that was *equal*, like I have now."

They looked at each other for a long time. Eventually, he felt her hand extend out to his and hold it firmly in her own.

"Lincoln, I know that you are a good person. Please don't think badly of the things we did together. I have learned since then that people do those things and they enjoy them. It just isn't right for me to hurt someone like that. It *never* was right for me. But that doesn't mean it was wrong. It just means that you have to find the right person to match you in what you need."

The comment made Lincoln sob loudly as he remembered the time with Diana, and how much she had seemed to enjoy hurting him. All along, *she* could have been his match, if only he could have seen…

Alexis felt her heart break. She had seen and heard how Anthony was when she had first met him, still heartbroken two years after his love had been lost due to an accident that took her life. But for Lincoln, it must be still so new … so *raw*.

"Lincoln, I know - I *expect* - that you have thousands of people who want to provide support to you, but do you have someone close to you, who is helping you through this?" she asked.

Lincoln smiled at her, seeing so many different things in her now. The question was disregarded for the moment.

"You are so different," he said. "It was the right thing to do when you left. It was the right thing for both of us. I don't know what it was, that connection we had, but it was *insane*," he continued, trying to make light of it. In the process, he made her giggle at the tone of his voice. It was a sound he'd not heard in so long. It prompted him to look more closely at her, remembering how she had been when he had first met her.

"I'm sorry I wasn't good for you…"

"Oh, Lincoln, I do think that you were *meant* to pass through my life. That time with you did give me an inner strength that I never had before I met you, and I feel like a stronger person now. I feel like a *better* person," she said and smiled at him. "For the very first time in my life, I feel *normal*."

Lincoln laughed out loud, still wiping his eyes.

~~~~~

From a distance, Anthony and Hannah both heard the laugh and turned their view to that direction. Inside, Anthony was fuming, and Hannah could see it.

"It's easy to see how much you love her, Anthony," she said. "What has you so upset that they are talking?"

Anthony turned toward the woman he didn't even know, but who had instantly inspired a level of trustworthiness in him.

"The things she did … the way she was the day I met her - I will never forget that, Hannah!" he said. "She would go into trances and not know where she was or who she was with. She was really screwed up. It was one of the scariest things I'd ever seen…"

"Then she is very lucky that you found her."

Anthony heard the comment but didn't reply further, instead resuming his stare toward the people he did not like seeing together.

~~~~~

"It's good to get to talk to you like this, Alexis. We didn't talk enough, and I am sorry for that. You might think that an old man like me might not still have hormones running through his body, but my God, when I was with you!" he said with a light-hearted tone in his voice, making her giggle softly again.

"But to answer your earlier question, yes, I have support," he continued. "It may not sound very professional, but my personal assistant, Hannah, has been there for me throughout this, right from the day that Diana died," he said. "She is a good friend, and that is what I need right now - just a really good friend." He paused and turned his hand, so he was holding hers before continuing. "I lost control when I met you. I wish I could go back and start over, with the ability to maintain my head during our time together, but of course I can't. I just hope that you know … that you *believe* … that I only wish the best for you, Alexis, and I really am so very, very sorry."

Alexis watched him begin to cry openly, but she held back her natural instinct to lean in and pull him close to her.

"Lincoln, I am fine," she said. "And you will be fine too."

He nodded at her, not feeling any of the desperation he had with regard to her in the past, but also not wanting the moment to end too soon.

"She was pregnant when she died," he said quietly and saw surprise on her face. "We had been married for twenty years, and she had always wanted to have a baby, but it never happened. And then it did happen, but now it's too late…"

Alexis could see that he was finding it more and more difficult to hold back his desire to let his emotions loose and sob.

"How could she fall pregnant, and then this happen? I don't understand how that could be. It just seems so *cruel*," he continued, now visibly crying in front of her.

"Oh, I'm so sorry," Alexis said, feeling tears threaten in her own eyes.

She watched him for several minutes as he seemed determined to gather himself together. He had already aged over their time together, and then afterward, but now she noticed he had aged again.

"Do you see an old man now, Alexis?" he asked when he saw her looking at him closely. In response, he saw her shake her head.

"No, I see a very attractive man who is suffering," replied Alexis. "You're not old. I *never* considered you old. And I think you have so much to offer the right person."

"Thank you," he responded, squeezing her hand tightly. "But I want to make things right with you. What can I do to make things right?"

"There's nothing you need to do. Move forward and try to find happiness - find the right *balance*," Alexis said and saw him nod while looking intently into her eyes. "And I haven't forgotten that you gave me all that money…"

On his face, she saw confusion.

"What money?"

"The money that was deposited into my account…" Alexis said and felt confusion herself at the level of confusion that he had on his face. "Lincoln, didn't you deposit $15,000 into my bank account a while back?"

Lincoln shook his head, not having any idea what she was talking about.

"No, I never put any money into your account."

"But the bank said the deposit came from Sunshine Supermarkets…" she informed him.

Lincoln pulled back his hand suddenly from hers.

"What?" he asked and seemed to instantly go white.

"Isn't that one of your companies? I assumed it was you…"

He had a look of horror on his face.

"No!" he breathed out heavily. "No, Alexis, Sunshine is under my umbrella, but I wasn't the one who had controlling power over that business. That was … I gave control of that business as a gift … to *Diana*," he continued as they looked at each other with a reflection look of surprise and uncertainty. "She must have … no, why would she do that? She didn't even know who or where you were…"

"Yes, she did," Alexis said, causing him to look even more confused. "She came to see me at my work."

"What?"

"Diana came to see me at my work," Alexis explained. "She approached me and made herself known to me."

"I don't understand. She never said anything…" he stopped. "What did she say to you?"

"She told me who she was, and she said she was thankful to me for being there for you so that you didn't have to ask her to … do … those things. I thought she must have been angry at me, but she seemed to have a look of true sincerity on her face when she said it. Lincoln, you're not saying that *Diana* deposited that money into my account…"

Lincoln's mind was working furiously. It didn't make any sense. Nothing made sense.

"What else could it be?" he asked. "You weren't owed that much by the supermarket when you left?"

Alexis laughed quietly at that idea.

"No, that would not be possible," she said. "I hardly earned $15,000 in a *year* there. There's no way they would have paid that to me when I left."

Lincoln was quiet for some time, just looking at her face while his thinking continued.

"She must have wanted you to have it," he said. "She must have been sincere. It wouldn't make any sense for her to give you such an amount otherwise. Diana wasn't fickle with cash, and she would never have used company money so easily if it weren't for something she felt strongly about."

Alexis watched his face and saw him grow resolved in the culmination of his analysis.

"Oh, Alexis," he said finally, sounding so very, very tired all of a sudden. "Sometimes I feel like I don't know myself … like I'm a stranger in my own skin. All the things I put you through … and all the things I put Diana through … I don't know when I became such a person to treat people like this."

He looked up at her after several minutes of silence.

"The past can't be changed, Lincoln," she said. "We can only learn from it and, from now on, move on to do things differently … better."

"You are so mature for your age," he said quietly. "Your soul is much older than your years, Alexis. Are you truly happy, where you are now?"

Alexis smiled at him softly.

"I am," she said. "I *am* happy, Lincoln. Because of that, I don't regret my time with you. If I'd not had that, I wouldn't be where I am right now. It was always meant to be - our time together - even if it wasn't meant to last."

He nodded at her and suddenly felt the time was right to end the conversation. He had nothing more he had to say to her. He'd voiced his thoughts, and she had listened. She'd said she didn't need his forgiveness or anything else from him to make things right. It was time to truly say goodbye to her completely.

Alexis watched him stand up, prompting her to stand up beside him.

"You are right. With you, I found a side to me that I didn't like, and I don't want to see again. But through that, I have learned a bit more about myself, and that will help me to find where I'm supposed to be, I am sure." He paused and then spoke again, all the while knowing she was looking at his face intently. "I am glad you're happy. If you need anything from me in the future, please do let me know. I know I put you through hell, but I am here as a friend if you need me."

Alexis saw the tears begin in his eyes, even though he tried hard to keep them away. She moved tentatively toward him, and he welcomed her as he held out his arms and wrapped them around her. They stood together, holding each other tightly. For the first time in doing so, they were both aware that there was absolutely no indication of arousal on him for her. It was something that shouldn't have been noticed in such a time, but was. It was a good sign that everything was absolutely finished. Whatever craziness they had shared together before - the animal attraction or whatever crazy thing it had been - was gone, and happily so.

Lincoln pulled back from her.

"I should find Hannah. I don't know where she's got to," he said as he started to look around, and finally saw her. "Oh, she's with your…"

"Anthony," Alexis finished for him, also seeing the two people in question sitting together, watching. She purposely did not ask - or even ponder - how he already knew who Anthony was and what he looked like.

"Yes, Anthony," he said and looked back at her. "Keep moving forward in your life, Alexis. Enjoy your time with him as it can be so short."

She nodded at him and moved away, him walking behind her without any thought whatsoever to all the times he had forced her to walk behind him … to *follow* him.

~~~~~

Anthony saw the two of them start to walk toward him and Hannah. He stood up to receive them, not knowing what to expect when he came face to face with the force of nature that was Lincoln Kokiri. He felt Hannah stand up beside him, also in anticipation, but he wasn't prepared for what followed.

Lincoln walked up to Anthony, stood right before him, and held out his hand.

"You are good for her, I know, Anthony," he said. "Make sure that you continue to deserve her. Don't ever take her for granted."
~~~~~

All four of them knew that the words could have been taken as a threat, made from Lincoln to Anthony. They weren't, and Anthony knew it. He knew it because at that moment, the two men were in a similar position, both having lost loved ones suddenly and without any warning.

Anthony held out his hand and shook the one before him.

"I am sorry for your loss, Mr. Kokiri," he said, not wanting to be on a first-name basis with such a powerful man.

"Thank you," Lincoln said, now ready to leave. "Hannah, please meet Lexi … *Alexis*."

Alexis held out her hand and squeezed that of the older woman in front of her, both of them recognising a certain, similar strength in each other, and an instant *liking* for each other.

"Take care of him," Alexis leaned in and whispered to Hannah, and saw her quietly nod and smile in recognition.

After one more glance at Lincoln, Alexis reached out and took Anthony's hand. The two of them walked away, that chapter finally behind them.

Anthony said nothing to her as they left the art gallery and made their way back to the hotel. He could tell she was deep in thought, and didn't want to invade her thinking. His own mind was working overtime. When they had left the hotel earlier that evening, he had just wanted to see her face when she saw the large photograph of him, which he'd known was going to be there. He had, in no way, anticipated running into that man, and her being confronted with memories of her time with him. He felt somewhat responsible for putting her through such emotional turmoil over the previous couple of hours, even though that made no sense.

After walking back to their hotel room and closing the door behind them, Alexis put her arms around him and held him tightly to her.

"Thank you for giving me that time with him, Anthony. I know it must have been difficult for you to watch…"

"It was," he responded, only wanting to be completely honest and not hide anything from her. "Hannah told me to stay back and let the two of you speak. It really wasn't me…"

"No matter what she said, you could have come and stood between us," Alexis said. "You could have tried to prevent us from talking. But you didn't … so it *was* you. And I thank you for that, because he needed to talk to me, and I needed to listen to him. Now you and I can relax with full belief that I really am free. I know we haven't had any reason to believe otherwise lately anyway, but it has still been there, in my mind … wondering if he'd actually given up."

Anthony nodded. " I know."

Alexis looked at him intensely and let thoughts of Lincoln flow out of her, to be placed in a box in her mind and finally forgotten.

"Wanna have a spa now?" she asked with a hint of suggestion in her eyes.

Anthony laughed as she instantly relaxed him.

"Oh, yes I do," he replied, smiling broadly at her and then kissing her deeply, fully intending to begin their night of pleasure in the beautiful hotel room they were in.

~~~~~

The next morning, Anthony woke up to the feeling of kisses on the back of his neck. He reached back, pulled Alexis closer against his back, and felt her arm wrap over and around him to hold him tight to her.

"I know what you need," he said to her with a sound of suggestive amusement in his voice.

"Oh, really?" she teased him back. "And what would that be?"

He turned over and kissed her deeply before pulling back and smiling.

"Breakfast in bed," he said, laughing loudly at her surprise. "Grab that room service menu, and let's order everything."

Alexis laughed at him but obliged as her tummy growled loudly, making him laugh even louder. How well he knew her body.

They ate together and stayed in the room until their 10am checkout, enjoying the spa and the bed until the very last minute when they would have to leave.

Before walking out, Alexis put her arms around him and rested there for a minute.

"Thank you, Anthony. This has been wonderful."

"Our time here isn't done yet, Allie. Our train doesn't leave until five, so we have all day, just about," he said and saw her smile in surprise. "We have things to do yet!"

~~~~~

As they left the hotel, Alexis didn't ask him anything about his plans, leaving it up to him what they would do. Walking along the riverfront, she was reminded of the night that they went to the restaurant in her town, and the level of passion she had felt with him when they'd kissed. She was so caught up in those thoughts that she had hardly noticed they were approaching a docking area of a large boat. It was only when she was walking up a gangway that she realised what was happening.

"Anthony, what..."

He smiled brilliant at her and held her hand up to his mouth to kiss it.

"A cruise down the river, Allie!" he said to her, loving the excitement he could see on her face.

"I've never been on a boat," she said quietly, in wonder.

"I know. You told me that a while ago," he replied and smiled at her as they found somewhere to sit quietly on board.

Alexis leaned over to him and kissed him. He revelled in the feeling.

Even taking into consideration the oddness of the night before, with her having seen that man, Anthony felt his heart soar. He knew he was ready to take another step with her.

As the boat moved, Alexis found herself immersed in the feeling of the movement on the water - something she had never felt before. Anthony enjoyed watching her face, full of expression of wonder. When they were well underway, he took her hand and kissed it, looking at her so intently that she felt like she could melt into him.

"Allie," he started, before kneeling before her and pulling out a small box. "Allie," he began again, and she saw a blush flow over him. "I absolutely love you. I thought I'd never find happiness again, but you make me incredibly happy. I want us to be together all the time, for our entire future. Will you marry me? Will you be my wife?"

Alexis felt surprised … shocked … stunned into silence.

For a moment, Anthony wondered if he'd made a mistake and misread *everything.* Then he saw her smile softly at him and slowly nod.

"Yes, Anthony," she said, leaning down and kissing him deeply as he continued to kneel before her. "Yes, I would very much like to be your wife."

He smiled at her, feeling his heart pounding in his chest as he nervously pulled the ring out of the box and slipped it onto her wedding finger. He then kissed her back while slowly raising himself up and pulling her up so they were both standing.

Around them, someone must have seen the action, as they became aware, all of a sudden, of people clapping. When they looked around, they were surprised to see people looking right at them as they did so.

Alexis laughed and resumed kissing him, not worrying at all about the crowd they had attracted.

CHAPTER 10

The Final Chapter

Alexis felt like a princess in her dress of flowing emerald green silk. It wasn't traditional, she knew, but she had seen the fabric in a local store when out shopping with Samantha, and it had immediately captured her attention. Of course, it probably should have been a fabric used for a bridesmaid's dress, but she didn't care. Samantha had taken so much care in designing it and sewing it for her, and Alexis loved it. It was her ultimate choice of dress for her ultimate day.

Samantha stood with her, laughing in excitement at the development of her being a bridesmaid for the first time in her life. Looking at Alexis, she felt thankful for having met such a good friend over the past year, but at the same time, she felt great pride in the dress that Alexis wore. Samantha was only beginning to find her way as a designer, but the dress would help to establish her.

"Oh my gosh, this is so exciting!" she kept saying, jumping up and down, and clapping her hands as if she were a child at Christmas time.

Alexis laughed at her. They had only found each other as friends fairly recently, but in the time she had known her, Samantha had proven to be an easy-going, fun, and trustworthy friend who Alexis had come to trust completely. She still didn't fully understand the relationship between Samantha and Tom. To her, it seemed like they were meant to be together. Regardless, she respected it and no longer tried to nudge the two of them together.

"Come on, you two!" Alexis heard Tom say as his head popped around the door. "Wow," he then said, seeing the two of them. "I am in heaven, getting to walk beside the two of you."

They laughed at him, knowing he was right. Alexis would have no traditional person walking down her down the aisle, but in recent months, Tom had earned a place as Anthony's friend as well as hers. He was a good choice for the job of giving Alexis away.

Tom walked both women out toward the back door of Anthony's home and saw Anthony's closest friend, Robert, step up and reach out his arm for Samantha to take. The two of them left the doorway together as bridesmaid and best man, and then Tom gave Alexis a friendly smile and nod as they stepped out next.

It wasn't a large area in Anthony's garden, but it was enough for the few people who were there. For Alexis, it was the preferred location for the occasion. She still loved the homestead, and could not have imagined a better location for such a special day.

As she and Tom walked around the garden path, finally the makeshift altar was in view. She saw Anthony turn and look at her, making her heart surge with the smile he gave her.

Anthony saw the vision and found himself breathless. He hadn't asked her about her dress, so the emerald green was a surprise, but a welcome one. His bride looked stunning. For a moment, he thought back to when he had met her. He could still visualise her trying so hard to look completely genderless in an oversized old jersey and old jeans, with her hair tucked inside a cap. He could not have anticipated then just how beautiful she was.

As Alexis approached, Tom carefully moved her hand from his arm to that of Anthony, giving him a smile and a nod in the process. Alexis sensed Tom fall into place beside Samantha and Robert.

As they said their vows, Alexis could see the combination of nervousness and desire on Anthony's face. She wondered if she was mirroring those same emotions back at him.

"Anthony, you may kiss your bride," the celebrant said.

Anthony immediately pulled Alexis into an intense hug and deep kiss, having wanted to do so for the past few minutes while the vows had been exchanged.

Alexis laughed at his enthusiasm as she also indulged in the feelings of bliss. If anyone had said to her five years earlier that she would get married to a good man who made her feel as whole as Anthony did, she would have laughed in the huge unlikelihood of that happening. Even two or three years earlier, when she was in the situation with Lincoln, she could never have expected to be where she currently was.

Apart from the gift that Lincoln had sent to them - the large photo of Anthony that they had previously seen at the gallery exhibition - she had not heard from him again, and didn't expect to. Over time, she had found a slight sadness about that. Yes, he had acted without reason toward her. Yes, he had frightened her in his pursuit. But when that had all cleared, after the death of Diana, she had seen a different person. That night, she had seen the person she had met right at the very beginning - the person who didn't need the delivery of pain for satisfaction. The person who had so much more to offer than just instructions and commands.

But she could not have any more regrets there. If things had gone on to be wonderful with Lincoln, she would never have been on the bus that day, desperate to get away, and she would never have met Anthony. And she never could have *not* met him. When they had met, they'd both had such pain inside of them - him from Cynthia's death, and her from her struggles with Lincoln. They had needed each other to work through those situations of pain.

~~~~~

"You look beautiful, Allie," Anthony whispered in her ear as they held each other closely in the dance under the small pop-up gazebo they had put up in the garden for the purpose.

Alexis looked at him and reached up to kiss him, something he still revelled in every time that she took the initiative. When it was her doing, he had confirmation that they were kissing because she wanted them to be kissing, and not because she thought *he* wanted it and that she should. He knew he no longer had to watch for such signs. He truly believed she was well cured from the trauma that seemed to have occurred in her during her time with Lincoln Kokiri. That didn't stop him silently monitoring her now and then, just in case there were still triggers that had not yet shown themselves.

"I'm going to make you so happy, Allie," he said to her, quickly discarding the thought that had just been plaguing his mind.

"You already make me happy, Anthony. I couldn't be any happier," she replied, looking into his eyes.

Anthony kissed her deeply, loving the feeling of her lips. It was a feeling he thought he would never get tired of.

"And I am very happy to be here, living in your beautiful home with you," Alexis continued.

He smiled at her, pleased with that sentence. She had resigned from her job two weeks earlier, but there had been a slight concern in his mind that she had done it for him and not for herself. One thing that he did truly believe was that she did love being in his family home with him. That had been evident the moment she had first set her eyes on the house.

"Hey! Stop hogging the dance floor," they heard Samantha say as she nudged them affectionately, making them laugh at her. She was holding Tom's hand, and Alexis could see the look on his face that she saw so often. Since Alexis had met her, she had asked Samantha many times if she ever even *noticed* the way Tom looked at her, but always Samantha laughed it off and disregarded the question. But Alexis could see his face. She could see the yearning he had for Samantha. Alexis found herself feeling quite sorry for him, to be silently in love with someone and. at the same time, be so fearful of declaring that love in case such a declaration would end a friendship.

Feeling eyes on him, Tom turned to see Alexis watching him with that same sad smile on her face. He was used to it now. He shrugged it off with a silly face, as he always did to make her laugh and not think about the subject he knew she was thinking of. There were things he wanted to say to Samantha, but they could wait for another time and another day.
~~~~~

Alexis turned her attention back to Anthony, vowing to only think of him.

"How many children do you think we could fit in this house of yours?" she asked and saw him smile brilliantly.

"A great many," he said and saw her laugh with him.

"When can we start working on that?" she asked him before he kissed her.

"About two hours from now, when I kick everyone else out and get you alone."

EPILOGUE

Lincoln sat in his office with a brandy balloon in his left hand, his left elbow resting on the chair armrest. He rarely drank alcohol, but that evening, he felt the need for it. The finest cognac suited his need perfectly. He'd moved his office chair right up to the window and was watching out over the vast, sprawling city that lay before him. The view reminded him of the vista from the apartment he had gotten for Lexi. He took a moment to remember how happy she had been then. It was a happiness that had lessened over their time together, until she'd not been happy at all. He still regretted that.

Today was her wedding day. He hadn't been invited. That saddened him, but he understood. Since the night they'd seen each other at the gallery, they had hardly spoken, except for a brief thank you from her when she'd received delivery of the large photograph of Anthony. It was a wedding gift to them from Lincoln. It was something she might have considered a gift of peace - an apology for all the times he'd scared her, and pushed her to leave her life in Melbourne behind to get away from him.

Although Lincoln had believed they'd both moved out of the realm of extremes that had possessed him over those three years, Lexi was on his mind again. The photograph hadn't been sent as a mere gift, out of the kindness of his heart. No, he wanted to make sure that she remembered him. In sending it, he had hoped she would place it somewhere in her husband's home, in pride of place. He anticipated that by sending the photograph, now and then she would stop and look at it - as would her husband - and they would remember who had given it to them.

He looked at his watch. By now, his Lexi would be wed. She would be someone's wife. She would have a husband. It wasn't right for him to think of her. He didn't want to think of her … but he was.

He remembered things about their time together. He thought of her kisses, her hands, her lips wrapped around him, and the taste of her as he had pleasured her. As he remembered, he subconsciously moved his right hand down and started to caress himself. At first, he was unaware he was doing it. He hadn't self-pleasured in a long while, having chosen instead to delve his mind into work, and his body into fitness.

Thinking about her having committed herself so fully to another man, Lincoln's mind was wandering and remembering. With those thoughts active, he began rubbing himself more fully through his pants. It was a mindless thing to do. His hand had acted without any conscious thought from him that he wanted to do it.

When he realised what he was doing, he let himself indulge in it. Once he started to really feel it, he stood to make his way to the bathroom that led off his office. He hadn't released in so long, but that night - on Lexi's wedding night - he would. He was as aroused as he could be. He needed to let go.

When he was midway from his desk to the bathroom door, his office door opened and Hannah, his personal assistant, walked in. She was as startled as he was, neither thinking the other was still in the office so late in the evening.

Lincoln was able to put on his professional face and move his thoughts to the present as he had always done. When the time called for it, his business face could show, no matter what he was feeling inside.

The professionalism he tried to exhibit, however, did not extend down his body. Standing in only his tailored suit pants and shirt, Hannah couldn't help but see that he was aroused - *highly* aroused. She blushed and looked away at first, but then considered her immediate options. She'd been his personal assistant since they were in their twenties. She had watched him through his marriage, she had watched him through his involvement with Lexi, and she had watched him - coddled him - since the death of Diana. She had never told him how she felt about him, and he had never seemed to notice that she was a woman at all.

Bringing her eyes back to his, she moved forward, needing to know how he would react to her making her feelings known.

As Lincoln saw her move toward him, he stood still, wondering what business she was bringing to him. When she stood directly in front of him, he saw her look down, making him blush, but also surprising him as he heard her voice.

"Let me..." she started to say as her hand reached out toward him, ready to touch him.

Startled by the movement and the words, Lincoln roused himself enough to grab her wrist before she could touch him.

"Hannah," he said quietly, wondering how to prevent what she wanted to happen, from happening, without hurting her feelings.

Hannah remained quiet for a moment as her breath held, horrified that she may have just offended her boss, and there might follow on repercussions from that. Then she felt him move closer and lean into her, talking to her with a high degree of softness and intimacy.

"Let me take you out for dinner," Lincoln said, trying to ease what he could see might result in a potential gap between them, and not wanting that gap to happen, let alone widen. "I have to finish some things up here, but I'll be ready to leave in about twenty minutes if you'd like to."

Hannah looked at him, blushing as she cursed at herself inside her mind for having been so stupid. She nodded and then quietly turned around and left the room, leaving Lincoln confused and uncertain how to move on from that moment with her.

As soon as the door closed, the moment with Hannah was lost. His thoughts instantly returned to Lexi, prompting him to resume his journey to the bathroom. He had to. Thinking about her had brought on too many feelings, and his arousal was insanely intense. Although he hadn't done it in a long while, he didn't hesitate to lower his pants and immediately stroke himself, forcefully and quickly, thinking over and over about her lips and her body. Finally, he reached that point, the orgasm so long overdue that his knees almost went.

"Fuck!" he called out, overwhelmed with the intensity of it. "Oh fuck, Lexi!! Sorry, but I just can't let you go yet."

He gathered himself up and looked in the mirror, assessing himself while finding the resolve to prepare to take Hannah out for dinner. He didn't know what she wanted, but he would give her the attention and time she needed. They would figure that out together. She had long ago earned his full trust, and he was overdue to consider moving on with someone new in his life. Yes, he would listen to her, and they would work it out.

But in the back of his mind, the more important issue was how was he going to get close to Lexi again ... *Alexis,* she had told him she wanted to be called, when she'd seen him at the gallery. Her wanting that was irrelevant. To him, she would always be Lexi. He realised at that moment that although he had resolved to completely let her go, he had indeed changed his mind.

He wouldn't scare her any more. He wouldn't stalk her. He wouldn't contact her. He would have to be subtle, but somehow, somewhere, sometime, he would find a way. They were meant to be together, and fate would bring them together again.

Because he wasn't prepared to walk away from her yet, after all.

~~~~~~~~~~~~~~

The End
~~~~~~~~~~~~~~

soon. I'll be ready to leave in about twenty minutes, if you would like?"

Hannah looked at him blushing, as she cursed at herself inside for [illegible] mind for having been so stupid. She nodded and then quickly turned around and left the room, leaving him confused and [illegible] may seem [illegible] that [illegible]

[illegible] thoughts [illegible] the bathroom [illegible] feel [illegible]

FRIENDSHIP OF DESIRE

~~ Book Three ~~

CHAPTER 1

The Formation of a Friendship

A Fairly Long Time Ago

Tom and Samantha. In their kindergarten years, they had been the two kids in their neighbourhood who seemed to repel off each other the same way magnets do when their polarity isn't the comfortable way around. In the kindergarten classroom, they would hit each other, they would yell at each other, and when one of them had that particular toy, the other suddenly had to have it. Parents and teachers looked at the two of them in constant wonder. To everyone, it was a mystery why they so regularly kept drawing toward each other, when it so obviously seemed that they should stay away from each other - *far* away.

Despite the repelling when they were in close vicinity, they did keep pulling toward each other in terms of the company they each kept. Through the kindergarten years, and on through the early years of schooling, they could rile each other up so well that no-one who viewed them could make any sense of it at all. Every time one had a birthday party, the other had to be invited. When the school holidays arrived, one ensured the other had to come for a visit. But always, their constant was the fighting. Sometimes it was physical. On many an occasion, either or both of them would end up crying to an adult about the other hitting them. Mostly it comprised a fairly steady flow of verbal attacks. It was like they thrived on it. It was almost as if their friendship *survived* on it - until high school.

~~~~~

Although close to the same age, it was obvious to all around them that they were maturing at different rates. Samantha was the first to ease off from the close-but-frayed friendship the two of them had shared for most of their lives to date.

"Samantha!" Tom would yell out to her from across the high school yard, eager to gain her attention and simply be able to talk to her. His efforts were rewarded by a look from her that, to many, wouldn't even be considered polite.

Samantha heard the voice and knew who it was, but being sixteen, things were changing inside of her. Suddenly she didn't know how to deal with the new thoughts inside her head. She was no longer sure of the way she felt about Tom. There was new confusion and uncertainty that
~~~~~

caused frustration in her. Dealing with him when she felt so confused about him was something she chose to avoid.

"He's following you again," her friend Tanya said to her one day when the two of them were sitting in the outdoor lunch area of the school grounds. "When are you going to talk to him and just put him out of his misery?"

Samantha let her eyes drift over to her lifelong friend. At the same time every day, he seemed to always patiently be sitting within close-but-not-too-close vicinity of her. It was a comfort and an annoyance, all wrapped up together.

"Stop it!" Samantha teased Tanya back, a soft laugh in her voice. "He and I aren't like that. I don't think he even looks at girls yet, so stop trying to cause trouble!"

Tanya laughed at her.

"You are so oblivious," she replied but let it go. The two girls had the same conversation almost every day, although occasionally Tanya let it go and kept quiet for a day or two. "But you know, he's absolutely gorgeous. Can you really not see that?"

Samantha heard the same words so often that she just sighed in reply. There was no point in trying to prevent her friend from always returning to the same conversation, but she did take a moment to look at Tom from the distance they were at. She knew him so well that it was difficult to carry out any kind of 'gorgeous assessment'. All she could see was the same face that she'd grown up with. It might have changed slightly over the years, but it was still the same face. There was nothing wrong with it. He wasn't ugly. But gorgeous?

~~~~~

Despite his efforts to still talk to her, Tom felt confused by the sudden intensity with which his lifelong buddy was rejecting him. Yes, they fought often. They always had. But why did she now so easily just ignore him? He didn't know what had happened. It seemed like one minute they were their usual selves, driving each other nuts with infuriation due to one thing or another. The next minute, she seemed to turn her back on him and not want to have anything more to do with him.

"Hi, Tom," he heard a voice say to him as it passed by.

He looked up to see a girl from his English class smiling at him.

"Oh hi, Kelly," he said mindlessly but with a slightly automated smile on his face.

"Oh, my god. Did Kelly Keri just say hello to you?" he then heard his friend, John, ask him in amazement as he took a seat beside Tom.

"Yeah, I think so," Tom replied with vagueness evident in his voice. He was still thinking of the ongoing sadness he felt about his seemingly lost friendship with Samantha.
~~~~~

John laughed at him.

"You think so?" he asked, disbelieving that Tom could be so blind. "Tom, that girl is hot, and she's into you. Aren't you at least a little bit excited about that?"

John watched as he saw Tom give him a look that said he just didn't comprehend what had just been said. John continued to laugh. They'd been friends only since the beginning of high school. They had a sound, easy-going, and fun friendship. That was something Tom hadn't had prior to meeting John, since his friendship with Samantha had always been anything but easy-going.

"Ugh," Tom said, shaking his head and smiling at his friend. "You think everyone likes me," he said as his smile transformed into a chuckle. "Well, guess what? They don't!"

"Oh, man, I swear you *choose* to not see the girls making a play for you," John responded, making the two of them laugh together.

Tom looked over at Samantha once more and saw her give him a slight glimpse. She could have waved. She could have smiled. Instead, she turned and left the area, with her friend following behind her.

There was just no denying it inside of him. He missed her. He knew they'd always been rocky in their treatment of each other, but he missed her fast quips at him. He missed her sarcasm. He even missed her odd punches on the sensitive part of his arm that had suffered immensely over the years they had known each other. He didn't know why, but quite simply … he missed her.

~~~~

Tom sat in English class and indulged in listening to the teacher at the front of the class. He didn't want to be a nobody when he finished high school. He wanted to go on and do great things. What great things, he had no idea as yet. What he did know was that sitting around, or standing around, doing a mundane job, was something he didn't want to do. He knew it was a snobby way to think, given where he came from, but he didn't care. He wanted more from his life. If he had to ignore every other student in order to concentrate on the teachers and learn everything he had to, he would. If that was what it would take to pass every exam and get out of school with the best academic record, he was going to do it. Nothing and no-one was going to distract him from that goal.

As he listened to the teacher talking about that night's reading assignment, he felt a nudge on his arm. He turned to see his classroom neighbour pass a note to him. Opening it, he let out a sigh.

'Going to Bobby's party tonight? I'll go with you … if you ask me. Kelly."

It didn't occur to Tom at all that the note was from who it was signed by. It was something that John would do, just to try and get a bite from
~~~~

him. Tom silently tucked the note into his jeans pocket and resumed watching and listening to the teacher.

~~~~~

"Haha, you are so funny," he said to John when he next saw him at the beginning of last period.

John looked up at Tom in surprise, not knowing what he was talking about.

"What?" he asked. "What have I done now?"

He saw Tom sit down beside him and give him the same old 'as if you don't know' look that he'd grown to know so well. In the relatively short time since the two of them had met, John had subjected Tom to a fair amount of pranks. It was more than a little expected that he was the troublemaker whenever something happened.

"You know," Tom said, shaking his head but smiling at his mischievous friend.

"No, I don't!" exclaimed John. "I swear! Why are you looking at me so suspiciously?"

Tom removed the note from his pocket and threw it at John. He watched as his friend picked it up, read it, and then looked at Tom with wide eyes.

"I didn't write this," John said. "I swear!"

"Uhuh. I know you," said Tom. "Who else would've written it?!"

John laughed at this quirky friend who had so recently come into his life.

"Um … perhaps Kelly?"

Tom laughed it off. It simply did not occur to him to believe it.

~~~~~

"Come on!" John yelled at Tom, frustrated at having to wait for his friend to be ready before they could head off to the party. "I still think you should have talked to Kelly," he said, watching Tom finally start to leave his house with him. "She is going to be *pissed* that you didn't take her."

Tom didn't know if John was being honest or indulging in another prank. Earlier, he'd been certain it was a case of the latter. At that moment, he wasn't so sure.

The two of them walked into the house. Already a crowd was amassing. Tom's first instinct was to look for Samantha. In doing so, his eyes glazed right over Kelly as she passed in front of him. Tom suddenly felt an almost painful nudge in his side.

"Dude!" he heard John say out loud with the sound of incredulity in his voice. "Seriously?"

"What?" Tom asked, oblivious to what his friend was talking about.

"Kelly just smiled and waved at you … and you looked right through her!"

"Oh," Tom said and immediately changed his focus to try and seek her out. He wasn't at all interested in her. As yet, he wasn't particularly interested in dating, if he was honest with himself. He just wanted his friend back.

"She's over there," John said as he pointed the way. "Will you please go and talk to her. Man, you are making that girl *suf-fer*!"

"Okay, okay," Tom said. He didn't understand why it was so important, but he was willing to believe his friend for once.

He spotted Kelly and walked toward her. Straight away, he saw her eyes contact with his and a smile form on her face as they did. Tom knew she was a girl in the school who was regarded by the guys as 'hot' and 'fine'. He'd heard many such descriptions about her in recent times. No such descriptions meant anything to him. To him, girls were still just other people, and could as easily be friends as guys could.

"Tom," Kelly greeted him when he reached her. "I thought you must have had a really good reason to ignore me since I didn't hear anything from you about my note today."

On hearing her words, Tom cringed inside.

"Ugh … sorry. I … I thought that was a joke from John. Sorry!" he said, feeling like the biggest idiot around.

Kelly watched his face and grinned.

"Ahh! That makes sense! I know what a trickster John is. I can totally see why you might assume he was setting you up or something," she said, smiling at him with amusement. "But rest assured, in this instance, it *was* me who sent that note."

Tom felt stupid. His friend had said it was probably Kelly who had sent the note. Tom hadn't believed him.

Kelly could see the embarrassment on Tom's face. She didn't often look at the boys in her school. She wasn't oblivious to the attention they sometimes gave her. Day to day, she tried to keep her head down and not look at any one of them in case they expected something from her all of a sudden. In contrast to the other guys, she liked the quiet strength that emanated from Tom. He didn't even seem aware of how good looking he was. Day to day, it seemed like it didn't occur to him that someone might like him. That made him different from the other boys in their year.

"Yeah," he said to her, blushing slightly. "Sorry."

"It's all good," Kelly replied as she laughed softly at him. "No worries at all. We're both here now. How are you?"

Tom had to think about that question before he answered.

"I'm doing okay, I guess," he started to say. Straight away, he saw her laughing softly at him again. He felt sheepish. "Nothing much happens in my life."

Just then, he lifted his head and turned it. Out of the corner of his eye, he noticed Samantha as she arrived. He watched her. She had turned up with her friend, Tanya. He watched as they made their way through the living area where he stood, and went into the kitchen.

Kelly followed the line of sight from his eyes, and recognised that he was looking at another girl. She didn't like that, even if it was that girl he'd been friends with forever.

"Tom, do you want to come outside with me?" she asked. She watched as he turned back to face her once again. "Just for a few minutes?"

Looking at her, Tom felt torn between the person who seemed to want his attention, and the one who seemed to not.

"Umm," he mumbled, looking back toward the kitchen one more time. "Yeah, okay."

Kelly smiled at him, not liking at all that he would be looking at someone other than her. She always drew attention. She didn't like not being able to hold the attention of someone she wanted to like her.

The two of them walked out the front door and around the side of the house, where Tom found himself suddenly pushed up against an exterior brick wall.

"Oh!" he exclaimed, not sure what was happening.

Kelly leaned into him and placed her lips on his. Even though only 16, she'd kissed loads of boys. He, at 16, had so far kissed no-one. So far, he hadn't *wanted* to kiss anyone.

For a few minutes, he remained still, wondering what he should be feeling in his first kiss. Being intellectual, he found himself considering how the two sets of lips felt as they sat against each other. He was surprised to find there was no real feeling in it - not for him anyway.

After a few minutes, Kelly pulled away. She looked at him with a surprised expression on her face. He hadn't kissed her back. Was that because he didn't know how to kiss, or was it because he didn't want to kiss *her*?

"What gives?" she asked him, surprising him in return.

"What..." he stammered, rubbing his lips with the back of his hand. "What do you mean?"

Kelly saw the movement. To her, it seemed like Tom was erasing the kiss. Suddenly she felt disgusted with herself. She never pushed herself on guys. She never *had* to.

"I like you, Tom. Don't you like me?" she asked.

On hearing her question, Tom felt a little sorry for her. He didn't want to kiss her, but he equally didn't want her to feel bad.

"Kelly, I'm ..." he started, before taking a deep breath. "I'm sorry. I'm just not ready for this kissing stuff. It isn't you..." he began to explain.

Before he could say anything more, she stormed off, leaving him alone.

He stood up against the wall, hating that he might have upset her. He hated to think about upsetting anyone. It was so difficult, going through that period of time. His friends all wanted to be doing kissing and stuff, but he still hadn't found any desire for it. He knew full well that he should want it. That didn't change the fact that he didn't.

Leaning up against the wall, he closed his eyes and listened to the music coming from within the house. Taking deep breaths, he tried to maintain calm inside of him.

"Oh!" he heard a familiar voice say. He quickly opened his eyes to turn in that direction.

"Samantha, stop!" he called out as he saw her starting to edge herself away. "Please don't go."

Samantha heard the pleading in his voice. She slowly and quietly walked forward toward him.

"I don't understand what's happened between us," he said, not making any move to get closer to her. "Please tell me what I've done…"

"You haven't done anything, Tom."

"Then why…?"

"I'm just not interested in you," Samantha said, straight afterwards feeling like the biggest idiot for even saying such a thing.

"You're not … *interested* … in me? What does that even mean? We've been friends since … forever. You seem to have just decided, all of a sudden, that I'm not good enough to be your friend anymore. Why?"

Samantha looked at his face closely. She was changing. She wanted a boyfriend. She wanted to find love. She just didn't want it with him.

"Tom, I'm never going to want you to be my boyfriend…" she blurted out.

"Boyfriend?! What are you *talking* about? When have I ever insinuated that I want to be your boyfriend?" Tom asked as he finally started to understand her coldness towards him. "I just want us to be friends, like we've always been! Why do you act like that has to change?"

"Because it does!" she shouted at him. The volume surprised both of them before she toned down her voice again. "Because we're changing, and it's time for us to be different. I want a boyfriend. You want a girlfriend…"

"No!" he exclaimed in reply. "No, I *don't!* Don't throw that at me. I'm not anywhere near wanting that! I just want friends. I want you back as my *friend*. You can put whatever conditions you want on that. I will only talk to you when we're alone, or I'll *not* talk to you when we're alone. However you want it, I don't care! Why does you wanting a boyfriend affect us?! I don't get it … I don't get it at all."

"I…" he saw her stammer with a look of confusion on her face. "I don't know! It just does!"

Tom suddenly felt angry at her. She was trying to give him reasons for her recent distance, but they didn't make any sense to him. All he could see was that his friendship must be worth extremely little to her. If it wasn't, why would she throw him away so easily after all their years of having been so entwined in each others' lives?

He knew then that he'd reached a breaking point. He'd watched her, and tried to coax her to talk to him, but hearing her words changed things. He heard her weak justification for throwing their friendship away, and it wasn't good enough. He had to accept that he was wasting his time trying to cling to a friendship that most definitely must be past its expiry date.

Samantha watched his face and felt bad, but at the same time, thought she was doing the right thing. She watched as he stepped right up to her. His face revealed a look she'd seen many times since they were young children. It was his look of disbelief and disappointment in her for acting as she was.

"Fine. You want me to give up and leave you alone? You have it. I give up," he said to her and walked off.

Samantha didn't turn to watch him leave. She did, however, feel a huge thud in her heart. It had been different when she'd been controlling them not spending time together. Hearing him sound so defeated and so uncaring was enough to bring her to tears. It surprised her as it was what she'd wanted. She was the one who had insisted he not want to spend time with her. Why, then, did it suddenly hurt?

~~~~~

Back inside the party, Tom sought out John.

"Hey, man. Where have you been?" his friend asked him as he placed his hand on his shoulder.

"Sorry, I'm going to head home," Tom replied. After his confrontation with Samantha, he was in a foul mood. It was something he rarely experienced. He didn't want to share it with anyone else.

"What?" asked John. "No, man. It's early…"

Tom shrugged away.

"Sorry, man," he said. "I'm not feeling too hot. I'll see you at school Monday, okay?" he said and walked off without even waiting for a reply.

Samantha saw him walking out the front door as she was walking in, but he didn't stop to talk to her. He saw her. She knew that. But for the first time in as long as she could remember, he ignored her completely. He walked past without one word leaving his mouth.

She stood in the doorway and watched him as he walked down the path, out the gate, and began his walk home. She felt like a piece of her heart had been yanked out of her chest. Even though it was what she'd
~~~~~

wanted, she had to question herself if she'd done the right thing.

~~~~~

When Tom got home, his mother was still up and looked at him with a surprised expression on her face.

"What happened to the party?" she asked.

At first, Tom didn't want to talk to her about it, so stood silently for a moment.

"Are you alright, honey?" his mother persisted.

"I just ... Samantha ... ugh!" he started to say, feeling frustration all over again.

"Come and sit down," his mother said, soothing him while she led him to the well-worn sofa in their living room. "Samantha ... what?"

Tom had to assemble words in his head before speaking.

"She's been ignoring me for weeks now, and I don't understand why," he said. "So tonight I asked her ... and she said it was because she wanted a boyfriend, but she doesn't want *me* as a boyfriend."

"Ahh, I see…" his mother said in her knowing voice.

"Do you? Because I don't! What does her wanting a boyfriend have to do with me? Why can't we still be friends? I don't understand…"

"Oh, wait. This isn't a case where she wants to have *you* as a boyfriend, but you don't want that?" his mother asked.

Tom looked at her, surprised.

"No! What? Why would you think that? Mum, no! She wants a boyfriend. I don't want a girlfriend. I just want her as a friend, but she seems to think I want more from her," he said and paused before continuing. "Why can't we still be friends? I just don't get it."

"I think perhaps the two of you are growing up at different rates, that's all," his mother said. "She might be already moving into the stage of wanting to find love. Are you in that stage yet?"

"Mum! No!" Tom exclaimed. "I know everyone else is there. Everyone keeps talking about kissing! I just want my friend back. I miss her."

His mother smiled knowingly.

"You two have always been different kinds of friends, that's for sure. Gosh, the way you used to fight!" she said, laughing softly. "None of us parents could ever understand why you both kept asking us to enable the two of you to see each other!"

They sat quietly together, each in their own thoughts, before she continued.

"Sometimes friends drift away from each other," she said. "That's just a part of life. It might resolve itself, or it might not. Unfortunately, you can't make it happen if she doesn't want it, Tom. Give her some space, and see where things go from there. I'm sure she hasn't done this to hurt
~~~~~

you..."

"Well, I *am* hurt..."

"Maybe, but I don't think she would intentionally do that to you. No matter how much you two have always fought - and gone out of your way to annoy each other at times - I don't believe Samantha would hurt you. Not like that. Puberty might be starting to play with her mind a bit, but it won't be intentional. Let her go for the moment. I think, in time, you'll see her find her way back."

They hugged before he stood up.

"Yeah," he said, eager to dismiss the conversation. "I'm going to bed. Goodnight."

~~~~~

Over the weekend, Tom concentrated on his study to try and keep Samantha from his thoughts. No matter what she did, or who she did it with, he was still going to get out of the place he was. He was going to do that by doing well at school, with or without her in his life.

~~~~~

At school for the remainder of the year, they didn't speak. Tom had resolved that their friendship was over. It was easy for him to believe that their friendship meant nothing to her, and that chapter had ended. He was completely oblivious to the fact that something had flipped. Now when he was around the school, hanging out with his friends and talking to other girls, *he* was actually being watched by *her*.

Samantha watched him from a distance. She continued to feel that longing inside of her. It shouldn't have been there, given that their distance was her doing. It was there, regardless. Over and over, she pushed it down, not wanting to feel it. In amongst the feelings of missing him, were also the feelings of having neglected and rejected a friend - a good friend.

To take her mind off him, she accepted the first guy who asked her to go steady with him. She wanted to find love. The only way to do that, it seemed to her, was to start dating guys, and the only way to figure out who she wanted to date was to date them.

When she was sixteen, she started seeing Paul. He seemed nice enough, and he was admired by her friends. When he asked her out on a date, she accepted. It wasn't perfect but, to her, dating someone because she 'may as well' was as good a reason as any.

~~~~~

At first, everything was simple between them, but when she was seventeen and the new school year began, she found herself pressured by him to have sex.

"What is wrong with you?" he taunted her. "Are you frigid? Fuck, we have been dating for almost a year. It's about time..."
~~~~~

"It will be time when I say it's time!" she screamed at him.

They'd been having the same argument for a couple of months, and his repetitive words were starting to anger her. They were at a friend's home with a dozen or so other kids. Alcohol was a common occurrence in the parties they attended. She didn't like it, but sometimes she took part in it. That night, she didn't want to. The more he pressured her, the more she knew it would be a bad idea for her to drink.

She suddenly felt like she was over the whole situation with him. She'd started dating him with some over-inflated expectation and desire to find love, but she didn't love him. Some days, she didn't even like him, and *most* days, she felt like he didn't particularly like her.

Resolved that she didn't want to be around him any more that night, she extracted herself from his arms and stood up in preparation to leave.

"Where do you think you're going? Sit down," he said to her, loud enough to demean her in front of his friends.

"No," Samantha responded. "I'm going home."

"I said … sit down!" he commanded at an even louder volume.

She looked at him with what she knew would be a look of hatred on her face.

"And I said, I'm leaving," she said. "See ya."

Samantha started to walk away. She made it to the doorway before he caught up with her. Just as she was about to walk out of the front door, she felt a hand grab her. It pulled her around to face him, while his other hand moved around and slapped her hard across her cheek.

She looked at him in shock. She could tell that the volume of voices stopping, and the room suddenly going quiet, meant that everyone had seen and heard the slap. Inside of her, she felt a mixture of anger, shame, and embarrassment.

"Get your ass back on the sofa. We're here together. You can't leave," he said with what looked like a snarl on his face.

Samantha couldn't believe what had happened, but when he spoke, her shock fell away from her.

"No. I've told you twice. Are you deaf?! I'm leaving," she said and tried to pull her arm away, but found he had it well restrained.

As if in slow motion, she saw his other hand move up again in preparation to deliver a second slap. Even though it must have only been a few seconds that the arm was moving, it was enough time for another hand to reach around from behind her and grab the hand that was, at that moment, making its way toward her face.

"Don't even think about laying another hand on her, asshole. She has told you she's leaving, and she is. Or do you always force girls to spend time with you even though they don't want to?"

Samantha knew the voice and, for the first time in over a year, was thankful for the sound of it being so close nearby. The room was silent, and the comment must have been something that Paul didn't want people to hear. He harshly let her arm go and shoved her backward into Tom's arms.

"Take her. I don't want her," he said with a vicious tone in his voice before turning and returning to his friends.

Samantha turned around and didn't have to think at all before pulling Tom close and encouraging him to hold her tightly. She didn't care what stupid reasoning she'd had for ending their friendship. What she did know about Tom was that he was a good person, and he would never treat anyone like Paul had just treated her.

Tom held her, also not caring about the time they'd spent apart, or the time that lay ahead. All he cared about was making sure she was safe.

"Come on. I'll walk you home," he said to her quietly.

Samantha nodded against his chest before they pulled apart from one another and walked out.

~~~~~

Neither said anything on the way to Samantha's home. She felt horrible about far too many things, and Tom didn't want to expect anything from the sudden closeness to her. He had rescued her from a horrible situation, but the next day, everything would return to normal. There was no point in thinking about it, and certainly no point in wishing things would change.

~~~~~

"Do you want to come in?" she asked him when they reached her house. Immediately she saw a look of surprise on his face.

"Samantha..." Tom started to say, not knowing what he dare say or ask her.

For a moment, she saw him look hopeful. The look passed as he moved his eyes downward and let out a deep breath, almost as if he were feeling completely and utterly defeated.

"No, thank you," he said. "I'm going to head home. Goodnight."

Against her wishes, he turned his back, walked down her path, and ventured home.

Samantha went to her room and lay on her bed, thinking about the evening's events and changes to plans. She thought she should feel some kind of sadness over Paul, but she didn't. Instead, she felt happy that she'd stood her ground and maintained her virginity, having refused Paul for so long. He wasn't the man she wanted to lose that to. Whoever claimed that would have to be someone far more special. That guy would be someone who treated her like a queen, not like a piece of trash.

~~~~~

The next day, Tom woke late to the sound of knocking on his
~~~~~

bedroom door. Thinking it was his mother, he turned over, pulled his pillow over his head, and pretended to be asleep. It didn't work. The knocking continued and only got louder.

"Mum! I'm trying to sleep!" he called out before hearing the door open.

He huddled down under the covers, not used to his mother walking into his room. With him being almost eighteen, they'd recently laid down some pretty hefty privacy rules that they both lived by.

"Um, actually, it's not your mum," he heard Samantha's voice say, making him self-aware and insecure.

"Hey, what are you doing here?" he asked, making sure he was sufficiently covered under the covers. They'd grown up together in each other's bedrooms, but the time apart, and the ages they were, resulted in him feeling shy in the situation.

"Can I come in?" Samantha asked, still standing in the doorway.

"Yeah, of course," Tom stammered out, completely unprepared for the situation at hand.

Samantha saw him lying under his bed covers and suppressed a smile of amusement. How many times had she seen him like that, and even in that moment, he looked like a little boy, the way he huddled down under them with only his head visible.

Tom saw her close the door behind her. She made her way over to his bed, where she sat on the edge and looked at him.

"I just wanted to say thank you for last night," she said.

"That's okay. It's no big deal…"

"Tom, it was a *very* big deal," she replied, cutting his sentence short. "Please don't undervalue it. He hit me once, and he was going to hit me again. It's a big deal that you stopped that."

Tom looked at her, his shyness melting away as he relaxed again.

"It's okay. I'm just glad you're okay, although why you were ever with him, of all people…" he started to say and saw her nod in response.

"I know. It wasn't for the right reason. I wanted to find love. I wanted someone to love me. He was just the first guy who seemed interested," she said and paused for a while before she continued. "I know I've been stupid, about that and about us. You were right. Making a decision to stop being your friend just because I wanted to find a boyfriend…" she said, feeling disbelief at her own actions. "How stupid could I be…"

"You aren't stupid, Samantha. Far from it," Tom replied, rubbing his eyes in an attempt to wake up properly. When he'd finished his rubbing, he was aware that she was watching his face closely, with a small, shy smile. "You're going to be okay. But I hope you won't go back there…"

"No! Oh, God, no!" Samantha exclaimed. "I would rather remain alone than put up with that! I know I can't have had much self-esteem to have stayed with him so long, but no. There is no way I would put up with someone hitting me."

"Good," she heard Tom breathe out in relief. "Because you are worth so much more than that."

They were silent for a while, thinking, before she spoke, her voice quiet.

"He wanted us to have sex," she said and saw a stunned look on Tom's face. "I didn't want to, though. That was the cause of our arguments. I'm just not ready for that, I don't think."

Tom nodded at her, just letting her speak.

"Are you?" she asked, confusing him. "Have you?" she asked again shortly afterward, confusing him more.

When she didn't elaborate on the wording, he questioned her.

"Am I? Have I … what?" he asked.

"You know!"

"No, I don't know! Have I what?"

"Had sex," she said quietly, as if there might be an adult in the room, listening to them having a naughty conversation.

Tom laughed at her softly with affection because of the way she had said it.

"No!" he answered. "God, no. I haven't even dated anyone yet…"

"But Kelly…"

Tom shook his head sharply.

"No, there is no Kelly!" he said. "She kissed me once, and that was that. I haven't dated or kissed anyone since then."

Samantha studied his face, confused.

"You haven't kissed anyone … for almost two years? How can that…"

Tom continued to smile and laugh softly at her expression.

"Samantha, I just said I haven't dated anyone yet."

"Well, yeah but…"

"There's no 'but'! When I meet someone who really wants to be with me - for the right reasons - I'm sure I'll change my view on dating and kissing. Right now, I just want to get through this last year of school, and get on with starting my life."

As Samantha watched him, he could feel her studying his face.

"You know, you've grown up looking pretty good," she said. Her words were received with him grabbing an extra pillow and thumping her with it. "Ouch! What was that for?" she asked, starting to laugh.

"You deserved that, and you know it," Tom said. "No more comments about what I look like! You know I don't like it. I never have."

Samantha realised, at that moment, just how much she'd missed him. Reminded of how well they did know each other, she nodded at him.

"I did know that. I'm sorry," she said softly.

Tom smiled sheepishly at her while shaking his head in affectionate teasing.

"Do you want to go and get some pancakes with me?" she asked him and saw his look of surprise.

"If you want me to…" Tom answered, uncertain.

When he saw her nod, and direct a beautiful smile at him, he felt himself melt slightly inside. It was a feeling he didn't want to feel.

"Alright," he said, expecting her to automatically remove herself from his room. When she didn't, he laughed quietly at her.

"Why are you still sitting there?"

"I'm waiting for you to get ready," Samantha said with a teasing look on her face.

He grabbed the pillow and let it thud across her arm again.

"I'm not getting out of bed with you sitting there!" he replied, laughing out loud. "Go and get out of my room so I can get out of bed and get dressed!"

Samantha giggled and stood up. She walked to the door and quietly removed herself, shutting the door behind her as she walked down the hallway.

Tom lay in bed for a moment, recognising the feeling he knew he didn't want to feel. He took a deep breath and focused on something else - pancakes! Finally, he pulled himself out of bed, showered, dressed, and made himself presentable before going to find her.

"Good morning, sleepyhead," he heard his mother say to him. She had a very distinct sound of knew-it-would be-alright amusement in her voice as he entered the kitchen.

"Morning. Samantha and I are going out. I'll see you later," he said, leaning in to give her a kiss on the cheek. He saw her wink at him in reply, smiling like she had a deep, dark secret that no-one else had.

Tom turned to Samantha, who had been sitting at the kitchen counter. She looked just as comfortable as if she'd never had any time away from the house that had almost been as much her home as his until two years earlier.

"Come on, you," he said. "I know your enthusiasm for pancakes."

~~~~~

For the remaining six months till the end of their schooling, Tom revelled in having her back in his life as his friend. Constantly he was teased about it - as he was sure she was also - but he didn't care. He considered he'd grown into somewhat of an expert at throwing quips back at his friends when they teased him.

"Come on, how can you not see what a hottie she is?" John especially would throw at him fairly regularly.
~~~~~

In those instances, Tom would grab John around the neck and playfully rub his hair as he held him in a vice-like grip.

"Retract that, my friend!"

"Okay, okay. I retract - retract!!" he'd say, laughing before Tom would let him go, both of them smiling.

"Good boy," Tom would say, laughing.

~~~~~

"Tomorrow is our last day at school forever," Samantha said to him as they sat on his bed the night before their high school education would come to an end.

"I know, and I still don't know what I want to do with my life!" he answered, making her laugh softly.

"Well, at least you have the job at the supermarket."

Tom groaned.

"Not quite my dream job," he said and assembled thoughts in his head. "The problem is that I don't know what my dream job *is*. What am I supposed to be doing? Which direction should I be moving in? I just … don't … know," he followed up, accentuating each of the last three words with banging his knuckles on his forehead.

He felt Samantha's hand reach out to touch him on his arm.

"Don't worry so much. You have a job, and you do enjoy it, don't you?" she asked and saw him nod.

"I do," he replied. "The people are great there, and I quite like interacting with the customers…"

"Well, there you go then," she said. "Why would you wish for something bigger and better when you are perfectly happy where you are?"

"Because I *should* be working toward something bigger and better?"

She laughed at him.

"You're such an idiot sometimes. Just enjoy it," she said. "If you can get enough shifts to live off, why would you look for anything else?"

"Hmm … maybe you're right. But what about you, though? Have you decided if you want to go to college, or get a job?"

Samantha shook her head and smiled sadly at him.

"I'm not as academic as you, as you well know," she said. "I want to study dressmaking, but I don't know if my grades will get me in…"

"Of course they will. You haven't failed anything, right?"

"Yeah, I know. Anyway, I did put the application in, so I should be hearing from that school any day now. Fingers crossed," she said, holding up her crossed fingers to his view.

Tom looked at her face. His feelings had levelled out, he realised. For a while, when they'd first resumed their friendship, he'd worried his feelings were going in a direction he didn't want them to. As he looked at
~~~~~

her, he could see and appreciate her just as a friend. That was how it was meant to be. Having had so much time without their closeness, he could only seize it and make sure he didn't suffocate it.

"Scott asked me out today," Samantha said quietly, lowering her eyes in concern of what Tom would think.

"Scott from school? Scott … Carpa?" he asked and saw her nod. "Oh."

"What do you think of him?"

Tom took a minute to consider his answer before speaking.

"He seems okay to me. I've never had any problem with him, and I haven't heard of anyone else having a problem with him," he said and paused. "But surely it's what *you* think of him that counts, right?"

Samantha looked at him, thoughtful.

"I wasn't such a good judge of character with Paul…"

"Well, Paul was just an utter asshole, excuse my French," replied Tom. "And don't forget you were only sixteen when you started seeing him. You are far more mature and worldly now…"

"Worldly?" Samantha asked as she burst out laughing, making him smile. "Oh, Tom! You do make me laugh sometimes." For a moment she was silent. "I don't think I can call myself worldly. I'm an eighteen-year-old virgin!"

"So am I! Are you saying that you don't think that *I* am worldly?!" he asked, teasing her. "Think carefully before you answer, Samantha Young!"

She laughed at him again before giving him a mock low bow.

"Oh, yes. Of course, Master Tom, oh worldly master," she said then paused for a moment before continuing. "Should I say yes?" she asked when she grew serious again. Seeing Tom's look of confusion, she went on to clarify. "To Scott."

"Oh, you need to decide that. Why would you ask me that?" he asked gently, unsure of what she wanted him to say.

"I value your opinion," Samantha said.

"Hmm. Well, I have nothing against the guy so if you're wanting me to say he's a creep, so you can avoid going on a date with him, sorry but I can't do that."

Samantha let out a deep sigh. She didn't know if she wanted to date anyone or not.

"Why do you still not date anyone, Tom? Don't you get … lonely?"

Tom was taken aback by the questions, and found himself flustered.

"How could I get lonely?" he asked. "I have good friends. I have you. I don't need anything more - not yet anyway."

They looked at one another for a long time before Samantha stood up.

"Okay, well, I'd better get home and have a decent sleep before our last day of the easy life tomorrow."

Tom stood up and hugged her, laughing.

"Last day of the easy life? Silly girl."

~~~~~

A week later, Samantha ran into the supermarket and signalled to Tom from the side of the checkout area, near where he was serving customers. Tom was trying to be polite to the elderly woman in front of him as he scanned the groceries and accepted her payment. In his peripheral vision, he could see Samantha waving her arms and smiling broadly at him.

Finally, the customer left. With no more customers waiting in line at that moment, Samantha rushed up to him and saw him laugh at her.

"What is up with you?" asked Tom. "You look like the cat who got the canary, or whatever that weird saying is that my mother keeps using…"

"I got in!" Samantha exclaimed, excited.

"You got in … where?"

"To dressmaking college!"

Tom looked at her and immediately ran around to the other side of the counter, not caring if his supervisor made a deal about it. Pulling her into his arms and hugging her, he felt her jump up and down in excitement, making him laugh hard. When they finally pulled apart, she was grinning widely as she looked at him with tears forming in her eyes.

"Oh, Tom, I can't believe it!" she said. "And with so many not-great scores from our exams too!"

He pulled her to him again and kissed her on her forehead.

"I'm so proud of you," he said to her.

Samantha revelled in the words and the feelings that came from them.

"We need to celebrate," Tom continued. "Tonight? Pancakes?"

Samantha pulled away from him, suddenly coming back down from her high.

"Oh, Tom. Sorry," she said. "Before I got this news, I'd already made plans to see Scott. We're going out for dinner, and to see a movie…"

"That's alright," Tom replied as he pulled away. "That's great! You and I will celebrate together another day. Go! Enjoy your time out with him."

She looked at him, uncertain if she'd hurt him in any way.

"Are you … sure? I mean, I could cancel…"

"No, Samantha," Tom said quietly. "You deserve happiness. You deserve love. Go and give him a chance."

They looked at each other, eyes locked, before she smiled sadly at him.

"Okay," she said. "But I'll see you tomorrow? Are you working?"
~~~~~

"No, I have tomorrow off."

"Pancakes for brunch tomorrow then?"

"Yep, that sounds good," Tom replied as he moved back behind his checkout counter.

Tom watched her walk out, wishing his heart didn't ache so much when he did only want her to be happy.

~~~~~

Samantha walked into the restaurant, settled herself in the seat at the table she saw him at, and looked at the man across from her. Scott had been in two of the same classes as her during their last year of high school. He'd been a student at the same school for long before that, but they'd only gotten to know each other in a peripheral sense - polite, but not quite friends.

As he smiled at her, she could see the nervousness on his face. The realisation instantly helped to ease her own apprehension.

"How was your day?" he asked.

Samantha smiled at him, the situation new to her.

"Actually it was excellent. I got my acceptance into dressmaking college!" she said excitedly. She was pleased to see him smile in a way that made her certain that he'd not only heard what she'd said, but also accurately perceived the heightened level of her excitement.

"Oh, that's amazing, Samantha!" Scott said. "Well done. And good on you for already knowing what you want to do. That's awesome."

Samantha grinned widely with her excitement.

"Thank you," she said. "What about you? What are your plans now that school is behind us?"

Scott blushed as he smiled at her.

"I'm heading off to do a year-long course in automotive mechanics. It won't be glamorous, but that is what I love to do - work on cars."

Before thinking about how it might sound to a guy she hardly knew, Samantha threw a suggestive quip at him.

"You must be very good with your hands."

Samantha saw Scott's head raise as he laughed out loud at the double meaning of her words.

"Oh … hmm!" he said quietly when his own laughing died down. He winked at her, assuring her that her suggestive wit was quite alright with him.

~~~~~

After their meal and movie, Samantha found herself nervous.

"Would you like a ride home?" Scott asked her at the end of the night.

Samantha nodded, finding that she had nothing to say for the moment. Once stopped outside her house, he turned the car off, unbuckled his seatbelt and turned to better face her.

"Thank you for a lovely evening. I've really enjoyed myself," he said to her, making her blush and smile in return.

"Me too."

"Can I take you out again?" he asked after leaning over and kissing her lips softly.

"Yes," Samantha breathed out heavily, the kiss still fresh on her lips.

She watched as Scott pulled away from her and got out of the car. She saw him move around to her side and open her door for her. The two of them walked up to the front door, where once again he kissed her softly before pulling away and removing himself, allowing her to move inside her home.

After she heard the car pull away, she leaned on the door and smiled to herself. Perhaps there was love to be found in the world for her after all.

~~~~~

"I'd like to cook you dinner. Can I pick you up and bring you to my place tonight?" Scott asked her when he called two weeks later. They had already been out together five times, seeing movies and going out for meals.

Samantha felt nervous at the invitation. She was enjoying time with him, and felt comfortable enough with the kissing they'd shared. But she was wary of being alone with him, out of the public eye. He hadn't given her any reason to be worried. She just was.

"Your parents' house?" she asked tentatively and heard his small, peaceful laugh in reply.

"No, Samantha," he said. "I moved into my own place as soon as school finished. It'll just be you and me, I assure you."

Samantha felt her anxiety increase even though there was no real reason she could identify to say that going to his home was a bad idea.

"Okay," she finally replied.

"Great. Shall I pick you up at your place, about seven o'clock?"

"Yeah, that sounds nice," she said.

"Okay. See you then," he said.

The line went quiet, leaving Samantha full of nerves.

~~~~~

As she stood at her front door that evening, Samantha was incredibly nervous, wondering what Scott would expect from her. They were the same age, so perhaps he wouldn't expect anything sexual. But then, he was living in his own place. That did set him apart from her in maturity and independence.

After his car pulled up, Scott jumped out of the car and opened the passenger side door for her. He leaned down to kiss her lightly on the lips before assisting her into the seat and closing her door.

"Are you okay?" he asked when he was behind the wheel again, and the car began to move. "You seem a bit apprehensive."

Samantha smiled at him, even though the smile did nothing to hide her nervousness from him.

"Yes," she said and then paused before deciding to be honest with him. "Actually, I *am* nervous, Scott."

"Are you?" he asked. "Why?"

"I ..." she stammered with the determination to push forward and simply speak. "I haven't been alone with you before ... not truly alone ... just the two of us."

He glanced at her briefly, confused.

"Samantha, we don't have to go to my place," he said quietly. "We can go out for dinner if you prefer..."

"No!" she exclaimed in reply. She'd known him long enough to not be worried. She wanted to face the challenge of her nervousness straight on. "No, it's fine. Just bear with me. I will relax."

He looked at her again, not wanting to make her feel pushed.

"Okay," he replied.

They said nothing more for the duration of the journey. Soon enough, Samantha saw a small apartment complex, before Scott drove the car underneath the structure and into the parking area.

"Are you sure you're okay?" he asked one more time before they got out of the car. "I really don't mind..."

Samantha put her hand out to him and grabbed his.

"Really, Scott," she said to reassure him and herself. "I'm fine."

He smiled and then led her from the car. Soon she was entering his apartment with him. It was a small area with a combined kitchen and living area in front of her as soon as they walked in the front door. There was no hallway at all. Off the living area that they were standing in were only two doors.

"Welcome to my home. That's the way to the bathroom," Scott said, pointing to one of the doors, making her realise that the other door must lead to his bedroom. The thought immediately made her blush.

"Right!" Scott exclaimed. "Dinner coming up. Would you like something to drink? Wine? Beer?"

"Actually, do you have something non-alcoholic?" Samantha asked, feeling like an immature girl for asking. She was relieved that Scott was gracious and smiled back at her.

"Yep! Orange juice or lemonade?"

"Juice would be great, thank you."

She watched as he served drinks for them both, and then began to cook food items that appeared to have been prepared ahead of time.

"Can I help?" she asked and saw him smile at her.

"Yep," he said. "You can talk to me while I whisk this amazing feat of culinary surprise up for you."

She laughed at him and instantly relaxed.

~~~~~

Sitting down on the small sofa, and eating a bowl of stir-fried vegetables and pasta, their conversation flowed easily. Scott was glad and relieved that she'd finally seemed to reach a place of relaxation.

"Yum. This is amazing!" Samantha said. "How have you come to be so independent so soon after high school, though? I don't understand how you can live like this already."

"I worked through high school in a local mechanics shop," he explained. "It was only on weekends, and Fridays after school, but it was enough money for me to stash away so I could move out of home as soon as possible."

"And you still work there?" she asked, not having heard any mention of the job since she'd met him.

"I do, but for now I'm only working when they need me," Scott said. "I'll go back to work on weekends once my course starts. For now, when I get the call, I'm happy to go, but I'm enjoying having time to do nothing as well."

He stood and took both of their empty plates to the sink, before sitting down with her again. He positioned his body so he could face her.

"Are you still nervous?" he asked, taking her hand in his and seeing her shake her head.

"No," Samantha replied in full honesty.

"Just because I'm living on my own doesn't mean that I'm in a great rush to grow up too much," he said quietly.

She looked at him with an enquiring look on her face, showing him she had no idea what he meant.

"I mean, we can move slow, Samantha. I don't expect anything … physical … from you," he continued with a slight blush on his face.

"I haven't…" she started to say - started to admit to him about her virginity - but he cut her off.

"That, to me, actually sounds really, really good. I…" he started to say.

Samantha didn't know if he'd accurately perceived what she'd been going to say to him. She remained quiet as he continued to speak.

"Last year, I was involved with someone a few years older than me, and we did get sexual … among other things," he said. "I don't feel the need to rush there again. So if you're happy for us to take things slowly - to get to *know* each other slowly - maybe we can both relax now?"

Samantha was temporarily silenced with his declaration, but nodded and smiled. "Okay."
~~~~~

Scott grinned at her before leaning in, ever so slowly, to kiss her, just as Samantha leaned in to him also. Their lips met slowly and softly. He wasn't going to push her. That was enough for her to let herself start to relax and feel.

~~~~~

When he dropped her off that night, he gave her a goodnight kiss on the doorstep of her home.

"Can I see you tomorrow?" he asked, already feeling eager to do so again.

"Oh, no," Samantha replied. "Tomorrow I have plans with my friend, Tom. What about the day after?"

Scott looked serious for a moment, before he backtracked to what she'd said.

"You and Tom are really close…"

Samantha wasn't sure if it was a question or a statement, but her answer was the same.

"Yeah, of course. Tom is my closest friend," she said, nodding in reply.

"But you two have never been … romantic?" Scott asked.

Samantha put her hands around his waist and smiled up at him.

"No, we are in no way romantic," she said. "He's my friend. Think of Tom as more like a buddy … a pal…"

Scott smiled at her. He'd seen the friendship between Tom and Samantha from a distance throughout their school years. He'd never had any problem with Tom. To him, he seemed like a good person.

"Of course," he said. "Sorry, I know there's nothing to be jealous of there."

Samantha reached up and kissed him.

"Good. Now, about the day after tomorrow?" she asked, trying to veer the conversation back and away from the subject of Tom.

"Day after tomorrow would be perfect," Scott answered, nodding. "Ring me when you know what time will be best for you?"

Immediately she nodded. "I will."

Lying in bed later that night, Samantha thought about the exchange. She hoped Scott wasn't going to be a guy who would ask her to make a choice. There was no way she wanted to make a choice between her boyfriend or her best friend.

~~~~~

"So, how's it going?" Tom asked her as they settled on the swings at a local park the next day.

Although they both thought they were too old for swings, it had always been a favourite place of theirs. It continued to be somewhere they found it easy to relax and talk when the weather was in their favour.

"It?" Samantha asked.

"You know … you and Scott."

Samantha looked at him closely but only saw friendly inquisitiveness on his face.

"It's fine," she said. "He's nice, and he isn't pressuring me to rush into anything physical, which I do appreciate … a lot!" She paused for a moment. "I do really like him, Tom. I think he might be one of the good ones."

Tom nodded at her, maintaining eye contact as he did.

"I think he is a good guy," he said. "Just enjoy it. You deserve it."

There was a long pause before Samantha replied.

"You deserve it too, Tom. Don't you think?"

"I don't think we were talking about me…"

"I know. But Tom…"

"No more on that subject please, Samantha. Just be happy yourself."

~~~~~

Samantha had another three weeks until her course would be starting. She was enjoying the time that she was getting to spend with Scott, knowing that once her dressmaking course started, she'd be working hard with studying. She was determined to do well at it, and work much harder than she ever had in high school.

"Samantha, I want to tell you about the last relationship I had," Scott said to her one night when they were cuddling on his small sofa. She was very familiar with the seat, already having experienced many conversations and kisses on it.

"You don't have to…"

"I know, but I want to," he said. "There were aspects of it that I want you to know about."

"Alright," Samantha said, feeling a slight unease about what he was going to tell her.

Scott inhaled deeply before seeming to assemble the words in his mind.

"The … woman … I was seeing … was a few years older than me," he started to say. "She was twenty-three, which isn't much older, I suppose, but she was very … experienced. So she was my first…" he started to say, his face full of blush. "But there were other aspects of our friendship apart from … sex."

Samantha listened to him, not sure why he was feeling so uncomfortable. She was a virgin, yes, but she was almost nineteen years old. She was certainly used to hearing about sex, even if she'd never done it herself.

"We started out just dating, but then she started taking me to a club," he said and cleared his throat, as if building to something that he was
~~~~~

finding difficult.

"Scott, I really don't need…"

"No, I really want you to know this about me," he persisted. "I think … it's … important." Silence. "This club that she introduced me to, I think she'd been going to for years, but being the innocent thing I was, I'd never heard of such a place. I was nervous, but I gave it a go, and I ended up loving it. I didn't know that I would, but she always said that she knew I was right for it."

"For what?" Samantha couldn't help asking. His words weren't making any sense to her, but her curiosity was piqued greatly.

"For BDSM," he said, looking closely at her face to see if it would scare her off.

"What is that?"

"It … the club … is where people go to … well, when we went, she - Jane was her name by the way - Jane would tell me what to do, and I would have to obey her." Scott cleared his throat, knowing his being so flustered was making him speak without any clarity. "Sorry, I don't know how to explain it, really."

"Well, what did you do when you were at the club?"

Scott gulped in nervousness. It had seemed a good idea to share that side of him with her. As he fought to find the words to talk about it, he questioned his sanity in bringing the topic up at all.

"She would use … things … on me … to make me feel…"

He stopped all of a sudden. Samantha could feel his frustration emanating off him.

"This is something to do with sex?" she asked, trying to prompt him along in his speech.

"No. Yes. Sometimes," he said. "Not specifically, but yes, sometimes it would lead to sex. Actually, it often led to sex, but that wasn't the point of it." He took one large breath and exhaled deeply. "She would use things like whips and things on me."

Samantha was surprised more than anything.

"She would hurt you?" she asked.

In hearing her question, Scott knew he'd have to be more forthcoming to explain.

"Well, I guess the act is that she was hurting me, but in reality I liked it," he said. "I liked the feeling of it on my skin, and I liked that she was in control, telling me what to do."

"How could you enjoy that?" Samantha asked, intrigued. "How could you get any pleasure from being hit with something?"

"I know it's a difficult thing to understand," replied Scott. "I don't understand how it works either. I just know that it does."

As he watched Samantha go quiet, he hoped, deep inside of him, that he hadn't scared her off.

"I don't expect *you* to do these things, Samantha," he said. "I'm just telling you because…" he began to say before finding himself unsure of the answer.

"Why, Scott? Why would you tell me something like that if you didn't hope that I'd want to do it too?" Samantha asked. When no answer was provided, she spoke again. "Why did you and this older woman stop seeing each other? Was it something to do with this?"

"No," Scott said at such a low volume that Samantha hardly heard him. "I stopped it because we didn't have anything in common apart from … that. At the start, everything was exciting, because I was new to sex, and then she introduced me to the club scene, and I enjoyed that. But she was older than me, and after a while, the sex and the playing just wasn't enough for me. I need more, I've come to realise."

"More?"

"Yes!" he exclaimed. "I want to go out to dinner, and go see movies at the cinema, and go for walks with the person I'm seeing. I want all these things that you and I have been doing together. It means far more to me than sex or the BDSM."

At that point, he said it because he really did, in the core of his soul, believe those words to be true.

CHAPTER 2

The Club

After seeing each other for six months, Samantha started to see cracks in the way Scott acted around her. At first, it was just small niggles. There were little things that made her feel like she was an annoyance to him. At that point, she would back away from him, not pushing to see him, and only seeing him when he initiated it.

During those times, Scott found that initially he would feel a euphoric and intense sense of freedom, and would embrace it. After a week or two, he would find himself missing her company so much that he'd call her and want to see her. Then they'd fall back into their routines together.

He hadn't tried to push her toward sex, although they did have plenty of hot and heavy groping sessions. Samantha knew she still wasn't ready to go there yet. Not with him. Not with anyone.

From an outsider's point of view, they looked like the perfect couple, but for both of them, something seemed increasingly not quite aligned. Despite their doubts, they kept going, month after month, both pretending that it was all okay - pretending that it was all quite a normal way to feel in a relationship.

~~~~~

"I don't want to keep doing this, Scott," Samantha finally said to him one night as they sat in his apartment. "I feel like I'm a yo-yo, or on a roller coaster ride or something."

"What do you mean?" he asked her, still not wanting to confront even his own feelings.

"We keep pulling together and then drifting apart, and then we come together again," she said. She paused before speaking again, taking his hand in hers. "I mean, do you even really want to be with me? Or am I here as a way to pass time until someone better comes along?"

Scott felt horrified, and it showed clearly on his face and in his voice.

"No!" he exclaimed. "How can you think that?"

"I can think that because something is off here," said Samantha. "And I think you feel it and know it too."

She saw him look away from her eyes and hang his head low.

"Yeah, maybe," he said. "But I'm not ready to walk away from this. I'm not ready to walk away from *you*."

"If you know what is wrong - what is missing - you should tell me,"
~~~~~

she encouraged him.

He looked at her, not wanting to speak. He had wondered himself if it was sex that he missed, but he didn't think it was. The emotions that came from that, he wasn't ready to face again yet.

"Is it this club thing you mentioned? Do you need to go there again?" she asked him.

Straight away, she saw him raise his head sharply once more, and look intently into her eyes.

"What?" he asked.

"The club thing!" Samantha said. "The whipping and spanking and stuff. Is that something you need?"

"No," he said, although sounding uncertain himself at his response. "I don't … think … so."

"Scott, I don't want us to split up," she said. "I don't think that I personally want to be whipped and flogged, but if it is something you need me to do to *you…*"

Scott felt a surge of energy stream through him. Adrenalin flowed. Suddenly he felt enthused, eager … aroused.

"Really? You would try it? You would use a whip or something else on me?" he asked. He saw Samantha nod even though her face also revealed uncertainty. "I … I don't know what to say."

"Well, we can give it a go, but I make no promises," she said. "And I'm not sure about being in front of other people…"

"We can try it here first, to see how we fit together like that," Scott said, his voice revealing his sudden enthusiasm and excitement. "We don't have to go to the club if you don't want to."

Despite her reservations, Samantha nodded slowly.

"Okay."

~~~~~

That weekend, in Scott's small apartment, Samantha found herself presented with an item with a small leather loop at one end, and a solid leather handle at the other. Holding it, she looked up at Scott with questions in her eyes.

"It's a riding crop," he said, feeling the extreme blush on his face.

"And I am to … whip you with this?"

He nodded, feeling a blend of embarrassment and eagerness in his body.

"Yes," he said. "Well, I guess more strike me with it."

"Okay," she said, not sure she could do it, but willing to give it a go.

"Try it with me dressed first," he said.

Samantha was surprised at the words.

"Will you *not* be dressed when I do it later?" she asked and watched him go a very deep shade of red.
~~~~~

"Oh … I didn't mention that the feelings are usually felt … on the skin?" he asked her.

Samantha didn't answer but instead stood up, ready to learn something new.

"Okay then," she said, breathing out heavily. "Let's do this."

Scott looked at her, uncertain in the position of being the teacher instead of the student, as he had been with Jane.

"Alright. I am going to … go down on the floor … on all fours," he said quietly, not able to hide his extreme embarrassment.

Samantha watched as he did so, wondering to herself how she had gotten herself into such a situation. Knowing she'd been the one to bring up the suggestion, she would see it through.

"Now, smack me with it," he said.

Samantha laughed inwardly at the absurdity of it. Sensing he wasn't in a humorous mood, she followed his instruction and struck the crop against the seat of his jeans.

"Try again," Scott said. "This time harder."

She repeated the action, this time trying to put more power into her strike. Although it must have been at least a bit harder on him, he could still hardly feel it.

"Samantha, if you are going to be my dominant, you need to be aggressive with me," Scott said. "Tell me what to do, and really hit me with that if you want to."

As soon as she heard those words, she immediately could see a problem in the making.

"But it isn't me that wants to do this, Scott," she said. "It's *you* who wants me to do it!"

Scott felt frustrated at the situation. If only she was already the dominating type, like Jane had been…

"I know," he replied. "But can you pretend that it *is* you who wants to hurt me?" he asked and heard her sigh.

"Alright," Samantha said and before striking him with as much force as she could muster.

She successfully took him by surprise. He could feel her strength growing.

"I want to take my jeans off," he said and waited to hear her response. He heard none. "It isn't meant as any kind of move toward sex. I just want to feel it more. I'll leave my boxers on."

"Okay," Samantha said finally, disbelieving that after all their time together, it would be the current situation that would make him present himself to her in such a way, instead of him trying to have sex with her.

She watched as he pulled jeans down just enough so that she could see his boxer shorts, and nothing more private. Once again, she delivered a blow out of the blue, with no warning. Hearing him moan drove her on to keep doing it.

"You'll tell me when you want me to stop, right?" she asked and saw him nod.

"Yes," he reassured her. "Don't stop yet. Keep trying to hit me harder and harder."

Without another word, Samantha put herself in the role, doing as he asked. Eventually, she found a position that gave her more power in her arm, and she started to feel a different kind of power flowing through her.

Even without having heard of the 'BDSM thing', she started to fit into the role, talking to him in a way that he was used to. He'd told her to be aggressive, so aggressive she would be.

"Are you enjoying this, Scott?" she asked him and heard him groan in reply.

"Yes."

"Don't talk to me," she said as she smacked him.

"But you asked…" he started to explain but felt another strike across his butt.

"I said, don't talk to me!"

Scott could feel arousal flowing through him. It was like a drug had just been released into his system after it having been kept from him for so long. She continued to strike him, until all of a sudden, he called out.

"Stop!" he yelled and then seemed to gather himself up and run to the bathroom without another word to her.

A few minutes later, he returned, feeling extremely uncomfortable. He realised as he returned to the living area that he hadn't quite thought through the flow-on effect from encouraging her to use the crop on him.

"Did you just…?" Samantha asked him, wondrous at the realisation that even though he had said it didn't have to be something sexual, perhaps that was something he couldn't actually control.

Scott sat down beside her, looking and feeling far more composed than he had a few minutes earlier.

"Yeah, sorry, I had to … release," he said, feeling his face blushing.

"You just … went to your bathroom … and … masturbated?" Samantha asked, not knowing how much clearer she could present the question to him. She saw him look uncomfortable and embarrassed.

"Yes," he responded.

"Me hitting you turned you on that much?" she asked. "So much that you had to do that?"

"Yes."

Scott watched her face, feeling a wide array of feelings all of a sudden. He felt released from the build-up in arousal, excited that she'd produced such a feeling in him, embarrassed at having had to go and release as he had, and worried that she'd think he was some kind of freak.

"Oh," Samantha said, at a loss of what else to say at that moment. "Okay."

Scott laughed softly with a sheepish but equally worried look on his face.

"I tell you I went to the bathroom to do that, and you just say okay?" he asked.

"Well, when you have to, you have to," Samantha replied.

He heard her words but was so surprised by them that he burst out laughing at her. He saw her instantly join in with him. When their laughter died down, he leaned in and kissed her, partly because he felt a need to, but partly because he wanted to see how she really felt about him after what had happened.

Samantha indulged in the kiss. What she'd done for him - *to* him - had driven him to need sexual release. She'd thought there was a chance that perhaps he wouldn't need her there after that, so the kiss was welcome to her. It was a way for her to be sure that she might still hold a place in his life, even if he needed that kind of excitement and release after all.

When their kiss ended and they broke apart, they looked intently at each other to assess how the other was feeling.

"Now, how about some dinner? I'm thinking cold cuts and salad. What do you think?" he asked her suddenly, as if nothing at all had happened.

"That sounds good," Samantha replied, smiling at him.

~~~~~

Over the weeks that followed, as Scott introduced Samantha to new things to try, she slowly gained confidence in using whatever he instructed her to.

"Would you feel confident enough to go into a club situation now, do you think?" he asked one evening.

"To do that to you in front of other people?"

"Yes."

"But what if you … you know," she said, curious.

Scott smiled at her.

"You'll see more than that there, I promise you. Some nights, there's nothing sexual. On other nights, sex is very full-on. You have to be open to seeing other people like that."

"But will I have to…?"

"No," he replied. "I've heard that some other clubs are extremely strict in their rules about sex, but the club I've been to is relaxed. People who want to get sexual, can and do. Others who have no desire for it, don't. Everyone respects those decisions."
~~~~~

"But will you expect me to…?"

"No, of course not," Scott said. "I can't help how I will be, though. My body might respond like that, but I think you're used to that now, right?"

Samantha nodded at him.

"If it happens, I'll do a quick run to the bathroom," he said, with a sound of amusement in his voice.

"Okay."

~~~~~

Another week later and Samantha found herself in his car, going to the elusive 'club' she'd heard so much about since she'd met him. Pulling up to the building, she was surprised when he told her they were there.

"But there's no sign or anything," she said, curious.

"No. It's a private club. They don't want people just walking in from outside. To get in, you have to go in with an existing member."

~~~~~

As soon as they walked inside, Samantha felt out of her depth. They'd gone early in the evening, so the crowd wasn't as big as Scott knew it could get, but there were still enough people to make her nervous.

Almost as soon as they got in the door, a man and a woman approached them.

"Scott," the man said, holding out his hand for a handshake. "It's good to see you. It's been a long while."

"Hi, Grant. Valda. Yeah, I took a break, but this is my partner, Samantha. She's new to this," Scott said.

The couple responded as if they knew exactly what that meant, although Samantha had no idea.

"Samantha," the woman said to her. "Welcome. Part of your initiation is that I will take you away from this main room and have a one on one chat with you out back. There are a few things that are always asked before we allow anyone to take part in the activities here."

Samantha looked at Scott for guidance. On seeing him nod, she let the older woman lead her away. They passed through the small crowd gathering in what appeared to be a large room, like a hall. Samantha could see a wide array of items placed around the outside of it. If she hadn't known anything from what Scott had told her, she might have thought she'd been taken into a torture chamber from medieval days.

"Come and have a seat," Valda said, inviting Samantha to sit on a small sofa with her. "Now, first of all, I need to make sure that you're here because you want to be here, and not because you feel pressured by Scott to be here. I know he's a nice young man. I watched him with his previous partner, and I never saw any issues there, but that doesn't mean that you necessarily want to do this," she said, looking closely at

Samantha to read her face. "Tell me a bit about what you know, and why you think you're here."

Samantha looked at the older woman beside her. The frankness of the words so far was a reminder of how odd the situation was to her, but she didn't sense any bad feelings coming from the woman.

"Scott told me a little of what happens here, and in his apartment, he has been … encouraging me to use things on him."

"Things such as?"

"A … riding crop? And a belt."

"Okay, good. And did you feel okay using them on him? Is there anything about it that worries you, or left you feeling confused?"

"Well, I don't understand why anyone would *want* to be hit like that. It doesn't make any sense to me," Samantha said.

Valda smiled at her, having had the same conversation many times since she and her husband had opened the club a decade earlier.

"It can be a trick of the mind, the whole pleasure and pain thing," said Valda. "Grant and I have been doing this for a very long time, but even we don't understand why some people perceive things to be painful, whilst others perceive the same things to be pleasurable. What we *have* learned is that the only way anyone can really know is by experiencing it. Here at the club, we only allow people to build up slowly in their levels of experimentation. There can be a psychological side to doing this kind of thing, and not everyone is well suited to it, but I think Scott bringing you here indicates that he at least thinks that you are."

"But what if someone does something and then it hurts too much?"

"Then they need to use their safe word to make sure the other person knows to stop. Have you and Scott talked about safe words?"

"Yes, he told me if I do something that's beyond what he's comfortable with, he'll use it, and I should stop doing whatever I'm doing at that time."

Valda nodded and smiled at her once again.

"Good," she said. "We're a fairly relaxed group here. We don't place as many restrictions on our members as some clubs do, but we do ensure that people aren't pushed past their own personal limits. Scott wants you to be his dominant? Is that right?"

"That is what he said, yes," replied Samantha.

"Then you need to remember that he is the one who controls how far you will push him," Valda said. "You need to keep your eyes and ears open and make sure that you identify when he is nearing his limit of what he can handle. You must train yourself to see that, even before he has used his safe word."

"Alright," Samantha replied, feeling only more confusion at the words being said to her.

"Now, I am happy with what you've told me, and I do believe you are here of your own accord," said Valda. "I trust Scott has told you about the sexual side of this club? We don't restrict people from being sexual, and we ask that people who don't wish to be around sex, keep an open mind to others enjoying it while they are here. Not everyone who takes part in this goes on to be aroused from it, or have sex, but a good proportion of the people who you will see here do, and they have the right to. If you feel uncomfortable about what you see, you - and anyone else - have the right to leave. Grant and I are both approachable, so if you have any concerns, you can come directly to us. Even if it looks like we're busy, if you need to tell us something or ask us something, it is our priority to respond, no matter what we're doing. This applies to all members in the club," she said and then looked closely at Samantha one more time. "How are you feeling now?"

Samantha smiled at the woman before her. It was hard not to when she could talk so easily about so many things that other people might regard as 'taboo' subjects.

"I'm fine," she replied. "I'll try this tonight, and if I don't like it, I'll tell Scott and he can decide what he wants to do about that."

"Some of the partners you see here tonight aren't partners in life," Valda said. "Some of them have wives or husbands who don't take part, but know their spouses are here, doing this with someone else. For some people, it is something they come to love and thrive off. For others, they can't stand it, and want no part of it. Neither side is right or wrong. Everyone needs to choose their own viewpoint on it, and equally respect the viewpoints of others. As part of our induction process, I will encourage you to just watch other people tonight, Samantha. Don't worry. It's something that everyone does when they first come here, so you don't need to feel like you are intruding by watching. It will help you to understand how it is for others, and give you an indication of things that Scott might want you to do to him in time."

"Thank you, Valda. You've been really good to talk and listen to," Samantha said and walked out with the older woman.

"How was that?" Scott asked when she rejoined him.

"It was fine," Samantha said. "I'm fine."

Seeing him smile brilliantly at her, she could see how happy her being in the club with him was making him.

"Come with me and I'll show you around," Scott said.

Samantha was led around the exterior of the room, seeing many things she hadn't known existed. Finding Scott informative about things, Samantha listened as if she were a scholar learning from a master. For that night, they weren't taking part in anything. It was a night where she could watch what others did. As they walked around, Samantha was very aware of all her senses going on high alert.

The near-nudity and full nudity, she found hard to watch at first. Men with obvious arousal, which there was no effort to try and hide, caught her attention, especially as a virgin who had hardly touched a man, let alone seen him like that. Scott watched her face, wondering what she thought of what was happening before her, particularly when, before them, they saw a guy go from whipping his partner, to being on his knees behind her and entering her. As that happened, Scott looked at Samantha and wondered if she'd get as aroused watching that as he did, but she looked more wide-eyed than anything.

Samantha was shocked at first. She'd never watched porn or had sex, so it was surprising to her, but at the same time, surprisingly interesting. She turned and looked at Scott, wondering if being around things like that happening would make him want to move things forward with them, or if he would start to pressure her into having sex with him. She wasn't sure what she saw on his face when she looked at him. Usually, he wasn't difficult to read, but that night he was.

What Samantha really wanted to see was women doing to men what Scott wanted her to do to him. When they saw couples in that position, she did stop for longer and take more notice.

The realisation that Samantha wanted to watch excited Scott - so much so that he knew he'd have to relieve himself due to the effect everything was having on him.

"I'll be back in a few minutes. Will you wait here?" he asked and saw her nod.

In the bathroom, Scott let go of the pressure that had been building. He didn't want to pressure Samantha to have sex, but at the same time, he was aroused so often that he was having to release more and more frequently. While she never said anything about it, he found he'd much rather do it when he was alone, like at the club, than when she was in his apartment, and he had to go to his bathroom there. She'd never made him feel like any kind of freak since that first time he'd run to the bathroom to let go, but to him, it still felt like some kind of betrayal to her. It felt like he was letting her down by him being so aroused like that so often when he knew she wasn't.

After he let go, he took a moment to look in the mirror before he returned to her. They were the same age, but sometimes it felt to him like he was years older than her. Sometimes he wished he was back there, where she was, before he'd ever had sex, or been introduced to the BDSM lifestyle.

Samantha was watching a woman using a riding crop on her male partner when Scott returned to her side once more. He'd worried she might wonder where he was, but when he reached her, he saw she was intrigued and completely caught up in what was happening before her.

When the woman saw Samantha, she motioned her to move closer. Samantha looked at Scott, who only nodded at her. As she stepped forward, the woman moved right up to her and held out her hand.

"I'm Angelica. You're new here, right?" she asked.

Samantha nodded as she shook the woman's hand.

"I'm happy to give you some guidance in the use of this if you want."

Samantha looked at the woman, and then at the woman's partner, but he kept his head down.

"He does what I tell him to do, don't you, Tony?" she said, running the end of the crop all over him from tailbone to chin as she walked around him.

"Yes, Mistress," he called out in response.

Angelica returned her attention to Samantha.

"It's just role-playing," she said. "Don't worry, when we're in our everyday lives, we don't treat each other like this, or tell each other what to do. But here, take this, Samantha. Don't worry. Tony is happy for you to practice on him. He often takes on this role for the new visitors. Now hold the crop like this. I find this is how I get the best power…"

Scott watched Samantha as she received instruction from the other woman. He was pleased to see her eager to learn new things, and take on board what was being said to her. As he saw her hit the man on the ground, he watched her face. That was something he could never see when they'd been doing the same kind of action in his apartment. He had thought she might not really enjoy it, but looking at her face as she brought the riding crop down on the man, over and over, he could see excitement on her face. That, in turn, excited him.

Samantha felt invigorated and alert. She'd already been doing the same thing to Scott recently, but there was a small piece of her that held back with him, because, she supposed, she cared for him so much. It felt different to be with someone she didn't know. As she delivered the blows, she found a new level of adrenalin rushing inside of her.

As she walked around the man, she could see the level of his arousal. He was completely naked, and there was no hiding it at all. It drove her on more, seeing how he was feeling. Without any warning, suddenly Angelica was on her knees in front of him, telling him what to do. Samantha saw Tony move into his partner from behind and almost instantly climax right before Samantha's eyes. That was before Angelica turned over and commanded Tony to place his head between her legs and use his tongue on her, an action that ended in a result that was equally almost instantaneous.

Samantha looked at Scott for guidance as she was holding their riding crop and didn't know what to do - or where to look. All she saw on his face was an intense look of amusement, mixed in with desire.

She was still holding the crop, looking at him, when Angelica jumped up and came up to her.

"Oh, sorry, Samantha. Sometimes we get carried away and forget about all the other people here!" she said, laughing out loud as she reached to take the crop from Samantha's hands. "I hope we didn't make you feel uncomfortable? It's never our intention," she continued. "Some people don't like nudity too much, but hey, it's who we are, and what we do."

"Oh, no. It's fine, Angelica. It's something new for me … to watch … that … but it is fine. And I feel more confident using the riding crop now, so thank you."

Angelica laughed at her.

"You and I are going to be great friends, I can tell," she said and winked at Samantha before giving Scott a knowing smile.

Scott veered her away, fearing that any more of that and he'd be aroused again, which he didn't want to be.

"You looked magnificent with that riding crop. How did you find using it the way that Angelica showed you?" he asked her and saw her look at him with an expression of surprise.

"I found that … really good," Samantha replied.

Scott couldn't be sure as he'd not seen it on her face before, but for a moment, he wondered if he wasn't seeing on her face, frank and blatant arousal. He pushed the thought from his mind quickly.

"Come on, let's go," he said. "It's best I drop you straight home to your house tonight, I think."

Samantha nodded, not arguing with him one bit, given how she was feeling, and how it went against how she wanted to feel.

~~~~~

In the following weeks, Samantha eased into enjoying herself at the club with Scott. They moved slowly when there. Scott never pressured her into exposing any part of her body that she didn't wish to. He didn't try to make her do anything she didn't want to. But at the same time, she was confused sometimes by his fairly constant 'tell me what to do' instructions, which seemed to go against her telling him the way things would be.

As she persisted, she grew to enjoy using different things on him. She was aware of how aroused he became, but she became more and more at ease with it, considering it more of a matter-of-fact type of occurrence than putting any more thought into it.

Overall, Samantha found that with her dressmaking skills growing, her spending time with Scott, and her attending the club, her confidence was slowly increasing. She enjoyed the feelings growing in her.
~~~~~

Suddenly the thought of becoming a dressmaker by trade didn't seem quite so impossible. The realisation drove her on to study harder, despite the joys she was finding in other parts of her life.

CHAPTER 3

The Induction of a Friend

"What?" Tom asked her, not believing what he'd just heard his closest friend say.

"I said, over the past few weeks I've been going to a BDSM club with Scott, and I'm really enjoying it."

Samantha watched his face. They were sitting in a café, catching up after a period of time apart.

"So, like, you let him … umm … whip you and stuff?"

"No, the other way round," Samantha replied.

Tom found himself astounded at what was being said to him.

"Scott lets you whip … him?" he asked.

Samantha laughed at him. One thing she never tired of with Tom were his facial expressions.

"No, not whip!" she said. "I have tried the whip, but haven't been able to master it, so we stick with the riding crop and a couple of floggers."

Tom was speechless.

"I'd like to take you one night," Samantha said. "Do you think you might like to try it?"

If he'd been speechless before, hearing her question left Tom dumbstruck. He became suddenly aware that she was laughing heartily at him.

"Oh, you were joking," he said, feeling sheepish all of a sudden.

"Oh, no, I was serious," Samantha said. "I didn't think I would like it, but I really am enjoying it. I'd love to take you along. There is a *lot* to look at, I can tell you!"

"Don't people usually go in pairs, though?" Tom asked. "I'd be a third wheel."

"No, I'd take you on a night where we could go together and just watch others, without doing anything."

"And how would Scott like that?"

"He would accept it," said Samantha.

Tom laughed at her. "I am not so sure about that!"

"Why wouldn't he? Lots of people go to that club, and some of them aren't romantically involved. Lots of people go with someone other than their romantic partner."

"Yeah, but…"

"But what?"

"I just don't think he'd like you to be there with me, that's all," said Tom. "Sometimes I'm not sure if I think he *is* truly accepting of me as your friend."

Samantha considered his words and suspected he wasn't wrong. Lately, Scott *had* been making references to her spending time with Tom, even though she'd hardly seen him in recent weeks. In Samantha's mind, Scott even mentioning Tom wasn't fair since he'd known the two of them were good friends long before he'd started dating her.

"Well, anyway, not worrying about what he thinks, what do *you* think?" she asked. "You'll see some sights, and they might be a bit … surprising … but if you're okay with that, I'd like to take you."

Tom looked at her. She was his lifelong friend who he usually thought he knew inside out, and yet she could still completely shock him on occasion.

"Alright."

~~~~~

Tom walked in with Samantha close by his side, at his request. Since she'd first gone to the club, she'd made friends and had grown to be regarded as a friendly person in the group. It was equally known that she didn't have sex there, or ever reveal private areas of her body.

As soon as they walked in, they were greeted by Grant and Valda. They introduced themselves just as they had when Scott had taken Samantha for the first time.

"Tom," they both said as he was introduced to them. "Welcome."

"Thank you," Tom said. "I'm just here at Samantha's request, to see the new hobby she is enjoying so much."

"Oh, a hobby?" Grant teased Samantha.

She smiled a brilliant smile at him, making Tom feel slightly jealous and insecure for a moment.

"I see!" Grant continued. "Well, regardless, Tom, we do have some protocols in place here so I'll sweep you away for a few minutes, please, and explain them to you."

Samantha watched as he was led away, just as she had been by Valda on her first night.

"So Tom is … your boyfriend?" Valda asked, curious all of a sudden at seeing Samantha with another man.

"Oh, no!" Samantha replied. "Scott's my boyfriend. Tom is a friend - my best friend really. We've known each other forever. I talk to him about so many things that I thought it might be nice to share this with him, and let him see what I do when I come here with Scott."

"Ahh," the older woman said with a gleam of amusement in her eye.

~~~~~

Tom was in awe in so many ways, due to what was happening before his eyes. He was still a virgin too, but had peaked at porn on occasion, even though it never held his attention for very long.

What was in front of him was different. The openness of people astounded him most of all. He wondered at how so many could be close to naked, and some completely naked, but not have any qualms about their bodies being seen by others. That, he found excessively intriguing, rather than arousing.

After a while, Angelica approached him and Samantha.

"Samantha, who is this lovely young man with you?" she purred, making Samantha laugh, and Tom cringe bashfully.

"Angelica, stop it!" said Samantha. "This is Tom. He's a very good friend of mine, so be nice."

Tom saw the woman relax and become more human as she greeted him in a friendly manner.

"I'm only teasing, Tom. I'm Angelica, and this is my husband, Tony."

Tom saw the man approach and was embarrassed to see he was not only wearing hardly anything at all, but was also very erect. Tom kept his eyes up, not knowing what to do in such a situation. Angelica and Tony laughed.

"Don't worry, Tom. We're all embarrassed by the lack of clothing at the start, but after a while, everyone realises that really, no-one cares. Now, how about I take you through some moves?" Angelica asked.

Reluctantly Tom nodded and followed her, leaving Tony and Samantha standing together nearby, watching.

"What do you think you would be most likely attuned to, Tom? Delivering pain? Or receiving it?"

"Oh, I don't know," Tom replied. "I don't think I could hurt someone."

"Right then," said Angelica. "How about we see if you like to receive it."

Tom was horrified for a moment, but with a glance and nod from Samantha, nodded at Angelica.

"First hold out your hand, palm up," she said and saw him do so.

Before Tom had time to think about it, she had smacked him with the crop in her hand.

"Is that okay?" she asked him and saw him nod.

"Get down on your knees," she said, making sure he could hear the authority in her voice. "I'm going to use this while you're fully dressed. If you feel okay with that, I'd like you to pull your jeans down and let me use it on you through your underwear."

Tom groaned at the thought. There was no way he wanted to do that in front of Samantha, but he did as he was instructed. He fully trusted Samantha. She'd asked him to try the activity out, so he would, no matter how embarrassed he got from it.

On all fours, he felt the strike against his jeans, but it wasn't painful at all. He understood why Angelica had mentioned the no-jeans try.

"How was that?" Angelica asked him.

"I couldn't really feel that," he said and saw her nod.

"Pull them down then," Angelica instructed.

Samantha held her tongue as she watched her friend do as he was told without any argument whatsoever.

"I'm going to hit you, Tom, softly at first, and then I'm going to intensify it," said Angelica. "You need to tell me when it's hurting you, and I'll stop. Do you understand?"

"Yes," Tom replied.

He felt the first one and recognised straight away the difference between the jeans being present and them not being. It hurt, but he allowed her to give him three more strikes - each more intense than the last - before he called for her to stop.

Samantha saw him look around him as if to check it was alright for him to get up. As he discretely pulled his jeans up and stood, he gave Samantha a shy smile.

"How did you like that, Tom?" Angelica was asking him, but he knew that he would never gain pleasure from the activity.

"It was okay," he said.

Angelica understood from the tone of his voice that receiving the strikes wouldn't be his thing.

"Here, take this and use it on me," she said, handing the crop to him.

At first, Tom was uncertain as he looked at Samantha, and then at Tony. On seeing Tony nod at him, he finally took the crop and followed Angelica's instruction about where to strike her with it - first on her hand, and then on her buttocks as she knelt on the ground.

"You can do it a bit harder, Tom," she said to him.

Tom increased his strike strength a bit more, but couldn't be enticed to keep going in his increases.

"I think that is all for me," he said, offering a hand to Angelica to help her stand up. She wasn't wearing much, and she certainly wasn't flat-chested, but being the gentleman he was, he managed successfully to not blatantly stare at her breasts or any other intimate part of her body. That didn't go unnoticed by her at all. "Thank you for making the time for me to ... experiment ... Angelica. It was lovely to meet you - and you, Tony."

Samantha said her goodbyes, equally happy to leave with him, but feeling like the evening had been a success.

As they sat in Tom's car, he remained silent, wondering what Samantha would have expected to come from the evening. At first, she seemed to not want to talk, but as he expected, once she found the courage, soon followed the talking.

"That was amazing, watching you, Tom," she said.

Tom blushed, not sure how he should respond. In his mind, all he kept visualising was him with his jeans down, and Samantha seeing that. It felt like another level of their friendship had definitely been defined at that moment.

"Did you enjoy yourself?" she asked and saw him smile at her and nod. "Enough to do it again?"

"Hmm … well, I don't feel the same enthusiasm about it as you obviously do, so I wouldn't rush to do that again, no," Tom said. "But I am glad that we went and I got to see what has had you so intrigued and engaged lately."

"But if I want to take you again?" Samantha asked.

She saw him look at her with a look of somewhat disbelief, as if exasperated by her.

"Samantha, you need to be doing that with Scott, not me," he said. "He's the one who's into it - *really* into it. That's the kind of person you need to go with, to something like that."

Samantha said nothing more until they pulled up outside her home. She turned to Tom to judge whether she might have upset him in any way.

"Are you okay?" she asked, but only saw him smile at her in his usual friendly way.

"Absolutely," he said. "I liked going with you tonight. Thank you for taking me."

He saw her smile, kiss him on the cheek, and climb out of the car. As he made his way back to his house, he was thoughtful about the evening. He hadn't seen Samantha do anything during the time they were in the club, so hadn't been able to make any judgement on how enthusiastic she truly was about it. The fact that she took him there must mean that she was honestly into it, he figured, but he believed he had no desire whatsoever to ever go into that world.

~~~~~

The next day. Samantha received a phone call from Scott. His voice immediately demonstrated the level of anger he felt.

"Everyone is talking about you being at the club with another guy! What were you thinking?" he seemed to scream at her down the phone line, stunning her.

"I don't understand what you're upset about," Samantha said. "I told you I wanted to take Tom…"

"No, you didn't!" Scott argued back.

"Yes, I did! We talked about it on the way home from the club the last
~~~~~

time I went with you. How could you have forgotten that conversation?"

"I haven't forgotten it because it never took place!"

Samantha couldn't understand what he was talking about, or why he was pretending they hadn't discussed it, when she remembered the whole conversation so vividly.

"Well, whatever," she said. "So what if I took a friend to the club? What's the big deal?"

"It's a big deal because you're my girlfriend!"

"And? You said lots of married people go there with people other than their spouses," she said and heard him sigh in frustration.

"That isn't the point," Scott said.

"Well, what *is* the point?" asked Samantha. "I have no idea why you're so angry. You know that Tom and I are friends. You've gone right through school with us from when we were at kindergarten, so don't act as if you only just found out that he and I spend a lot of time together..."

"This is different."

"Why?" she asked.

"It just is."

Samantha reached a point of frustration that she knew she had to try and defuse. She took a deep breath and a moment to think before she spoke again.

"You aren't making any sense, Scott," she said. "You're angry about something that doesn't deserve your anger. Tom is my best friend. He always has been, and he always will be. Just accept it, because that aspect of my life isn't going to change."

To that remark, she heard the sound of the dial tone. He'd hung up on her with no goodbye, no see you later, and no advance warning that he was going to end the call at all.

Samantha stood with the phone in her hand, looking at it in disbelief. When she'd met him, he hadn't been moody at all. Over time, his moods had started to become more intense and more frequent. In one way, it concerned her. In another, she found that she just didn't care. She didn't care about his moods, and perhaps the reason she didn't care about his moods was that she didn't really care about *him*.

~~~~~

Later that day, she received another phone call from him, his voice deep with apology.

"Look, I'm sorry," he said. "I know you and Tom have been best friends forever. I had no right to say anything about your friendship, so I'm sorry."

"Is that what it was about?" Samantha asked. "My friendship with Tom? Because you said it was about me taking him to the club. Which is it?"
~~~~~

She wasn't talking to him with a friendly tone, and she knew it, but he'd riled her up. When she got like that, she needed time to sort through her feelings and thoughts before being approached again. That was just one of the many things that Tom knew about her, that Scott still didn't and possibly never would.

"I was embarrassed when people told me you were there with another guy…"

"What people?" Samantha asked, wondering if he even had a real point of argument.

"I don't know … just people."

"You don't know who you spoke to, that told you this?"

As she started to hear his voice grow frustrated and annoyed all over again, she wished she'd just hung up on him … or something.

"What does it matter?" Scott asked. "The point is…"

"The point is that you hate that I have a best friend who's a guy," she said. "You're jealous of him, when you have absolutely no reason to be… "

"No reason to be? Are you kidding me? He is Mr *Perfect*," Scott said. "Everybody likes him. Women look at him when he walks down the street. Even people at the club are still talking about him going there, and he was only there for one short time!"

Suddenly Samantha heard a different situation entirely.

"So *that* is what this is about?" she asked. "You're jealous of Tom?"

There was silence for a while until finally Scott spoke again.

"Of course I'm jealous of him," he said. "He knows you better than I do. Hell, he knows you better than *anyone* else does. How could I not be jealous of him?"

"Umm … maybe because I am involved with you, and not him? Maybe because I am *dating* you, and not him. Maybe because I am *kissing* you, and not him."

"I know!" Scott yelled down the phone, once again frustrated. "I know it's illogical and stupid, but it's how I feel."

"Well, if you want this relationship to continue, you are going to have to get over that, because Tom isn't going anywhere," said Samantha. "He's my friend, and he will always be a priority to me."

"I don't expect him to go anywhere!" Scott said. "I just don't think you should have taken him to a club where you and I go as partners!"

Samantha groaned inwardly as the conversation seemed to be taking another turn. She was weary of it, not knowing what was at the heart of his being so angry, with all the different angles and objections he'd made to her during not one but two phone calls.

"Scott, I have to go," she said. "I'll talk to you later."

"We haven't finished talking…"

"Yes, we have."
And with that, she hung up on him.

CHAPTER 4

The Break-Up

"Samantha, be more aggressive with me! I want you to tell me what you want me to do, and what you want to do to me!" Scott yelled at her, as was his way more and more frequently.

"I am trying to tell you what I want you to do, and what I want to do to you, but you keep contradicting what I say," replied Samantha. "Which is it? Do you want me to have the control or not? Because you keep saying you do, but then you get angry at what I say I want!"

"Ugh! I'm tired of this conversation," he said and walked away from her. They were in his apartment, but more and more, it wasn't an enjoyable experience for either of them. "Let's get some food and then just chill with a movie."

Samantha was annoyed at him but nodded. She, too, was feeling frustrated at almost every interaction they had together.

~~~~~

"He drives me nuts with all this 'you be the dominant' crap," she said to Tom as they sat on the swings in their local park the next day. "He wants me to take charge, but when I take charge, he doesn't want me to take charge like *that*. He wants me to take charge how *he* wants me to take charge. So you tell me, how can I be in charge if he keeps telling me what I have to do to be in charge?!"

"It does sound a bit strange," Tom replied noncommittally.

"Strange? Strange?! He drives me bonkers!"

Tom sat quietly, unsure if she expected him to say anything, or whether it was one of those times where she just needed him to be a sounding board for her frustrations.

"What do you think?" she asked, forcing him to respond.

"What do I think … about what exactly?" he asked.

"You know, about me breaking up with Scott!"

Samantha saw him look sharply at her with a shocked look on his face.

"I didn't know we were talking about you breaking up with Scott!" Tom said. "Do you not think you could have led with that instead of your issues with the BDSM club thingy?!"

"Yeah, well, anyway, what do you think about me breaking up with him?"
~~~~~

Tom looked at her. It was definitely one of the many days of their lifelong friendship where she was on one track of conversation, and he was on another. Even though she was indicating she wanted his opinion on something, he knew it was likely she didn't want to hear what he thought about the subject at hand.

"Samantha, what do you want me to say?" he asked. "Apart from this issue, I don't know how things are with you. Are you unhappy? Does he treat you badly?"

She took a few minutes to think about the questions presented to her. "No."

"No - you aren't unhappy? No - he doesn't treat you badly?"

"Both."

"Are you being intentionally vague today? Because I feel like you're baiting me by asking me questions but not telling me anything."

Tom watched as she suddenly stopped her swing from moving, then stood up and turned to face him front on.

"I just wanted you to give me your opinion on what I should do…"

"How can I give you an opinion when I don't know what is going on in your relationship, that is making you question if you should break up?"

At that point, Samantha felt frustrated with him so walked off.

Tom was well used to such action, so let her go. When she was ready to talk to him, she would see him and do so. He knew from many years of being her friend, that trying to talk to her when she was in such a stubborn place, never did any good.

~~~~~

Over the following month, Samantha concentrated on her dressmaking course. She knew she was losing enthusiasm for spending time with Scott, but they still saw each other a couple of times over weekends. She still went to the club with him, but even in that, something was starting to feel out of kilter. She enjoyed the action itself, but was enjoying it less and less in his presence.

One evening, when Tom was at the supermarket, about to leave work, he saw her approach his checkout counter.

"I need a good friend to talk to," she said to him. She felt shy as she'd pulled back from him in recent weeks too, full well knowing she wasn't treating him well. As always, she needn't have worried.

"Then you have come to the right place, Miss Young, for I do believe that, for you, I am a very good listener!" Tom said, grinning at her.

"Thanks," Samantha replied, smiling as she relaxed.

Tom was used to her drifting away and then returning when she needed a friend. He knew some people wouldn't endure such a friendship, but he was only happy to have her back.

"I need another ten minutes to close up. Can you wait by the front
~~~~~

door for me?" he asked and saw her nod before moving away.

He completed his final chores of the day. After cleaning down the checkout, doing his till reconciliation, and handing the float to his supervisor for locking up in the safe, he found her outside.

"Right. What's up?" she heard him ask.

Rather than answer the question with words, she pushed herself close to him. It was a move she knew Tom would recognise as her needing him to put his arms around her and hold her tightly. They stood close together, hugging until he felt her pull away from him.

"Oh, Tom, I don't know what to do!"

He saw her confusion, and a slight tear begin to form in her eye. He happily put his arm around her shoulder to lead her away.

"Come on," he said. "Come with me to my place, and tell Uncle Tom all about it."

Soon they were in his bedroom, sitting up on his bed.

"Are you going to tell me what has you so upset tonight?" he asked.

"I ... I think I want to split up from Scott," Samantha said, almost resolved to do what she was thinking of doing, but at the same time thinking she might be making a mistake.

"Right," Tom said as he nodded. "What are you finding difficult about that? Are you unhappy with him?"

"No. Yes. Oh, I don't know!" she said. "That's the problem! Sometimes we are good together, but so often now, we argue all the time. I feel like I don't want to be around him."

"Then don't be," Tom said.

She looked at Tom and laughed softly

"You make it sound so easy."

"No, not easy, but if you aren't happy, why would you think it could be a good thing to stay with him?"

"Because I know he's a good person."

Tom felt a physical feeling as if he'd been kicked in the stomach.

"There are a lot of good people in the world. That doesn't mean we're supposed to be romantically involved with them," he said quietly.

Samantha heard the depth of what he was saying, and instantly felt sadness. Tom was one of the good ones - the *best* good one, in her eyes - and yet love never seemed to come his way. Or at least, he never seemed to recognise it, even when he was looking right at it.

"I know," she said. "But he doesn't really give me any reason to end the relationship."

"Well, I can't pretend to be an expert since I am not experienced in relationships, but I would think that not being happy in it probably *is* reason enough to not be in it. Wouldn't you agree?"

"Yeah, I know you're right," Samantha said. "I think I've just been putting it off, not wanting to hurt him, but maybe he'll be glad for it to happen. Maybe he wants the decision to be taken out of his hands."

"Perhaps," she heard Tom say as if he were deep in thought. She couldn't know how torn he always was, wanting in part for her to be happy, even if that meant with someone else, but also wanting her to be single so that there might be some chance her view would change and she would finally see him differently.

"I should get going. I have to get up early in the morning for course," Samantha said as she stood. Turning to him, she appreciated again how lucky she was to have him in her life. "Thank you, Tom. I know I'm always going on about one drama or another…"

He stood up and put his arms around her.

"No, you aren't," he said. "And I'm always here for you."

"Goodnight," she said before pulling away and heading out his bedroom door.

~~~~~

The following day, Samantha tried to maintain focus on her course studies, but her mind kept drifting to Scott.

"Where is your head today?" her design classroom partner, Emma, asked. "You looked like you didn't hear anything in that lecture, which isn't like you."

The girls were sitting in the cafeteria at lunchtime, together but not having talked yet.

"Oh, sorry, Emma. I think I'm going to end my relationship, and the decision is plaguing me," Samantha replied.

"Oh, hell," said Emma. "Been there, done that! It sucks, making that kind of decision, doesn't it! But if you are having doubts about the person you're with, walk. I've struggled with those decisions in the past, but I can tell you that after the talk has been had, and I've walked away finally, I've never regretted it."

"Really?" Samantha asked.

"Really! Making the decision seems like a big deal, but if you were that happy, you wouldn't be thinking about ending it at all, would you? That's my opinion on it, anyway."

Samantha lodged the words into her memory to consider later, then changed the subject. Talking about anything else would be better than talking about Scott for the rest of the day.

~~~~~

As she walked out of her classroom at the end of that day, she was surprised to find Scott waiting for her outside.

"Hey, what are you doing here?" she asked him and instantly could feel that something was up.

"I want to talk to you," he said. "Can I give you a ride home, and talk on the way?"

Samantha nodded, feeling the ominous mood coming from him.

Once in the car, Scott turned on the engine, as if he had full intention of driving her home as he'd said. Then he turned it off again and turned to her.

"Samantha, I'm so sorry," he said, confusing her. "I … last week I received a call from Jane - my ex. She wants us to get back together. I didn't think I would ever want to go back there, but she…"

Samantha sighed, not letting him sense that she was feeling inside of her a hint of relief and happiness.

"Well, the two of you are better suited to what you need, Scott," she said. "It's okay, I understand."

"I'm so sorry. I would never want to hurt you. I have loved spending all this time with you," he said, looking at her face and seeing her nod.

"We gave it a good go, but even though you are the same age as me, you are worlds ahead in the essential aspects." She laughed all of a sudden and then smiled at him. "It's all good. Thank you for meeting me and telling me in person. Take care."

With that, he saw her climb out of his car and walk away without looking back.

CHAPTER 5

The New Play Partners

In the weeks after Scott had told Samantha he didn't want to see her anymore, Samantha kept her head down and refocused on her studies. She was even more determined to work harder toward her goal of becoming a recognised dressmaker. It was her dream, and she'd become distracted from it, but she would work hard and get herself back on track.

During that first month, she didn't talk to Tom as much. Things felt a little raw between them. They had done since the night she'd asked his opinion about her breaking up with Scott, and him not telling her exactly what she'd wanted to hear. She knew it was unfair of her, but she didn't care. For the moment, she wanted space from him. She wanted space from everyone, so she was going to take it, just until she could get her head where it needed to be. She wasn't sad about the break-up, but it still consumed her thoughts on some days.

Meanwhile, Tom waited patiently. From their years as friends, he was very familiar with her periodically taking time out from spending time with him. As always, all he could do was wait and see if she would eventually find her way back to him.

~~~~~

As the second month began, Samantha started to feel like she was desperately missing Tom. She thought she should be missing Scott, but no, it was definitely Tom she was missing the company of. As often was the case when she had time away like that, she reached a point where she could hardly remember why she'd thought she was annoyed at him at all.

On a weekend morning, she made her way to his house in the hope of catching him at home.

"Samantha!" Tom's mother greeted her at the front door of their home, as she always had. "Tom's still in bed, but go and wake him up."

Samantha laughed and nodded. "Okay."

She walked up to his door and knocked gently.

"Hmm?" she heard a mumble from the other side of the door, and she opened the door a small amount.

"It's me," she said quietly, in case he was sleeping, but instantly she saw his head come up and look at her.

"Yep, I'm awake," Tom said. "Come in, stranger."

She approached the bed, as always loving looking at him as he lay
~~~~~

with only his head visible, due to the care he took to make sure all of his body was covered.

Tom watched her close his door and approach, looking shy and young at that moment.

"What's up?" he asked, encouraging her to be the one to start the conversation.

Samantha sat on the bed and looked down at him.

"I just missed you," she said.

Tom was surprised to see her eyes glistening. He held out his arms to her, and she let herself be pulled down into them, neither saying anything. At that moment, they both felt complete once more. When she pulled away from him, they looked at each other before she spoke.

"I'm sorry I haven't wanted to talk," she said. "I did split up with Scott, and I just wanted some time to myself."

"That's okay," Tom said. "How have you been, though?"

"I'm okay. Actually, to be honest, the day that I was going to split up with Scott, he broke up with me."

"Oh! Did it take you by surprise?"

She nodded, moving her eyes away from his.

"It did surprise me, but I wasn't sad about the relationship ending. I think I was angrier at myself for now having been in two such waste of time relationships," she said and paused before continuing. "Silly, huh?"

"No, not at all," he said, smiling sadly at her. "No more B … D … S … M then?" he laughed softly, taking his time spelling the letters out.

Samantha looked at him, having forgotten about that aspect of her time with Scott.

"What?" Tom asked, seeing her depth of thinking on her face. "No! You want to keep doing that?"

She hadn't given it any thought, but after Tom put the idea in her head, she looked thoughtful.

"I … don't … know."

Tom said nothing, silently wishing that he hadn't brought the topic up at all.

"Would you?" she asked him, confusing him with the question.

"Would I … what?"

"Would you like to give it another go?"

Tom was surprised by the turn of conversation, but determined to not read anything into it.

"With … you?" he asked tentatively, uncertain where the conversation was going.

"Yes! Oh, Tom, what a good idea!" Samantha said. "What do you think? You and I could be play partners at the club!"

Tom sat up suddenly, not caring about keeping every inch of himself covered up.

"What? Samantha, you must be joking! Right?"

"No. Why?"

"I know I tried it that one time, but I really don't want to be hit!"

Samantha thought about the possibilities opening up before her. She could try things differently if she went to the club without Scott. He had always been so rigid in everything, and that had kept things from being relaxed and easy. With Tom, it could be so different.

"No, we could be in opposite roles," she said. "You felt okay using the crop on Angelica, didn't you?"

"Yes…" Tom replied quietly, finding himself not believing where their conversation was going.

"Then you could be the dominant, Tom," said Samantha. "I don't mind trying to be the submissive…"

Tom suddenly laughed at her.

"You?! A submissive? Being told what to do?"

Samantha laughed with him.

"Yes! I am sure I could … adapt."

Tom looked at her, wondering where her latest thinking was coming from, but knew he was already resolved to try whatever she was going to suggest, just as he always had been.

"Will you? Can we?" she asked.

Tom took a moment to think about it.

"Samantha, I don't think I could hit you…"

"You were fine with Angelica…"

"She isn't you!" he exclaimed.

"Well, what difference does that make?"

"It … just … does."

They sat in silence for a while, their minds both working in their own spaces, at their own paces.

"I'm going to have to get ready for work soon," Tom said, looking at the time and finding relief that he had a valid reason to cut the conversation short.

"Okay, I will leave you, but will you think about it?" she asked.

"Yes! Now go away," Tom said fondly before he saw her smile at him and leave as quietly as she had arrived.

~~~~~

Later that day, while working on the checkout, Tom found his mind wandering to her question. He didn't know if she had been serious or not, but a part of him hoped she'd been joking. He could still remember how Angelica and other women in the club had looked when he'd gone there - and how little they wore. The thought of him seeing Samantha like that was enough to concern him. It was hard enough at times to keep his
~~~~~

feelings straight about her. He wasn't sure how his body would react to seeing her dressed like that - or not dressed, as the case may be.

~~~~~

When the discussion finally sparked again some weeks later, Tom found that he equally was and wasn't surprised by it.

"What have you decided?" Samantha asked him without reference to anything in particular, but he knew what she was talking about.

"Are you really serious about this, Samantha?" he asked. "Please tell me straight. Don't joke about this."

"No, I am completely serious," she replied. "I want to try this with you."

He looked closely at her, so many thoughts going through his head.

"I don't know if I could hit you..." he said quietly and received a hug from her in reply.

"You'll only do what I'm comfortable with, and I won't push you to do more to me than you want to," she said.

"But this dominant thing. I was doing some research and I'm supposed to make all the decisions."

"Yes, traditionally," Samantha agreed.

"I couldn't do that," said Tom. "I'll only agree to try it if we agree that you'll choose what's used, when it's used, and how hard it's used."

"Alright," Samantha said, a smile growing on her face. "I agree to those terms. I don't think it's traditional, but we don't need to worry about that. Plenty of people at the club aren't doing what is time-honoured in a club such as that, I've been told, and the people there seem nice. You know Angelica and Tony..." she said and immediately saw him blush and roll his eyes, making her laugh.

"You better not expect me to dress like Tony!" he said, making Samantha laugh even harder.

"No! No, thank you. You can keep your clothes on!"

"And you?" he asked, teasing her. "How many of your clothes will come off?"

Samantha replied with one of her now-infamous punches on his arm.

"Ow! It was a legitimate question," Tom said, grinning. "Look at what Angelica wears ... or doesn't wear as is more the case."

Samantha laughed harder at him.

"No, I am not going to have my ... chest ... on full display, thank you very much," she said. "The most you will see is my cute butt."

Tom had to control his blush, working hard to prevent himself from thinking anything about any part of her body. Samantha could see him trying to do the best he could to maintain focus on the right things.

"Well, you had better appreciate me as the very best friend you've ever had, if you are going to force me to look at your cute butt!" he
~~~~~

finally said.

Samantha laughed at him again, putting him at ease.

"Will we see Scott there, though?" Tom asked. "What should I expect if that happens?"

Finally, he saw her simmer down with a serious look on her face.

"I would like to go on a different night to him," she said. "I know that he and I both wanted things to end, but I don't want to see him if I can help it."

"Alright," Tom said. "Well, you need to work out what night we'll go, so I can rearrange my work schedule if I need to, cute butt girl."

"Oh! Thank you!" Samantha said, excited by the prospect.

"But listen, I'm going to look at some apartments this weekend," said Tom. "Do you want to come along and look around to help me choose?"

"You're moving out of here?" Samantha asked and saw him smile.

"Yeah, I think it's past time to be in my own space. Do you want to look with me?"

She nodded enthusiastically.

"Absolutely!"

~~~~~

That weekend, the two of them looked at three apartments, and Tom found one that was ideal for him, for cost and location. Although it would be his home, it was Samantha who appeared most excited, jumping up and down like a child at Christmas.

"Oh my gosh, this is so exciting!" she said as she grabbed his arm and jumped around, making him laugh at her. "Can I help you buy stuff for it, too?"

He couldn't help but catch on to her enthusiasm as he nodded at her.

"Sure. Of course you can tell me what to spend my hard-earned cash on. What else are friends for?" he teased her as she laughed more.
~~~~~

CHAPTER 6

The Test of Friendship

After moving into his apartment, Tom found a steady routine with his work and his time with Samantha. Now that he had an apartment, she seemed to visit him far more often during the hours when he was off work and she was free from her course.

When the time came for her to take him to the club, he felt extremely anxious about it.

"What are you worried about?" she asked him softly when they were about to leave his apartment to head there.

"It's just new to me," he said. "I don't want to hurt you."

Samantha hugged him tightly - something he never got tired of.

"We'll just ease into it," she said. "They have all sorts of things there that we can try. I'll pick one thing at a time, and we can work it out between us."

"Okay."

When they arrived, Tom was greeted again by Grant and Valda, and welcomed to the club as a participant. After that, Angelica and Tony approached them.

"Tom! You are here at last. I knew you had it in you," Angelica gushed at him, making them all laugh in understanding there was nothing behind her outrageous flirting with people in the club. She then became quieter. "But listen, let me introduce you to the smaller, easier things first," she said, leading him away with Samantha and Tony following behind.

Tom looked at things she picked up and showed him the use of, but he kept referring back to Samantha.

"Which of you is going to choose what's going to be used each time?" Angelica asked.

Tom was relieved the question had come up.

"Samantha is," he said. "I want her to tell me what she wants me to try on her. We'll work together to figure out what level of strike I'll use on her, that we'll both feel comfortable with."

"That's good," Angelica said. "It's easy to think that you can handle receiving or delivering the pain, but sometimes it can come as a surprise, being on either side of it. Working up to things slowly is a good approach. You two will be fine."

After a while, she and Tony left, and Samantha moved closer to him.

"Well, Miss Cute Butt, which is it going to be to start with?" Tom asked.

Samantha looked at the range of items along a wall set up with racks and displays, and picked a crop first.

"You've used this before," she said and saw him nod. "Will you try this on me?"

Tom took a deep breath and took the item from her.

"Okay," he breathed out slowly.

They found their spot among the growing crowd, and Tom watched her, taking her as the lead even though he knew he was supposed to be. Being in the role she wanted him to be in went against who he, was with regard to how he preferred to treat women, but she was his friend and she knew what she wanted. That was all he had to keep telling himself. She was his friend, and she knew what she wanted.

Samantha suddenly felt shy. It had been different with Scott as he'd introduced her to the club. With Tom, it was more a case of Tom being Tom - her friend. Since she had suggested it, she would keep moving forward with their plan, even though she knew Tom would happily walk out with her any time she wanted that.

Tom watched her as she moved over to a steady surface to lean against, and then turned to him.

"Before I pull my skirt up, will you try it here to see how it feels at this angle?" she asked.

Tom blinked in surprise at what she'd asked. His focus was naturally on the aspect of her pulling her skirt up. He had to realign his mind to change his focus to her request for him to try and strike her as she stood before him. As he focused on the question, he nodded at her and watched her move so she was supported properly. With her body angled so that her rear was to him, she looked sideways at him and nodded at him.

"I'm ready, Tom," she said.

Tom looked at her with such a mixture of feelings that he found it quite overwhelming. Looking into her eyes and seeing her desire, he roused himself to move forward with her request.

Getting his stance set up, he brought the crop around and struck her buttocks with it through her clothing. He watched her face to try and read anything, but she only looked eager for it to happen again.

After a handful of tries, and her feeling his confidence growing in it, Samantha spoke again.

"I'm going to pull this up, Tom. Don't worry, I have full cover underwear on, and that is staying on!" she said.

Tom knew she was only teasing him, but he found himself wanting to groan at images running through his head. He watched as she slid her skirt up so that it was bunched around her waist, and she stood before him. She had full briefs on so nothing was visible, but it was still enough to arouse him.

Samantha saw it in his jeans, but looked away from him to let him have his privacy. Sometimes in their friendship, things could be teased about, but she didn't want to tease her good friend about that.

"Do it," he heard her say.

He instantly repeated the action with his hand and crop, hearing the difference as it struck the flimsy cotton. He looked at her face and saw a smile, so repeated the action. With every strike that was a little stronger, her smile grew, and he could see her lips part as if she were in deep arousal. He thought she probably had chosen the underwear as they were safe, being plain, full and cotton, but with them being light in colour, the more he struck her, the more evident he could see them starting to show some wetness. It was a discovery that only aroused him even more.

Inside, he felt like he was in heaven, looking at her like that. At the same time, he also felt like he was being some kind of freak for enjoying looking at his best friend in that way. He could feel straining in his jeans, and desperately wished for that to go away, but could only concentrate on her at that moment. The option of thinking about anything else just didn't seem possible.

That night, they only stayed an hour or so, using only the crop. They went through the motions a small number of times until Samantha said she didn't want any more. At those words, Tom felt relief, although he was still highly aroused and hoped that would fade soon enough once they got out of there.

~~~~~

In the following months, they kept going, and slowly they found their flow. They figured out what she liked and how much he could handle, delivering to her in his strikes. Always he got aroused, watching her as her face revealed so much about what she was feeling. He didn't understand it, but he did believe she was gaining something from it, and wasn't being hurt by it.

One night, when in the club, Samantha felt enough courage to remove her skirt altogether and stand in only a corset, stockings, garter belt, and briefs. Slowly but surely she was becoming more confident, and building up her comfort in wearing less and less, although the most private parts of her body she kept covered. Those areas weren't for everyone or anyone to see yet. No matter how much she was around all the people in the club who were so comfortable with nudity - no matter how comfortable she was finding she could be *around* their nudity - she had no desire or intention to put herself on display like they did. She was glad that Tom seemed reluctant to see her like that also. She knew he got
~~~~~

aroused when in the club, but not once did he ever try to act on it in any way. If anything, he seemed embarrassed about it, as if he wished his body wouldn't react in such a way.

As he watched her strip down to the corset set she had recently bought, Tom felt himself wondering how much more he could take, seeing her like that week after week. She was his friend, and he wasn't allowed to have certain feelings about her, but even holding onto the 'she's just a friend' insistence in his mind, when he saw her that night, he couldn't seem to stop his body acting like it did. He knew he was in a fortunate position to be able to keep his clothing on since other men in his position in the club eventually wore very little.

When she stripped down, Tom immediately felt like someone had turned the heat up in the room, and found himself sweating. He tried to ignore it for as long as he could, but eventually knew he had to take a breather. He just had to, even before he could pick up the whip she wanted him to try that night.

"Wait a minute, Samantha," she heard him say.

She watched as he turned and stepped away from her for a minute, as if to take a deep breath. When he turned back, he seemed to have found some resolve to move forward, but not before he peeled off his t-shirt to let out some of the heat inside of him. He stood in front of her in only his jeans. It was a sight she'd seen periodically throughout all of their lives, but she couldn't help but acknowledge that his body was changing. Without her even having realised, his body had moved from being the scrawny, skinny thing it had always been, to muscular and toned.

Tom didn't notice how she was looking at him at all. All he could focus on was the whip he'd picked up and was holding. He was determined to not look at her too much in the state she was in. If it did, he'd be rethinking their friendship status, and he couldn't do that.

To keep his mind off her, he put his effort into trying to get the whip to work. She watched him as he tried to flick it this way and that.

"How do I use this thing?" he finally asked no-one in particular, slight frustration becoming evident in his voice.

As if already having been watching him, Angelica approached him.

"Let me help you with that, Tom," she said, unintentionally eyeing up his torso as if he were a perfectly cooked steak. She gave him a look that was completely missed by Tom, but not by Samantha. She saw exactly how her best friend was being looked at.

Tom handed Angelica the whip. Between the two of them, he slowly managed to get it to crack as it needed to for the purpose it was about to be used for.

"Samantha, are you ready?" Angelica asked.

Samantha nodded. She was confused by feelings that she suddenly felt must only be jealousy.

Getting her head back into it, she moved down to the ground on all fours and waited as Angelica showed Tom the angles that she found easiest to use the item. Soon Samantha found herself in that place again, where she felt a sting on her skin that to her was an extreme pleasure and left her wanting more.

Tom thanked Angelica and hardly noticed her move away. Even with her wearing outfits that were designed to openly reveal her breasts, over time Tom seemed to have become immune to the power of the image. For all he noticed her body, she may as well have been fully clothed in jeans and thick jersey, topped off with a ski jacket.

As the evening really began, Tom focused on giving Samantha what she desperately seemed to want. Needing to concentrate so much on using the whip and getting it to work well, his focus was less on her and more on the action. He found that to be a very welcome distraction from looking at her body as a whole, instead focusing on getting the whip to hit the one small spot that she wanted it to.

When she called out to him later to say she had reached her limit, Tom was relieved. He eagerly turned away from her to put on his t-shirt. He didn't want to look at her as she put her clothes on. He'd often been eager to get out of the club due to extreme arousal, but that night was another degree altogether. That night, he found himself almost wanting to run from it and never look back.

~~~~~

Sitting in his car as they left the club that night, Tom and Samantha both found their individual minds working overtime. As such, nothing was said as he drove her home. When he pulled up outside her place, he turned to her, hoping he looked like he usually did in their simple friendship mode.

Samantha turned also to look at him, aware that something was starting to feel different inside of her, but not wanting to feel it at all. She leaned in toward him and kissed his cheek before saying a simple 'goodnight' and then climbing out.

~~~~~

That night as he lay in bed, Tom tried hard to file away the images in his head. It had been odd enough for him at the start of their club visits, having to see so many other bodies in the room. Over time, he had grown to accept nudity and the different acts that occasionally would occur right before his eyes. All of the things he had witnessed hadn't made him any more eager to become sexual himself. If anything, it had reinforced his resolve to wait and make that something special with one person, and not be so easy about it.

But seeing Samantha in certain ways - even without her ever being naked or revealing as much as the other women in the club - was another challenge altogether.

CHAPTER 7

The Growth of Two Souls

"Tom," his manager said to him as he called him into his office within the supermarket.

Tom walked into the office, feeling like he was about to be reprimanded for something, even though he couldn't think what he might have done. He worked pretty steadily on checkout, and as far as he knew, he was always polite to customers.

"Sit down, please," his manager said with a no-nonsense tone that alarmed Tom even more. "I've had some reports from customers," he continued, making Tom gulp in fear, but then the man before him smiled brilliantly. "And they are all very impressive. You've been here for a long time now, Tom, and I would like to offer you a supervisory position. How would you feel about taking on such a role?"

Tom was stunned, realising at that moment how close he'd just been to wondering if he was going to be fired.

"I can see your surprise, but you know the checkout processes inside out now. I think you would do well as a checkout supervisor, providing guidance and training to new checkout operators as we employ them, while generally keeping the checkout area flowing smoothly."

Tom heard the words and finally felt a warmth grow inside of him.

"Thank you, Sir," he said. "I am surprised but thankful that you consider me able to do a job like that."

"You sound like you want to turn down the opportunity," his manager said.

"No!" Tom said as he smiled. "No, thank you, Sir. I would be very eager to take on such a roll whenever you feel I'm ready."

"Good, because I think you're ready now," his manager said. "So if you agree to take on this position, with the increased responsibility, I would like you to start tomorrow. Kathy, your current supervisor, is rostered on tomorrow from 10am, and she has agreed to train you. So go home now, and come back for a 10am shift tomorrow. I'll liaise with HR, and they'll contact you with your new pay rate as well."

"Thank you!" Tom said, instantly recognising that he was being dismissed, as if that was his time up with his manager.

He walked out of the office, maintaining his composure. As soon as he was clear, a broad smile graced his face as the feeling of excitement flowed over him.

With it being later in the afternoon, and knowing Samantha would be finished with her course for the day and soon going home, he went to his apartment just long enough to shower and change. He then went to her home. In his life, he hadn't often just turned up at her house, but he had something to share with her.

As he approached the driveway, he saw her also making her way there.

"Tom," Samantha said as she ran to him and let him embrace her. "What are you doing here?" she went on to ask as she put her key in the door and let them both in.

"I wanted to share some news with you. I got a promotion today!"

Samantha almost fell over from the level of excitement coming off him. Tom was many things, but it wasn't often that he exuded such energy about anything that happened in his own life.

Tom welcomed her arms around him. She jumped at him and hugged him, giving him a big sloppy kiss on his cheek, and making him laugh in the process.

"Oh my gosh, that is so exciting! Come with me up to my room so I can get changed and you can tell me all about it," she said.

The words suddenly made Tom shy and stop walking.

Samantha turned, looked at him, and gave him one of her classic looks of fond frustration.

"Tom, you aren't afraid to come to my bedroom, are you? After all the hours that I've spent in yours?"

He looked at her face and saw her eyebrows go high, knowing she was teasing him. Logically, he knew she was right. If they were both in his bedroom, or both in her bedroom, what did it matter?

Samantha saw him take a deep breath and finally start following her. He took her hand as she held it out for him, as if to help him across a horrific gap he was fearful of.

When they walked into her bedroom, Tom was reminded of so many memories from their childhood. In recent years, he hadn't stepped foot in there, with her most often visiting him rather than the other way around. As he entered the room, he felt a fond calm flow over him.

Samantha watched his face as he walked around, first looking at her bookcase, still with so many children's books that they'd once fought over to read. Next to that was her large wooden toy box that her father had made for her one year as a birthday gift. Tom remembered being jealous that she had something so big, because having such a big toy box must mean that she would have many more toys than he ever would. He could almost see the memories vividly in his head, like watching a movie rolling behind his eyes. He laughed softly as he felt a sliver of emotion pass over him.

Samantha left him for a moment and quickly changed as his back was to her. No other man would she trust with such a move, but she knew him. She knew that even if he happened to turn around by accident, he would quickly look away again and give her privacy. It was just the kind of person he was.

Tom could sense what she was doing so kept looking at things while facing away from her. Her toys, her dolls, her books, her large dollhouse - everything was so like it had been when they'd been kids, he was quite blown away by it. One difference was that one wall had been converted into a large pinboard. On it, were dozens of sketches of clothing. Tom stood before it and just looked.

"Samantha…" he seemed to breathe out as he looked at the images before him. "These drawings … your designs … they are amazing. *You* are amazing."

Samantha looked at him, but instead of moving toward him, sat down on her bed and waited for him to look back at her.

When Tom turned around, he saw her on her bed, and noticed the oversized teddy bear beside her. He laughed as he walked to the bed and climbed up on the mattress. Sitting beside her, he grabbed the bear in his hands before hugging it to him.

"My fuzzy," he said.

Samantha laughed out loud at the sudden memory of him doing that often when he'd visit her home when they were little.

After sharing a laugh with her, Tom continued to hold the bear but grew serious once more.

"You really do have amazing talent," he said. "Those sketches are phenomenal. I'm sorry. I thought you'd be good, but I really didn't know you were *that* good."

Samantha felt herself blush suddenly, looking from him to the designs and then back to him again.

"It's nice having you here again, Tom. You've always been there for me when I've needed you, either at your family home or your apartment, but it feels good to have you here, in this room with me," she said, reaching out and taking his hand in hers.

Tom let the action happen and revelled in her words, but didn't want to take the moment too seriously.

"Your room is just the same as I remember it," he said. "It's amazing that you've been able to keep it like this while you've grown so much as a person. So many people would throw special things like all of this out, but you are just so amazing. I really am in awe of you, Samantha Young."

"Well, now I am in awe of you!" Samantha said. "Getting a promotion

- wow! What will that entail, exactly?"

"Well, as of tomorrow, I am going be undergoing some training to become a checkout supervisor, so I'll be supervising all the checkout operators," he said with a shy look on his face. "Not a dream job, I know…"

"Why do you keep saying that?"

"What?"

"Ever since we were leaving high school, you've been saying that your job at the supermarket isn't a dream job, but you are happy there, aren't you?"

"Yeah, of course I am," Tom said. "The people - the staff and the customers - are all incredible."

"Then why say it isn't a dream job? You enjoy it. That is much more than many other people ever say about the job they do. Tom, you are an incredible worker, and your bosses must see that. That's why they're promoting you. Please don't insinuate that it's a nothing job. You are doing great, and you're being recognised for that," she said, watching his face as he seemed to intently look at her in return. "Be proud!" she added as she finished with a now-traditional jab onto his arm.

Tom was silenced by her speech for a few minutes before he roused himself to respond.

"Thank you," he said.

"You are welcome. Now give me my fuzzy," Samantha said as she held out both hands.

Tom held the bear tighter to him, laughing softly and with affection toward her.

"No," he said with mock seriousness. "He wants to come home with me."

Samantha laughed loudly at him, remembering the same argument from many times over the years.

"You are crazy," he heard her say as she gave up trying to get her bear back. She instead lay down along the length of the bed, on her back, looking at the ceiling. "I still love this room. I know that we're all supposed to want to grow up, but I don't want to rush to be an adult. I'm just not ready for so many things."

As she spoke, Tom looked down at her face from his position sitting up beside her. Silently, he wondered how many people got to grow up like the two of them had, knowing each other from so young, and still growing together as they moved into adulthood.

"Well, there are good things about adulthood too," he said.

Samantha looked at him. If he was any other guy, she knew she'd expect a macho remark about sex to follow. With him, she knew it was highly unlikely that Tom would do that. Other guys, yes. Tom, no.

"I like living in my apartment, having my own space," Tom continued. "Not that my mother ever made me feel claustrophobic, but it is nice to have a space that's just mine to do what I want with. And I do like working. You are right. I shouldn't demean what I do at all, because I do love it, and that does make me pretty lucky."

"Not to mention the sights you get to see at the club your best friend takes you to," Samantha added, making him laugh out loud.

"Yes! What would my life be like without seeing those! Especially Tony and Angelica!"

Samantha laughed but realised the moment had finally arrived where she could naturally ask him something that she'd wanted to since they'd started going to the club together.

"When you look at Angelica, doesn't it … you know?" she asked.

"Quit with the 'you know's, Samantha," Tom said with affection. "*You* know that I hate when you say 'you know'. When I look at Angelica, doesn't it what?"

Still looking at her face, he saw a slight blush appear over it before she finally seemed to find the courage to speak quietly.

"You know - turn you on," she said.

"Oh!" Tom said, feeling a small amount of amusement at her question.

"I mean, she never has her chest covered. Does it affect you?"

"Samantha, when we're there, there are lots of people who aren't wearing much…"

"I know, but she seems to pay particular attention to you," Samantha said.

Tom considered that. It confused him as he didn't think that was true, but it seemed to be an irrelevant viewpoint with regards to her original question, so he disregarded it.

"I think when we first went, I was more shocked by what everyone was doing, rather than turned on," he said. "I don't really notice it now."

"But how can you *not* notice it?"

"Well, do you get turned, on looking at the men in the club? Tony?" he asked.

Samantha burst out laughing, making him smile.

"Eww! No!"

"Well, there you go then," said Tom. "What's the difference?"

"Tony doesn't look at me the way that Angelica looks at you."

Tom was confused by her statement, and Samantha could see it on his face.

"I don't know what you're talking about," he said. "We're all there for the same thing. Other people are just taking the sex side of things to different degrees, that's all. I don't think anyone is looking at anyone outside of their own partner, to be honest."

"But you *do* get turned on, Tom," she said and instantly saw a different look on his face, as if he'd been caught out doing something naughty.

They looked at each other. Samantha wanted to know who it was that affected him so much, so often. Tom wanted to not say anything at that point.

"Tom."

"What?"

"Do you get turned on when Angelica approaches you or is nearby?" Samantha asked.

"No, I don't get turned on by Angelica," Tom honestly replied.

"Then, who? I know that you *do* get aroused. I've seen it."

Tom felt his face go extremely red. He wished he hadn't rushed over to her house to tell her his news after all.

"Please stop, Samantha," he said as he stood up in natural reaction to want to leave.

"Why?" she asked, knowing full well she was riling him up, but not stopping herself regardless.

Suddenly he looked at her with a look that almost emanated anger. It was an emotion that she'd rarely seen on his face in their entire lifetime together to date.

"Because you won't like the answer!" he said, his voice full of passion and power. "You are asking this question, but you know as well as I do that it's a question that if I give you an answer to, you aren't going to want to have heard it. And then you'll do that thing where you take yourself off and not talk to me for however long, like you're punishing *me* even though it was *you* who pushed me to say it," he said to her loudly.

Samantha was surprised into silence. Although he then toned his voice down slightly, she could still hear the emotion in it.

"You have to stop asking me questions that you really don't want the answer to," he said. "Just stop."

Samantha watched as he all of a sudden seemed to deflate. It appeared as if he'd said all that he could, and now he was prepared for something to happen from the words he had spoken.

"I have to go," he said quietly and made for the door.

"Tom!" she called out but his mind was obviously made up. She watched as he walked out and closed the door behind him.

Samantha sat on her bed once more, and felt tears come to her eyes. She suddenly felt incredibly angry at herself. He was right. She had known what she was doing, and in her heart, of course she knew the answer to the question. She'd wanted to bait him, as she had done hundreds of times before over their long friendship, and it wasn't fair that she had done it. It wasn't fair any time that she did it, and especially over something so personal.

She lay down and hugged the large bear close to her, regretting how she had just treated her best friend yet again.

~~~~~

Tom marched out of her house, full of anguish and embarrassment. He knew that she'd known how aroused he got when they went to the club, but to hear her bring it up in conversation was beyond what he could handle. He was well used to her doing things like that - picking a subject that she knew would affect him so much - but that was the most personal thing she'd used to upset him about.

As he walked away from her home, he felt his mood quieten, and his body relax. He cursed himself inwardly for his body being so reactive to everything. It wasn't as if he *wanted* to be turned on when he was around his closest friend. She must have known that. Why did she have to bring it up and taunt him with it as heavily as she had?

Entering his apartment, he knew he had to push thoughts of her aside. The following day, he would be beginning training for his new position in the supermarket, and he couldn't - wouldn't - be distracted by her. Their friendship would weather the uncomfortable moment, as it did everything else, but for the first time in as long as he could remember, he found himself making the decision to actually take a break from seeing Samantha. She had done it many times during their friendship, but he knew it was time for *him* to take a break from *her*. If he didn't, damage would be done, and he knew it was only a matter of time before even small amounts of temporary damage in their friendship might become permanent. He couldn't help that happen. Breaks were one thing. The thought of losing her as his friend forever was something completely different. It was something he couldn't even let himself ponder, the idea hurt so much.

~~~~~

The next day, Tom began a new stage in his life as a checkout supervisor. He was determined to work as hard as he could in whatever he did, and to treat people as best he could. He easily fitted in to the role, finding pleasure in assurances from his manager and other staff that he was going to be just fine in a supervisory capacity, with his easy-going nature but advanced knowledge about the systems.

He didn't contact Samantha in the following weeks, nor did she contact him. He was okay with that. He missed her, but knew that sometimes, in order for them to remain friends, they had to have time apart. It was always a lonely time for him, but he would endure it, just as he always had. Having the new job to help occupy his mind was his saviour for the moment.

~~~~~

A few weeks into his new position, Tom was setting up tills for an upcoming shift changeover when his manager approached him with a young woman at his side.

"Tom, this is Alexis. She has worked on checkouts in another supermarket before, and has come in today, asking if we can offer her two days of work experience. If things go well, we could have her taking over Tina's role when she goes off for her maternity leave," he said and saw Tom nod. "Can you please show Alexis around, and arrange the hours she'll work over the next few days?"

When the manager moved away, Tom looked at the young woman.

"Alexis. Nice name! I'm Tom," he said as he wrapped up his till count and held his hand out to her.

Alexis slowly and reluctantly touched and shook his hand, still feeling untrusting of people in general even though it had now been a while since she had run from Melbourne and from Lincoln.

From that moment, Tom recognised that she was someone who had secrets, and he suspected that some of them were not good. He didn't push her for any personal details, and over time, the two of them slowly formed a friendship as she was offered full-time employment in the supermarket.

~~~~~

Samantha let a month pass before she contacted him. She felt guilty about having treated him so badly, and she knew from his absence in her life that she'd hurt him. Regardless, she gave him space while she put her head down and focused on her learning. She used her frustration in herself to create more designs, some of which were becoming extremely intricate, and starting to attract the attention of her class tutors.

"I think someone is going to be passing this course with the title of Best Student," her friend Emma teased her at lunch one day.

Samantha smiled at her friend, used to the remark that Emma delivered often.

"Well, I suppose someone has to, but we don't know who that person is yet, do we?" Samantha retorted.

Emma laughed at her.

"You'll get it, I'm sure," she said. "Your drawings are incredible, Samantha. I mean we're all doing okay, but you're in another league altogether."

Samantha remained quiet, her mind wandering back to Tom, as it often did when she wasn't caught up in designing or studying.

"What's on your mind?" Emma asked. "You are always so thoughtful at lunchtimes these days, girl!"

"I argued with a friend of mine last month, and I miss him," Samantha said.

"Then call him and tell him that."

Samantha looked at her in surprise.

"You reckon? You were the one who said we should walk away from people, when I was talking about breaking up with Scott."

"Oh, boyfriends are different," said Emma. "Throw them away whenever you can, I say. No, friends are always important. If this guy is someone you truly do value as a good friend, make the effort. Life is too short to let the good people slip away, and the more time that passes, the harder it is to make it up to people."

That day, after she finished her course hours, Samantha walked into the supermarket and looked around for Tom.

"Can I help you?" a young woman asked her, and pointed out where Tom was when Samantha told her she wanted to see him.

Samantha walked toward the area she had been directed to, and finally, he came into view. He was talking to someone but seemed to just see her out of the corner of his eye. Instead of smiling at her, he moved so he was between her and the person he was talking to, with his back toward her.

Instantly Samantha felt a tear come to her eye as she regarded the action as a shun. She saw it as a way for him to tell her that he didn't want to see her. He didn't want to know her. The thought was incredibly sad for her, but she accepted it and turned away to return home.

~~~~~

Tom saw her in his peripheral vision. His heart instantly began beating too loudly for him to be able to concentrate on what his manager was saying to him. He had to manoeuvre himself so he couldn't see Samantha anymore. He knew the conversation he was taking part in would only go for another minute or so, so he just had to hold his concentration for that long, giving his manager his full attention until he could get away.

As the conversation wrapped up, he looked again to the area where Samantha had stood. She was no longer there. Panicked, he walked as fast as he dared without attracting too much attention, and made for the front door of the supermarket.

Outside, he saw her walking along the peripheral edge of the car park.

"Samantha! Wait!" he called out and saw her stop before slowly turning to look at him.

He ran to her. As he got closer, he could see the redness of her eyes and the fresh tears.

"What?" he automatically asked her, instantly worried that something serious had happened to her. "What has happened to make you cry so
~~~~~

much?"

Samantha looked at him, not at all surprised at his caring tone and concern for her. She looked up into his face and couldn't stop a heavy and very audible sob from coming out as she tried to articulate words.

"I upset my best friend and now … I … I miss him so much," she said.

Straight away, she saw his face change from concern to a smile before he leaned in and pulled her tightly into his arms, kissing her forehead softly.

"Oh, you silly Samantha," he said, feeling a tear threaten in his own eyes. "I'm right here. I've missed you too."

They held each other for a long time until he felt her body move from being rigid with the occasional sob passing through it, to finally relaxing against him. When she pulled away from him, he looked into her eyes and saw the most regret he'd ever seen on her face.

"I'm sorry, Tom," Samantha said. "I was being a cow, and not thinking about how much it might hurt you when I was asking you those questions."

"You were winding me up, I know," Tom said, nodding. "And usually, I can overlook it as a joke, but some things are too personal for me, Samantha. There are some lines that we just can't cross in our banter. I can't stand being put in those situations with you."

"I know," she replied. "I'm sorry. I won't do it again."

"Yes, you will," he said but with affection in his voice. "But it's okay. Let's just put this behind us, please. I've missed my best friend too."

They held each other for a while longer before he pulled away. In doing so, she felt his hand move up to lightly touch the side of her cheek and push a stray hair from her face.

"I have to get back to work," he said with some reluctance noticeable in his voice.

Samantha nodded and smiled sadly at him.

"It's Saturday tomorrow. Pancakes?" he asked.

She laughed softly, finally starting to feel relaxed.

"Yes, please," she said quietly.

Tom leaned in once more to kiss her on her forehead before smiling and walking back toward the supermarket doors.

~~~~~

The next morning, when Tom heard his apartment buzzer sound, he reluctantly drew himself out of bed and headed to the door. When he opened it, he saw Samantha looking extremely shy and uncertain. He opened the door wider and welcomed her in, not thinking anything of his attire.

Samantha saw him in the doorway in just boxer shorts, and was again
~~~~~

reminded of how much his body had changed over recent years. She didn't want to look at him like she knew she was, but her eyes were drawn to his chest, shoulders and arms.

"Come in," she heard him say. The words were enough to draw her attention back to his face. She felt embarrassed by her blatancy in having looked at him in such a way, but he seemed completely oblivious to it.

"I just need to have a shower before we go," Tom said and then looked at her more closely. "Are you alright?"

Samantha nodded at him, focusing on his face out of fear of what looking at his body was doing to her. Even in the club, when he'd taken off his t-shirt, she'd been stunned by his body. At least he'd been wearing jeans then. Seeing his upper torso and his legs as well did start to affect her. She made sure not to let her eyes fall to his boxer shorts. Thoughts passed through her head quickly, but they were enough for her to feel a slight blush move over her cheeks. As usual, Tom appeared oblivious to her reaction to him, as he was to any woman who reacted to him.

"Okay. Make yourself at home, and I'll be back in a few minutes," he called out as he walked away from her, presenting her with a solid view of his back … and down.

Tom was still somewhat sleepy as he climbed into the shower. For him, it was easy to shower, dress, and then get back to her without really thinking much at all.

But while Samantha sat on his sofa, waiting, she had to proactively stop her thoughts from venturing where she knew they mustn't. By the time he returned, fully dressed in jeans and a well fitted long sleeve t-shirt, she appeared completely normal.

"Shall we go?" he asked her.

Samantha nodded, smiling at him as if her mind had been completely blank for the previous twenty minutes.

~~~~~

Over their regular 'dining out' food of pancakes, they resumed talking as if nothing had happened between them.

"I am enjoying supervising the other checkout operators, and we have a couple of new staff members, so I've been helping them to settle in," Tom said. "I'm actually really enjoying being in this supervisor role. I didn't know if I would, but I am."

Samantha smiled at him, happy that she'd taken the time to visit him the night before in an attempt to resurrect their spending time together again.

"I'm glad you're enjoying it," she said. "And of course you're good at being a supervisor. You're good with people, so why wouldn't you be?"

Tom looked at her, glad she was before him once more, even though their recent time apart had been his doing. He was happy to be with her
~~~~~

again, but knew he had needed them to have a break from one another.

"Thank you."

From that moment on, life seemed to settle back into normality for both of them, that feeling of something missing finally disappearing once they relaxed fully around each other once more. Talking was back to normal. Hanging out in his apartment was back to normal. Attending the club was back to normal - not any easier, particularly for him, but certainly back to normal.

~~~~~

Tom continued to grow in his new role as checkout supervisor in the supermarket, and he was enjoying interacting with other staff on a different level. One day, he gave Alexis a ride to the bank after work, during which she saw his whip and flogger in the back seat. They were things Samantha had suggested they buy so he could practise using them on her in his apartment as well as at the club.

When Alexis freaked out, Tom was initially angry at himself that he'd left such things out in the open. Moving past his discomfort, he found he was more curious about her reaction to them. The conversation that followed secured another stage in them moving toward forming a mutually respectful and trustworthy friendship. She had something in her past that was intriguing to him, and she seemed equally intrigued about the club that he went to with Samantha, and the things they did there.

Inviting her to his place for dinner and introducing her to Samantha was the natural next and final stage in them securing each other as good friends. He could see that Samantha took to her instantly. That reassured him in his assessment of Alexis as a friend who would become someone very special in their lives.

~~~~~

Samantha had never been a girl who had lots of female friends. A few of them had continued to remain in the outskirts of her life after their high school years. As she'd left school behind, although she'd met plenty of other women on her design course, Tom was always the only person she truly regarded as a great friend.

When she met Alexis, she felt different, maybe because of the experiences Alexis had gone through. Although Alexis never gave full details about her experiences, she'd said enough for Samantha to know she'd been left somewhat traumatised by her time with whoever the man had been, and it had been due to the constant delivering of pain to him. The concept struck a nerve with Samantha, especially with Tom being in that position with her. It prompted many conversations between the girls that offered Samantha a different viewpoint to things that she and Tom did.

~~~~~
~~~~~

"Tom, Samantha, this is Anthony," Alexis said to them one weekend when the four of them went out to dinner at a restaurant together.

Tom immediately gave the stranger a once over and then caught himself out in surprise of himself for doing so. Something about Alexis made him feel protective over her. As the evening wore on, all Tom could see about the relationship between Alexis and her man was that it was mutually respectful. Tom found himself slightly jealous of it. Sitting across from them, watching the way they looked at each other, he couldn't help but yearn for that kind of relationship himself. He quietly wondered if it would ever happen to him.

Samantha also watched the couple and found herself wistful. Not only were they such a stunning couple to look at, but there was something very loving about their manner with each other. Even with all the teasing they gave each other - the laughter, the jokes, the quiet quips and jabs at one another - none of those things could hide the level of love on display. It affected her, as it was also affecting the man next to her.

Neither knew the other felt exactly the same.

~~~~~

"Thank you for putting the time aside to have dinner with me and Anthony the other night, Tom," Alexis said to him at work the next workday they were on together.

Tom looked at her, still finding himself thoughtful about so many things to do with her. Sometimes it felt like she was someone who had come into his life for a reason, although if that were the case, he had no idea what the reason could be.

Alexis saw him smile at her shyly.

"It was a pleasure to meet Anthony, Alexis. You two are … inspirational … to look at really," he answered with a tone of sadness in his voice.

"Inspirational? Explain," she pushed him to see how he would expand on the sentence. In response, she saw him blush a small amount.

"I just … I guess I just felt a little bit jealous really," Tom said, being honest but knowing he could sound like an idiot for saying such a thing. When he looked at her face, he only saw surprise. "I sometimes wonder if I'll ever find someone who'll love me, Alexis. When I was looking at you two, seeing the way you are around each other - even just the way that you look at each other - I don't know. A part of me wishes I could find that."

Alexis smiled at him and moved closer to talk to him more quietly.

"Are you sure you haven't already found it?" she asked and then smiled at him again before they were approached by the manager so ended the conversation.

Her question stayed with him for the rest of the day.
~~~~~

~~~~~

"When we were in Melbourne at the weekend, he asked me to marry him, and I've said yes!" Alexis said to Samantha and Tom one night over a dinner they were enjoying in Tom's apartment.

Samantha immediately jumped up and hugged her.

"Oh, Alexis! I'm so happy for you!"

Tom stood and moved to hug her as he kissed her cheek.

"Thank you," Alexis said, still feeling the warmth from the time she'd spent in Melbourne with Anthony, and the moment of his proposal.

She turned to Samantha and took her hands.

"But Samantha, I need a wedding dress and I would be honoured if you would design and make it if you have the time."

"Me? Oh, but it's such a special day for you…"

"Yes, it is," said Alexis. "That's exactly why I want you to design and make the dress for me."

"But I'm still only learning…"

"Can you sew anything that you've designed?" Alexis asked, knowing full well that Samantha had been making her own clothing for ages.

"Yes…"

"Right then, let me give you a rule of customer service, that I have no doubt Tom will agree with," she said, looking to him for support. "That being that the customer is always right. What they want, they should get, and what I want is for you to design and make me a dress. It doesn't have to be fluffy and grand with a one-mile train or any of that rubbish. I want a dress that I can wear on the day, knowing it is original and simple, but I could also wear again to whatever fancy occasion may present itself in the future. I don't know - going to the opera or something."

Samantha heard the spiel and then smiled.

"Alright," she said. "But you'll give me input into the design sketches, and you'll come with me to buy the fabric so you definitely have what you want."

"Agreed," Alexis said and hugged Samantha. "Oh, thank you!"

~~~~~

A month later, the dress design was finalised, and the girls headed off to search for the perfect fabric. Walking into the large fabric outlet store, Alexis felt overwhelmed. At the same time, Samantha felt like she was in heaven, being surrounded by such a wide plethora of textures and colours.

"Oh, that's it, Samantha," Alexis exclaimed after they'd been walking primarily in the wedding fabric aisle of so many shades of white and cream.

Samantha turned and followed the eye line of her friend. She thought she must be missing whatever Alexis as looking at, given that there was nothing either white or cream in front of them.

"What?" she asked.

"There!" Alexis said, pointing forward and then moving forward and taking a piece of fabric in her hands to feel it. "Here."

"But Alexis, that's ... green."

Alexis laughed at Samantha.

"I don't care," she said. "My wedding. My wedding dress. This is the fabric, Samantha. Everyone else can have their creams and whites, but this ... this is *my* fabric."

Samantha was stunned, but seeing the look on her friend's face, forced herself to relax and smile.

"You're right. Who says you have to wear the same colour everyone else wears on their wedding day?" she said and instantly touched the fabric herself. "It will work well with the design, and this colour is going to look amazing on you with your skin and hair colouring."

After shopping, the girls sat down for lunch in a nearby café.

"So, we are having the wedding at Anthony's house, as you know," Alexis said and saw Samantha nod in affirmation. "But we thought you and Tom might like to come down next weekend for a visit. What do you think?"

Samantha instantly considered the logistics of such a trek, one aspect in particular on her mind. Alexis, being as perceptive as she was, picked up on it.

"There's more than one spare room in Anthony's house, if that's what you're worried about," she said. "Will you talk to Tom about it and see what he thinks?"

~~~~~

Another week later, Tom and Samantha were on the train, travelling on their journey down to the town where Anthony lived.

"Are you okay?" she asked him, sensing his nervousness.

"Yeah, I'm just not used to this ... visiting ... thing," he replied. "I know we know Alexis and Anthony, but it feels strange to be going to stay in his house."

"I know, but they're having the wedding there, and we'll have to stay there for that weekend anyway," said Samantha. "At least this time you can have your own room. When the wedding's on, you and I are going to have to share..."

Tom looked at her sharply, the news being completely new to him.

"What?"

"Alexis didn't tell you?" Samantha asked and saw Tom shake his head. "They're having a few people to stay, so you and I will be in one room."

Tom was quiet, trying desperately to not think about the possibility of
~~~~~

sleeping close to her.

"What's worrying you about it? I've seen your undies heaps of times…" Samantha said cheekily and immediately received a less-often-felt punch on her arm. "It'll be okay. You'll be quite safe, I assure you."

Tom had to smile at her, knowing that it was important for them to be at the wedding, so he wouldn't mention anything to Alexis. After all, it wasn't her fault how he felt about Samantha. She had no way of knowing how much torment could come to him, sleeping in the same room and the same bed as her.

~~~~~

"Oh my holy cow, what an amazing home, Anthony!" Samantha exclaimed as soon as the homestead came into view. The four of them had walked up from the train station, where Alexis and Anthony had met Tom and Samantha off the train.

Anthony smiled at her and then looked at Alexis, who squeezed his hand in agreement. She felt exactly the same way about the house that would soon be her home.

When the four of them walked inside, Anthony showed Tom to his room as Alexis showed Samantha to hers.

"I've assumed you don't want to share," Alexis said quietly to Samantha as they walked into the room Alexis had used when she'd first met Anthony.

"You assumed right, even though I know you think it should be differently!" Samantha teased Alexis back, smiling. "But don't worry. The weekend of the wedding, Tom and I shall be good and share a room."

"Does he know about that?"

"Yeah, I told him on the way here," Samantha said, laughing softly.

"And his response? I am sure he'll be in heaven…"

Samantha laughed more loudly.

"He was embarrassed and a bit surprised, but he'll be okay," she said. "It will all be fine."

The two of them moved out of the bedroom and back to the living room, where Samantha's eyes fell immediately on the large photo hanging over the fireplace.

"Anthony! Is that you?" she asked, looking at him and seeing him blush as he smiled shyly and nodded. "Oh my gosh, that is amazing! But where did you get that done? It looks so professional."

Anthony looked at Alexis, a look passing between them that caused Samantha and Tom both to be curious.

Finally, it was Alexis that spoke.

"It was an early wedding gift from someone from my past," she said, silently begging Samantha to not ask any more questions.
~~~~~

Samantha picked up the cue and quickly stopped the automatic question that would have left her mouth then, from escaping.

"Well, Anthony, that is stunning. Quite a handsome lad in your baker's outfit, aren't you?" she said and then thought about what she'd said. She instantly backtracked a bit, making everyone laugh. "Not that you aren't a handsome lad *without* your baker's outfit, of course!"

Anthony laughed out loud at her, glad the moment had passed with a small amount of humour. Accepting the large photograph into his home had been difficult for him, knowing who had paid for it and sent it to them. Alexis had worked him until he acknowledged that it was a photo of him, not of the person who'd bought it - Lincoln Kokiri. While he didn't particularly need a photo of himself in his home, he knew it did make Alexis happy, so he'd let her convince him it should be hung with pride of place. He couldn't tell her that sometimes looking at it kept his memory alive with the one person from her past that he desperately wished they could both forget.

~~~~~

Tom felt out of his element in the situation, having never been a person who had lots of friends. Even as well as he knew Samantha, they hadn't had 'sleepovers' since they'd been very young as kids. Despite his initial discomfort, especially since he didn't feel he knew Anthony that well, he got through the afternoon and evening. He was confident he'd be fine getting through the wedding weekend also. It was just one more challenge that he could overcome, just as he had overcome so many in recent months.
~~~~~

CHAPTER 8

The Wedding

Present Day

Tom stood in the bathroom of Anthony's family homestead and looked at himself in the mirror as he prepared to collect the girls from the room they were readying themselves in. He never knew how others viewed him - particularly women, having not yet had a real relationship. Looking at himself in the mirror, clean-shaven and suitably groomed in the wedding suit he had on, he thought he looked okay. He didn't see a Prince Charming, but he equally didn't see an ogre. As far as he was concerned, he was just an average guy - nothing more, nothing less.

Finally, he was ready. He knocked on the bedroom he knew the groom had been forbidden from entering. When the door opened, and his view fell to the two women inside, his breath was stilled. It should, of course, have been the bride that caught his eye and made him breathless, but while he did acknowledge that Alexis did indeed look beautiful, it was the woman standing beside her - his lifelong best friend - that his eyes automatically went to. Samantha looked incredibly beautiful. He had to wonder yet again how she had come to be his friend when she was as stunning as she was.

Pushing unwelcome thoughts out of his head, he invited both women to join him so he could walk them out to the back door of the home. There, Samantha was handed over to John, a close friend of the groom.

Smiling proudly, Tom quietly led Alexis down the aisle through the garden, and silently smiled at Anthony as he moved her hand from his arm to that of her soon to be husband.

The vows were read, followed by a lengthy and indulgent kiss from the groom to his bride. The groom led his bride for a dance under the makeshift gazebo they'd all had fun erecting that morning.

Tom saw Samantha approach him and give him an eyebrows-up look and brilliant smile. It made his heartbeat speed up before he saw her move her head sideways as an indication to join her on the dance floor.

Instantly he moved forward toward her, very happy to be able to hold her in his arms. It felt like a magical moment, until she revealed her sometimes bossy and boisterous self.

"Hey! Stop hogging the dance floor," he heard her say as she nudged the bride and groom affectionately, making everyone laugh at her.

Tom looked closely at her face. She had been his friend for as long as he could remember, and had proved on many occasions that she was completely trustworthy and loyal to him. He valued that friendship above everything, no matter what his heart told him to do, and no matter what his heart told him things could be like. He wouldn't threaten their friendship. He couldn't.

Feeling eyes on him, he turned to see Alexis watching him with that same sad smile on her face. He'd grown used to it so shrugged it off with a silly face, as he always did to make her laugh and not think about the subject he knew she was thinking of. It was something that he couldn't think about, even though many people had asked him right through from their teenage years why he didn't make Samantha his girlfriend. As if anyone could *make* Samantha do anything. She was such a powerful person, Tom was fairly sure it would take a very definite kind of man to even be able to turn her head, let alone influence her in any way.

After a while, the photographer approached to lead Alexis and Anthony away for some photos, removing them from the crowd for an hour. The few people that were at the wedding hardly noticed they'd left, before the bride and groom were back again, taking part in their ceremony celebration once more.

They danced and eventually sang, but all through the evening was the sound of people laughing. Tom could see how happy his new friends, Alexis and Anthony, were in each other's company. The sight made him happy, but it also made him feel incredibly lonely. He knew he had choices. There had been times since his teenage years when he could have been in relationships, and he'd made a conscious decision not to be. But sometimes he equally felt desperation inside of him - an itch that he so much wanted to scratch.

~~~~~

Later into the night, Tom excused himself in need to be alone.

"Alexis, Anthony, I'm heading off to bed," he said, shaking Anthony's hand and kissing the cheek of Alexis.

They said their goodnights, and then he left the festivity and made his way to bed. It was the same bed Alexis had slept in many times, but that night, Tom and Samantha were sleeping in it. No-one questioned them being okay sleeping in the same bed. They had said they'd be alright doing so, and since it made it easy to house everyone in the homestead for the wedding, no-one tried to talk them out of it.

Tom lay in bed in his t-shirt and shorts, and thought about the day. He knew things had to change in his life. Nothing was wrong, but he didn't want to be alone forever. The loneliness unexpectedly and silently crept up on him as he felt a few tears begin slowly, followed by a flood. He was like that, trying to bury his face in his pillow, when he heard the
~~~~~

bedroom door open and then close again. That was followed by the feeling of weight on the other side of the bed. He remained still, not wanting to upset Samantha with his seriousness. He hoped she would believe him to be asleep. It was a silly thing to hope for. Samantha was accurately perceptive - that was one thing he loved so much about her.

"I know you aren't asleep, so don't even try to pretend you are," he heard her voice say.

"I wasn't pretending to be asleep," Tom muttered back, keeping his eyes out of her view.

He felt her get off the bed, and then heard her changing before she climbed under the covers, the weight on the mattress shifting once more.

"What's up?" she asked him softly from her far side of the bed.

"I'm fine. Just tired and needing sleep, I think."

"Tom, I saw you before you came in here. You weren't fine. Please turn over and talk to me."

Reluctantly, he turned but held his arm up so his eyes were covered. In usual Samantha style, he felt her hands pulling on that arm until he finally looked right at her. Samantha saw the redness of his eyes and immediately felt protective of him.

"Why have you been crying? I mean I know people say that everyone cries at weddings but…" she started to say, trying to lighten his mood. On seeing he wasn't in the mood for humour, she continued to speak more from her heart. "Tom, what is it?" she asked softly.

He turned on his other side so he could look directly at her, and saw her do the same. Facing each other, but with a large gap between them, he considered for a moment how that pretty much summed up their friendship. He always wanted to be on her side, but she was always just out of reach to him.

"I don't want to talk about this right now," he said. "Please don't ask me to. There are flow-on effects from things on my mind, and now isn't the right time for me to voice them."

"But whatever it is, it's upsetting you."

"Yes, but talking about it won't make it any better, and it could make things much worse. So please, not tonight."

Samantha looked at his face and knew not to press him.

"Okay," she said, worried but respecting his request.

It was the first time they'd slept in the same bed together for many years. Tom was very aware of her, but knew he couldn't be - wasn't *allowed* to be. He saw her lean over and turn off her bedside lamp, making the room go dark. Then he turned over to move to the very edge of the bed, and lay still, hoping she would fall asleep quickly without hearing the heavy thumping of his heart.

CHAPTER 9

The Declaration

Tom woke up the next morning, feeling the extreme tiredness that came from lying awake well into the night. He'd heard the moment that Samantha drifted off to sleep, and found listening to her breathing to be comforting to him, despite his emotions having been extremely alert and busy inside of his mind.

"Good morning," he heard the voice beside him say, startling him. He turned over to see Samantha lying where she had the night before. She was still a distance away, and still lying on her side, watching him. "I've been waiting for you to wake up," she said quietly, almost as a whisper.

Tom watched her face before speaking. Even waking first thing in the morning, she looked outstanding.

"Why?" he asked and saw her present a sad smile.

"Tom, you were upset last night," said Samantha. "I'm not going anywhere until you talk to me. Come on, let's have it. You've always been there for me when I've needed to talk. Now let me be there for you."

He took a deep breath and found conflict in his mind. If he told her how he felt and those feelings weren't welcome, the level of damage that could be placed on their friendship deeply concerned him.

"It isn't quite the same thing…"

"Well, why not?" she asked. "Why should it be different for you to share things with me, in the same way that I share things with you?"

"Because this is *about* you," he said and immediately saw a startled look on her face.

"Me? What did I do? I didn't think I drank that much…"

Tom looked at her, concern growing in his heart and his head.

"Samantha, you didn't do anything."

"This is worrying me," she said. "Please tell me what is on your mind."

She spoke at such a quiet and peaceful level that it felt extremely intimate to him. Finally, he took a deep breath and decided he had nothing to lose. All he could do was hope that if their friendship was strong enough, it would withstand his honesty.

"I don't know exactly at what point," he started, and watched her face as she intently began listening to him. "But somewhere along the way, my feelings for you have … changed."

Samantha heard the words and held her breath. Whatever it was that he had to say, she had prompted him to speak, so she couldn't tune out and ignore the words that might come.

"I'm sorry if they're not welcome, but Samantha…"

Suddenly he saw her hand go up and he immediately stopped speaking.

"Stop," she said. "If you are going to walk away from our friendship, I couldn't stand that, so take a minute before you do that, please Tom."

"What?" he asked, confused by where she had thought the conversation was going. "No, I wasn't going to say that! Why would I say that?"

"I know I can be annoying," she started to say.

Tom cut her off immediately with a 'don't give me that rubbish' look that she knew so well. She then remained quiet and encouraged him to keep speaking.

"I've never been with a woman, not for sex and not for … dating," he said. "I want you to know and understand that you are the reason for that."

"I've never stopped you from dating…"

"No, you misunderstand me," Tom continued. "*You* are the person I want to be with. I want you to be … more than my friend, Samantha. I want you to be the first person I … have sex with. I want you to be the first person … in everything."

He paused and let her absorb the words he was saying to her.

Samantha heard the words, but something wasn't quite registering with her. It couldn't be as he was saying. He had always been her friend. That was all he'd ever wanted them to be. She looked at him, the confusion evident on her face.

"I don't…" she started to say, but the words drifted off and she saw him look down and nod his head.

"I know," Tom said. "I know that you don't feel the same way. I get that, and I respect it, but I can't help how I feel. I've tried to hold back from saying anything because I don't want to risk losing your friendship…"

Samantha knew from that sentence that she couldn't be misinterpreting what she was hearing. He then started talking again, making her heart beat faster.

"I really don't want to ruin our friendship," Tom said. "You mean too much to me…"

He was mid-sentence when he became suddenly aware that she was moving closer to him - *much* closer. Then he felt her arm move over his, pulling herself even closer still, until they were facing each other, their faces only a breath apart.

He held his breath, too many emotions flowing through his mind and his body. Nothing had prepared him for her leaning in and kissing him.

Samantha didn't care if she'd heard incorrectly. The moment was there, and she was pretty sure she had understood correctly. It was a revelation that made her heart sing, and she had to kiss him.

As their lips touched, Tom was aware of how different it felt to be kissing her, from the initial kiss he'd experienced in high school. Back then, it had been lips touching lips in a practical sense, with no more attachment in it. Samantha kissing him was different.

He pulled away and looked at her face, and was shocked to see the look on her face. Slowly he moved in toward her again, taking his time to make sure she was aware of what was happening, but she didn't push him away, and she didn't stop him.

She felt him find his way in the kiss, remembering that even though she'd still not been sexual with anyone, she had shared many kisses with Scott, and Paul before him. She felt Tom's hand come up and touch her cheek, then run through her hair, as if it were the most natural thing in the world for him to do.

They remained like that for a long time, lying close to one another and kissing softly, both surprised that the other wasn't pulling away. When they came apart, they remained as close, looking into one another's eyes before Samantha spoke.

"I haven't been with anyone either," she said.

"But … Scott … and the club when you guys were going?"

"No," Samantha replied, shaking her head. "He wasn't the right person for me. I think I knew that all along, just as I knew Paul wasn't right for me before that."

Tom felt confused.

"You're still a virgin too?" he asked and saw her nod at him, making him catch his breath.

"Tom, don't you know?" Samantha asked, grinning. "*You* are the person I have always been waiting for."

"I've been right here."

"Yes, but … you never seemed … interested in me. Not like that anyway."

She saw him express a look of horror at the realisation, and she laughed at him softly.

"I know that we've always had our moments - ones that other people could never understand - but Tom, you are the best man I know. You're the best man I have *ever* known."

~~~~~

After lying in bed for a long while, enjoying just holding each other, Samantha and Tom heard life start to emerge outside their door as other
~~~~~

people began to get up.

"We need to get up," Tom said to Samantha finally, having listened to the sounds outside. "Can we talk about … us … when we get home?" he asked her, uncertainty clear in his voice.

"Yes, today is still a wedding day," replied Samantha. "Let's just enjoy it with Alexis and Anthony, and maybe not act as if anything is … different?"

Tom nodded in agreement, and that was the end of the conversation … after Samantha leaned in and kissed him once more.

~~~~~

Throughout the morning, Tom and Samantha acted as they normally did, hoping that no-one would see anything different when they looked at them. The only person they weren't sure about was Alexis, who sometimes seemed to have a sixth sense about things, and had always been suggestive about Tom and Samantha being meant to be together.

Finally, the time came for the two of them to catch their five-hour train journey back to their home city. On the platform, Alexis hugged Samantha.

"Thank you so much for being here, and for designing my dress!" Alexis said. "I know how much work you put into it."

"It was my pleasure," Samantha replied. "You looked so beautiful in it, it was you who made it really, not me."

Alexis turned to Tom and, as always, loved the feeling of his arms wrap around her. As they hugged, he heard her very distinctly whisper in his ear, in a way that no-one else would hear.

"I think you might have some gossip for me next time we catch up."

She could feel him smiling against her cheek. When he pulled away, he had a bashful look on his face even though he was trying hard to hide it.

Anthony moved forward and said goodbye to the two of them, and then Samantha was leading Tom to the train.

As they settled back into their seats, Tom tentatively reached out his hand to take hers, stopping short just in case it wasn't welcome. He smiled as she reached out hers also, and confidently took his hand and held it tight.

~~~~~

Back at his house, Anthony found himself pulled aside by Alexis.

"I have an idea that I want to ask you about. You might not like it…"

Anthony looked at his new bride and was alarmed at her choice of words, but let her lead him into their bedroom.

"The dress - my wedding dress that Samantha made for me," she started and saw Anthony nod with a confused look on his face. "I want to use … contacts … to get it into a women's magazine, to help Samantha get some attention for her work."

Anthony analysed the words said to him and, at first, didn't understand which part of her speech that he wouldn't like. Then it hit him fully.

"You want ... Lincoln ... to help you?"

Alexis nodded with uncertainty clear on her face.

"Yes," she said. "I know it isn't ... ideal ... but he has contacts and resources, Anthony. If you really don't want me to, I won't. I just feel like she's so talented. If there's any chance I can help her..."

Alexis found her words cut off by him kissing her all of a sudden - deeply. When he pulled away from her, he saw she was slightly stunned, which made him smile.

"I don't like what you went through with him, but I agree with you. If you can make a call, and that results in a friend getting her work being seen by others, I support you in that - but only if you feel comfortable doing it, Allie. You wouldn't contact him if you were still scared of him, right? Not even for a friend..."

Alexis kissed him.

"Not even for a friend," she said. "I'm okay. When I talked to him at the gallery, it was alright. It will be okay, I promise. And now that I think about it more, I'll try and do it through Hannah, rather than directly talk to him."

"Okay," Anthony said and paused, stroking her cheek lightly with his finger. "You are such a generous, wonderful woman, my lovely bride."

~~~~~

On the long train journey home, Samantha was quiet - a fact that was very noticeable to Tom. He wanted to wait and see if she would bring up their conversation of that morning. When she didn't, he took the initiative and broached the subject.

"Are you okay, Samantha?" he asked. "Are you having regrets about what we talked about?"

Samantha looked the man she had known for more than twenty years.

"No, no regrets," she said. "I think my emotions have gotten away on me a bit. I just want us to ease slowly into ... whatever it is that we both want to happen."

Tom felt her tighten her hold on his hand and took it as reassurance that all would be well.

"Alexis looked beautiful in your dress," he said, purposely changing the subject to help her relax.

"I know!" Samantha responded, immediately transformed into the lively and energetic person he knew her to be when she was at ease with everything. "I wasn't sure about that colour for a wedding dress when she chose it that day, but she looked stunning in it. I think that no matter
~~~~~

what happens with my career - if I *have* a career in dressmaking - that dress will always be my favourite."

~~~~~

A week later, Samantha sat with Tom in the local café where they often went for pancakes, when she felt vibrating in her pocket. When she reached in and took out her mobile phone, she saw an unknown number on the screen.

"Hello?"

"Samantha Young?"

"Yes."

"Hello, Samantha. My name is Hannah. I am calling you on behalf of Lincoln Kokiri. Mr. Kokiri saw photographs of a wedding dress you recently designed, and would like to meet with you to talk about having your work - particularly that dress - featured in a magazine article he is currently negotiating, showcasing up and coming fashion designers."

"What?"

Samantha heard the woman on the other end of the phone laugh at the sound of Samantha's evident shock.

"Sorry, I know you don't know me, so I understand this is probably unexpected," said Hannah. "I would like to arrange for you to come to Melbourne to meet with Mr Kokiri, to discuss how this could work for both of you. He will pay for your travel and accommodation for one night, and you are welcome to bring a partner or friend with you also."

"I ... I don't know what to say."

"It is a big decision, of course," Hannah said. "Can I leave it to you to think about it for a couple of days, and then call you again? The article is due in the magazine out month after next, so there are approximately four weeks until the final proofs need to be submitted to the company for review. If you could come up next week, that would be ideal."

"I'm in my last year of study, and attend course full-time, Monday to Friday. I shouldn't really take any days off..."

"That's fine. Mr Kokiri anticipated that, and is happy to meet with you over a weekend. I can arrange for you to fly here Saturday morning and then return Sunday evening."

"Okay..."

"Okay ... you are saying yes? Or okay, you'll think about it?"

"I will think about it for the next couple of days and then give you an answer," said Samantha.

After formal goodbyes, Samantha looked at Tom. He could see she'd received some kind of shock.

"What is it?" he asked. "Bad news?"

"I ... I don't know. It was a woman who said she works for Lincoln Kokiri, and that he wants to feature the wedding dress I made for Alexis,
~~~~~

in a magazine."

Tom looked at her, considering the name she had said. He remembered the day he'd come face to face with Lincoln Kokiri in the supermarket. That was the moment when he'd looked like he was charging toward Tom, as if to punch him. Alexis had later explained that Lincoln had been upset because he'd seen Tom give her a ride in his car.

"Maybe it's some kind of joke?" Samantha was asking, then presenting a face that said she thought she'd been pranked. "Of course it was a joke! Oh, I am so stupid to think something like that could happen to me."

"No, wait, Samantha…"

"It's alright, Tom. I'm just being silly … I mean, Lincoln Kokiri is a great businessman - a multi-millionaire. Why would he look at my…"

"No, you don't understand, Samantha," said Tom. "*Alexis* knows Lincoln Kokiri."

"What?"

"She never told me how she knows him, but she definitely does," Tom said. "He came into the supermarket to find her one day."

Samantha looked at him as if she couldn't understand what he was saying, but then she saw his hand reach out and take hers.

"I'll ask Alexis, but I think you'll find it's legit," said Tom. "What else did the woman say?"

"She said they would fly and pay for accommodation for me and a friend to travel to Melbourne for a night so I could meet him."

Tom smiled at her.

"Really? You get to go to Melbourne, all expenses paid? And you get to take a friend? A *good* friend?" he asked, winking at her.

Samantha finally began to let herself believe what was happening. She smiled at him, still with a slight doubt inside.

"Ring Alexis and ask her," Tom said. "Go on. Do it now. Otherwise, you are going to burst, wondering!"

Samantha picked up her phone again and dialled the number of her friend.

"Alexis, I just received a call, and I think it's probably some kind of prank but … is there any chance that you spoke to Lincoln Kokiri about the wedding dress?" she blurted out in one long sentence and question. The response was Alexis at the other end of the line, laughing.

"Oh, Samantha! Yes, of course I made a call," said Alexis. "You did me such a great favour, making such a beautiful dress. I didn't know if anything could come from me mentioning it, though. Was it Hannah who called you?"

"Yes…" Samantha replied quietly, still in shock.

"It's all good, Samantha," Alexis said. "I just made a phone call. Now it's up to you to do the work, to see them, and convince them that your pieces should be considered for whatever they're planning to do with it."

"Thank you."

After they finished their goodbyes, Tom saw a brilliant smile appear on Samantha's face.

"It *is* real," Samantha said.

Tom laughed at her.

"Of course it is," he said. "You need to have more faith in your talent. Now, about that all expenses trip for you and your best friend…"

~~~~~

Two weekends later, Tom escorted Samantha onto a small plane bound for Melbourne. They'd been through a great deal, and done much in their years as friends, but travelling was something they'd never done - either alone or together.

Settling in their seats on the plane, he could sense her nervousness. He laughed with her as he took her hand in his.

"You are going to do great," he said. "No matter how Lincoln Kokiri knows Alexis, I don't believe a businessman like that would put time and money into something he didn't regard as being a good business investment. Relax. It's all going to be fine."

~~~~~

When they arrived in Melbourne, they were surprised by a man in the arrivals area holding a large sign saying one name - 'Samantha Young.

Samantha and Tom walked to the man and introduced themselves.

"Ms. Young, welcome to Melbourne. I'm Toby and I will be driving you to your hotel, where Hannah and Mr. Kokiri will meet you later today."

Soon they found themselves being whisked away to a limousine, which in turn drove them to the Grand Hyatt Hotel.

As they climbed out, the driver not only came around to open their door for them, but continued to walk them into the hotel and introduce them to the staff at the front desk.

"This is Ms. Young and her partner. Please make all services available to them, and bill their expenses directly to Mr. Kokiri," Toby said with authority in his voice, as if he did such things all the time for business propositions.

"Of course," the exceptionally groomed woman behind the front counter said.

"I shall leave you now," Toby said to Samantha once more. "But please come down here to the lobby at 3pm to meet Hannah and Mr. Kokiri. They are eager to meet you, and discuss your business."

"Thank … thank you," Samantha stammered, feeling nervous and excited, but well out of her depth.

~~~~~

When Tom and Samantha entered their room, Samantha almost fell over, with its high standard of beauty and luxury. Tom watched her as she walked in and just stood in the middle of the room. When she turned to look at him, he saw the shock on her face.

"I can't believe…"

Tom moved to her and put his arms around her.

"You're here because you're becoming a great designer, Samantha."

She looked at him with so much doubt that he almost gave her one of the fond arm punches he'd suffered from over their years as friends.

"I'm here because he wants to do something nice for Alexis…"

"No, he wouldn't do this just for Alexis," Tom retorted. "He's too savvy in business to make bad business decisions. Just meet the man and listen to his ideas, at least. No harm can come from that, right?"

Samantha nodded and moved closer to him, holding him tightly as she dared to let herself feel hopeful that something good was going to come from the upcoming meeting.

~~~~~

Later that day, Samantha came face to face with the powerful presence of Lincoln Kokiri, and his personal assistant, Hannah.

"Samantha, it is a great pleasure to meet you," Lincoln said as he reached out and shook her hand.

As he turned to Tom, Lincoln only then realised who he was. He felt awkward as he remembered the day he'd gone to approach Tom in the supermarket Alexis was working at. Thinking about it through the slight haze of his memory, he could still remember the rage he'd felt at the thought of someone - Tom - touching his 'Lexi'.

Tom was also not sure what to expect, given the explanation Alexis had given him about that day when he'd thought Lincoln was racing toward him with the intention of punching him. Regardless, he had to respond when he saw the great man hold his hand out to him.

"Tom," Lincoln said with a sheepish smile on his face. "I am glad to make your acquaintance in this different circumstance."

Samantha looked at Tom with an 'is there some story here' kind of question of her face. He felt guilt over not having told her that he had met Lincoln kind of, in a different time and place.

"It is my pleasure to properly meet you, Mr Kokiri," Tom said. "Thank you for providing this support to Samantha, and allowing me to come with her."

Lincoln nodded and then turned his attention back to the designer before him.

"Samantha, this is Hannah, who you've been speaking with. Shall we grab a seat and make ourselves comfortable?"

Once seated around a four-seater table in the hotel lounge, Lincoln was straight down to business, as always.

"I saw the photos of the wedding gown you designed and made for Alexis. I believe it will fit in very well with a spread I'm organising in a women's magazine next month. I believe there is much talent out there, waiting to be discovered, so we - my company - are eager to help people such as yourself to get noticed so that your career can take off. How do you feel about that?"

Samantha was in awe of the man before her. In addition to him being so staggeringly gorgeous to look at, he had such an aura about him. He was much older, and yet extremely attractive. He was like a magnet, pulling her in to want to be closer to him. It was a power that intrigued her, but equally frightened her. She unconsciously moved a bit closer to Tom's side with the discovery.

"I … I am very thankful for the opportunity, Mr Kokiri," she said, but suspected she sounded like she had doubt in her voice.

"You are uncertain of something. It is best that you voice it before we move forward," Lincoln said bluntly, not in any way unfriendly, but far more businesslike than Samantha had ever had to deal with.

"I just … I know that you and Alexis are friends, and I…"

"You wonder if I'm putting your dress in the magazine spread as some kind of favour to Alexis."

"Yes."

Samantha thought Lincoln might be offended, but he only smiled at her, mesmerising her completely.

"I can understand why you might think that," Lincoln said. "Yes, your dress came to my attention because Alexis wore it, and she did call Hannah to ask if there was anything we could do for you. I will not keep that from you, Samantha. But none of the dresses in this magazine spread will be from designers who I do not deem worthy of such a showing, due to the high calibre of their work. It would not matter how well you know Alexis or anyone else that I know. If you didn't look like someone who has the talent to succeed in such a cutthroat industry, I most certainly would not be featuring you."

Samantha nodded. She felt timid, but grateful that Tom was there to lean on as she felt him squeeze her hand under the table.

"Thank you," she said.

"Now there is another part to this spread. We will be showing the wedding dress, and Alexis has agreed to let that be brought to Melbourne for a professional model to wear for photos," he said, putting Samantha further at ease that he wasn't using it as a way to see Alexis. "But we would also like to take photos of *you*, and have a journalist interview you. You'll have your own half-page feature, as will each designer."

"What will they ask me?" asked Samantha.

"Mostly about who you are, and what your aspirations are as a designer. Perhaps what inspires you in your creations. They won't ask anything personal. The journalist has been instructed to be careful where they let their questions venture to. If you *are* asked anything that makes you feel uncomfortable, you have the right to refuse to answer. This isn't an exercise in looking for dirt on people. It's to highlight the strengths of each designer to their best advantage."

Tom watched the face of the man speaking. He had seen his look of power that morning in the supermarket, although Alexis had certainly taken control of that situation - and the man - at that time. Tom had never asked the name of the person Alexis had experienced so much mental trauma with due to her delivering of pain, but he had wondered if the great businessman in front of him was the one responsible for that situation. Looking at him, Tom found himself conflicted in his thoughts. On the one hand, Lincoln was so much older than her. In that regard, and knowing how happy Alexis was with Anthony, it was difficult to think that she would have been with a man of Lincoln's age group. On the other hand, there was something extreme about Lincoln Kokiri that made even Tom feel pulled toward him. He exuded charisma, or some kind of power. Tom couldn't put his finger on what the feeling was. He just knew it was there.

"Why are you doing this for people who are not known, Mr Kokiri?" Samantha asked. "It cannot be a business decision..."

"I assure you it *is* a business decision, Samantha," Lincoln replied. "My company is exploring branching into new avenues, and I am seeking talented individuals to invest my time and money into, to help them grow as business enterprises themselves. It is not an act of kindness or generosity on my part, I assure you. I am looking for people who I can invest in, who in the long run, I believe will generate enough business that they will become an active, contributing income for my company."

Samantha was blown away. It felt like every word he said to her, she had to blink and wonder if she had just heard correctly.

"You want to ... invest ... in me?" she asked.

"If interest is shown in your work, yes, that will be something I would like to talk to you about, but the first step is getting the magazine article up and ready. So how do you feel about that? The first thing you need to consider is if you want the wedding dress to be photographed and put in the magazine spread with nine other unknown designers. You also need to think about whether you're comfortable talking to a journalist to answer some questions," Lincoln said and then went silent as he waited for her to answer.

Samantha was so stunned that she forgot to answer straight away. She heard Hannah laugh softly as if to nudge her.

"This really is happening, Samantha, but if you don't feel comfortable, or you do not wish to do it..."

"No! I mean, yes!" said Samantha. "Thank you - yes, thank you. I would very much like to be a part of this. When would you need me to be available for a journalist, though? I'm not sure when I'll be able to come back to Melbourne..."

"You won't have to," said Lincoln. "I have the photographer and journalist on call for this evening, and can arrange for them to be here at, say, 7pm if that suits you?"

"Alright," Samantha responded, feeling all of a sudden like she was Dorothy from The Wizard of Oz, having travelled through a tornado and woken up in Kansas.

Lincoln then stood up with Hannah by his side, declaring by doing so that the meeting was over. He held out his hand to Samantha.

"I look forward to seeing the finished article, Samantha, and watching your career as it develops," he said. "That wedding dress was phenomenal, and Hannah has told me how much it means to Alexis and how pleased she was with the finished result. With the right coverage, I believe you have what it will take to go the distance and become known."

"Thank you," Samantha replied, relieved that the powerful man before her was going to walk away and leave her and Tom to relax and breathe easy.

Tom watched Lincoln and Hannah walk out before he turned to Samantha and hugged her.

"It's happening for you," he said, grinning. "Your dress is going to be seen!"

No words were said in response to that. All he did see was her suddenly jumping up and down with the most excited look on her face that he had ever seen.

~~~~~

With precise timing, at 7pm Samantha opened their hotel room door to be greeted by a makeup artist, hairdresser, photographer and assistant, and the journalist. After introductions, she was put through the experience of how she thought a princess or a debutante might feel, being groomed and dressed until she looked exactly as the photographer wished her to look. While that was happening, she was interviewed. It was another new experience that pushed her in her comfort levels, but the interviewer was respectful and completely steered clear of personal questions.

While everything was going on, Tom stayed back and just watched. To see her go through such a visual transformation was incredible for him to watch. He enjoyed the facial expressions she gave to him now and
~~~~~

then, as if to say 'stop looking at me', but he only laughed at her and kept watching.

When it was all over, and the hotel room door was closed, Samantha took a deep breath and closed her eyes, not moving for a moment.

Tom watched her and left her to her moment, instead lying back on the bed and closing his eyes also. As he felt the bed move, he turned to look at her, and moved with her so that he could hold her as they lay together.

"What an amazing day!" he said and heard her laugh out loud as she looked at him.

"That is an understatement! Oh my holy cow, my dress is going to be in a magazine!!"

Tom laughed at her. He never tired of her funny little expressions.

"Well, not only your dress. You know that *you* are going to be in the magazine too, right?" he teased.

They both turned and faced each other, lying close. Since Tom's declaration at the wedding about his feelings, the two of them had been moving very slowly out of their friendship comfort zone and on toward the slowness of letting desire build at a pace they were both comfortable with.

"Thank you for coming with me to do this," she said to him and lightly kissed his lips.

Tom revelled in the feelings. He had only kissed one other person in his life, apart from her, and he didn't place any emphasis on that since it hadn't even been his choice or desire. As he kissed Samantha, his lips woke up and felt like hers were the exact lips his had always been meant to be paired with.

He didn't pull away - he couldn't. Always when they kissed, he just wanted to sink into it, like sinking into the warmth of a bath. The way she moved her lips … the way she tasted … her lips … her tongue … he returned her kisses over and over and heard her start to moan softly.

Samantha let herself move into that zone - the one where she was kissing Tom, her lifelong friend. She'd had to take some time to adjust and come to terms with the change in their friendship, fearful of what might happen between them, but even she couldn't argue that it felt right. The two of them shared a light and yet intensely loving kiss. She had gone much further with Scott, and Paul before him, but she was thankful that Tom didn't push for anything else. Even his hands were well behaved, and she found that she enjoyed the return to just kissing. It didn't feel like they had to rush.

When they parted, they looked at each other intently.

"Samantha, before I ask you this. I want to say that I don't necessarily mean now, or even soon … but…" Tom started to say, moving his hand to take hers in his, and bring it to his lips. "Will you marry me?"

He watched her face as he spoke, hoping so much that he wasn't going to ruin everything. On her face, he saw nothing - not surprise, not concern, not happiness, but, equally, not anger. He continued, feeling like he might need to make a case for the question he had just presented to her.

"I'm not going to pressure you, and I don't mind how long you might need before you're ready, but I do love you, and I know that I want you to be my friend for life ... my best friend ... and my lover. I want us to start a new chapter..."

Suddenly he was forced to stop speaking as Samantha leaned in and kissed him aggressively. It was new to him, but he went with it, letting her lead the way. Eventually, he felt her ease back.

"You were saying too much," she said as if that answered his unspoken question, but it only left him confused. He found himself in one of the hundreds of confusing moments she had led him into over their years as friends who could so easily infuriate each other.

"Oh, no, you don't, Miss Young. You don't get to just shut *this* conversation down!" Tom said forcefully but with affection, making her laugh softly at him. "I asked you a question, so just bloody well answer it."

Samantha kissed him again, her face full of a broad smile.

"And?" he asked when she'd finished, teasing her further.

Once again, she smiled and kissed him.

"And?" he asked once more in his exaggerated mock frustration at her.

Finally, she laughed out loud.

"Alright! Yes, I will marry you! Now shut up!"

~~~~~

The following month, the magazine was released and Samantha was immediately approached by prospective clients, eager to have her design gowns for their upcoming weddings.

"Thank you so much, Alexis. I know this is all your doing," she said to her friend who had travelled up by train to spend the weekend with her as Samantha moved out of her family home and into an apartment.

The two young women were moving things around, finding places for all of Samantha's personal items while also creating a workspace for her.

"It is *not* my doing, Samantha!" said Alexis. "*You* did the work on that dress, and now you are being recognised for that work. Stop trying to deflect from your success, and just enjoy it."

Samantha laughed at the bossy sound of the voice that had been speaking.

"Yes, Ma'am!" she said, making Alexis laugh with her.
~~~~~

"Now, what about your own wedding dress? How is that going?"

Alexis saw Samantha's face light up instantly.

"It will be simple. I don't need anything grand. I just want…"

"Yes?"

"I just want to marry Tom."

Alexis held back the 'I told you so' that automatically wanted to jump out of her mouth. The two women had become so relaxed with one another since Tom had introduced them that quips were common and always greeted with humour, but Alexis didn't want to tease her friend in that instance.

"Not long now," she said.

"I know," Samantha replied, a sigh visible in her voice.

Alexis laughed at her.

"Why the big sigh?" she asked. "You guys have known each other your whole lives. You must already know each other inside out…"

"Yes, all except one way," Samantha said quietly, almost as if to herself.

Alexis said nothing, not wanting to ask for clarification on that, so changed the subject.

"And the wedding itself?" she asked and saw Samantha look excited but also a little doubtful.

"You know that Mr. Kokiri arranged everything, right?" Samantha asked. "The hotel rooms for everyone, and the room for the wedding ceremony itself. I don't understand why he has done that…"

"I am sure it's a business decision…"

Alexis saw Samantha looked at her with an indefinable look on her face.

"Are you really sure about that, Alexis?"

"What else could it be?"

"Alexis…"

"Yes?"

"What is it with you and Lincoln Kokiri? I've never asked before, because I know you're a private person, but what…?"

"Samantha, that is irrelevant to your wedding, I assure you," Alexis replied. "He is a businessman, and his company frequently invests in other businesses. If he is doing something like this, trust me - it *is* for a good business reason."

Samantha felt the conversation close and let it go, not wanting to make Alexis any more uncomfortable than she already looked.

"Can I show you my dress design?" she asked, in determination to help relax the situation.

"Yes! Of course I want to see it!" Alexis said, also eager to move their conversation anywhere else.

She watched as Samantha pulled out her sketchbook and brought it to the sofa, where she sat down and opened it up to scroll through the pages as Alexis sat beside her.

"Samantha! Oh, stop flicking through those pages and go back to the start!"

"What?" Samantha asked as she did as she'd been instructed.

As she turned the first page, she saw Alexis view the drawings before her with a look of awe on her face.

"I haven't seen your work in this form before, except for the dress you made for me," said Alexis. "I want to see all of these, so turn the pages slowly."

As Samantha turned the pages, Alexis felt a slight shade of envy at the obvious creative talent before her. That was shaken off with the happiness for her friend.

"You are so talented. You deserve all the success that will come to you, Samantha. Even if you do get a helping hand now and then by a rich benefactor - by *anyone* - it doesn't matter because this ... this is your work, no-one else's, and no-one will buy your work just because you know someone rich. This is all on *you*, so don't ever ask how much Lincoln or anyone else is making this happen for you. The only person making it happen is you. Look at these - oh my God, they are incredible."

Samantha listened, smiled at Alexis, and then finally turned to the page of her wedding dress design.

"This is it."

Alexis looked at her and then grabbed the book to pull it closer, and look closer still at the design.

"You are going to look so beautiful," she said with a sound of excitement that made Samantha giggle slightly. "Tom is going to ... oh! Tom is going to melt on the spot when he sees you!"

"I can't wait for that day, Alexis," Samantha said softly.

When Alexis looked closely at her, she was sure she could see a stray tear trying to escape. She reached out, took Samantha's hand in hers, and squeezed it tight.

"I'm sure that Tom feels exactly the same way."

CHAPTER 10

The Final Chapter

Alexis and Samantha readied themselves in a small hotel room of the Park Hyatt Hotel in Melbourne. It was yet another generous offer of Lincoln Kokiri. With Samantha's designs having proven to be popular, he was starting to earn money off his investment in her. As a reward, he'd offered to put the bride, groom, and their friends and family up in the hotel, and pay for the reception.

Although her pride had been too high to accept initially, eventually Samantha accepted the offer. She was still convinced that a large part of Lincoln Kokiri's generosity was due to whatever it was that he and Alexis had shared. Regardless, with her gowns and dresses selling on their own accord, she finally believed that she had talent and could start to take some pride in her achievements.

Standing in one of her own dresses - a simple but elegant strapless gown of the purist white - Samantha looked at herself in the full-length mirror. She was deep in thought when Alexis came up behind her.

"You look beautiful, Samantha," she said.

"Thank you," Samantha replied. "If anyone had asked me a year ago how my life would be right now, I wouldn't have even dreamed that I would be here, in this beautiful hotel, standing in a wedding dress that I designed and made, and marrying Tom. How did my life come to change so much over such a short period of time, Alexis?"

"It has changed because you have worked hard to make it change," Alexis said. "You're talented, and people are now beginning to see that. You're only going to get busier in your dressmaking, I'm sure. And as for Tom - well, I think you and Tom just happened to be the last two people on the entire planet to know that you were always meant to be together."

Samantha laughed at her.

"He is wonderful, isn't he? You don't know how often I treated him badly, completely turning my back on him at times. But he has never once made me feel like I was doing anything wrong. He's always been so accepting of who I am."

"He knows you're a good person…"

"Maybe."

Alexis looked at Samantha's face and could see anxiety.

"Are you nervous about the ceremony?"

Samantha smiled at her.

"No, that I am fine with," she said and blushed as she continued. "It's afterwards … tonight … that I'm uncertain about."

Alexis was surprised by the words. She and Samantha had never talked about anything intimate, but she had assumed that Samantha and Tom had been sexual.

"What are you uncertain about?" she asked.

Samantha looked at her friend intently, blushing profusely.

"We've never … I've never … he's never…"

"You can't mean that you're both … virgins?"

Samantha laughed softly and nodded her head.

"Yep, we both sure are. You sound surprised."

"Well, you and Tom are so … intense!" said Alexis. "Whenever I've been around the two of you - even right from that first dinner at his home - I've always thought I was witnessing open desire and passion that you shared together. The two of you really do look like you're sharing and enjoying really hot sex!"

Samantha laughed out loud.

"Perhaps it has been more a case of sexual frustration," she teased Alexis back, making them laugh together.

"Come on, then," Alexis said. "Let's get you to your groom-to-be so that you can become his wife, and then we can all let you guys get on with your night!"

Hearing a knock on the door, Alexis opened it to see her husband Anthony.

"Oh, geez," he moaned softly as he looked at her. "How do you keep getting more beautiful? Can you and I just stay here instead?" he asked with a mock sadness before a broad grin spread on his face, making Alexis laugh as Samantha threw in her conversation from behind his wife.

"No, you can't, you horny bugger. She is required right now, as are you!"

Anthony laughed out loud and leaned in to kiss Alexis softly before moving forward and kissing Samantha on the cheek.

"Alright bossy, you win," Anthony said. "Come on. There's a very eager lad downstairs!"

Escorting the two of them out of the door, Anthony saw Samantha's uncle approach to give her a wink and a smile before taking her arm as her choice to be led down the aisle with.

In a small conference room that had been magically transformed for the occasion, a small number of guests were assembled and waiting. As Alexis and Anthony started to walk down the aisle, Tom turned and gave Alexis a small, nervous smile, watching as she moved with grace and confidence. She was such a different woman to the one he'd met when she'd begun working in the supermarket he was a supervisor at.

As Alexis walked down the aisle, another set of eyes followed her. He wasn't at the wedding for her. He was there for Samantha, due to her business success, and her gratitude to him for helping her to get started. When Lincoln saw Alexis, he felt a familiar pang in his heart. He'd thought those feelings had all gone, and he'd been glad they had gone. The feelings that had flowed on from his attraction to her had led to them both becoming screwed up, although in different ways. His heart sank as he looked at her and saw how beautiful, confident, and poised she was. He knew she was happy, and he had no reason to dislike her husband. It was due to Anthony that she had finally recovered and changed, but he couldn't help his heart. No matter what happened for the rest of his life, she would always be his greatest regret.

Feeling Hannah's hand take his, he looked at her and knew she was a good woman. In the months that they had drifted from simple employer/employee relationship to good friends and then more, he knew he was in a good place with her. But just as he had thought when he'd first met Alexis - when he had been married to Diana - the same thought passed through his mind once more. 'She just isn't Lexi'.

Hannah watched his face and felt some concern at his facial expression as Alexis had walked by. She knew how they had affected each other over those three years, but she had believed he'd recovered from that. Looking at him at that moment, she wondered…

Tom watched his best man and Alexis reach the end of the aisle and then part as Alexis moved to one side, and Anthony moved to stand next to him.

Next, he saw his bride approaching with her uncle walking beside her. Tom felt his heart completely melt. He was nervous about them finally taking the step from being just friends, to becoming so much more, and from anticipation of the night to come.

The vows were said, and the magical words finally arrived, permitting Tom to disregard everyone else, take his bride into his arms, and give her the kiss he'd been desperate to give her ever since he had seen her walking toward him.

The room had been set up so that everything was carried out in the one area - the wedding vow exchange, the dancing, tables and chairs for dining, and a buffet off to the side.

Tom and Samantha moved forward to have their first dance as husband and wife.

"You look so beautiful," he whispered to her.

Samantha felt her body react to his as she moved closer to him.

"I'm nervous … about tonight," she said quietly with a slight blush on her face. In response, she saw him look at her with similar nervousness.

"Me too, but I will have fun exploring…" he said with a cheeky grin on his face, making her laugh as she punched him on the arm, just as she had been doing for twenty years. "I love you, Samantha. Thank you for saying yes," he whispered in her ear.

Samantha fell against him. He was Tom - her friend forever, now her husband, and soon to be her very first lover.

Anthony led Alexis out onto the dance floor while watching Samantha and Tom.

"They look outstanding together, don't they?" he said as he moved her around the floor.

"They do," Alexis replied, also watching the newlywed couple. "They always did, I think. Although, as much as I love having Tom as my friend, I don't think he looks as outstanding as you do, my lovely husband. You, I could look at all night."

"Oh, is that so?" Anthony asked, grinning.

"Oh, yes."

"Then I had better keep you up all night so that you can," Anthony replied and leaned in to kiss her.

Soon Tom and Samantha were approached by their photographer, who moved them this way and that, to this location and that, with this person and that, so that a full photoshoot could be done, both for their own record and for further promotion of her work.

As the evening wore on, guests were sometimes eating, sometimes just talking, and sometimes dancing, with Tom and Samantha both doing the rounds to talk to everyone. When they approached the table where Lincoln and Hannah sat talking business to other likeminded people, Samantha saw Lincoln stand up and shake Tom's hand before he turned to hug her.

"You look beautiful, Samantha," Lincoln said. "Thank you for inviting us to come and attend this. We are very grateful for the invitation."

"Oh, no! You did all of this," Samantha said. "You couldn't seriously think we wouldn't invite you to attend!"

Samantha saw the usually power-exuding man suddenly look a little shy - something she hadn't seen on him before.

"Well, I thank you anyway, and I do wish you both the very best," Lincoln said. "I have no regrets about investing in you. You are an incredible designer, and Tom here is a very lucky man."

Tom watched the interaction and felt at ease with it. He still didn't quite 'get' Lincoln Kokiri - an older man who could produce such strong feelings in people. Although he wouldn't mention it, he hadn't forgotten the morning Lincoln had forcefully walked toward him in the supermarket, before Alexis had stepped in and dragged him away. Something about that interaction continued to stick with him as a bit of a mystery, but he couldn't doubt the generosity of Lincoln, and the way that he was helping Samantha to move forward as a designer. Tom justified that was more important than the uncertain feelings he had toward the man because of that one moment in time in the supermarket.

The married couple smiled and moved on to the next table. As they did so, Hannah saw Lincoln's eyes fall once more to Alexis and Anthony on the dance floor.

"Would you like to dance, Lincoln?" he heard the voice beside him ask. In response, Lincoln nodded and instantly became the confident, debonair gentleman that he was. He held out his hand to welcome her up and onto the dance floor with him.

~~~~~

Shortly after taking some time to talk to all of their guests, Tom pulled Samantha into his arms.

"Samantha. My lovely bride. My lovely wife. I don't think you and I need to be here any longer. Do you?" he asked her quietly.

Samantha looked closely at him, blushing but nodding, just as eager for the two of them to be alone.

"I would like to be alone with you," she whispered in his ear.

On hearing the words, Tom felt such a level of desire that he thought he might burst with longing.

"Shall we say something to our guests?" Samantha asked. "I don't know what's the right etiquette."

She looked at her husband and lifelong friend, Tom, who had always been dependable and had always put other people first.

"Maybe if I just tell Alexis quietly, but then not announce it," she suggested and saw him smile.

Tom nodded and watched her walk over the dance floor and whisper something in their friend's ear. Tom saw Alexis turn and give him a knowing smile and nod before Samantha returned.

Taking his hand in hers, the two of them walked out quietly, noticed by some guests but not by others.

In the elevator, Tom pulled her close and kissed her deeply, feeling her body instantly melt against his as if she had been waiting for that moment all night long.

"No holding back tonight," she said suggestively.

Tom knew what she meant. They had been holding back, out of fear of ruining their friendship, for far too many years.

"No holding back," he reassured her before kissing her again and continuing to do so until the elevator door opened at their floor.

As Tom pulled the key card out of his pocket, he found himself
~~~~~

shaking so much that he couldn't at first align the card with the slot it had to move down into. It was then that Samantha realised just how nervous he was. In that, they were so different, she realised. Although both virgins, she found she was more excited rather than nervous, as if her body had always known that night was coming.

Tom felt sheepish as Samantha reached out and placed her hand over his to push the card down into the slot smoothly. He looked at her face as they heard the click of the door unlocking, and found himself in awe of her. He had known her all his life, but something was about to change between them forever.

Once in their room, he found himself presented with her back as she moved her hair out of the way and asked him to unzip her dress. In doing so, Tom felt his hands shaking even more than they had in the previous moment at the door lock. He'd seen her wearing so little since they'd become play partners at the BDSM club, but that was different. Even just removing her wedding dress, he felt his arousal heightened to a point that he hadn't before realised he could reach.

Once Samantha stood before him in her underwear of white strapless corset and briefs, she turned to him and pulled him close to her to re-engage their kissing. Tom let her set the pace of undressing him when she was ready to. Once they were naked and lying together, he revelled in letting her take control of everything initially. Then his confidence grew, and he knew he needed to have his own share of being in control.

As she lay back on the bed, Tom took his time and raised himself onto his knees as he looked at her from head to toe and back again.

Finding her body then being lightly kissed on every little part, Samantha felt like she was a cat, wanting to stretch out and purr at the glorious new feelings. She was used to him touching her to a degree, and him seeing her wear very little, but being kissed lightly everywhere was new for her. She felt like she could lie still all night indulging in it.

Together they explored, touching, kissing, and learning much about how it felt to touch and be touched. Tom was in heaven. Even though he was inexperienced, he was at least knowledgeable enough to know what to try, which resulted in Samantha having her first orgasm.

Tom watched her face as she recovered from it. When she opened her eyes, he was close to her, smiling broadly in the knowledge that he had done pretty well for a first try.

Samantha knew the look well and laughed at him. Lying on her back, she guided him over her and between her legs but before he moved forwards and inwards, she saw a serious look appear over his face.

"We haven't talked about the timing of children yet," he said and felt her lightly stroke his face as they looked at one another. "I'm in no hurry, and I think your career is just starting to take off. Should we wait?"

Samantha nodded at him.

"Yes, please. Sorry, we should have had this discussion so we could be prepared…" she started to say.

Tom instantly moved off her. For a moment, Samantha thought she'd upset him. Then she saw him returning with a large smile on his face and a box of condoms in his hand.

"I'm prepared!" he said happily, making her laugh out loud before she looked down his body and smiled cheekily at him.

"Yes, I can see that you definitely are," she said and saw him blush deeply before he laughed out loud at her suggestiveness.

It took some time for them to figure out how to put the condom on. It was a process that had them both laughing in the embarrassed relaxation that came from them being such good friends, trying something completely new for both of them. Finally, Samantha lay back and let him take control of what came next.

Tom kissed her deeply and slowly edged forward, hoping everything would literally fall into place. He soon experienced a new feeling as he was welcomed inside her. He watched her face and saw her eyes focused on his.

"Oh, Samantha … oh, I've never felt anything like … oh! Are you alright?" he asked her softly.

Samantha kissed him in acknowledgement, adjusting to the new feeling. She felt happy that despite all their years of fighting in the beginning, despite the times they'd stopped being friends, and despite the men she'd dated and been involved with before the two of them finally accepted each other, Tom was the man she shared her first time with.

Tom moved inside of her, excited but soon finding the new sensation overwhelming. It wasn't long before he was experiencing his own climax. He lay on top of her, feeling the sensations flowing through his entire body while Samantha held him tight. Finally, he pulled his head away from her shoulder and looked at her. He wanted to speak to her, but his head was fuzzy, and he couldn't find any words.

"Hmm," he said simply, making her giggle at him, which in turn made him smile broadly at her and kiss her again.

Samantha happily lay under him. For the most part, during their friendship, she had been the dominant one. She'd always been the one who'd said when they would spend time together and when they would have time apart. She'd been the one who'd said what they would do, and where they would do it. Regardless, she was happy to let Tom take on the stronger role as her husband. She watched him as he carefully withdrew from her, immediately noticing the feeling and moaning at it at the same time.

Tom held up the condom, wondering what to do with it before he finally stood up and took it to the rubbish bin in the bathroom. When he returned, he saw Samantha still stretched out, looking like she might never want to move.

Samantha felt speechless at being naked in a bed with Tom beside her as her husband. She wanted to be happy, but suddenly her emotions overwhelmed her. Tears flowed as Tom lay down with her and pulled her close.

"Did I hurt you?" he asked, concerned at the appearance of tears, but saw her smile at him and place one hand against his cheek before she kissed him.

"No," she said, sounding like she was laughing and crying at the same time. "I just feel so happy!"

Tom laughed at her and kissed her forehead like he had done so many times before.

"Oh, my beautiful wife Samantha, you are a weirdo to be laughing when you're crying," he said to her, suddenly feeling tears threaten in his eyes too.

"Now *you're* crying!" she cried out.

For the next few minutes, they enjoyed having their simple giggle together before Tom really looked at her and kissed her again.

"I love you, Samantha. I've always loved you."

Samantha felt a tear run down her face, which she didn't even bother to wipe away.

"I love you too."

~~~~~

Downstairs on the dance floor, Anthony held his wife tight, breathing in the scent of her.

"I want to tell the world of our news," he said quietly and saw Alexis laugh softly at him.

"Well, we aren't doing it at Tom and Samantha's wedding!" she exclaimed in mock seriousness. The look she received from him almost melted her, it was so full of love.

"Do you think it'll be a girl or a boy? Should we find out, do you think?" Anthony asked.

Considering the question, Alexis beamed at him.

"Oh, I hope it is a little Anthony, but if we have a baby girl, I'll be just as pleased with that," replied Alexis. "After all, it's only the first of many, right?"

Anthony smiled brilliantly at her and kissed her again.

"Too true," he said. "Yes, we must keep working on that - keep up the practice to keep the production line moving along smoothly, and all that."

Alexis laughed at him, happy that she was pregnant to a man who so eagerly wanted to be a father.
~~~~~

"May I cut in?" she heard a male voice - *the* voice - say. She looked at Anthony to see how he would react. He simply nodded and let Lincoln move to put his arms around Alexis, as Anthony moved to quickly save Hannah from having just been stranded on the dance floor.

Hannah was surprised and a bit saddened by the action of her partner.

"Do you remember what you said to me that first night I met you?" Anthony asked her, seeing the expression on her face. "When the two of them were talking at the art gallery? That nothing will happen between them again, and there is nothing to worry about."

"I know, and I know there is nothing to worry about, but sometimes..." Hannah started to say but immediately realised she couldn't - *shouldn't* - say anything about her doubts and concerns, since Alexis and Anthony were so obviously in love.

"Hannah, you are a beautiful, gracious woman," Anthony said. "Did you never marry?"

"No, I was always too into my ... work."

"Your work? Or your boss?" Anthony dared to ask, but saw that she wasn't offended by his straightforwardness.

Hannah smiled at him.

"Yes, it could be that I worked so close to him all these years that other men who approached me never stood a chance," she replied. "Even when Diana was alive, my thoughts were ... forbidden."

"But now things have changed between you, I sense," Anthony said. "Since that first time that I met you."

"Yes, the employer / employee line has definitely now been well and truly crossed, no doubt about that," she said softly. "But if I'm honest with myself, Anthony, I don't know if he really is into being with me, or if I'm just the woman who is there. Sometimes I feel like I'm just a 'she'll do' woman, filling a gap in his life."

Anthony looked at her sharply.

"You shouldn't feel like that, Hannah," he said. "You deserve so much more."

Hannah went quiet in his arms. She had thought the same thing to herself at times, but still, even at her age and having known Lincoln for so much of her life, trying to keep perspective about him and make decisions was still difficult for her. A part of her wished he would ask her to marry him. A greater part of her knew that he never would.

"You are a very mature young man, Anthony," she said. "Alexis is very lucky to have found you."

"No," he said. "*I* am very lucky to have found *her*. And if you aren't being treated as well as you deserve to be, you should let another man find you, Hannah."

At that moment, Hannah, despite being so much older than Alexis, found herself extremely envious of her. Despite her youth, Alexis had broken away from Lincoln when she knew she had to. She'd known her life would never be normal if she didn't. She'd known that there was something - *someone* - better waiting for her out there.

"Thank you, Anthony. I appreciate you dancing with me and saying such things."

Anthony looked at her face, all of a sudden feeling concerned for her. He remembered his first impression, when they'd met at the gallery, was that she was older than him but still so beautiful and gracious. To hear her talk as if she held no value was a horrifying thought to him. He quietly wished for the evening to be over, so he didn't have to look at - or even think about - Lincoln Kokiri anymore.

~~~~~

Lincoln held Alexis in his arms. He hadn't been thinking about her in a long while, and when he had thought about her, it hadn't been in a romantic or sexual context. Looking at her on that night, something had changed in him, and he knew it. He shouldn't have approached her, feeling like he was, but he'd been drawn to her with the need that he'd felt so many times in the years before. He hadn't even given Hannah another thought. Even though the four of them were on the dance floor, he had no awareness whatsoever about his partner being led around in the dance by another man.

Alexis let him lead her, at that moment not feeling anything but gratitude toward him for all that he had done for her friend.

"You are very generous to do this for Samantha," she said to him.

When he looked right into her eyes, Alexis recognised something different in his eyes, and in the way he was looking at her. For a moment, it startled her before she told herself she must be imagining it, and it must be a residual fear from long ago.

"I'm not doing this for Samantha," he said, leaving the words open to interpretation, almost as if he knew it might fluster and confuse her. After a moment of silence, he moved on from those words and spoke again. "It's good business, Alexis. Investing in her is already paying off for my company. Helping her with something like this isn't just a kindness. It's another part of my investment."

Alexis said nothing, suddenly feeling a slight panic inside of her. There was no reason to be panicked. Since they'd seen each other at the art gallery the night before Anthony had proposed to her, they'd hardly spoken. When they had, he'd always been civil. It had almost seemed like nothing bad had ever happened between them - like they were just old friends or old colleagues.

But at that moment, she felt something happening and changing. She wasn't sure if she was imagining it or it was real. She chose not to
~~~~~

noticeably react, or give any outward indication of what she was feeling, especially with Anthony and Hannah being so close by. As the seconds passed, Alexis felt the hairs on her arms and the back of her neck start to rise. She knew and remembered the feeling well. She fought to remain calm, despite what her body was telling her. She kept telling herself, over and over, that it must be her imagination. It *must* be.

Lincoln, meanwhile, revelled in being so close to her. He tightened his hold on her as he pulled her closer into his chest. He felt like he was getting drunk on the feeling of her being in his arms - like a drug he'd once tasted but not had recently was finally starting to flow through his veins once more, slowly at first but quickly picking up momentum in accessing part of his body and his mind.

He had forgotten Hannah. He had forgotten Anthony. He had forgotten every other person in the room. As he concentrated on the adrenalin running vigorously through his system - when he could hold back no longer - he leaned in even closer to whisper in her ear.

"I want you."

EPILOGUE

As Alexis opened her eyes, she was struck by the bright light. At first, it confused her. As her consciousness slowly returned, she realized she was in a hospital.

Looking around, she saw Anthony sitting by her bed, appearing to doze in an armchair that didn't look particularly comfortable. For a moment, Alexis studied him, smiling as she did so. He was the man she loved, and the man she wanted to spend the rest of her life with. She wanted him to be her husband, her lover, and the father of her children. There was no other man like him.

Briefly, her mind cast back to her last memory. She and Anthony had been at the wedding of Samantha and Tom. She'd been dancing with Anthony, and then she'd been dancing with Lincoln. That was the last thing she could remember - except for the thoughts she'd had when she'd been in his arms.

The more her consciousness awoke and sharpened, the more she could remember how she'd felt as he'd held her close. The dance had begun with her feeling like they were two old friends, and nothing more. As the minutes had passed, she'd recognized feeling like she had in the past. It hadn't been difficult to feel her body wanting to do as it had always done - fall to the ground and wait for an instruction. She clearly remembered feeling like she was heading into a daze.

As she came to that realization, Alexis felt startled. It was at that moment that Anthony woke and saw her face.

"Allie!" he exclaimed as he stood up and moved to sit on the side of the bed, taking her hand in his as he did so. "Shh. It's okay. You're going to be okay."

"What happened?" Alexis asked, fearful that not only had she thought she'd felt like her body wanted to do as it had always done when in the presence of Lincoln, but that it *might* have done that - right there, in front of everyone, at her friend's wedding. The thought was not a pleasant one for her.

"You fainted," said Anthony. "It's alright now though. The doctor said your blood sugar got too low, that's all. Everything is okay now. They're blood-sugar-ing you up still, but the doctor said you should be good to leave in a few hours."

Alexis forced herself to smile at his attempt to deliver some humour into what he'd told her. Low blood sugar. That was all it was. She smiled further as she convinced herself that was all that she'd felt at all when she'd been in Lincoln's arms. It hadn't been some weird return to how she'd been before - affected by him in that way. It had just been her body reacting to the running around she'd been doing at the wedding, and her not paying attention to what she and her unborn child had needed.

"The baby?" she asked.

"She is fine," Anthony said, grinning.

"She?" Alexis asked as she took in the beauty of the smile he was giving her.

"She," Anthony answered before he leaned down and kissed her lips.

Alexis finally relaxed. She was fine. Her baby was fine. Her husband was fine. She needed nothing more.

Allowing herself one final thought about Lincoln Kokiri, she was resolved. Maybe he hadn't caused her to faint, but being close to him wasn't a good idea. She'd never again contact him. She'd never again ask him for anything. They'd had quite a journey, and it was a journey that could have ended much sooner. She couldn't regret that she'd contacted him again - not after seeing how much he'd helped Samantha in her career - but it was time to completely close that chapter of her life.

Smiling, she pulled Anthony down for another kiss as the memory of Lincoln Kokiri was placed in a box in her mind, and put on a shelf that would become dusty in time.

"I love you, Allie," she heard Anthony say as he pulled away.

"And I love you," she reassured him. It was the stark, honest truth. She was in love, she was loved, and she *deserved* to be loved and in love. For the first time in her life, that was something that Alexis truly believed.

~~~~~~~~~~~~~~~

The End
~~~~~~~~~~~~~~~

THANK YOU!

Thank you so much for reading this story. If you enjoyed this book, I would greatly appreciate you leaving a review at the retailer you purchased it from, or at Bookbub.

~~~~~

Every second month, I send out a newsletter to my subscribed readers, enabling them to learn about new releases and freebies, and take part in the odd opportunity to win items such as books, Amazon gift cards, and Kindle e-readers. If this sounds like something you might be interested in, you can sign up at http://eepurl.com/ca559H.

~~~~~

If you would like to make contact with me, please:
Follow me on Bookbub
https://www.bookbub.com/authors/ann-m-pratley

Follow Me On Twitter
https://twitter.com/runkiwiwriter

Visit my Goodreads Author Page
goodreads.com/author/show/14777236.Ann_M_Pratley

Thank you,
Ann M Pratley

www.ingramcontent.com/pod-product-compliance
Lightning Source LLC
Chambersburg PA
CBHW020247030826
48979CB00030B/2645/J

* 9 7 8 1 9 9 1 1 6 4 6 8 1 *